Praise for Laura Griffin

TOUCH OF RED

"Griffin never disappoints with her exciting, well-researched, fast-paced romantic thrillers. . . . An engrossing story full of twists, turns, and sexy interludes."

—*Publishers Weekly*

"Scorching-hot chemistry and a happily-ever-after you'll enjoy rooting for."

—*Kirkus Reviews*

"A carefully constructed mystery with high-stakes tension throughout will have readers eagerly turning the pages. Once again, Griffin delivers another top-notch thriller."

—*RT Book Reviews*

"Masterful writing."

—*The Romance Reviews*

"A killer mystery makes hearts pound faster . . . a fast-paced thrill!"

—*BookPage*

AT CLOSE RANGE

"A compelling mystery that will grip the reader from the start with her crisp storytelling, natural dialogue, and high-stakes tension . . . fiercely electric."

—*RT Book Reviews*

"Explosive, seductive, and totally empowering . . . *At Close Range* has it all."

—*Romance Junkies*

DEEP DARK

"A book to be devoured and savored with each new development. It is the perfect combination of mystery, terrifying suspense, and hotter-than-hot romance."

—*Fresh Fiction*

SHADOW FALL

"An expert at creating mystery and suspense that hook readers from the first page, Griffin's detailed description, well-crafted, intriguing plot, and clear-cut characters are the highlights of her latest."

—*RT Book Reviews*

"Great lead characters and a spooky atmosphere make this a spine-tingling, stand-out novel of romantic suspense."

—*BookPage*

BEYOND LIMITS

"A page-turning, nail-biting thriller from the very first scene to the very last page."

—*Fresh Fiction*

FAR GONE

"Perfectly gritty . . . Griffin sprinkles on just enough jargon to give the reader the feel of being in the middle of an investigation, easily merging high-stakes action and spicy romance with rhythmic pacing and smartly economic prose."

—*Publishers Weekly* (starred review)

"Crisp storytelling, multifaceted characters, and excellent pacing. . . . A highly entertaining read."

—*RT Book Reviews* (4 stars)

"Be prepared for heart palpitations and a racing pulse as you read this fantastic novel. Fans of Lisa Gardner, Lisa Jackson, Nelson DeMille, and Michael Connelly will love [Griffin's] work."

—*The Reading Frenzy*

"A tense, exciting romantic thriller that's not to be missed."

—Karen Robards, *New York Times* bestselling author

"Griffin has cooked up a delicious read that will thrill her devoted fans and earn her legions more."

—Lisa Unger, *New York Times* bestselling author

MORE PRAISE FOR THE TRACERS SERIES

"Explodes with action . . . Laura Griffin escalates the tension with each page, each scene."

—*The Romance Reviews*

"Has it all: dynamite characters, a taut plot, and plenty of sizzle to balance the suspense without overwhelming it."

—*RT Book Reviews* (4½ stars)

"The pace is wickedly fast and the story is tight and compelling."

—*Publishers Weekly*

"With a taut story line, believable characters, and a strong grasp of current forensic practice, Griffin sucks readers into this drama and doesn't let go."

—*RT Book Reviews* (Top Pick)

"The perfect mix of suspense and romance."

—*Booklist*

"The science is fascinating, the sex is sizzling, and the story is top-notch, making this clever, breakneck tale hard to put down."

—*Publishers Weekly*

Books by Laura Griffin

The Tracers Series
Touch of Red

At Close Range

Deep Dark

Shadow Fall

Beyond Limits

Exposed

Scorched

Twisted

Snapped

Unforgivable

*Unstoppable**

Unspeakable

Untraceable

Also by Laura Griffin
Far Gone

Whisper of Warning

Thread of Fear

One Wrong Step

One Last Breath

Deadly Promises (anthology)

The Alpha Crew Series
*Alpha Crew: The Mission Begins**

*Cover of Night**

ebook only

Desperate Girls

Laura Griffin

GALLERY BOOKS

New York   London   Toronto   Sydney   New Delhi

Gallery Books
An Imprint of Simon & Schuster, Inc.
1230 Avenue of the Americas
New York, NY 10020

First Gallery Books hardcover edition August 2018

GALLERY BOOKS and colophon are registered trademarks of Simon & Schuster, Inc.

For information about special discounts for bulk purchases, please contact Simon & Schuster Special Sales at 1-866-506-1949 or business@simonandschuster.com.

The Simon & Schuster Speakers Bureau can bring authors to your live event. For more information or to book an event, contact the Simon & Schuster Speakers Bureau at 1-866-248-3049 or visit our website at www.simonspeakers.com.

Interior design by Davina Mock-Maniscalco

Manufactured in the United States of America

10   9   8   7   6   5   4   3   2   1

The Library of Congress has cataloged the trade paperback edition as follows:

Names: Griffin, Laura, 1973- author.
Title: Desperate girls / Laura Griffin.
Description: First Gallery Books trade paperback edition. | New York : Gallery Books, 2018.
Identifiers: LCCN 2018001856 (print) | LCCN 2018004930 (ebook) | ISBN 9781501162428 (ebook) | ISBN 9781501162411 (paperback)
Subjects: | BISAC: FICTION / Romance / Suspense. | FICTION / Suspense. | FICTION / Romance / Contemporary. | GSAFD: Romantic suspense fiction.
Classification: LCC PS3607.R54838 (ebook) | LCC PS3607.R54838 D47 2018 (print) | DDC 813/.6—dc23
LC record available at https://lccn.loc.gov/2018001856

ISBN 978-1-5011-9038-4
ISBN 978-1-5011-6241-1 (pbk)
ISBN 978-1-5011-6242-8 (ebook)

For Tracy

Desperate Girls

1

J EN BALLARD planned to get lucky tonight.

The thought made her heart do a little hopscotch as she slid her Volvo sedan into the driveway and checked her surroundings. No news vans. No beat-up hatchbacks belonging to reporters. She skimmed the street in both directions but saw only familiar cars in familiar driveways. She glanced in the rearview mirror at the driveway across the street, but it was empty—which might or might not be a good sign.

Jen pulled into her spacious garage. She gathered her groceries off the passenger seat as her phone pinged with an incoming text. David.

Running late. ETA 20 min.

She breathed a sigh of relief. Now she'd have time to shower and change into something more alluring than the charcoal pantsuit she'd worn to work.

She slid from the car and hurried into the house. Even laden with groceries, she felt empty-handed this evening. She had no briefs to read, no pretrial motions to consider. She'd left everything at the office, including her laptop, which felt good for a change.

Jen stashed the steaks and the salad ingredients in the fridge, then washed the potatoes and put them in the oven. She checked the clock. Fifteen minutes. She uncorked the merlot. It needed to breathe anyway. Really. She poured half a glass, then made her way to her bedroom as she sipped a little liquid courage.

David liked merlot. And he was allergic to bees. Funny the things you learned about your neighbors over the years. She also knew he was divorced, no kids, and he was one of the top cardiologists in Dallas.

Jen set her glass on the bathroom counter and turned on the shower, twisting her thick hair into a bun because she didn't have time to dry it. She stripped off her clothes and stepped under the hot spray.

A date. *Tonight.* Her stomach fluttered with nerves, and she wished she hadn't sampled the wine.

She'd bumped into David at Home Depot last week, and he'd asked her out right there in the lightbulb aisle.

We should have dinner sometime, he'd said with his easygoing smile.

She'd been so shocked that she stood there staring at him for a full five seconds until *I'd love to!* popped out of her mouth.

It was impulsive. And ill timed. But once the words were out, there was no going back.

She'd told him they should probably wait until her trial was over, but his blank expression made her realize he might not even know about it. How could he not, though? Didn't he read the papers? Maybe he was too busy saving lives to take notice of the media circus that had been going on in her courtroom for the past four weeks.

His utter obliviousness to her professional life appealed to her. A lot. She liked the prospect of seeing someone who didn't think of her as Judge Ballard or Your Honor. Most men were intimidated by the robe, and she hadn't had a single date in the two years since she'd been elected to the bench.

Jen stepped out of the shower and wrapped herself in a towel. Nerves fluttered again as she opened her closet and skimmed the endless rack of suits.

"Crap," she mumbled, combing through the hangers. Everything was drab, even her weekend clothes.

Very few women could exude sex appeal in the courtroom and still be taken seriously. Brynn Holloran came to mind. The auburn-haired defense attorney wore low-cut blouses and spike heels, and everyone knew she was a force to be reckoned with. Jen had always dressed down, in muted colors and sensible shoes, even during her prosecutor days. She wanted people to focus on her brain, not her boobs, but lately she'd felt sick to death of the whole conservative-jurist shtick.

Her gaze landed on the coral sheath dress she'd worn to her niece's graduation. It was pretty. Feminine. She remembered feeling confident in it. She grabbed the hanger and, before she could change her mind, slipped into a lace thong and pulled the dress over her head. She tugged up the zipper and rearranged her breasts because the tight fit didn't leave room for a bra.

Jen checked herself out in the mirror. Not bad. She freshened her makeup and fluffed her hair into a breezy style to match the dress. She slid her feet into sandals and downed a last sip of wine.

Her phone chimed from the bedroom, and she rushed to check it. Maybe another update from David. But instead it was Nate Levinson, a former colleague. What would he want? She'd missed two calls from him while she'd been in the shower, as well as a call from a Beaumont area code. She let Nate's call go to voice mail. It was business, no doubt, and she was taking the night off.

She glanced at the mirror one more time before heading into the kitchen. The house felt warm, and she stopped at the thermostat to turn up the AC. The clock read 7:25. David would be here any minute, and she still needed to season the steaks and throw the salad together. She walked into the kitchen and felt a crunch under her feet.

She looked down. What the . . . ?

Glass. All over the floor. She looked toward the patio, and a warm waft of air turned her blood to ice.

"Hello, Jennifer."

She whirled around to see a black pistol inches from her face. Her heart leaped as she looked at the man holding the gun. *Dear God, no.*

The calls from Nate, from Beaumont, all made sense now.

The man stepped forward. "On your knees."

"Don't hurt me."

"*Now!*"

Her legs folded, and she was on the floor, chunks of glass biting into her skin. *This can't be happening. How can this be happening?* Her heart hammered wildly in her chest.

"Don't hurt me." She gazed up at him, and the utter calm on his face made her stomach quiver.

He brought the muzzle of the gun to her forehead. It felt cool and hard, and bile rose in the back of her throat.

"Please," she croaked. "I'll do whatever you want, just—"

"That's right." His eyes were flat and soulless. "You will."

Brynn Holloran dipped her fingertips in the warm water and eyed the clock.

"What's your mood today?" Chrissy spun the nail-polish carousel and glanced at Brynn's ivory blouse. "Nude? Blushing bride?"

"Oh, no." Brynn picked a bottle and plunked it on the table.

"Cha-Ching Cherry." Chrissy smiled. "You must have a trial today."

"Monday."

Chrissy nodded. "You'll win," she said, snipping away at Brynn's cuticles. "Red's your lucky color."

Brynn darted another look at the clock as nervous energy buzzed through her. She appreciated Chrissy's confidence, but it did little to quell her stress. Nothing would until she stepped into that courtroom.

"Big case?" Chrissy asked.

"Yes." Big was an understatement. "It's a murder trial, and I haven't gone up against this prosecutor before."

Chrissy swiveled in her chair and took out some hot towels. Wrapping Brynn's hands, she studied her face through the steam. "You'll do great. He won't know what hit him."

Chrissy had been a fierce supporter ever since Brynn repped her in a dispute with her toad of a landlord, who was jerking her around over the rent. Brynn hadn't even represented her officially, just sent a nasty letter on firm stationery. The toad had backed down, and Chrissy had offered Brynn a lifetime of free manicures—which she wouldn't take, of course. Brynn would never hit Chrissy up for freebies, but she wasn't above coming in on a busy Friday and asking to be squeezed in.

Chrissy unwrapped the towels. She pumped lotion into her hand—eucalyptus mint—and started massaging Brynn's forearms. It felt so good she wanted to drop her head on the table and weep.

The massage was over way too soon, and Chrissy thwacked the bottle of polish against her palm before twisting off the top.

"The trial's in Dallas," Brynn said. "I have a thousand things to do, but I couldn't leave town without stopping in."

Chrissy raised a sculpted eyebrow. "Not if you're going to *Dallas*," she said, expertly stroking red over a nail.

She understood the importance of appearances. She was in the image business. Thanks to skin treatments and relentless workouts, the sixty-two-year-old salon owner didn't look a day over fifty, and Brynn hoped to be as lucky someday.

If she didn't work herself into an early grave first.

A text landed on Brynn's phone from Ross, her law partner. She swiped the screen with her free pinkie.

Perez is missing.

"Damn it." She looked up. "I have to make a call, sorry," she said, tapping Ross's number.

He picked up on the first ring. "Where are you?" he demanded.

"In a meeting. What do you mean, 'missing'?"

"We were supposed to have a video conference at nine to practice his testimony, but he blew it off, and he's not answering his phone."

"Try his girlfriend."

"I did. That's what worries me. She hasn't seen or heard from him since Tuesday, and she has no idea where he is."

Brynn bit back a curse. "Did you tell Reggie?"

"I'm headed to the office."

"I'll meet you there," she said. "We'll figure out what to do."

As soon as the phone was down, Chrissy took Brynn's hand and swiftly finished the first coat. She examined her work and did a quick second coat before switching on the drying lamp.

"I have to run. I—"

"Five minutes." Chrissy's stern look shut down any objections. She borrowed another lamp from a neighboring table and arranged Brynn's other hand beneath the heat before walking into the back room.

Brynn gazed longingly at her phone. She wanted to call Reggie. And check her e-mail. *Shit.* How could Perez be missing? Maybe he wasn't. Maybe he was sleeping off a hangover somewhere. But a tight ball of dread formed in Brynn's stomach as she thought about all the implications. Her eighteen-year-old client was going on trial for his life, and their star witness was MIA.

She took a deep breath and tried to relax, letting the lingering eucalyptus scent calm her. That worked for about a minute, and then she cast a furtive look over her shoulder. Chrissy had disappeared, and Brynn made a break for the cash register. She pulled out the credit card she'd left on top of her purse so she wouldn't have to rummage with wet nails. After leaving an extra-big tip and signing the bill, she stepped from the cool salon into the sweltering summer heat.

Brynn slid into her black SUV and headed across town, which wasn't a long drive. Pine Rock was a sleepy bedroom community just north of Houston—six stoplights and two churches.

Her sister's Wonder Woman ring tone emanated from the speakers, and Brynn answered.

"Have you left yet?" Liz asked.

"We leave Sunday."

"Perfect!"

"What is it?"

"Mike's got a college friend in from out of town. We're taking him out for Tex-Mex tomorrow night, and we want you to come."

"I wish I could, but I'm slammed," Brynn said.

"You're just saying that because you think it's a setup."

"Well, isn't it?"

"It's Tex-Mex and margaritas. Totally casual. And this guy's cute. I know you'll hit it off."

Liz and Brynn had a special language when it came to men. "Hot" meant drool-worthy alpha. "Cute" meant a teddy bear, and the last "cute" guy her sister had set her up with had been three inches shorter than Brynn.

Not that it should matter. Who cared what he looked like if he was decent and smart and managed to get through the evening without burping or bad-mouthing his ex? Brynn was the problem.

"I really have to work," Brynn said. "I have a whole new fire drill, as of ten minutes ago. Our star witness is missing."

"Damn. Really?"

"Really." She turned into the parking lot beside her building and whipped into her usual space.

"Well, call me if you catch a break and want to go out tomorrow."

"I will. Love you."

Brynn strode across the lot, careful not to catch her Jimmy Choo sandals in any of the potholes. She dropped her phone into her purse as she mounted the steps to the converted Victorian that housed the offices of Blythe and Gunn.

Reggie had bought the property three years ago when he moved his law practice from Dallas to Pine Rock. From the street, the place looked charming. But years of dealing with leaky windows and temperamental plumbing had dampened Brynn's enthusiasm for the architecture. The building was originally a boardinghouse, but Reggie had renovated it to accommodate six lawyers, two paralegals, an administrative assistant, and a receptionist—not to mention the steady flow of clients who drifted in and out seven days a week. Big trials were the firm's gravy, but Saturday-night arrests were its bread and butter.

The waiting room was empty of tearful mothers and hand-wringing spouses this morning. The receptionist's chair was empty, too, and Brynn followed the smell of fresh coffee to Reggie's office.

Faith sat behind her mahogany desk, dabbing her eyes with a tissue. Brynn stopped short. Reggie's assistant never cried. The mother hen of the law firm was unflappable, no matter how crazy things got.

Brynn stepped over. "Faith?"

She glanced up, startled, and her usually perfect mascara was streaked down her cheeks.

It was Faith's boys. Had to be. Her two teenage sons were constantly getting into trouble, and Faith had started to worry that the older one was on drugs.

Brynn knelt beside her. "Faith, what happened?"

Faith squeezed her eyes shut and shook her head.

"Brynn!" Reggie boomed from his office. The door jerked open, and her silver-haired boss stepped out. "Brynn, get in here."

She shot him a glare and returned her attention to Faith. "Are you all right?"

She dabbed her nose. "Yes, just . . . go on."

Brynn stood and followed Reginald H. Gunn, managing partner, past the nameplate bearing his title. Shelves crammed with law books lined the walls, and towers of file boxes crowded every corner. Reggie walked behind his cluttered desk, and Brynn noted the pin-striped suit jacket hanging on the back of his chair. The pink silk handkerchief in the front pocket told her he planned to be in court later.

"Close the door, would you?"

She followed his gruff command, taking one last peek at Faith as she eased shut the door.

"Sit down," he said.

"I'll stand. What's up?"

Reggie's leather chair creaked as he sank into it. He ran a hand through his thick hair.

"Nate called me. Jen Ballard was killed last night."

Brynn sagged back against the wall. "What—"

"I don't have all the details yet, but she was murdered sometime yesterday evening in her home."

Murdered.

Brynn's blood turned cold. Beautiful, witty Jen Ballard *murdered.* The words didn't belong in the same sentence.

She stepped closer to Reggie's desk. "How?"

"I don't know, okay? I haven't even had time to call the police up there. And there's something else—"

A sharp knock came at the door. Ross leaned his head in and immediately zeroed in on Brynn. "You tell him yet?"

"Tell me what?" Reggie asked.

Ross stepped into the office, oblivious to the tension hovering in the room. "Perez is missing. We were supposed to run through his testimony at nine, but he blew off the appointment."

"Try his girlfriend."

"She hasn't seen or heard from him in days." Ross looked at Brynn and frowned. "What's wrong?"

She cleared her throat. "Jen Ballard."

"What about her?"

"She was murdered," Reggie said.

Ross's face went slack. "*What?*"

"She was killed in her home last night. Up in Sheridan Heights, right outside of Dallas," Reggie told him. "I just got off the phone with Nate Levinson twenty minutes ago."

Ross shot Brynn a look, as if she might somehow make sense of what he was hearing, but she couldn't. The forty-two-year-old woman who'd once been their boss, their mentor, and their *friend* was dead.

"What's the other thing?" Brynn asked Reggie. "You said there was something else?"

Reggie stared at Brynn. A veteran trial attorney, he had a talent for creating drama, but the solemn look on his face was all too real.

"What is it?" Ross asked.

"James Corby is out."

Brynn's eyebrows shot up. "*Out?*"

Beside her, Ross made a strangled sound.

"He escaped."

"Are you fucking kidding me?" Ross clutched his head with his hands. "*How* do you escape a fucking maximum-security prison?"

Reggie's gaze locked with Brynn's. "I don't know."

But he *did* know. And so did Brynn. As an assistant prosecutor, Brynn had tried James Corby's case alongside then lead prosecutor Jen Ballard. Brynn had learned that James Corby was not only violent and sadistic but also smart. Frighteningly smart. And the prospect of him slipping out of prison had lurked in the darkest corners of Brynn's mind for years.

Her chest felt tight. She placed her hand on her sternum and tried to breathe. But it was Ross who bent at the waist and looked like he was going to puke.

"Shit!"

"Hey," Reggie snapped. "Don't throw up in here."

Ross straightened and shook his head. "This is insane. Where the hell are the marshals?"

"They're on it," Reggie replied. "That I *do* know. Nate tells me they've been working this thing from the beginning."

"And when was that?" Brynn asked.

"Wednesday."

"He escaped *Wednesday*, and we're just now hearing about it?"

Beside her, Ross let out a blistering string of curses.

"What does this mean for us?" Ross asked. "Our trial begins in Dallas in *three days*, right down the goddamn road from Jen's murder—"

"It means we have to take action," Reggie said. "I've already started."

"What do you mean?" Brynn couldn't keep the skepticism out of her voice. She'd dealt with plenty of criminals and considered herself fairly streetwise. But what kind of "action" did Reggie think they were going to take here? Was he planning to jump into his Mercedes and hunt down an escaped convict?

"I'm hiring protection," Reggie said. "The best money can buy."

"Bodyguards?" She blinked at him. "You can't be serious."

"I am." He checked his watch and picked up the phone.

"Wait, stop." Brynn held up her hand. "Before you rush off and hire anyone, we need to talk to the sheriffs up there about protection. This falls on them, doesn't it? Our courthouse is in their jurisdiction."

Reggie gave her a dark look. "This law firm doesn't exactly have a lot of friends up there. As you well know."

"Reggie, they hate us up there," Ross said.

"Exactly my point. We can't count on the locals to do anything for us."

"Yes, but it's their *job*," Brynn said.

"Yeah, and it's our job to win this trial. I won't have my two top attorneys worried and distracted."

Brynn was still in shock. But not so much that she couldn't imagine the major pain in the butt having a bodyguard trailing her around was going to be. This was the biggest case of her career. Reggie had put her in charge of everything, from jury selection to the closing statement. She'd spent countless hours preparing and still had work to do.

"Yes, but . . . bodyguards? As in plural?" She played the money card. "That sounds expensive."

"It is."

"Listen, Reggie, I appreciate the thought." She glanced at Ross. "We both do, but—"

"No buts. And it's not a thought. I already made the call." He looked at Ross. "Now, about this Perez thing, did you get Bulldog on it?"

Ross shook his head, and Reggie jabbed at his desk phone.

Bulldog, aka Bull, aka John Kopek, was the private investigator Reggie kept on speed dial. Brynn shook her head. She felt like she'd been sucker punched, and her boss was already back to business.

"Bull, it's Reggie. I need a locate." He muffled the receiver against his shirt and gave Brynn a sharp look. "You've got a trial to prep for. Better get to it."

Erik Morgan was almost out when everything went sideways.

An earsplitting *boom.*

A billow of smoke.

He halted in the narrow corridor and adjusted the body slung over his shoulder. The air around him swirled with grit. Sweat seeped into his eyes. But he pushed the distractions out of his mind as he and his teammates moved into position.

Weapon raised, Erik darted around the corner, instantly spotting two silhouettes. To his right, a man holding a pistol. To his left, a teenage girl holding a cell phone. Erik fired two rounds at the man, hitting him square in the chest.

"Clear!"

He ran for the door, stopping at the threshold to scan for hostiles.

"Clear!" he repeated, then took off down the stairs.

One flight. Two. A door slapped open above him.

Boom!

Dust rained down as Erik adjusted his load and kept moving. They were running out of time. He could feel it. More smoke, more shouting. He heard his teammates' footsteps behind him.

"Go, go, go!" someone yelled.

Boots thundered as four men carrying more than eight hundred pounds of dead weight bounded down the stairwell. At ground level, Erik stopped at the plywood door. His teammate kicked it open and peered out to scan the area.

"All clear!" Hayes yelled.

Erik followed him through the door, exiting the kill house with a cloud of smoke and dust. He sprinted the last fifty yards to a concrete barricade, then dropped to a knee in the dirt and lowered his load to the ground.

"Two minutes, forty-six seconds."

Erik glanced up to see Jeremy Owen looming over him with a stopwatch. The former Marine sharpshooter did not look happy.

The man playing the role of Erik's protectee groaned and sat up. "What the fuck happened back there?"

Hayes shook his head. "I couldn't see." He glanced back at the kill house, a building made up of rooms, hallways, and stairwells where they practiced closed-quarters battle and rescue scenarios. Flash-bangs and smoke grenades were tossed into the mix to ramp up the chaos.

Erik had watched Hayes work, and visibility wasn't his only prob-lem. Hayes's protectee had a paint splatter on his shirt the size of a soc-cer ball. If they'd been facing live rounds, the man would be dead.

"Okay, everybody up," Jeremy ordered. "Hit the hoses, and we'll reconvene on the south range at fifteen hundred."

Erik got up and helped his teammate to his feet. He wiped the sweat from his face with the back of his arm and glanced at the sun. It was ninety-eight today—hotter inside the kill house—and his clothes were saturated.

Everyone grabbed the gear and moved out. Jeremy caught Erik's eye and signaled for him to walk back with him on the trail.

"How'd it go with Becker?" Jeremy asked when they were deep in the woods.

Hayes Becker, twenty-six, of Roanoke, Virginia. As a team leader, it was Erik's job to help evaluate candidates who wanted to join the elite ranks of Wolfe Security, and Hayes had made it to the final round.

"He's not ready yet," Erik said. "But he's getting there."

"What's your take on his skills?"

"His tactical driving's good. PT scores are off the charts. It's his shooting that needs work."

Jeremy grunted. "That's the problem with these FBI hires."

"So we're keeping him?"

Jeremy nodded.

They made their way along the running trail and O-course. Set among the towering East Texas pines, the course had been modeled after the SEAL obstacle course at Coronado. The pinnacle in terms of height and effort was a seventy-foot cargo net, which a couple of new recruits were clawing their way up right now. They wore olive-green

BDUs to differentiate themselves from real Wolfe agents, who wore all black.

Erik reviewed this afternoon's session, making a mental list of the areas where Hayes needed work. Any team they deployed on a job was only as good as its weakest member, and new hires either had to get up to speed or get out.

"I'll spend some time with him," Erik said. "We can burn through some mags on the range, see if I can pinpoint his problem."

"Good. I'll give Liam the heads-up."

Erik walked into the clearing as a silver 5-series BMW sped by, leaving a cloud of red dust in its wake. It curved along the dirt road and pulled up to the sprawling log cabin that served as their business headquarters. A man climbed out from behind the wheel. Average height, medium build. From his Ray-Bans and his suit, Erik pegged him for a corporate executive. Then the passenger door opened, and a woman slid from the car.

Erik halted. Her long red hair caught the sunlight as she turned around. She wore tight black jeans and a silky white shirt, and she had a big leather purse slung over her shoulder. She was several inches taller than the guy with her, partly because of her mile-high heels.

"Who is that?" Erik looked at Jeremy.

"No idea."

They got all kinds of VIPs at the compound. Pop stars, politicians, athletes. Some of their clients were just ordinary rich people who'd picked up an enemy along the way and decided they needed protection. Judging from their looks, this couple fell into the last category. They mounted the steps to the building, peeling off their shades as they went inside.

"Yo, Erik."

He turned to see Tony Lopez jogging up the trail. In a black T-shirt and tactical pants, he was dressed just like Erik, only he wasn't sporting a layer of dirt and soot.

"The chief wants you in his office," Tony said.

"Now?"

"Yeah, ASAP."

Erik's gaze narrowed. "This have to do with the five-series that just pulled in?"

"You got it."

"Know who they are?"

He smiled. "I hear they're a couple of hotshots from Dallas."

"Shit."

"Think they're attorneys," he added.

"*Shit.*"

Tony grinned and slapped him on the shoulder. "Better you than me, bro."

2

THEY WAITED a good ten minutes before Liam Wolfe met them in the lobby of his office, which was nothing like Brynn had expected. The building looked like it was made of Lincoln Logs, and a huge stone fireplace dominated the lobby. After reading that Wolfe Security was one of the top personal security firms in the country, Brynn had expected something slick and modern, not what could have been a hunting lodge tucked deep within the piney woods.

The CEO wasn't what she'd expected, either. Brynn had spent way too much time last night surfing around and only managed to find one photograph of Liam Wolfe, a paparazzi shot of him helping some young starlet into a limo. The picture didn't begin to do him justice, probably because he wore sunglasses that concealed his striking green eyes. They were sharp eyes. Warrior eyes. Brynn had read that the man was some sort of special ops badass, but it turned out you actually had to see him in person and shake his hand to get the full impact.

"Nice place you have here," Ross quipped as Liam led them down a hallway. "Was that a firing range we heard on the way in?"

"It was."

"Sweet," Ross said, and Brynn tried not to roll her eyes. Her partner wasn't exactly a gun enthusiast. But he was probably trying to fit in at what was obviously a boys' club.

Brynn followed Ross into a conference room and stopped short. Five men stood around the table, each one more ripped than the last. Some had military haircuts, some had scruffy beards, but all wore the same black commando-style clothing.

Liam made introductions, and everyone nodded. The silence stretched out, and Brynn realized they were waiting for her to sit down.

So she did.

The conference room had modern furnishings, including a long glass conference table and black leather chairs. A giant LCD screen dominated the far wall. Pulling a legal pad from her bag, Brynn smiled and glanced around the table, trying to project more confidence than she felt.

"Thank you, Mr. Wolfe, for agreeing to meet us here this afternoon," she said.

He nodded. "Typically, we go to the client's home base, but we're happy to accommodate you."

Ross shot Brynn a questioning look that she pretended not to see. She hadn't told him that coming out here was her idea, not Reggie's. She was trying to get ahead of a situation that was rapidly spinning out of her control. Despite three intense debates, Brynn hadn't persuaded her boss to ditch the bodyguard plan. She'd resigned herself to the fact that these men had been hired, but she was here to negotiate terms. As always, the devil was in the details.

"Gentlemen—" She looked around the room, slightly dazed by all the testosterone. These guys were seriously jacked. "I'm sure you're as busy as we are, so I'll get right to the point—"

The door opened, and a man stepped in. He was huge—even bigger than the rest—and Brynn's heart gave a little lurch as he zeroed in on her.

"This is one of our team leaders," Liam said. "Erik Morgan, meet Brynn Holloran."

The man gave a brisk nod.

"And her partner, Ross Foley."

Another nod. All the chairs were taken, so he slipped to the side of the room and leaned against the wall.

Brynn cleared her throat. "So I—or *we*—would like to thank you for being available on such short notice."

She wondered if Liam Wolfe caught her underlying message. She had no doubt he'd researched his new clients and knew that Blythe and Gunn represented several NFL players with very fat salaries. Liam had probably jumped at the chance to take this job because he was thinking about future referrals.

But his expression gave nothing away. "Short notice is pretty typical for us. Threats like this tend to catch people off guard." He paused. "I understand you'd like an overview of the security plan?"

"Exactly."

"First question is *when*," Ross said. "I don't know if you realize this, but half our office is driving up to Dallas tomorrow morning."

Brynn's stomach knotted just thinking about the whole operation: two lawyers, a paralegal, and a private investigator who still hadn't managed to locate a witness critical to the case.

"We're aware," Liam said. "We're also aware that your trial starts Monday. We're used to moving quickly, so it's not a problem." He looked at Brynn. "We're finalizing your security plan today, and your agents will be ready to go in the morning. Meantime, I understand the two of you are staying at a hotel instead of your private homes?"

"Reggie's idea," Ross said. "The hotel isn't exactly Fort Knox, but no one knows we're there."

Brynn glanced at Erik Morgan, who was watching Ross with a carefully blank expression on his face. The man wore all black and stood with his arms folded over his chest, making his muscles strain against his shirt. His close-cropped hair was dark. And wet, she noticed, as though he'd dunked his head in a bucket of water on the way over here. A thin layer of dust covered his body, which made him look like he'd just come off a construction site—except for the pistol on his hip. The big black weapon looked perfectly natural there, and Brynn had a feeling he knew how to use it.

She tore her gaze away from Erik's gun to focus on the plan Liam was outlining.

"I'm sorry." She leaned forward. "Did you say *your* vehicles?"

"That's correct. Two full-size SUVs, both armor-plated and with bulletproof glass."

"Armored cars? You're kidding," Ross said.

"No."

Brynn started to laugh but then caught herself. There was nothing funny about this. Not at all. One of the least funny things was the money this had to cost.

Brynn shook her head. "Two vehicles is totally unnecessary. Ross and I are staying at the same location." Reggie kept several corporate apartments in Dallas because the firm had frequent business there. "Not only that, but we'll be going to the same place every morning— the courthouse—at the very same time. One vehicle is plenty."

"Not for a three-man package," Liam said.

Brynn stared at him in disbelief. "Three agents for two lawyers?"

"No, three for each of you."

"*Six* men? You can't be serious."

"Each of your teams includes three agents on a rotating shift, two on, one off, around the clock."

"Around the clock," she repeated.

"That is correct, ma'am."

———

From his spot against the wall, Erik watched her reaction to his boss's plans. And those were just the ones he'd mentioned so far. She didn't know the half of it.

Brynn Holloran didn't like this setup at all. Maybe she was one of those people who was sensitive about privacy. Or maybe she thought this thing was going to cramp her lifestyle—whatever it was. Erik had seen all kinds of reactions since he'd started this job, and he was definitely accustomed to getting a cool reception. People didn't like change. But when Erik and his guys went to work on something, change was pretty much guaranteed, so like it or not, she was going to have to deal.

"Mr. Wolfe . . ." She seemed to be struggling to keep her voice friendly. "If we go along with this—"

If? She still didn't get it.

"—we're going to need your guarantee that your agents won't impede our work in any way." She glanced around the table, looking at everyone but Erik. "No offense, and I'm sure you're all *very* good at your jobs. But you have to understand that we have a job to do, too. Our client's future is at stake, and we can't afford any distractions right now."

"We always aim to keep a low profile," Liam assured her. "The objective is to protect the client with as few disruptions as possible."

He wisely didn't say *no* disruptions.

"Good." She smiled. But it looked fake, and Erik wondered what she looked like when she smiled for real. "Glad we can agree. With that in mind, we should reconsider the staffing level." She flipped to a new page of her notepad and brushed a lock of that shiny auburn hair over her shoulder. "Six agents is excessive. Blythe and Gunn is a small firm, as you know. We're used to doing more with less. That said, I'm sure you can see the logic in scaling back the number of agents."

"Six *is* scaled back," the chief told her. "My original recommendation was eight."

"*Eight?*" She looked at him like he was crazy. "Mr. Wolfe, I understand a lot of your clients are politicians and celebrities. Have you ever worked for people involved in a trial before?"

"Yes."

"Okay, well, then you know how it is. It's a grind. Long hours, few breaks. We'll be holed up in a corporate apartment every night going over files and eating takeout. We hardly need six full-time people to get us to and from the courthouse every day."

Ah, shit. Erik suppressed a smile as he watched his boss.

"Ma'am." Liam leaned his elbows on the table. "Let me be clear. We are not a taxi service. Ensuring your personal security"—he glanced at Ross—"and yours goes way beyond getting you safely from point A to point B, although we will do that. Your firm has hired us to provide comprehensive security for you twenty-four/seven. That includes securing your residence and your communications, as well as protecting you personally, whether you're at home or on the move or at work. Comprehensive security means everything. It's a lot to cover, and frankly, six men for two principals is stretching it thin, even for us, and we've got the best people in the world doing this job."

"I hear you." She smiled. "Really, I do. But couldn't some of this be done through technology? How about a few of your agents, plus some strategically positioned security cameras that could be monitored at a central location? That would require less manpower."

She gazed at Liam with those pretty baby blues, as if every word out of her mouth made perfect sense.

"Security cams are useful," Liam said, "and we plan to have some in place. But in the event of an attack, a camera isn't going to do much to save your life."

"An attack? You really think—"

"Yes, I do." Liam paused and gave her one of those hard stares he was so good at.

She stared right back.

"You know, I spent a good chunk of my morning on the phone with the Sheridan Heights police chief," Liam said. "When I got off with him, I talked to the supervisory deputy U.S. marshal overseeing the search for escaped convict James Corby. Local law enforcement is not up to this task. It's clear to me that until Corby is apprehended, you and your colleagues are going to need outside resources to ensure your safety. That means us. And that means whatever level of manpower we believe it takes to get the job done."

Brynn's smile was gone, and from where he stood, Erik could see that she was simmering.

She was hot. And headstrong, too, which, unfortunately, was a combination that really did it for him. The only woman Erik had ever seen challenge Liam head-on was his wife, and she was on a freaking SWAT team. Liam was intimidating, but that didn't stop Brynn from trying to negotiate the terms of what she obviously viewed as a prison sentence.

"Could you go back a sec?" Ross said. "You said something about communications. You mean phones? Computers? What?"

"All of it," Liam told him. "Your cell phone is essentially a tracking device. We'll provide each of you with a new, clean device." Liam looked at Brynn. "You'll be able to keep your number and your contacts."

"Fabulous," she said. "But what if I don't *want* a new device?"

Liam glanced at Erik. As of ten minutes ago, Erik was the leader of Brynn's detail, so many of the technical aspects fell to him.

"I'll talk to Skyler," Erik said. "She might be able to examine her phone, clear it for use." He nodded at Brynn. "You'll have to leave it here overnight."

She looked at him as though he'd asked her to leave her arm on the table.

"Your call."

She shrugged. "Fine, no problem." Although it clearly was. "It's password-protected, though."

"Send me your code, and I'll give it to Skyler," Liam said.

"Hey, I wouldn't mind getting a new phone," Ross said. "I just need my contacts and my number."

Liam glanced at his watch. "One more issue. I already discussed this with Reggie Gunn, but I'd like to get your take on it." He looked at Brynn now instead of her law partner. "What can you tell me about your connection to the murder victim?"

Pain flashed in her eyes. But she folded her hands in front of her and seemed to shake it off. "We worked for Jen Ballard when she was a prosecutor. The time span covered hundreds of cases, including James Corby's. Jen tried the case and got him put away for life, no parole."

"And we helped," Ross said. "As assistant DAs, we were all part of the prosecution team that got him locked up, so we could be on the guy's shit list."

Liam nodded. "I understand your current trial in Dallas has no connection to Jennifer Ballard or James Corby?"

"Right, there's no connection," Brynn told him. "Different judge, different side of the aisle, different everything."

"We're at the defense table now instead of the prosecution," Ross said.

Liam kept his focus on Brynn. "When you were trying Corby's case, did you ever receive any personal communication from him?"

"No."

"Anything after the trial?"

"No."

"And have you ever received any threats related to work?"

"Ever? Yeah, of course," she said. "I was a prosecutor for four years, goes with the job. But recently? No."

"Any unusual phone calls lately, letters, or threatening messages on social media?"

She hesitated a beat. "No."

"You're sure?"

"Yes."

Erik watched her, not sure why she was lying. Or even if she *was* lying. He didn't know her well enough yet to tell. But he would. By the time this job was over, he would know everything there was to know about Brynn Holloran, including plenty of things she was going to wish he didn't.

Liam watched her for another moment, then looked at Ross. "What about you?"

"Nothing. Why? Did Jen get something?"

"I don't know," Liam answered, but Erik could tell he was hiding something.

Brynn's gaze narrowed, as if she could sense it, too.

Liam steered the conversation back to the security plan, outlining all the basics as Brynn jotted notes on her legal pad. Finally, they discussed a pickup time in the morning, and everyone stood.

Erik hung back, waiting for the room to clear so he could keep his distance as he got the hell out of there. He was acutely aware of how rank he smelled after a four-hour training session.

But Brynn stayed by the door, digging through her purse. When the room was empty, she walked over and gazed up at him. She didn't have to look far—she was nearly six feet tall.

"Erik, is it?"

"Yes, ma'am."

She reached out her hand, and he started to shake it, but she handed him a sleek new iPhone in a designer case.

"Thanks," Erik said, sliding the phone into his pocket. "I'll get it back to you tomorrow."

"Please do. Half my life's on that damn thing."

She left the room, joining her partner in the hallway, and Erik trailed behind them.

Skyler crossed the lobby, and her eyes darted in Erik's direction. Judging from the smirk on her face, she'd heard about his new assignment. Erik needed to get Skyler on this thing. He could use her insight. It was clear this new client was going to be a handful.

Ross paused at the end of the hallway as Skyler disappeared into the computer room. He looked at Erik. "Hey, any chance you guys bring your admins along on the job with you?"

Brynn glared at him. "Jesus, Ross."

"What?"

She turned to Erik and rolled her eyes. "Please excuse us. We'll see you in the morning."

They tromped down the stairs together.

"What was that about?" Ross asked.

"That woman's a bodyguard, Ross. Open your eyes."

"Her?" He glanced back over his shoulder. "She was maybe five-two."

"Yeah, and did you see the pistol strapped to her hip?"

Brynn squared her shoulders as they headed for the car. What a meeting. Brynn couldn't remember a time when she'd lost so much ground in so little time.

Actually, the ground had been lost beforehand. She just hadn't realized it.

Six agents. Two armored cars. People following her everywhere she went. The only concession she'd managed to get was a vague assurance from Liam Wolfe that his team would cause "as few disruptions as possible." Which amounted to a pile of crap. Brynn had nothing in writing, and the logistics of this operation were worse than she'd ever imagined. She couldn't believe Reggie had agreed to all this.

Ross popped the locks, and they slid into the BMW. Brynn stowed her purse on the floor and automatically reached to check her phone, which of course wasn't there. Had she really handed it over to a perfect stranger?

"This is crazy," she said.

"Which part?"

"All of it. Six bodyguards? That's ludicrous. And it's got to be cost-ing the firm a fortune."

"What do you care?" Ross backed out of the space. "Reggie's pay-ing out of his drawing account. It's not going to affect your salary one bit."

Ross drove past a row of pickups and looped back onto the dirt road.

"It's wasteful," Brynn said. "Our firm's bleeding money, and why? So Reggie can make some kind of statement to Dallas law enforce-ment."

"He's got a beef with them. Fact is, they hate him. *And* they hate us for working with him."

"Still, this is over the top. We don't need this level of security."

"Brynn."

"What?"

He cut a glance at her. "Did you even read about Jen?"

"Of course I did." Brynn's blood chilled. She'd read everything she could get her hands on. A judge's murder anywhere, let alone an afflu-ent suburb of Dallas, was big news across the state.

"It was bad," Ross said.

Bad? It was a horror show. Brynn looked out the window and tried not to think about the details. *The victim suffered multiple gunshot wounds and was rushed to the hospital, where she was declared dead on arrival.*

Brynn shuddered. Jen wouldn't have been rushed anywhere if her date on Thursday evening hadn't been a doctor. He'd shown up soon after the attack and kept Jen hanging on by a thread until the para-medics arrived.

"Honestly, I'm glad Reggie hired these guys," Ross said. "Every last one of them. I don't know what it costs, and I really don't care. That guy's a sadist. Jen proved that at trial."

"He has antisocial personality disorder."

"Well, what difference does the label make if he comes after one of us? If Corby shows up in your living room, are you really going to care about his clinical diagnosis?"

"He's not going to come after us. Reggie's overreacting."

"Overreacting? Jen is *dead*."

"I know," she snapped. "I'm aware of that, okay? But everyone's jumping to conclusions about who killed her. Jen was a prosecutor for four years. You know how many people she helped convict?"

"No."

"Hundreds. When we worked for her, she was averaging ninety-five felony cases a year. Add misdemeanor filings, and her caseload was nearly four times that. Jen made a boatload of enemies, and any number of those guys could be out on parole and looking for revenge. God knows plenty of them are unstable."

"Yeah, but think about the timing. James Corby just escaped from prison."

"True. And he was one of her most high-profile cases. Maybe someone heard about it and decided it was the perfect opportunity to settle a score."

Ross shook his head. "Who would do that?"

"I don't know. But you have to admit it's a possibility. And now here goes Reggie, mobilizing an army of bodyguards. All this drama so he can make a point to Dallas law enforcement that they're not competent to do their basic job."

"He wouldn't do all this just to make a point."

"He absolutely would. He's manipulating the press, ginning up publicity for us right before a big trial. You know as well as I do that he never misses an opportunity to shine a spotlight on himself or the firm. When we show up with this entourage, people will notice. I mean, really, *six* bodyguards, Ross?"

They neared the gate to the property. No guardhouse, no keypad, not even a sign, just two plain black panels that slid open when they got close.

Ross rolled through the opening, and Brynn watched in her side mirror as the black gates glided shut behind them. Liam Wolfe's compound—like the man himself—was practically invisible unless you knew where to look.

Ross turned onto the highway and hit the gas, and the V-8 engine gave a throaty growl.

"Lemme just say this." Ross looked at her. "James Corby is a sick son of a bitch. Whether he killed Jen or not, I'll sleep a hell of a lot easier when they collar him up."

Yeah, sure. Like they could just pluck him off the street, a man who'd slipped out of a maximum-security prison.

"Me, too," Brynn said. "But first, they have to find him."

3

BRYNN SAT amid a mountain of pillows, her files spread out around her on the king-size bed. She was supposed to be prepping for trial tonight, but she'd spent the past two hours digging for info on Jen's case.

A shrill noise made her jump. She looked at the phone on the nightstand. No one was supposed to know she was here.

Another cringe-inducing sound, and she grabbed the phone. "Yes?"

"Hey, it's me." Bulldog.

She slid her laptop aside and leaned back against the pillows. "How'd you find me?"

"Are you kidding? I'm a fucking detective. How's the Ritz?"

Ha. She and Ross were holed up in an extended-stay hotel north of Houston with a bunch of cranky businessmen.

Not that Brynn had socialized much. She'd purchased dinner in the gift shop before coming straight up to her room.

"It's peachy," she told him. "Where are you? And please tell me you've got something on Perez."

"I do, but you're not going to like it."

"Damn." She grabbed the single-serving wine bottle on the night-stand and took a swig.

"I talked to his baby mama again this morning. She still hasn't seen him, but I tracked down one of his buddies, and sounds like Perez was talking about Vegas."

"Vegas?" Brynn plunked the bottle down on the nightstand. "Tell me you're kidding."

"No. I'm working on confirmation."

A sharp knock sounded at the door.

"Bull, hang on, okay?"

She crossed the room and peered through the peephole to see Ross standing in the hall, wearing jeans and his SMU Law T-shirt and hold-ing a pizza box. Brynn unlatched the door and let him in.

"Bulldog's on the phone," she told him. "He thinks Perez might be in Las Vegas."

"Vegas? What the hell?"

She grabbed the phone again and sat on the bed. "I thought he lost his job last month," she said to Bulldog. "How does he have the money for Vegas?"

"I don't know, but I plan to find out."

Ross walked over and tapped the button for speakerphone. "Bull, hey, it's Ross. Are you going up there?"

"If I have to."

Ross looked at Brynn. "Reggie's going to freak."

"*I'm* freaking," she said. "This guy's our key witness. Without him, our defense collapses."

"Calm down," Bulldog said. "I'll find the guy. You won't need him until week two, earliest."

"Yeah, but I can't refer to his testimony in my opening statement and then have him not show up." Brynn squeezed her eyes shut and tried to breathe.

"He'll be there," he said. "But I might have to go get him, all right? So put in a word with Reggie for me."

Brynn gritted her teeth. She didn't need this right now. Now, on top of everything else, she had to persuade her boss to cough up money for a trip to Las Vegas.

"Brynn?"

"I'll talk to him," she said. "If he won't cover it, I will. We need that testimony."

"I'll find him. Trust me."

He hung up, and Brynn looked at Ross.

"If Bulldog doesn't find him, we're screwed," he said.

"I realize that. I'll pay for the trip if Reggie won't."

"It's not the cost I'm worried about."

She could tell Ross was worried about the same thing she was. How did their deadbeat witness suddenly rustle up the cash to go to Vegas? The timing was beyond convenient.

Ross's gaze landed on her luggage.

"*Three* suitcases, Brynn?"

"Yep."

She didn't mention she had a hanging bag in the closet, too.

"And what's with all the bankers' boxes?"

"Case files."

"I thought Nicole had everything?"

Nicole was the paralegal coming to Dallas with them. She planned to be there for the beginning phase of the trial and then head back to Pine Rock.

"She has some of it," Brynn said. "The most important stuff is with me."

"Wolfe's crew is going to need a moving van for all that. Ever heard of packing light? All I have is a garment bag."

"Yeah, and you're a guy. I need more than two ties and a pair of wingtips."

She refused to feel guilty. She liked to have choices. She'd packed nine suits, twelve blouses, and a mere seven pairs of shoes. And she wasn't ruling out going back for more if the trial dragged on.

Ross shook his head, and his attention landed on the computer sitting open on the bed. She watched his brow furrow as he read the headline on the news article. He leaned over and tapped open another article. And another. He clicked the page for the medical examiner's office, and his frown deepened.

"Don't tell me you're looking for the autopsy report."

"I just want to understand the basics," she said. Which was more or less true. But the basics had led to some very disturbing details.

"Don't do it." He shot her a worried look. "You were friends with her. We both were. You shouldn't read that stuff."

Brynn closed her computer. She didn't want to tell him it was too late. She'd already talked to a contact in the Sheridan Heights Police Department who had shared preliminary details from the autopsy over the phone. Jen had suffered two gunshot wounds to the abdomen, point-blank range.

"It doesn't feel like Corby to me."

Ross rested his hands on his hips and tipped his head back. "Brynn, come on."

"Just listen."

"I don't want to hear this. I don't want to remember her this way."

"Neither do I, but I'm sorry, there are some things you have to know." She waited for him to look at her. "Jen was shot at close range, for one thing. She nearly bled out on her floor and then died on the way to the hospital. That's what the investigator told me."

Ross just looked at her.

"Corby likes knives. We know that. This MO doesn't fit with him at all. And where'd he get a gun within twenty-four hours of escaping from prison? It doesn't add up. Plus, his were sexual homicides. All of his victims were raped. Jen wasn't." Brynn shook her head. "I don't think this is Corby. It's someone else, and everyone's caught up in this manhunt for Corby, assuming *he* did this, when the person who really killed Jen could be walking away scot-free."

"You really believe that?" Ross asked.

"We're defense attorneys. You, of all people, should know we can't rush to judgment, especially not at the beginning of an investigation."

Ross picked up the pizza box.

"Where are you going?"

"To my room to work," he said. "I know you, Brynn. It's pointless to argue when you get this way. You get some idea, and you're like a dog with a bone." He held up the box. "Last chance for mushroom double-pepperoni. Want any?"

"No."

"See you tomorrow. And you really should stop reading those reports about Jen. It isn't healthy." He walked out without looking back. Brynn stared at the door for a few moments, then latched it.

She went to the window and peered through the thick curtains at the crowded parking lot. Beyond it was an interstate busy with Saturday night traffic, people headed out to bars and restaurants. She thought of her sister and her brother-in-law's college friend. She could be having Tex-Mex and margaritas right now, but instead she was working. Again. And it wasn't just because of the trial Monday. Not even her sister knew that she'd worked every Saturday for the past seven months. It was her routine. Her choice.

Her coping mechanism.

When she worked, she didn't have to think about what a mess she'd made of her personal life.

Another shrill noise made her jump. Cursing, she grabbed the phone. "Yeah?"

Silence.

Then "Ms. Holloran?"

"Yes?"

"This is Erik Morgan."

"How did you—" She didn't finish. Of course he knew where she was—he was picking her up in the morning.

"Everything all right there?"

"Fine. Yes. I'm just getting some work done."

"I won't keep you," he said. "I wanted to let you know we processed your cell phone, and everything looks clean."

"Clean?"

"No bugs or viruses or extraneous tracking software."

She sank down onto the bed, unable to believe she was having this conversation. Sure, she knew phones could be used to track people, but she couldn't really believe someone would do it to *her*. This whole thing seemed surreal. Imaginary.

But there was nothing imaginary about Jen's death. Because of her job, Jen had always been careful about her security. And yet someone had broken into her home and shot her.

"Thanks for the update." Brynn tried to sound casual.

"I'll have it back to you in the morning."

"All right."

"Eight o'clock," he reminded her.

"I'll be ready," she said with confidence.

But she wasn't ready for any of this.

Lindsey Leary knew it was bad the second she set foot in the house. The humid air was thick with the coppery scent of blood. Lindsey made her way down the hallway, her paper shoe covers rasping softly against the hardwood floor.

She stopped in the doorway, and the officer behind her whistled.

"Damn. You ever seen so much blood?"

She tore her gaze away from the stain on the floor to look at the shattered patio door. A sheet of black plastic had been taped over the opening.

"Linds?"

She glanced at Dillon. "Huh?"

"You ever seen anything like this?"

"No."

Although, actually, she had. Looking at the floor again, she remembered visiting her uncle's farm in South Texas. He'd just slaughtered a pig, and Lindsey had arrived in time to see it being butchered in a giant cast-iron kettle by the back porch. The blood on the ground had been a similar shade of dark red, and Lindsey hadn't been able to eat bacon for years.

She stepped closer to the stain. Bandages and other detritus from the paramedics lay scattered across the floor, and Lindsey didn't envy the CSIs who'd had to sort through all this mess.

Dillon stepped back, covering his nose. "This heat isn't helping."

No, it wasn't. Lindsey looked across the room at the busted-out door. Gaps in the plastic had let flies inside and let the air-conditioning escape. Today's temp had hit one hundred degrees, and the interior of the house had probably gotten close to that.

Lindsey dug into the pocket of her blazer and realized she'd left her flashlight in her car. Before she could ask, Dillon handed over the Maglite from his duty belt. It was big enough to double as a club.

Lindsey scooped her long brown hair over her shoulder to keep it out of the way as she crouched down to examine the floor. Normally, she wore a ponytail to work, but she'd been on her way out to a bar when she'd gotten the call from Max Gorman. The veteran detective had asked for Lindsey's take on the crime scene, and she'd been so flattered that she'd snagged a patrol officer and come over here on her night off.

"What's with the glass there?" Dillon asked as she swept the beam of light over the shards. "That's got to be, what, fifteen feet from the patio door?"

"I was just wondering that." Lindsey stood up. She walked into the kitchen, where yellow evidence markers denoted places where CSIs had collected evidence.

Lindsey pulled her phone out and scrolled through the photos from Max. She found the one she was looking for, a shot of a mostly full bottle of merlot that had been sitting on the counter beside a bottle opener when detectives arrived at the scene. The bottle was now at the lab, being run for prints.

In Lindsey's mind, what was more interesting than what had been found at this crime scene was what *hadn't* been found: fingerprints, footprints, hair from the perpetrator. They'd found no murder weapon, slugs, or even shell casings. No communication from the killer, such as a note or a symbolic object, which might have been expected if you bought into the working assumption that Judge Ballard was murdered by the vengeful escaped convict James Corby.

But Lindsey didn't buy into that. Not yet. And she didn't like assumptions. Max didn't, either, which was why he had wanted her opinion on this case.

She looked at the bottle opener again. "You know anything about wine?" She glanced at Dillon.

"I'm a Bud man." He smiled and patted his gut. "Can't you tell?"

"Yeah, I'm not much of a wine drinker, but this looks pricey." She walked over and showed him the photograph of the bottle, something from Argentina.

Dillon shook his head, and Lindsey stepped over to open the fridge. Not much in it besides a few diet sodas, a Caesar salad kit, and a package of expensive T-bone steaks. Looked like Jen Ballard was trying to impress her date. On a hunch, Lindsey stepped over and peeked inside the oven, where she found two charred potatoes. A detective or a CSI had probably switched off the oven after showing up at the scene.

The wine told a story, Lindsey felt sure. She headed back through the living room, careful not to step on any shards of glass, and went back to the bedroom wing of the town house. The first bedroom had been converted into an office. The second was the master suite, which included a seating alcove and an attached bath.

Lindsey stepped into the bathroom, noting the Oriental rug on the floor. She couldn't imagine springing for something like that and then sticking it in her bathroom, where it was sure to get trashed from all the dirt and grossness she routinely brought home on her shoes.

A hairbrush and a tube of lipstick sat atop the granite vanity alongside a neat row of perfume bottles, all French. Lindsey eyed the hairbrush and thought about Jen Ballard standing here brushing her hair in the final minutes of her life.

Lindsey stepped into the closet. Floor-to-ceiling shoe cubbies, built-in dresser. The closet could have been in a magazine, except that it was filled with dark pantsuits and boring black pumps. She opened the top dresser drawer.

The judge's lingerie was another story—lacy and lots of colors.

She slid the drawer shut, feeling inexplicably guilty. She was a detective, for heaven's sake.

"Anything interesting?" Dillon asked from the doorway.

"Maybe."

Lindsey stood for a moment, staring at the vanity and remembering the crime-scene photo of the wineglass that had been sitting there. A bath towel lay crumpled on the floor beside the shower.

"So, I'm thinking she comes home, pours herself a drink, and puts the potatoes in the oven. Then she comes back here to shower and get ready." She walked back down the hallway, retracing her steps to the bloodstain near the kitchen. "She reaches the living room, and he confronts her."

"So the question is, was he here already, or did he break in while she was showering?" Dillon said.

That wasn't the only question.

"Would have been noisy, breaking through that door," Lindsey said.

"Maybe she didn't hear him because of the running water." Dillon leaned against the wall. Despite the beer paunch, he was a nice-looking man, with clear blue eyes and a trustworthy air about him. Not that Lindsey was looking or anything, because although they'd started in the same academy class, she now outranked him.

"I don't know," she said. "I'm leaning more toward him breaking in beforehand at some point, maybe while she was at work."

He tipped up an eyebrow. "Then lying in wait?"

"Possibly."

Lindsey crossed the living room, stopping beside a piano. The bench was pulled out, and on it sat a booklet of sheet music. Lindsey leaned closer. "'Für Elise,'" she said, switching on the flashlight to reveal tiny bits of glass on the paper.

"What's that?"

"The song."

"You play?"

"No."

Taking out her phone, she went through the living-room shots Max had sent. No one had photographed the sheet music, or if they had, Max hadn't thought it important enough to send.

"Hey, you mind holding the flashlight?" She handed the light back to Dillon. "Shine it at an oblique angle, so the glass shows up."

Dillon crouched beside her and held the light as Lindsey snapped several photos with her phone.

"You've got a theory, Linds. I can tell."

"Maybe." She stood up.

"See?" He smiled and stood, too. "This is why you're the detective and I'm still a lowly uniform."

She shot him a look. "You're a uniform because you like women falling at your feet." She took the flashlight back and returned to the patio door, sweeping the beam over the floor.

"You think the crime-scene techs missed the bits of glass on the sheet music there?" Dillon asked.

"It's possible."

"So . . . you're thinking what?"

"I'm thinking . . ." She glanced around. "Questions, mostly. Why is there glass on the floor here by the door, but there's none on the floor by the piano? And then there's more glass there by the kitchen, where she was shot and killed?"

"Maybe the guy tracked it in with him?"

She walked over to the piano bench and stared down at the sheet music.

"Linds, come on." Dillon checked his watch. "We're not getting any younger, and I've got to get back."

"I'm thinking . . . she comes home, pours a drink. Maybe she's distracted or in a hurry, and she doesn't notice the patio door is busted out."

"So the killer's already inside. Why doesn't he ambush her right then?"

"I don't know. Maybe he wants to draw it out. So she goes back to the bedroom to get ready for her date. Maybe he watches her undress and get in the shower. Then he comes back in here, scoops up some glass with the sheet music, and scatters it here on the floor where she'll notice it for sure when she walks back into the kitchen. When she does, he's waiting there. Her look of surprise, her *fear*, that's what gets him off."

Dillon stared at her. "Scary."

"What?"

"The way your mind works." He shook his head. "How do you come up with that?"

"Just . . . look at the scene." Lindsey swept the flashlight over the floor, and something glinted under the piano. She crouched down and aimed the beam at it.

"*Dillon.*"

"I'll be damned." He knelt beside her. "How the hell did they miss that?"

4

BRYNN RUSHED to the elevator and spilled coffee on herself as she lunged to catch the door. She rode downstairs, blotting her jeans with a tissue. When she reached the lobby, she spotted the luggage cart beside the front door, where she'd left it under Ross's watchful eye.

He was nowhere to be seen, though. She glanced around with annoyance as she crossed the lobby. A white Chevy Tahoe had pulled up to the entrance.

One of the commandos-for-hire stood beside it. Tall build, impossibly wide shoulders. Erik Morgan was dressed like a civilian today, in jeans, work boots, and an untucked gray T-shirt. The look might have been casual if Brynn hadn't noticed the bulge of the gun at his side.

Okay, this was happening.

Brynn walked outside, and Erik opened the SUV's cargo hatch.

"Morning," she chirped. She couldn't see his eyes behind his mirrored aviators, but he gave a brisk nod. "Sorry I'm late. I was watching Drew and Jonathan while I waited for my curling iron to cool."

He stared at her.

"You know, *Property Brothers*? Forget it." She sighed and looked around. "Have you by chance seen Ross?"

"He dropped off his bag."

Brynn noticed a second SUV, a silver Ford Expedition, parked in front of the Tahoe. The rear door was open, and she saw Ross's garment bag inside. Where the hell was he?

Erik moved past her to grab the luggage cart. Someone must have broken the news that all this stuff was going to Dallas with them, but he didn't say a word as he pulled the cart over and started loading file boxes into the Tahoe.

Brynn set down her coffee cup and grabbed one of the boxes, which were even heavier than they looked.

"I can get that." Erik reached for her box.

"I can do it." She stepped toward the car, but he blocked her.

"Ma'am. I need you to wait inside with Jeremy."

Understanding dawned as she stared at her reflection in his shades. He wanted her indoors. Away from the open parking lot, where—she glanced around—exactly zero people were lurking on this quiet Sunday morning.

She handed him the box, then turned on her heel and strode back into the lobby, seething with irritation. She spotted Ross lounging on a sofa near the restaurant. He was scrolling through his phone, oblivious to Jeremy, who stood beside him with his arms folded over his chest like a sentry. Jeremy wore the same pseudo-civilian clothes as Erik and probably had the same serious firepower concealed under his shirt.

This was so weird.

Brynn walked over, and Jeremy acknowledged her with a nod. Ross didn't look up from his phone as she sat down. She wanted a slug of coffee, but she'd left her cup outside. She distracted herself by going through her purse to make sure she hadn't left anything in the room.

A shadow fell over her. "Ma'am, we're ready."

Erik exchanged a look with Jeremy before leading Brynn and Ross across the lobby to the packed SUVs. The Tahoe's front passenger door was open. Brynn saw that her coffee was now tucked into the cupholder, which dissolved a teeny-tiny bit of her annoyance.

She slid inside, closing her door before Erik could, and then watched as Jeremy and Ross climbed into the SUV in front of them.

Jeremy was Ross's team leader. Erik was Brynn's. All this had been explained to her yesterday by Liam Wolfe.

"Where's everyone else?" she asked.

Erik started the engine and adjusted the air vents as Brynn waited for him to answer.

"They went ahead with the advance team."

"Advance team?"

He looked at her. "Our tech people are already up there, getting our systems in place."

Systems. She could only imagine that meant the security cameras and . . . what? Some sort of special communications? Brynn gritted her teeth and looked out the window. She didn't know what all this entailed, and she dreaded finding out.

"Ready?"

"No." She turned to look at him. "We need to get clear on a few things first."

He watched her for a moment, then peeled off his sunglasses. It was the polite thing to do, so she could see his face while she talked to him. And *wow*, she hadn't really noticed his eyes before. They were brown with flecks of gold in the irises, and his lashes were thick and dark.

"It's Brynn. Not *ma'am*."

He stared at her for several seconds. "All right."

"Do you want me to call you Erik or—"

"Erik."

"Good. Fine." She took a deep breath. "I appreciate you loading my bags, Erik, but I can handle my own stuff. I don't take more than I can schlep around by myself, and you're not a bellboy."

One of his eyebrows tipped up with what might have been amusement.

"And you're also not my boss, so don't start giving me orders," she said. "I don't like being bossed around, so . . . don't, okay?"

He gazed at her for a long moment. Then the sunglasses went back on.

Was that an *okay*? A *say whatever you want, but I plan to ignore it*? This man was tough to read.

The SUV in front of them started moving, and she expected Erik to follow. Instead, he reached into his pocket and dug something out.

Her phone. She felt a ridiculous wave of relief as he handed it over.

"Skyler says you're all set." He shifted the SUV into gear and got moving.

"Thank you." Brynn turned the phone over in her hand, searching for any sign that it had been examined by a tech expert, which she assumed Skyler was. It looked exactly the same, though, down to the beach-at-sunset photo on her home screen. She'd taken it on her last vacation two years ago.

She dropped the phone into the other cupholder and leaned back as they turned onto the frontage road. Half a mile later, they eased onto the interstate. Traffic was light, and Brynn figured they'd arrive well before noon, barring accidents or road work.

She glanced at Erik beside her, with his bulging arms and short-cropped hair. Everything about him screamed ex-military. She looked over her shoulder. He'd folded down the middle seat to make room for all her boxes and suitcases, and every item was packed in tight.

"Didn't you bring anything?" she asked.

"It's back there."

She looked ahead, then reached over to adjust the vent. He had the temperature set to seventy degrees and the radio turned off.

Erik shifted into the far-left lane and picked up speed.

Brynn felt edgy. And it wasn't just because she'd gotten a paltry three hours of sleep last night.

"You okay?"

She looked at him, surprised by the concern in his voice. "I'm just . . . restless, I guess. I do this drive all the time for business, and I've got it down pat. I even have a playlist for it."

"Really?"

"Starting at my house, I make it to the interstate by song two. Song sixteen, I stop at Luv's Truck Stop for a barbecue sandwich. On a Sunday, the whole trip takes me two hours and fifty minutes, assuming it's not a holiday weekend and there aren't any accidents on the way."

"We can stop if you're hungry."

"It's not that. I'm just not used to having a chauffeur."

He shot her a look. "I'm not a chauffeur."

"A driver. Whatever."

"Not whatever. I'm head of your security detail."

"My *point* is, I'm used to being in the driver's seat."

"Yeah, I get that." He glanced at her, and she wondered if he really did.

This whole thing felt unnatural. A heavy weight settled in her stomach as she thought of Jen. What was more unnatural than a perfectly healthy woman having her life brutally ended in her own home?

Multiple gunshot wounds. . . . Her doctor friend tried to stop the bleeding, but she was too far gone.

Brynn looked out the window, trying to get that homicide detective's words out of her mind. Researching the case had kept Brynn up most of the night, and now she was behind on her own work.

She snatched up her phone and combed through her missed calls. She had several from her sister but nothing from Bulldog. She saw that Erik's gaze was trained on the road, so she called her sister back.

"Hey, it's me."

"Hey. We missed you last night."

Liz sounded relaxed, and Brynn pictured her sitting on her back porch, where she liked to drink coffee and work the Sunday crossword. In ink, of course, because besides having two beautiful children and being married to an unbelievably nice guy, her sister was also wicked smart. She was an HR manager for a Houston hospital.

"Sorry to miss you guys," Brynn said. "I had to work."

"Any word on Jen's case?"

Her stomach tightened. "No news. I'll let you know if I hear anything."

"You doing okay? You sound stressed."

"I'm fine. What's up with you?" Brynn could tell something was off.

"Well . . . I'm sure this is probably the last thing you want to think about right now, but we bumped into Adam last night."

"No kidding?" Brynn reached for her computer bag in the back seat.

"He was with someone."

She tensed. That explained the tone of Liz's voice. And she knew what was coming next.

"She was wearing a ring, Brynn."

She took out her laptop and powered it up.

"Brynn?"

"Yeah, I'm here."

"Did you know about her?"

"I heard something about it a while back."

"Brynn! Why didn't you tell me?"

"Because it doesn't matter." She darted a glance at Erik. He was staring straight ahead, but she knew he was listening.

"Brynn, come on. I know you're upset."

"Actually, I'm not." It was the truth. She wasn't upset. Mildly curious, maybe. But not upset.

"Do you know her name?" Liz asked.

"No."

"Well, don't you even want to hear what she looks like? Wait. Don't answer that. She's short and has a bad dye job, and you're ten thousand times prettier than she is."

Brynn felt like she was in high school listening to this.

"I saw her in the ladies' room at the restaurant, and I wanted to pull her aside and tell her what a prick she's marrying."

"Lizzie, please. I don't care. Really." She looked at Erik, whose eyes were still glued to the highway, as if he couldn't hear a word of the conversation. "Listen . . . can I call you back later?"

"Why? Oh—is your *bodyguard* there?"

"Yes."

"Oh my God, that's so weird. Okay, call me when you can talk."

"I will."

She ended the call and dropped her phone into her purse on the floor. The last thing she wanted to think about was Adam and his impending nuptials. Or maybe not impending. Who knew? Brynn had spent two years with the guy, and they'd never even talked about marriage. So maybe he wasn't in a hurry to get hitched.

Brynn logged on to her computer and opened a document Ross had sent her late last night. She started reading, but her thoughts soon strayed.

Adam was getting married. Why should it matter? *She* sure as hell didn't want to marry him. So why did it bug her that Liz knew? Probably because now it was only a matter of time before Brynn's mother knew, which meant she'd be calling Brynn to talk about it.

After reading the same sentence three times, Brynn gave up and glanced at Erik. He looked so serious. Was he annoyed that she'd dragged out her computer?

She cleared her throat. "So, this setup. How's it going to work exactly?"

"You mean the rotation?"

"Yeah, I guess. I already heard about the three-man package. I mean the rest of it."

He kept his eyes on the road, evidently in no hurry to answer. He seemed to select every word carefully, taking his time. "The advance team will have all our comms set up," he said.

"Comms. Like radio communications?"

"Yes."

Whoa.

"Also, our security cams, which will be placed at key entry points, as well as the lobby of your apartment building, the Atrium."

"You have authorization for all this?"

"That's correct." He glanced at her. "I haven't been to the courthouse yet, but that's on my list today. I set up a meeting with the security chief over there to review their procedures."

Interesting that it was Erik who'd set up the meeting and not Liam or Jeremy. Brynn was trying to get a feel for the pecking order at Wolfe Security in case she needed to take issue with something at some point—which she surely would.

"It sounds like you're taking the lead on all this."

He didn't comment.

"We're in Judge Linden's courtroom."

"I know."

"And if you plan to be in there at all, you may want to arrange to reserve a seat," she added. "There's a limited number open to the public, and this may get some media coverage, so—"

"It's taken care of."

Well, alrighty then. Sounded like he had everything mapped out.

"What about sleeping arrangements?" she asked.

He looked at her.

"Both apartments have two bedrooms," she told him. "Ross and I were each planning to set up a home office, but we can use the dining tables instead, so your guys can have a place to sleep."

"Your off-shift agent will be in a hotel down the street. Whoever is on won't be sleeping."

"But what about at night?"

"We don't sleep on duty."

"So . . . we're going to have two guards glued to us at all times, even in the middle of the night?"

"One will be with you, and one will be elsewhere on the premises, either stationed someplace or on patrol."

"That's really . . . amazing." Amazingly wasteful. Just thinking about the money made her want to pick up the phone and get into it with Reggie again.

"Standard procedure for us."

"Yeah, well, in this particular situation, it sounds like overkill. Don't you think you're going to be bored out of your mind?"

"Bored?"

"Yes, *bored.*"

"That's not something I worry about."

Brynn checked her watch and blew out a sigh. She tried again to read, but she couldn't concentrate. Screw it. She snapped shut her computer.

"I need to be honest with you. I'm not bought in on all this," she said.

"What?"

"This security arrangement."

"Reggie's bought in."

"Yes, obviously. And I think it's sweet of him to do this, but you don't know Reggie like I do."

"You think Reggie is paying our rates because he's *sweet*?"

She set her laptop on the floor. "No, I think he's paying because he's paternalistic and overprotective, especially when it comes to me and Ross. *And* because your involvement will generate publicity for him."

"If you're so opposed, why didn't you refuse protection?"

"Reginald Gunn is a hard man to say no to."

He looked at her. "How long have you known him?"

"I met him in Dallas seven years ago when I was fresh out of law school. Back then, we were on opposite sides. I've worked for his firm for three years." She shifted in her seat to face him. "And I'll save you the guesswork—I'm thirty-three. But I bet you already read that in the big fat file you probably have on me, right?"

"We're the same age," he said, dodging the question.

"I know. I have a big fat file on you, too."

———————

Erik tried to hide his annoyance. He'd underestimated her.

"I had a friend run a criminal background check on you and your teammates." She paused. "What? I'm not about to shack up with a bunch of strange men twice my size without checking them out first."

"So how'd I check out?"

"All clear. Except for last year's speeding ticket in Virginia. Congratulations, you've been vetted."

Vetted. She had no idea how much vetting he'd gone through during the course of his career.

She cast a sideways look at him. "You're smiling. Something funny?"

"No."

"You think I'm paranoid."

"No, caution is good. Especially for someone like you. I wish more people would take commonsense precautions."

"Someone like me . . . meaning a single woman living alone?"

He caught the defensiveness in her voice.

"Someone in your job. Anyone involved in the criminal justice system needs to be careful. In my opinion." He glanced at her. "Your picture's been in the news, too, so that doesn't help."

He didn't add that her boss was the worst kind of client. The man was a publicity hound, and his law firm was frequently in the media. Erik didn't know if Brynn was like that, too.

"On the contrary, publicity helps a lot," she said.

And there was his answer.

"How?"

"My client is young," she said. "When we win this trial, he has a life to go back to, and I want to help him rehab his image. This kid is more than just a mug shot everyone's seen on TV. But I digress." She smiled. "We were talking about *you.*"

She seemed to like needling him.

"I also know you're from Rockville, Maryland, and you were in the Marines before joining the Secret Service. Very impressive." She paused, as if she expected him to say something. "How come you quit?"

The word "quit" rankled.

"Various reasons," he said.

"So . . . the hours? The travel? Better money in the private sector?"

He could tell from the spark of interest in her eyes that she wasn't going to let it go. And this was why he hated small talk.

"Something like that."

"Sounds like there's a story there."

"There's not."

"Hmm. Well, I've spent a whole lot of time deposing people, and I happen to be pretty good at sensing when they don't want to talk about something."

"Maybe another time."

"I knew it. But just tell me, you weren't one of those guys who got fired for partying on the job, were you? Drugs and prostitutes?"

He shot her a look.

"Didn't think so."

She sounded pretty pleased with herself for boxing him into a conversational corner. And she sounded something else, too. Flirty? Maybe he was imagining it.

She slipped off her sandals and shifted on the seat, tucking her feet underneath her, and he noticed her red toenails.

Erik cleared his throat. "So tell me more about this trial you plan to win."

"Nice redirect."

He waited for her to answer, but she just looked at him. She'd been doing that all morning, and it was messing with his head.

Erik's last client had been a tech CEO, and he'd spent every minute of every car ride glued to his phone. But this client was a lawyer, which meant she got paid to talk, and she evidently enjoyed it. Erik hadn't counted on so much conversation. He hadn't counted on any of the things that were making this the car ride from hell.

First problem, she smelled good. Not perfume but something sweet and subtle, like maybe her shampoo.

Second problem, she looked good. He'd known that going in, but he hadn't realized how hard it would be to be cooped up right next to her without getting distracted. She wore skintight jeans—dark blue today— that showed off her killer legs and high-heeled sandals again. Yesterday's were thin and strappy, but these had big, chunky heels that gave her an extra few inches. Not that she needed it. She wore a white button-down shirt that could have been a man's, only there was something feminine about it—but damned if he could pinpoint it. It was too loose to reveal her shape, but he kept getting glimpses of her collarbone.

He needed to get his head out of his ass. He shouldn't be noticing her clothes or her legs or her freaking collarbone. She was his client. Period.

"First, tell me why you care so much about my trial," she said.

"Call me curious."

"Nope."

He cut a glance at her. "*Nope?*"

"You're obviously not much of a talker, which is fine, but I don't believe you just want to listen to me rattle on."

He had to give her points for being perceptive.

"It's relevant to the job I'm doing, so I want to know more about it."

She turned to face him, and her shirt shifted again. "How is it relevant, exactly?"

"Your name's been in the news. You're my client. Anything that draws attention to you right now is relevant."

"Well, what did you see in the news?" she asked.

Great, she was going to answer his questions with questions. This could take all day.

"Not a lot," he said. "The defendant's some wealthy drug dealer."

"Wrong on both counts. In fact, he's flat broke. Reggie took the case pro bono."

"Nothing's ever really pro bono."

She arched a pretty eyebrow at him. "Cynical, aren't you?"

"I'm realistic."

"Well, in this instance you're right. The firm's getting free exposure out of it. This case has garnered some media attention, as you've noticed."

"So why isn't Reggie handling it instead of you?"

"He's tied up with something big right now."

"Bigger than this?"

"Yes. Anyway, I offered to take it."

"What about Ross?"

"Ross is second chair. I've got more trial experience, so I'm taking the lead. It's a good opportunity for me."

Interesting. He would have thought uprooting her life temporarily and moving up to Dallas wouldn't be much of a plum assignment.

"What's that look?" she asked.

"Nothing. You were telling me about your case?"

She sighed and looked ahead. "Justin Sebring. He's charged with first-degree murder in the shooting death of a college student named Seth Moore outside a pizza restaurant."

"Sounds serious."

"It is. But he's innocent."

"They all are, right?"

"No, actually, some defendants are guilty as hell. I take it you don't like defense attorneys?"

"I didn't say that."

"Doesn't matter. I'm used to it. But everyone has the right to due process. That's in the Constitution for a reason. It keeps those in power from running roughshod over people's rights."

"So if your client's so innocent, why is he going to trial? I thought prosecutors generally try to cut a deal if they don't have a strong case."

"That's where it gets sticky. Justin's not a drug dealer, but the prosecutor is saying he was working for a local distributor and killed the victim during a botched drug buy. The DA's office is playing hardball, hoping we'll cave and give them something on the big fish in exchange for a light sentence."

"And?"

"And what? It's not happening." Her voice took on an edge. "Justin is eighteen. He was three months shy of graduation when his life got derailed. Now he could spend the rest of his days in prison for something he didn't do. I can't let that happen."

He heard the determination in her voice, and he had to respect it. He also respected that she had the guts to take on such a high-pressure case. The stakes were high, which meant stress for her, which Erik understood, because his job was high-stakes, too. They both operated in a world where their performance had life-and-death consequences. So many people didn't.

She shifted her legs out from under her. Then she looked at her watch, as if she'd lost patience with the conversation.

"Hey, any chance we can pull over soon?"

"Why?"

"Um, because I'd like to use the ladies' room."

"Don't you mean because you want to sneak away and call Liz back?"

She looked ticked off, and he knew he'd nailed it. "Who I call is none of your business."

Erik took his phone from his pocket and sent a text to Jeremy. He exited the highway and pulled into the first gas station. It was busy with weekend travelers, and he veered around the pumps to swing into a space by the convenience store.

Brynn grabbed her purse.

"Wait." He caught her arm before she could jump out.

She glanced down at his hand, and he let her go.

"We need to get clear on a few things," he said, tossing her own words back at her.

"Like what?"

He waited for her to look at him and held her gaze. "I know you don't like this. And I know you're used to being in control. In every area of your life, I'm guessing."

She didn't respond to that, just watched him with those deep blue eyes.

"Your private life is private. Full stop. You don't have to worry about me, or anyone on my team, sharing your personal information with anyone. Our job is your safety. But we can't keep you safe if you won't let us near you."

He paused to let that sink in.

"You don't need to run away from me to make a phone call or have a personal conversation or conduct a business meeting or whatever. Just forget I'm here."

She scoffed. "You're two feet away, but I'm supposed to pretend you're blind, deaf, and dumb?"

"Pretend whatever you want. The point is, don't compromise your safety by avoiding me because you're trying to hide the details of your personal life. I've seen all this before, Brynn. I know how people react in these situations—"

"Like having a close friend murdered and then being forced to smile and act normal while a posse of armed bodyguards follows me around everywhere?"

"Yes."

She looked away. Erik waited.

"Okay, fine," she said. "I hear what you're saying. And you're right, I *was* planning to step away and call my sister to hear more about my ex-boyfriend, who I know I shouldn't give a damn about, but for some crazy reason I do, all right?"

"Call her from the car. I'll put my earbuds in if it makes you feel better."

She just looked at him. He saw a trace of vulnerability in her eyes, and he wondered what her ex had done to her.

"Okay," she said. "But as long as we're here, we may as well make a pit stop. Can you let me out of your sight for three minutes, or do you need to follow me into the bathroom?"

"I'll wait in the snack aisle."

"Fine." She dug into her purse and pulled out a twenty. "You can pick us up some Pop-Tarts."

5

BY 6:15, Brynn had knocked out everything on her to-do list. She'd unpacked her bags, organized her case files, and even squeezed in a grocery run to pick up necessities, all the while being shadowed by muscle-bound security agent Trent Reese, who'd uttered a grand total of six words during their outing.

Brynn emerged from her bedroom and found him at the breakfast bar, hunched over a laptop. He looked up as she walked into the kitchen.

"Hi," she said.

Like the rest of the corporate apartment, the kitchen had an impersonal, catalog feel to it, right down to the empty pewter bowl in the center of the granite island. Everything was relentlessly beige—the paint, the sofa, the carpet—and Brynn longed for her cluttered bungalow with its rich wooden floors and antique rugs.

Brynn grabbed a water bottle from the fridge. "Where is everyone?" she asked.

"Across the hall. We're about to change shifts."

They were doing rolling shift changes, staggering the start times for security reasons.

"Erik's on his way over," Trent added as he flipped shut his computer and stood up.

"Isn't he done for the day?"

"No, ma'am. He's on until midnight."

A brief knock at the door, and then Erik walked in. Brynn was still getting used to the fact that all these people had a key to her apartment. It made sense, she supposed—especially if they were going to be coming and going at all hours—but she wasn't crazy about not being able to walk around in her underwear whenever she wanted.

Erik looked her up and down. "Where are you going?" he asked, noticing her workout gear and earbuds.

"Out for a run."

He shot a look at Trent.

"And after that, I'm going *out* out. Ross and I are having dinner at Otto's Tap Room."

Erik's gaze narrowed. "I thought you were working tonight."

"Nope. We always take the night off right before a trial." She didn't mention that she was prone to anxiety attacks if she worked the night before. "I go for a run to clear my head, and then Ross and I head over to Otto's for burgers and beer. It's kind of a pretrial ritual we have together."

Erik just looked at her.

"Are you going to tell me that's not allowed?" she asked.

"No. But there's a fitness room upstairs with a treadmill. Three, in fact."

"I knew you were going to say that." She plunked her hand on her hip. "Treadmills make me feel like a hamster. I prefer to run outside, in the park. On an actual *trail* surrounded by birds and trees and fresh air. Can't someone come with me?"

He glanced at Trent, and Brynn felt her irritation rising.

"Look, Liam said as few disruptions as possible," she reminded him. "And I know this may seem like nothing to you, but my pretrial routine is important. It's how I get my head in the game."

Erik didn't say anything.

"Actually, I was up there earlier," Trent said, drawing Brynn's gaze away from Erik. "It's a really nice fitness center. They even have a rooftop pool."

"No, she's right," Erik said. "We'll figure it out. Where's Jeremy?"

"Putting gas in the Expedition," Trent reported.

Erik looked at Brynn. "Give me twenty minutes. I need to go change. I'll have Jeremy scope out the route on his way back here. Draw it out for me, and I'll text him a picture."

"*Scope out* the route?"

"Yes."

She stared at him. It was a battle of wills, and he had the upper hand, because he wasn't actually insisting that she do what he wanted. No, he was offering to let her go, but it was going to be a huge pain in the ass if Jeremy had to scope out her pathetically short jogging path.

"Forget it," she said. "I don't want to waste time with all that. I'll use the treadmill."

"You sure?"

"Yes, let's go."

She stuffed her earbuds in her ears, and Erik had the nerve to look smug as he followed her out.

As workouts went, it was ugly. Four miles, and she was soaking wet by the end. Usually, she only ran two, but with Erik there, she felt like she had something to prove.

Which didn't make sense, really. He was her bodyguard. And he'd told her to pretend he wasn't there. But that wasn't happening, especially when it was beyond obvious that he and his team were in peak physical condition. Brynn had a competitive streak, and knowing Erik could probably run four miles uphill without breaking a sweat made her push harder.

Finally, she hopped off the machine. They rode the elevator back down, and she kept her distance, even though Erik seemed unbothered by her sweat-drenched state. Back inside the apartment, a new agent was seated at the breakfast bar in front of a computer. Hayes Becker. Brynn had read his background, too. At twenty-six years old, he was the youngest member of the team, and he looked it, too, with his blond hair and dimples.

Brynn retreated to her room to clean up and then stood in front of her closet, debating. Otto's was casual, so she settled on jeans and a stretchy black top that accentuated her boobs. She put on some makeup and did a quick blowout, deciding to leave her hair down. Then she sent a text to Ross: *Ready in 5?*

It didn't take him long to respond: *Staying in tonight. Not up for Ottos.*

Brynn stared down at the phone. *U ok?* she asked.

Working.

She grabbed her purse off the bed and returned to the living room, where she found Erik and Hayes gathered around a laptop, discussing something. Brynn recognized surveillance footage of the lobby down-stairs.

"Ready?" she asked Erik.

"Yeah."

"Hayes, can we bring you anything?"

"He's driving," Erik informed her.

Hayes grabbed the keys to the Tahoe and followed them into the hallway. Brynn made a beeline for Ross's apartment. Unlike everyone else, it seemed, *she* didn't have a key, so she had to knock.

Skyler answered the door. Her long dark hair was pulled up in a ponytail, and she wore black jeans and a Wolfe Sec T-shirt.

"Hi," she said, glancing over Brynn's shoulder at Erik. "What's up?"

"I need a word with Ross," Brynn said.

He came to the door, and Skyler returned to the living room, which was identical to Brynn's across the hall.

"Hey, sorry to bail," Ross said.

"What the heck? Are you sick?"

He shrugged. "Just tired. I thought I'd stay in and go over a few things. Anyway, I'm not hungry."

"You cannot get sick, Ross. We need you tomorrow. Want me to get you some Alka-Seltzer or something?"

"You're the one who gets the pretrial heaves, not me."

Brynn glanced toward Skyler and lowered her voice. "You'd better not be staying home to hit on her."

"Get real."

"I mean it. She works for us, and it would be completely unethical."

"Don't worry about me." He looked over her shoulder at Erik wait-ing patiently in the hallway, listening to every word. "You guys have fun." He patted her shoulder. "Keep the tradition alive."

Otto's Tap Room wasn't what Erik had expected for Dallas or Brynn. Located on the outskirts of downtown just beyond the railroad tracks, it looked like a run-down warehouse. Only a blue neon sign and a row of pickups out front hinted that the place was open for business.

Hayes pulled up to the entrance, and Erik got out to open Brynn's door.

"I'll text you when we're done," he told Hayes.

"Roger that."

"Wait, aren't you coming in with us?" Brynn asked.

"I'll keep an eye on things outside."

"Are you sure? Best burgers in town."

"I'm sure."

Brynn slid out and stood on the sidewalk, looking uneasy as the Tahoe pulled away. "Has he had dinner?" she asked Erik.

"He probably ate before his shift."

Erik crossed the sidewalk and opened the door, letting out a gust of cool air and loud music. The place smelled like barbecue. People were crowded around the bar, watching the Rangers game, and Brynn led him to a high-top table in back.

"This one's better," he said, touching her waist to steer her to a corner table.

"Don't like your back to the door?" she asked as she took a seat.

"That's right."

"What was I thinking?"

Over bluesy guitar music, Erik could hear the sharp crack of a pool game in the back room. It was Erik's kind of place, and under different circumstances, he would have liked to come here with Jeremy to put away a few beers and win some money at nine-ball. Right now, he was working, though, which meant focusing on Brynn and all the heads she'd turned since walking in here.

A young waiter came over. "Get you folks something to drink?"

"I'll have a Guinness," Brynn said.

"And you, sir?"

"Water."

The waiter looked at Brynn. "Any wings or nachos tonight?"

"I'd like the Otto Burger, no cheese, please."

"I'll have the same," Erik told him. "And one to go."

When the waiter was gone, Brynn looked at him. "For Hayes?"

"Skyler. She texted me in the car."

Brynn put her elbow on the table and rested her chin on her hand. "So let me guess, no drinking on the job?"

"That's right."

"What else don't you do?"

"What do you mean?"

"You guys seem pretty disciplined. No drinking on the job, no sleeping. Anything else off-limits?"

"No tobacco, no stimulants."

"What, like Red Bull or something?"

"Anything with caffeine."

"No way." She leaned closer, and Erik tried not to glance down her shirt. "You don't drink coffee?"

"No."

She shuddered. "I would die. No, first I would turn into a complete hell-bitch, and then someone on my team would shoot me. You don't drink coffee at all? Not even in the morning?"

"Never."

"Is that by choice, or is it some kind of rule?"

"It's in my contract."

"*Seriously?*" She leaned back. "You need a new lawyer. And Liam sounds like a control freak."

"Doesn't bother me. I gave all that up when I joined the Secret Service."

"Why?"

He smiled at her look of disbelief. "You really want to know?"

"Yes, I do."

"It messes with my focus," he said. "Coffee, sugar, junk food. Anything that gives you a short-term buzz eventually wears off and causes cravings. You're better off without it."

"Speak for yourself."

Shouts erupted from the bar as the Rangers scored a run, and Brynn turned to look at the TV.

"No, it's true," he said. "Imagine you're protecting someone. You need to be completely in the moment. Every moment. You can't be distracted because you're jonesing for a cigarette or a hit of something. You have to be focused on the principal and the surrounding environment, ready to tune into any threat, at any time."

She stared at him. There was something smoky and sultry about her eyes tonight. And then there was that shirt. He was trying hard not to stare, but it was nearly impossible. Had she worn that for him?

No. She'd planned to go out with Ross tonight. So was there something going on between them? The guy didn't seem like Brynn's type, but Erik had only known her for two days. Anyway, if there was something going on, he'd find out. That was how these things went. Everything came out eventually—affairs, rivalries, grudges. Erik was trained to observe people and pick up on precisely the things they wanted to hide.

Such as the guy at the far end of the bar in the leather biker jacket. He had a gun tucked in the back of his pants, and Erik was keeping an eye on him.

"So . . . 'be in the moment.' " She gave him a long look. "Interesting philosophy."

"It's more of an operating principle."

"What else?"

"What else what?"

She smiled. "I want to hear more about your operating principles."

Did she really? He watched her expression, but he couldn't tell.

"Wolfe Sec is the best in the field," he said. "Liam's put together a workforce of highly trained, intensely focused operators who will go to any lengths to protect a principal."

"Any lengths . . . like jumping in front of a bullet?"

He nodded.

"Really? I mean, come on. I can see why someone might do that for a president. But a rock star? Or a lawyer?"

Erik sighed. Here was the trust issue again. "Ideally, nobody's jumping in front of bullets," he said. "The best security is preventive. First and foremost, that requires having trust with the client. Meaning you."

"Hmm. That's a tough one, because I hardly know you."

"You don't have to know me. You have to know that your safety is my top priority. You have to know that I'm thinking about your case around the clock."

"Even when you're off duty?" She sounded skeptical.

"That's the point. I'm never really off. None of us is. While we're working for you, you have our full attention."

The waiter dropped off their drinks. When he was gone, Brynn clinked her glass against Erik's.

"Thanks for coming out with me." She sipped the foam off her beer.

"No problem."

He hadn't been thrilled with the idea, but now he was glad to be here. There were things they needed to talk about, and she seemed more relaxed away from all her case files and legal pads.

"Are you ready for tomorrow?" he asked.

"Yeah, but I don't want to talk about it. That's bad luck."

He smiled slightly.

"What?"

"You're superstitious," he said.

"Isn't everybody, at least a little?"

"No."

"Well, if I sit around hashing through the case the night before, I get all wound up and have trouble sleeping. It's better if I take the night off so I don't overthink it. Maybe it's weird, but it's my thing. And I've got the best win record at the firm, so I'll stick with what works."

Erik was impressed, but he kept it to himself. She had plenty of confidence already.

"So what happens tomorrow?" he asked.

"Voir dire. That's lawyer-speak for jury selection," she added. "We go through every potential juror, one by one, and each side has a limited number of opportunities to strike someone from the pool."

He watched her talk, paying attention to her body language—something else he'd been trained to pick up on. She made lots of eye contact, which probably helped her win people over in the courtroom.

"What makes you strike someone?" he asked. "Race or age, I'm guessing?"

"Actually, no. I mean, race is a factor, sure. Sebring is mixed race, so we definitely don't want an all-white jury. But more important, I'm looking for mothers."

"Mothers," he repeated.

"Preferably mothers of sons. They tend to be sympathetic."

Erik lifted an eyebrow.

"What, you don't believe me?"

"I didn't say that."

"I can see it in your face." She tipped her head to the side. "You have any brothers?"

"Two. And my mom was tough as nails when we were growing up."

"Well, I bet she gets picked for jury duty a lot. She ever mention it?"

"Actually . . . yeah, come to think of it." Erik folded his arms over his chest. "I always thought it was because she was a teacher."

"Teachers are good, too. They tend to be fair-minded. What does your mom teach?"

"She's retired. But she taught middle-school science."

"I'd definitely want her on my jury, then. She'd pay close attention to the physical evidence." She picked up her beer. "But hey, we're not talking about the trial tonight, remember? It's bad luck."

The waiter returned with two big plates. The hamburgers were about six inches tall, but Brynn didn't hesitate to pick hers up and dig right in.

"Mmm." She closed her eyes and moaned.

Erik tried to keep his mind out of the gutter as he started on his food. For a while, they ate without talking, and he kept his gaze moving between the bar's two exits.

"So Brynn, I need to ask you some things."

She looked wary. "You want to know about Corby."

"That's right."

"You have a file on him, don't you?"

"Yeah, but I want to know from you."

She sighed. "Know what?"

"I want to know why, exactly, you don't think he killed Jen Ballard."

She looked at him for a long moment, then took a sip of beer. She placed her glass on the table.

"The police think he did," she said.

"What do *you* think?"

"I don't know. The timing's pretty uncanny, if it wasn't him."

"True."

"But something feels off with it."

"Off how?"

"Well . . . if you read about Corby, you know his MO. Every one of his victims was raped and choked, and then he slit their throats. So this thing with hunting down Jen and shooting her? It doesn't add up." Brynn shook her head. "I mean, if this is about revenge, wouldn't a knife be his weapon of choice?"

"I don't know."

Erik knew someone who would, though. Liam's brother was a criminal profiler, and they needed to get him involved in this.

"Corby killed that prison guard with a homemade shank," Erik said.

"Yeah, that's my point. He has a thing for knives. And torture. So he spends three years in prison fantasizing about getting revenge on the woman who helped put him there, and then he tracks her down and shoots her? And also, where'd he get the gun?" She tipped her head to the side. "You know a lot more about guns than I do, in your line of work. Wouldn't it be a stretch for a convicted felon to get a firearm so fast?"

"With money, anything's possible. He could have a connection in prison who told him where to go."

"That's the other thing," she said. "He'd just escaped. If every cop in the state is looking for him, you'd think he'd want to keep a low profile."

"You're assuming he's logical."

"Fair point. He might not do the logical thing. But he *is* smart. I know that firsthand from the trial." She poked at her french fries, but she seemed to have lost her appetite.

"Sorry to have to ask you about this," he said.

"It's all right."

Still, he felt like shit for bringing it up. "Were you and Jen close?"

She didn't talk for a moment, just stared at her plate. Then she looked up.

"Jen mentored me when I was just out of law school and working for the DA's office. We got to be friends. She took it hard when I went over to the dark side."

"The dark side?"

"Criminal defense work."

"Why'd you switch?"

"Reggie made me a good offer."

"You said he's hard to say no to." Erik watched her reaction, trying to get a read on their relationship.

"Also, I like the people—Reggie, Faith, Nicole. Plus Ross and the other lawyers. The firm is like the big, noisy family I never had. And there's the money, obviously. I've got a ton of loans to pay back." She shrugged, like changing sides was an easy decision, but Erik would bet it was more complicated.

Erik had gone to the "dark side," too, when he left public service for the private sector. Most people assumed he'd done it for money, and he didn't waste his time trying to convince them otherwise.

Brynn pushed her plate away. "You know, Corby was my last case working for the prosecution."

Erik hadn't known that.

"You know his nickname in prison?" she asked.

"What?"

"The Champ. You know why?"

Erik tried to imagine. Despite his history of violence, Corby wasn't a big man, only about five-five, one thirty. Erik couldn't picture him being a champ of anything that involved physical strength.

"Chess," she said. "He was the reigning champion. No one could touch him, or so I've heard."

"Maybe they were scared to try."

"Or maybe he's just smart."

"Did he ever reach out to you?"

The question caught her off guard, and Erik saw her try to cover it.

"Seemed like you had something on your mind when Liam asked you."

She took a deep breath. "It's probably nothing."

"It's not nothing, or you wouldn't have thought of it."

She watched him, as if weighing what to say. This woman had trust issues, and he was going to have to find a way past them.

"I got a note once," she said.

"Where?"

"On my car."

"*On* your car?"

"Tucked under the wiper blade. *Blade.* I just realized that." She shook her head and looked away. "Not that that means anything, but—"

"What did it say?"

"No envelope, no return address, just a folded note. It said, 'I'm watching you.' And at the time, my mind went straight to Corby, because it was the one-year anniversary of his conviction."

"Shit, Brynn. What did you do with it?"

"What do you think? I took it to the police."

"And?"

"There were no prints on it besides mine. Not Corby's or anyone's. Which isn't really surprising, right? Corby couldn't exactly put a note on my car if he was sitting in prison in Beaumont."

"And yet you originally thought it might be from him. Why?"

"I don't know. Just the way he was at trial." She leaned back in her chair. "He used to look at me, you know? *Stare.* The 'I'm watching you' thing made me think of him."

"So the police have the note."

She shook her head. "They returned it to me. It's in a file at my office."

"I want to see it."

"Why? It doesn't prove anything. The detective I gave it to thought I was totally paranoid."

"Because you believed it was important, or you wouldn't have saved it." He leaned closer. "Don't discount your instincts. You helped prosecute this guy. You know him. You got a note, and you immediately thought of him. You shouldn't ignore that."

She watched him. He hated the fear in her eyes. But he liked that his words had an effect on her. She wasn't arguing with him, for a change.

"I'll ask someone to send it up," she said.

"Do it soon. I'll get the marshals to look at it, too."

She looked down at their half-eaten burgers.

"New topic," she announced. "What do you think of Otto's?"

"It's pretty good."

"That's it? I take you to the best-kept secret in Dallas, and you give it a 'pretty good'?"

"It's not what I pictured for you."

"Oh, yeah?" Her eyes sparked with interest. "What did you picture?"

"Something . . . I don't know, sophisticated. A wine bar or something. Maybe some lawyers hanging around the bar, talking shop."

"So you think I'm a snob."

"I didn't say that."

"Sure, you did."

———

Brynn watched Erik polish off his burger as the bar filled up with regulars. She signed the check and left a big tip as Erik texted Hayes that they were ready to leave.

Erik led her through the crowd to the door, and the Tahoe was parked right out front, engine running. Hayes jumped out and opened the passenger door for Brynn, while Erik went around.

"You, step *back*!" Hayes yelled.

"But—*oof!*"

Brynn whirled around as something slammed against the car. Her heart lurched.

"Stop!" Brynn jumped out and grabbed Hayes's arm. "That's our *waiter*!"

Hayes had him pinned against the SUV, his face pressed against the window. At Erik's sharp command, Hayes released the guy and stepped away.

The flush-faced waiter shot a panicked look at Brynn and then Erik.

"Are you all right?" Brynn reached out, but he jerked away.

"Yeah. Jesus." He looked at Erik as he smoothed his shirt. "You forgot your to-go."

"Thanks." Erik snagged the bag off the ground.

"I'm *so* sorry," Brynn said. "Thank you."

The man hurried away, darting a scowl over his shoulder as he reached for the door.

"What the hell was that?" Brynn demanded.

"Get in," Erik said, helping her.

Batting his hands away, Brynn climbed into the back seat. Erik closed the door, cutting off further conversation.

Hayes slid behind the wheel. As soon as Erik closed his door, they were moving. Erik stashed the to-go bag on the floor and calmly fastened his seat belt.

"Um, hello? Someone want to explain what just happened?"

Hayes glanced at her in the rearview mirror. "He rushed up to you."

"Yes, and thank God you were there." She looked at Erik. "You think you guys might want to take it down a notch?"

"He was doing his job. He intercepted the threat."

"Threat?" Brynn leaned forward between the seats. "That kid's barely out of braces. He could press charges for aggravated assault."

"I hardly touched him," Hayes said.

"You *shoved* him against a vehicle."

"'Aggravated'?" Erik gave her a skeptical look.

"Hayes is armed."

"His weapon wasn't out. The guy didn't even see it."

"His body could be considered a deadly weapon," she said. "So could yours."

Erik set the thermostat to seventy degrees. "Well, if he presses charges, you can represent us."

"Ha! You couldn't afford me." Brynn leaned back and folded her arms over her chest, not just pissed but rattled. She'd nearly jumped out of her skin when she heard Hayes's booming voice behind her.

The ride back was silent and uncomfortable. Hayes seemed embarrassed. Erik seemed tense. Brynn stared through the tinted back windows at the downtown streets, trying to get her head around this new reality. She'd thought going to Otto's would settle her nerves and help her feel normal on the eve of a big trial. But nothing was normal when she was surrounded by armed men twenty-four/seven.

Brynn closed her eyes and pinched the bridge of her nose, feeling a headache coming on. She thought of Jen and wished she and Erik hadn't talked about her. Ross was right. She shouldn't have talked to that homicide detective, because now she had all the lurid details of Jen's murder filling her mind.

She took out her phone and sent a message to Faith. Reggie's assistant had known Jen from the law firm's early days up in Dallas, and she was shocked by the murder. Everyone in the legal community was, from both sides of the aisle.

Brynn told Faith about the anonymous note and asked her to overnight it to Dallas. Faith was the only other person at the firm who understood Brynn's haphazard, somewhat alphabetical filing system. The note she'd received on the one-year anniversary of Corby's conviction was in its own manila envelope within a file marked "D Com" for defendant communications.

You believed it was important, or you wouldn't have saved it. Brynn looked at Erik in the front seat, and she knew he was right.

Hayes pulled up to the front door of the building to drop them off before heading to the parking garage. The whole door-to-door service thing made Brynn feel spoiled. But Erik kept insisting, and she needed to pick her battles with him.

She swiped her way into the building with her key card and strode past the gurgling marble fountain in the lobby. Growing up, Brynn had lived in a series of apartments, none of which had a posh lobby or a rooftop pool or a fitness room. Brynn wasn't footing the bill for this place, but still it seemed wasteful.

She and Erik rode the elevator up without a word and went straight to Ross's to deliver the to-go bag.

As Erik let himself into the apartment, Brynn got a text from Bulldog: *Meet me in the lobby.*

She stared down at her phone. *Where r u?*

Downstairs.

Brynn glanced around. Ross and Skyler were both on the sofa with their laptops out. Erik leaned over Skyler, pointing at something on her screen. Hayes was in the hallway with Brynn, his shoulder propped against the wall as he checked his phone.

"I'll be across the hall," she said.

Hayes looked up and nodded.

Brynn slipped out and returned to the lobby, where she found Bulldog waiting beside the fountain.

The PI was short and stocky and proportioned like a bulldog, hence his name. He wore his usual cheap suit, no tie. Twenty years as a cop and five as a private detective had put a permanent frown on his face, but he looked especially unhappy tonight.

"Where's Ross?" he asked.

"Upstairs. What are you doing here? I thought you were in Las Vegas."

"I'm on the red-eye out of DFW. Had to catch you before I left. It's important." He glanced over her shoulder. "You got a problem, buddy?"

Brynn turned to see Erik standing behind her looking like a thundercloud. Good, she'd ticked him off.

"Erik, I'd like you to meet John Kopek, also known as Bulldog. John's our private investigator."

"I know. Otherwise, he'd be in handcuffs." Erik looked the man over, no doubt noticing the Ruger under his jacket. He turned to Brynn. "You told Hayes you were across the hall."

"Bulldog stopped by to tell me something important." She turned to him. "What's going on?"

At the look on his face, Brynn braced herself.

"Michael McGowan is dead."

6

BRYNN'S STOMACH clenched. "*Mick* McGowan?"

"That's right."

Brynn stared at him.

"Who's Mick McGowan?" Erik asked.

"The lead homicide detective who worked on the James Corby case," Bull said. "He was found at his house this morning. Gunshot wound. Investigators are looking to see if it's connected to Jen's murder."

A woman breezed past them, looking alarmed at the word "murder."

Bulldog turned to Brynn. "Hey, mind if we take this upstairs? We don't need to tell your whole building this shit."

Erik led the way upstairs, and Brynn was too stunned to talk. *Mick McGowan. Gunshot wound.* The words looped through her mind as she retraced her steps to Ross's apartment.

When they walked in, Ross seemed startled to see Bulldog.

"Hey, what's up? I thought you were in Vegas running down Perez."

Bull looked to Brynn, in case she wanted to break the news. She didn't.

"Mick McGowan is dead," Bull said.

"*What?*"

"He was shot in his home," Brynn added.

Bull sat down on an ottoman near Ross. Brynn took a seat on the sofa beside him while Erik remained standing.

"What the hell happened?" Ross asked.

"You remember Max Gorman with the Sheridan Heights Police Department," Bull said. "He's the lead on Jen's case."

Brynn nodded. "I talked to him last night." Had it really only been last night?

"Mick's been retired two years now," Bull continued. "Gorman stopped by Mick's place to talk to him about Corby. Found him in his kitchen."

Ross shook his head. "How—"

"Shot dead with his own gun," Bull told him.

"When?"

"The ME's guy said it looks like he's been dead a few days. The body's in bad shape."

"His own gun." Brynn tried to get her mind around the idea. "So you're saying—"

"They're thinking Corby broke in, got hold of the gun, then got the drop on Mick somehow. Shot him in the head right there in his kitchen, then went over to Jen's place."

Brynn looked at Erik, who seemed impossibly calm in the wake of this news. He was watching Brynn's reaction, but he shifted his attention to Bulldog.

"Any ballistics to confirm this?" he asked.

"Not yet," Bull said. "But Mick's gun is missing. So is his vehicle. A white Dodge pickup."

Brynn let out a laugh, which was completely inappropriate for the moment. "Oh my God, *still*? That thing's older than dirt!"

Bulldog looked at her warily. "It's a ninety-five." He glanced at Erik. "So you guys keep your eyes peeled for the truck. There's a BOLO out on it already."

"You tell Reggie about all this?" Ross asked.

"Talked to him on my way here."

Silence settled over the group. A hundred questions swirled through Brynn's mind, but she couldn't focus on any of them as she pictured the veteran police detective she'd worked with on so many cases dead on his kitchen floor.

Mick had white hair and an easygoing smile. He was a widower. And a grandfather. And a Cowboys fan. Brynn pinched the bridge of her nose as the details flooded back.

Bulldog stood up and checked his watch. "I need to get to the airport. But I wanted to tell you."

Brynn and Ross got to their feet.

"Thanks for coming by," she said.

"Yeah, no problem." He shot a look at Erik, then turned to Brynn and Ross. "You two watch your backs."

Erik found her in her kitchen with Hayes. He was leaning back against the sink, drinking Gatorade as Brynn crouched inside the pantry.

She stood up with a bottle of wine in her hand. She set it on the counter, then pulled open a drawer and took out a corkscrew.

"Get you anything?" she asked Erik.

"No." He looked at Hayes. "She fill you in?"

"Yeah. I was about to call Liam and give him the update."

"Good plan."

Hayes walked out, and Erik turned to Brynn. "You okay?"

"Fine, why?" She opened a cabinet and took out a wineglass. "I mean, here I am standing in my kitchen without a bullet in my brain. I'm doing great."

She filled her glass. It was white wine, and it probably would have been better chilled. But she didn't seem to care as she took a sip.

"John Kopek is on our list," Erik said. "But we didn't know about his concealed-carry permit, and we definitely didn't know he was stopping by here tonight. He should have called first."

"Next time he drops by to tell me someone I know's been murdered, I'll be sure to remind him of the procedure."

"That's not the point. If he can get in, so can someone else." Which was Erik's problem, not hers. He needed to talk to Jeremy.

Brynn was far from *fine*, and she looked like she wanted to talk.

"Is there anyone you want to call right now? Maybe your sister or—"

"God, no. She'd freak." She set the wine on the counter, then combed her hands through her hair. "I can't believe this. It's like . . . like he's going down a hit list."

She was right. And it was very possible her name was on it, along with Ross's.

"I can't believe this," she repeated. "Really, I mean, I thought Reggie was wrong." She looked up at him, wide-eyed and in shock.

Erik stepped closer. "I know you're upset."

"*Upset?* I'm beyond upset. I'm . . . I don't even have words for what I am right now."

"Brynn, listen to me." He waited for her to look at him. "There was some good news mixed in there, too."

Her eyes widened.

"We have a vehicle now. That's an important lead. The marshals will be all over that, along with every other badge in the state. They'll track him down, I promise you."

"How can you possibly know that?"

"Because that's what they do. And they're the best in the world."

He watched her, battling the urge to wrap his arms around her because she looked so vulnerable standing there staring at him like he was crazy.

The other good thing that had come from all this? She took him seriously now. This threat to her life—and it was a very real threat—had her full attention. Which meant he was going to get her cooperation.

He wanted her trust, too, but that was another matter. Trust would come later. And he was going to have to earn it.

"I guess Reggie was right. You, him"—she nodded toward Hayes on the phone in the living room—"Skyler. We really do need all of you."

Erik nodded.

She closed her eyes. "This is unreal." She let out another laugh that was totally at odds with the situation. It seemed to be her reaction to stress. "You know what else is unreal? I have to be in court in a few hours. What the hell am I thinking?" She picked up her glass and dumped the rest of her wine down the sink. "I need to go to bed." She looked at him. "Will you be here a while longer?"

She asked it casually, but he saw the tension in her face.

"Until midnight."

"Great. Thank you. Well, I'm going to turn in, so . . . get some rest." She gave him a fake smile. "I'm sure I'll see you tomorrow."

She walked out, and he watched her disappear into her bedroom.

Erik muttered a curse and scrubbed his hands over his face. This job sucked, and he was only one day in.

And it was going to get worse before it got better.

A brief knock came at the front door, and Jeremy stepped inside, pocketing his key.

"Hey, Skyler needs to talk to you," Jeremy told him.

Erik darted a look down the hallway. "Brynn went to bed. You got this covered?"

"Yes."

Erik hesitated a moment before heading across the hall. Ross was in the kitchen now, standing in front of the open refrigerator with a blank look on his face. He seemed to be in shock. Erik found Skyler in the spare bedroom, where they'd set up a computer and printer, along with several monitors for their surveillance cameras. Skyler sat at the desk, frowning at the screen as she fast-forwarded through video footage.

"How'd he get in here?" Erik asked, referring to the PI.

"Still working on it." She grabbed a stack of papers off the desk. "Check it out. The marshals just sent these."

Erik thumbed through the pages, which showed the possible faces of escaped convict James Corby. Beard, no beard, goatee, no goatee, mustache, long hair, short hair, no hair. With his average build and unremarkable facial features, Corby was the sort of guy who could blend into a crowd. Erik muttered a curse.

"I know, right?" Skyler glanced at him. "Could be anyone."

He flipped through again, pausing on the shaved-head picture with the goatee. Before his escape, Corby was wearing his hair short but not shaved. After his escape, maybe he'd shaved it for a quick disguise.

"So how's the client?"

He glanced up. "Fine."

"She's attractive."

"And?" Erik returned his attention to the paperwork.

"She seems to like you, I couldn't help but notice."

"Actually, she thinks we're a pain in the ass."

"Not us. *You.*"

He flipped through the pages again. Skyler loved to tease him about being aloof with women. Clients sometimes flirted with him, but he never went there. It was one reason Liam had trusted him with this particular job.

"Of course, maybe I'm imagining it," she said. "Could be she's got a thing with her boss. The man's spending a fortune on her security."

Erik didn't react. The thought had crossed his mind, even though the guy was old enough to be her father. No way he was immune to her. The man would have to be dead.

"On the other hand," Skyler continued, "he's paying for Ross, too, so maybe it doesn't mean anything. Reggie Gunn strikes me as a businessman, so could be he's just protecting his investment."

Erik looked up. "Is there a point to this?"

She smiled sweetly. "Just giving you a hard time. And reminding you to keep your eye on the ball." Her look turned serious. "I heard about Otto's. How bad was it?"

"Minor."

"Hayes said Brynn was pissed."

"She'll get over it." Erik held up the stack of papers. "We need to show these to her and Ross. They need to memorize these faces. We all do."

"That's why I made copies. Those are yours."

He folded the papers and tucked them into his back pocket. "And my eye *is* on the ball, Sky, but thanks for the advice."

"Anytime."

7

BRYNN WAS dressed for battle.

She slipped on the jacket of her favorite Armani suit, midnight blue. The silk lining was like a whisper against her skin. Whenever she wore Armani, she felt wealthy and successful but also a touch guilty. She adjusted the jacket and then slid her feet into Louboutin pumps that cost more than the weekly paycheck her mother had used to raise two girls.

Mary Holloran had spent thirty-two years at a Houston law firm, starting as a receptionist and retiring as the legal secretary to the firm's senior partner. Brynn had worked in the soaring glass building as a temp in the summers and learned all the most important things about being a lawyer. Her mom taught her how to be cool under pressure and handle calls from assholes and deal with handsy men. She also taught her how to look good on a shoestring budget. Brynn remembered nights up late in their little apartment, watching her mother fix runs in her panty hose with nail polish and color her roots with Nice'n Easy.

Brynn leaned toward the mirror and smoothed Chanel lipstick over her mouth. She'd come a long way. She didn't wear panty hose, but spike heels that made her legs look miles long and the amount she paid to have her hair done would leave her mother speechless. But Brynn gladly shelled out the money. She knew the importance of not just looking good but feeling strong. Confidence was everything, especially in a courtroom and especially on day one.

Brynn checked her watch. She took a last slug of coffee and grabbed her leather attaché case. She rode the elevator down with Hayes, who wore a dark gray suit. The Tahoe was waiting, and Trent—also in a suit—opened the door for her, looking remarkably alert for a man who hadn't slept last night.

Brynn had barely slept, too. She'd been up most of the night, tossing and turning and thinking of Mick McGowan.

"Where's Ross?" Brynn asked as Trent got behind the wheel and Hayes took the shotgun seat.

"They just left," Hayes said.

"And Erik?"

"At the courthouse with Joe."

Who's Joe? she wanted to ask. But she couldn't worry herself with the security details—she had her hands full with the case.

Trent eased into downtown traffic, and Brynn spotted Ross's SUV several stoplights ahead.

She nestled her attaché case beside her. The accessory served the dual purpose of toning down her stilettos and making her look prepared. Which she was. She knew all the evidence inside out. She knew every deposition inside out. She knew her case strategy inside out, starting with voir dire. The only wild card, at this point, was Robert Perez, her missing witness. She was putting her faith in Bulldog. He'd sworn he'd take care of it, and he'd never let her down.

She took a deep breath and tried to relax as Trent navigated the morning rush hour. She stared through the tinted window, feeling more disconnected from the city than usual. Whenever she came here, she always felt like a visitor, and she knew she wouldn't feel at home until she stepped into the courtroom.

The bright green foliage of the park across from the courthouse came into view. She recognized the shiny silver Airstream, where a long line of people stood waiting for breakfast tacos.

Several news vans were parked nearby, and a police unit was stationed at the corner. Brynn's nerves fluttered as she spotted Jack Conlon on the courthouse steps. The assistant district attorney was surrounded by a scrum of reporters, and they moved with him en masse as he made his way up.

"Damn it, Jack." She gripped her briefcase.

Up ahead, Ross's driver put on his turn signal.

"Where are they going?" Brynn leaned forward.

"Around back," Hayes said. "Erik's arranged for us to drop you guys off in the prisoner bay."

"What? Why?"

"It's a concealed entry point."

"Stop the car."

Trent glanced over his shoulder. "What?"

"I don't want a concealed entry point."

He ignored her and started turning.

"*Stop*, God damn it, or I'm jumping out!" She clutched the door handle, and Hayes reached back.

"Ma'am, you can't—"

Brynn shoved open her door. Trent screeched to a halt. Horns blared as she jumped out, followed by Hayes.

"This way," she told him, dashing across the street just in time to miss a speeding car.

"Wait!" Hayes yelled.

She paused, looking up the steps to see Conlon enter the courthouse. Hayes caught up to her, darting his gaze around as he adjusted his earpiece.

"Let's go." She hurried up the steps, her attention focused on the doors ahead of her. She passed through a pair of tall columns.

"Ms. Holloran!"

Finally.

She pretended not to hear the voice as she reached for the door handle.

"Brynn!"

She stopped and turned around. A reporter rushed up to her. She didn't recognize him, but he was trailed by a cameraman.

"Ms. Holloran, have you talked to your client this morning? How is he feeling?"

"Justin and I spoke earlier," she replied. "He's relieved to finally have his day in court."

Another reporter joined them, and Brynn guided them out of the traffic flow.

"Conlon says your client gunned down Seth Moore in cold blood and that he intends to get justice for this heinous crime. Would you care to comment?" The reporter tipped his microphone toward her.

She smiled. "I have no comment other than to thank people for their outpouring of support. It means a lot to Justin and his family."

She reached for the door, but Hayes beat her to it and managed to stay close behind her as she walked through.

The courthouse was cool and dim compared with outside. As Brynn's eyes adjusted, she glanced around and noted the long line at the walk-through metal detector.

"Crap," she muttered. "We're going to be late."

She spied Conlon up ahead, talking and laughing with one of the courthouse security guards. The guard handed Conlon's briefcase off to the woman manning the X-ray machine and then waved the prosecutor through.

Brynn strode across the lobby, trying to remember the guard's name. Steve? Stan?

"Jeremy's at the back entrance," Hayes informed her. "There's no line at the checkpoint there."

"We're going this way." She cut a glance at Hayes. Sweat beaded on his forehead, and he looked stressed. If she'd gotten him in trouble, she'd smooth it out.

Brynn looked ahead and caught the guard's eye. "Sam, how are you?"

He smiled. "Haven't seen you in a while. How you doing this mornin'?"

"Late for court, I'm afraid." She held out her attaché case, and he put it on the X-ray machine. "He's with me," she said, nodding at Hayes.

"Your bodyguard, huh?" Sam's jovial expression faded. "I heard about all that."

A barricade made of two metal poles and a nylon strap prevented people from walking around the metal detector. Sam unhooked the strap and waved them through.

"Thanks, Sam."

"Y'all take care now."

Brynn collected her attaché off the X-ray machine as Hayes glanced around anxiously. Not a rule breaker, this guy.

At the far end of the hallway, Brynn spotted Ross and Nicole and a pissed-off-looking Jeremy. She hurried to catch up to them. They had exactly four minutes to get to Linden's courtroom on level two, and the judge was a fanatic about punctuality.

Ross stood tapping his foot at the base of the marble staircase. "What the hell? Why'd you go through the front?"

"Conlon was out there."

His eyebrows arched. "Any reporters?"

"Two. We got a good sound bite."

He smiled. "All right. Off to a good start, then. You ready, tiger?"

She started up the stairs. "Let's go."

———

Lindsey found Max in the police department garage, hosing down the back door of his unmarked Taurus. She got a whiff of vomit as she approached him.

"Ew. Drunk suspect?"

"Shit-faced." He looked at her. "I heard about those shell casings. Good find."

"Thanks. Any word back from the lab?"

"Not yet." Max closed the car door and stepped over to shut off the hose. "I don't expect much, though, do you?"

"Not if Mick kept the gun loaded."

"How many cops you know keep an unloaded weapon around?"

"None," she said.

"Exactly." Max rolled up the hose, taking care not to get his slacks dirty. Judging from his dress shirt and tie, he probably had to testify later today.

Lindsey studied her former mentor, who'd been through three marriages, two since she'd known him. He was pushing fifty, but he looked good, and he knew it, too. He kept himself in shape, and his salt-and-pepper hair made him appear experienced rather than past his prime.

"So we know for a fact the gun came from Mick?" Lindsey asked.

"Looks that way." Max leaned a hand on the roof of his vehicle. "'Course, we don't know for sure, because the weapon's still missing, but the casings and slugs fit that scenario. Why? What's on your mind?"

"A lot."

"Good. That's why I brought you in on this."

"Okay, here's one thing bugging me," she said. "No fingerprints at the judge's crime scene."

"He's careful. Didn't you read about him? He raped and murdered four women without leaving behind prints or DNA. The guy's meticulous."

An unmarked unit pulled into the garage, and Lindsey stepped out of the way.

"Yes, but why now?" she asked. "He's on a revenge spree, right? Everybody knows it's him, so what's he trying to hide?"

"Maybe nothing. Maybe it's his MO at this point. No trace left behind. And I'm not holding my breath on lab work, because odds are Mick McGowan loaded that gun himself, so Corby's prints won't be on the shell casings. So once again, no physical evidence linking him to the crime."

"Here's something else bugging me," she said. "Where the hell is he?"

"Think the marshals are wondering that, too."

"Obviously. But I mean, *where* the hell is he, like, right this minute? Eight forty-six on a Monday morning. Where's he sleeping? Eating? Taking a leak? Where's he parking this old truck everybody assumes he stole from Mick McGowan? It has to be inside a garage, or we would have spotted it by now."

"You think he's staying with someone?"

"It would make sense. We're talking about a guy who escaped from prison, traveled three hundred miles north, killed a cop and a judge, and then dropped out of sight. Someone has to be helping him."

He watched her, and she couldn't tell whether he liked her theory or not.

"Corby's been sitting in prison for three years," she pressed on. "This whole thing has been planned out, right down to the last detail. We need to understand him if we're going to get a step ahead of him and figure out his next move."

"I like the way you're thinking, kid."

The term irked her, which was why Max used it. She did better work when she was out to prove something.

"I want you to be my partner on this," he told her.

"But I'm buried with cases. I thought you wanted me to *weigh in*?"

"I talked to the LT. You're with me until we wrap this thing."

Lindsey watched him, flattered that he'd asked for her and annoyed at being treated as a rookie. She'd learned a lot since her uniform days when Max had been her training officer.

"One condition."

He smiled and shook his head. "You're setting conditions now?"

"That's right. You're not my TO anymore. You want a partner, you've got one, but we get equal say *and* equal credit."

"Done."

"Good." She checked her watch. "Let's go. We need to canvass the neighborhood. We'll interview those residents, see if anybody saw someone in a white Dodge pickup near Jen's house on the day of the murder."

"It's been done."

"We need to do it again."

He smiled. Max knew her because he'd mentored her. And he knew that once she got her claws into something, she wouldn't turn loose.

"What?" she asked. "Are you with me or not?"

He held up his hands in surrender. "Hey, I'm with you. You drive."

———————

Hayes picked up Brynn and Trent at the back entrance. As soon as they were moving, she dug her phone out from her attaché case. She'd kept it on silent all afternoon, because the only thing Linden hated more than tardiness was a cell phone going off in his courtroom.

Brynn had two messages from Reggie and called him back without listening to them.

"How'd we do?" he asked eagerly.

"Eight women, four men, two female alternates."

"That's good."

"I know."

She gave him a rundown of everyone, including race, education, and occupation.

"Two teachers. I like that," Reggie said. "Any moms?"

"Seven of the eight."

"Even better. So opening statements tomorrow?"

"That's the plan," she said. "Although Conlon's already started his show. He was grandstanding in front of the courthouse this morning."

"Yeah, I saw that," Reggie said. "You both had nice sound bites, but his was longer."

"Big surprise." Brynn peeled off her jacket and tossed it over the seat. "How'd it go with Sheffield today?"

Daniel Sheffield was a major league baseball player facing assault charges after punching a photographer outside a nightclub.

"I'm still working on him," Reggie said.

"Really? I thought his agent recommended us."

Her phone beeped with a call from Erik, but she let it go to voice mail.

"He did, but you know how it is with these guys," Reggie said, meaning athletes with huge egos. "I'll let you know how it develops. Any updates on Jen's case?"

Brynn's stomach knotted. She'd managed to get through eight hours without thinking about the murders. When she was in court, her case had her undivided attention.

"Nothing new," she said. "But I'll give you a call if anything comes up."

"Okay, keep me in the loop."

"I will."

Hayes turned into the Atrium's driveway and parked right in front of the door. Brynn slid from the SUV. Jeremy stood beside the Expedition talking on his phone. No sign of Erik. No Ross, either, so he must have gone up already.

Trent followed Brynn to her apartment without conversation, and she wondered if she might be getting the cold shoulder.

"I'm going to change and work out upstairs." She tossed her attaché case onto the sofa. "I'll just be a sec."

He nodded and stood silently beside the bar.

Brynn went into her bedroom. She kicked off her heels and sank onto the bed to massage her sore feet. It had been a good first day, better than she'd expected. Jack Conlon wasn't happy with the jury, which made Brynn happy.

She changed into a black Speedo swimsuit and threw on some sweatpants before grabbing a towel and heading up to the fitness center with Trent at her side. All the treadmills were full. She pushed through the glass doors and stepped onto the blessedly empty patio.

Brynn closed her eyes and stood there, letting the sun warm her shoulders. She tuned out the traffic noise at street level, the distant clamor of a construction site, her hovering attendant. She dropped her sweatpants and towel onto a lounge chair and stepped to the pool. The concrete apron felt hot beneath her feet, and she gripped the edge with her toes as she gazed at the shimmery blue. She pulled her arms back and drew a deep breath of chlorine-scented air. Then she plunged.

The first silent moment was her favorite—the cool glide, the nothingness. She broke the surface with a smooth stroke, reaching and pulling as she set a rhythm. She timed her breaths, then curled tight for the turn, pushing hard off the wall with the balls of her feet. She torpedoed through the water and broke the surface again.

She thought of Erik. She hadn't seen him all day. She hadn't really been looking, but she'd thought she might catch a glimpse of him, maybe on her lunch break. Could be he was mad at her.

Brynn wasn't sure what he thought of her. There was the buzz of attraction, yes, but beyond that. What did he think of her as a person?

She sensed an underlying disapproval that seemed to go hand in hand with the attraction thing, and she couldn't figure it out. Not that she wanted to. She was slammed with work and had plenty of things that needed her attention more than he did.

Which explained why her love life had been nonexistent since her breakup with Adam. She'd been buried with work. All the time. Every weekend. She'd made sure to be so she wouldn't have to think about her woefully empty personal life.

It wasn't that she wanted Adam back. But their breakup had shattered her illusion that she could have normal things. Lasting things. A regular relationship, like her sister had with Mike. Sure, it had been a bit . . . flat. But it had been stable. As stable as a relationship between two self-absorbed workaholic lawyers *could* be, which wasn't stable at all, as it turned out.

So maybe Brynn wasn't meant for normal or lasting. Even when she had a boyfriend and a steady paycheck and a nice car in the driveway, she was still a pretender.

She did another flip turn, and a pair of shiny black shoes caught her eye. Trent? As she surfaced, the shoes followed her. It wasn't Trent but Erik, keeping pace with her along the side of the pool. He looked like 007 today in a black suit.

Brynn reached the side and stopped. "Hi," she said, gasping for breath.

Erik glared down at her, arms crossed, blocking out the sun with his big shoulders. "I need to talk to you."

"Four more laps."

"Now."

She dipped under, pushing off the wall. When she reached the other end, the shoes were waiting.

"Now, Brynn."

"In a minute."

She ducked down. Two big hands like shovels scooped under her arms and lifted her from the water. Erik plunked her down in front of him, dripping and sputtering and blinking water from her eyes.

"What the *hell* is wrong with you?"

"I need to talk to you."

"Can't it wait a damn minute?"

"No."

She squeezed the ends of her hair, drizzling water all over his shoes. "*What?*"

"You know damn well what."

She crossed her arms, refusing to feel self-conscious about standing there in front of him in a swimsuit.

"I spent half my day on damage control because of your little publicity stunt this morning."

"Excuse me?"

"Your press conference in front of the courthouse," he said. "Not only did I get my ass chewed out by my boss, but I also had to deal with a pissed-off security chief who staffed an extra man at the prisoner bay this morning, at my request, to deal with your arrival."

"I didn't ask you to do that."

"You didn't have to. We're professionals. That means we plan these things without being asked, because we know what constitutes good security."

"Well, I never agreed to all this."

"Doesn't matter. Your boss agreed when he hired us and tasked us with the job of keeping you safe."

"Um, *wrong*." She fisted a hand on her hip. "It absolutely does matter. It's called consent, and I didn't consent for you to interfere with my job."

"You're interfering with *my* job. You think fifteen seconds of publicity for your law firm is worth some nutcase taking a shot at you?"

"Maybe."

His eyebrows arched. "Are you freaking insane?"

"No."

Erik looked around and seemed to notice that they were attracting attention from the treadmill hamsters. He took her by the elbow and steered her away from the windows.

"It's not just about the firm," Brynn said, shaking her arm free. "It's about my client. His entire future's at stake, and he's been sitting behind bars for five months. This kid has no voice, and it's my responsibility to make his case not just in the courtroom but in the court of public opinion."

Erik didn't respond, just glowered down at her.

"I'm his spokesperson. It's my job to make a positive impression on the public to help offset all the negative things the prosecutor's already planted in people's minds through all his leaks to the media!"

"And it's *my* job to keep you alive."

She tipped her head to the side. "Come on, Erik, let's be real. I researched you guys. You work for celebrities. Do you tell your NFL clients they can't sign autographs outside the stadium? Do you tell your pop divas they can't walk the red carpet at the Grammys? Do you tell your senators they can't give stump speeches? My job is every bit as important as theirs—I'd say more so—and I can't do it effectively if you make me invisible."

Erik stared down at her. "Are you done?"

"Yes."

"Good. Then you can listen."

"I—"

"Hey." He held up his hand. "I listened to you."

She huffed out a breath and crossed her arms.

"We are not a PR firm," he said, trying to keep his voice even. "You didn't hire us to put you in front of a camera."

"I didn't hire you at all."

"Are you saying you want to fire me? Because I strongly *don't* recommend it."

"I'm not saying that. I'm saying I want input. I told you in the beginning, I don't like being bossed around. It pushes my buttons."

Erik clenched his teeth. Drops of water slid down her neck, disappearing between her breasts, but he managed to keep his focus on her face.

"I'm saying we need to talk about things ahead of time," she said, "instead of just springing things on me in the moment."

"I agree."

She blinked. "You do?"

"Yes. I'm willing to explain our security plans ahead of time and the rationale behind everything, and you can weigh in. But what you *can't* do is change the plan and threaten my guys—"

"I didn't—"

"If you have a problem with something, you take it up with me."

"Fine."

"Another thing? Your phone. I have to be able to reach you, so don't ignore my calls. I won't contact you unless it's important."

She looked suspicious, and he could see his willingness to compromise had caught her off guard.

"Do we understand each other?" he asked.

"Yes."

"Good."

She reached for the towel on the chair and patted her arms dry.

"So what's wrong?" he asked. "You seem stressed."

This, too, seemed to catch her off guard.

"I *am* stressed. It was a long, tedious day. I came up here to blow off steam and get away from annoying *people*." She wrapped the towel around her waist and glared up at him.

Her skin was flushed, and it wasn't just from exercise. She was all fired up, and maybe he shouldn't have plucked her out of the pool, but he'd had it with her ignoring him. That shit was over, as of right now.

Brynn twisted her hair into a knot. "You said there was something important. What is it?"

"You have visitors downstairs."

"Visitors?"

"Homicide cops," he said. "They need to talk to you."

8

LINDSEY WAS expecting business attire, but Brynn Holloran showed up in a damp swimsuit and sweatpants, with a towel around her neck and her supersized bodyguard trailing closely behind her.

Max tried to cover his surprise as he stepped forward to shake her hand. "Ms. Holloran, I'm Detective Gorman. We spoke on the phone the other night. Thanks for meeting with us."

"Of course." The lawyer looked at Lindsey. "And you are?"

"Lindsey Leary. I'm pitching in on the case."

"Great." She glanced around the apartment, which looked about as homey as a dentist's waiting room. "We can sit in here," she said, leading them to a long table.

Brynn took a seat at the head of the table opposite Jeremy, the bodyguard who had let them in here. Everyone claimed a chair except for Erik Morgan, who leaned against the bar. Lindsey had just met the man, but she pegged him for ex-military based on his perfect posture, short haircut, and steely gaze.

"So what can I do for you?" Brynn asked.

"We hear you're on the Sebring trial," Max said.

"That's right."

"Conlon trying that one?"

"He is."

"Tough case."

"Yes. But I assume you're here to discuss *Jen Ballard's* case?"

"We are." Lindsey scooted her chair in. "We believe you can help with our investigation. I understand you and Jen were friends?"

"Yes."

Lindsey flipped open her book. "And . . . I understand you were on her team for the James Corby trial?"

"That's correct."

Lindsey glanced at Max, whose gaze was glued to the attorney—which shouldn't have been surprising. The woman definitely made an impression.

Lindsey waited for her to elaborate on her answer, but she didn't. Defense attorneys tended to hold their cards close.

"Listen, Ms. Holloran," Lindsey said, "I'll cut to the chase here. We're a small department. We're understaffed and underfunded, and we've got a crapload of cases to deal with. So we could really use your help on this one."

"I'll help however I can, but what is it you want, exactly?"

"It's more what we *don't* want," Lindsey said. "We don't want to re-invent the wheel here, in terms of our investigation. I'm sure you know our prime suspect—actually, our *only* suspect, at this point—is James Corby. You prosecuted the man. You know him. It's possible you know him better than anybody, now that Jen Ballard and Michael McGowan are dead."

Brynn's brow furrowed at Lindsey's words. "And?"

"We'd like you to tell us more about his MO," Max said. "You helped convict him of four homicides—"

"A jury convicted him."

Max nodded. "Well, what's his trademark? What should we look for to link him to these crime scenes?"

"Nothing."

"There's got to be something," Max said.

"No, that's just it. *Nothing* is his trademark." She looked at Lindsey. "He leaves behind no trace of himself whatsoever. No prints, no semen, no hair or fiber evidence. He's meticulous. That's what made him tough to prosecute."

Max leaned back in his chair, watching her. "That's been our problem so far. CSIs have been over both victims' houses, and they haven't found dick, if you'll pardon my language."

"That doesn't surprise me," Brynn said.

"What about people?" Lindsey asked. "Is there anyone he's close to who might be helping him, giving him refuge? You've probably heard that Mick McGowan's killer stole his guns and his truck, and there's been a BOLO out but no sightings."

"Wait, *guns?*" Erik cut in.

"He cleared out McGowan's gun cabinet," Lindsey said. "The door was open, and everything was missing."

"I need a list of those weapons."

"We're working on it. We've made contact with McGowan's son, and he's supposed to get us a list of everything that could have been in there."

Based on his intensely unhappy expression, this was the first Erik was hearing about the gun cabinet.

"He takes trophies."

All eyes turned to Brynn.

"From his victims," she elaborated. "A chunk of hair, a bracelet. He takes a souvenir from each of them, sometimes two. In Lauren Tull's case, she was missing a necklace. Investigators found it in Corby's possession, which was how they finally nailed him."

"We read about that," Lindsey said. "We've checked for anything missing at the judge's house, but so far nothing that anyone can pinpoint." She flipped through her notepad. "What about relatives? Do you recall anyone who attended Corby's trial?"

"No."

"Friends? Girlfriends?" Max persisted. "Maybe someone who just showed up for a day?"

"Not that we ever knew about."

"That old truck of McGowan's is distinctive," Lindsey said. "I keep thinking he has to be hiding it in a garage someplace, or we would have had a call on it by now."

"We believe someone must be harboring this guy," Max added.

But Brynn was shaking her head. "I wouldn't assume that," she told them. "Corby's a loner. I mean, in the extreme. He's an only child, he never knew his father, and his mother's been dead for years. The guy's alone in the world, which—if you believe the shrink who evaluated him—is part of his problem. There's nobody. His coworkers at the cable company said they barely knew him, that he kept to himself. No one posted his bail or attended the trial to support him. He had no visitors in prison, with the exception of a few curious reporters who were hoping to write a book." She sighed. "The man is antisocial, in every sense of the word."

Lindsey glanced at Max. They'd really been hoping for a name or a place that might provide a new lead.

"Back to the guns," Brynn said.

"What about them?" Max asked.

"That whole thing seems off. All of his sexual homicides, he killed them with a knife. If he's on some sick revenge quest, then I'd expect him to use a blade and not a bullet."

Lindsey looked at Max. "You didn't tell her?"

"We were keeping it under wraps."

"Tell me *what*?" Brynn leaned forward, her sharp words at odds with the fear in her eyes.

"Jennifer Ballard . . ." Lindsey hesitated.

"Jen died of gunshot wounds." She looked at Max. "That's what you told me on the phone."

"Yes, but her killer didn't just shoot her," Max said. "He cut out her tongue."

9

AFTER THE detectives left, Erik reviewed the new camera setup with Jeremy and then went across the hall to look for Brynn.

"Where is she?" he asked Hayes.

"In her bedroom."

Brynn stepped into the hallway. She wore jeans and a white T-shirt now, and her damp hair was loose around her shoulders. She walked into the living room and grabbed a pair of sandals from under the table.

"Going somewhere?" Erik asked.

She slipped her feet into the shoes. "Getting some dinner. Who's coming with me?"

Erik nodded at Hayes. "Bring the car around."

"Sure."

"It's right next door," Brynn added.

"Which place?" Erik asked. "One of us can run out for you."

"No, *I* can run out." She picked up her purse. "I refuse to be a hostage here."

Erik looked at Hayes. "They need you at Ross's to review the new camera setup."

"Got it," Hayes said, looking all too relieved to duck out the door.

Brynn grabbed her cell phone off the counter and tucked it into her back pocket. Erik followed her out and waited while she locked the apartment. Then she headed for the elevator and jabbed the button before he could reach for it.

They rode down in silence.

"Want to talk about it?" he asked.

"About what?"

"What's bothering you."

The door slid open, and she stepped out.

"Brynn?"

"I'm *fine*."

She headed for the back exit. Erik strode in front of her and pushed open the door, scanning the surrounding area before allowing her to step out.

"Bamboo Palace," she said. "It's just past the yogurt shop."

Farther than next door, but Erik let it go. She was already in a pissy mood. He skimmed the street as they walked without talking. They passed shoppers, dog walkers, even a few joggers, although the pavement was still hot enough to fry an egg.

The restaurant was sandwiched between a chiropractor and a pet groomer. A swag of red paper lanterns hung over the hostess stand. Beside the register sat a happy Buddha statue and a bowl of fortune cookies.

"Two for dinner," Brynn told the hostess.

Erik had assumed they were picking up food, but Brynn had other plans, apparently.

The hostess showed them to a red vinyl booth next to a fish tank. Erik took the seat facing the door, and Brynn slid in across from him.

Erik noted people and exits. An elderly couple had a booth beside the window, and a lone businessman sat at the bar near a line of to-go bags waiting for pickup.

Brynn already had her nose in a menu.

"Sure you don't want to talk about it?" Erik asked.

"I told you, I'm *fine*."

"You're upset."

She slapped the menu down. "How the hell would you know?"

"You get snippy when you're upset."

"Don't you mean 'bitchy'? How original. That's definitely something I haven't heard in my seven years as a female practicing law."

"That's not what I said."

"That's what you meant."

The hostess reappeared with a notepad in her hand. She pulled a pencil from behind her ear and looked at Brynn. "Something to drink?"

"Two Tsingtaos." She gave Erik a sharp look, daring him to object.

The woman jotted it down and walked away.

Erik rested his arms on the table. "You're under a lot of stress. I get it, Brynn."

She stared at the murky fish tank. "What they said about Jen . . . I had no idea."

Erik watched her, wishing she didn't look so anguished.

"I've been kidding myself. All this time." She looked at him, and the vulnerability in her blue eyes put a pinch in his chest. It was such a contrast to her usual brash confidence.

"I thought maybe it wasn't him." She shook her head. "I know— crazy, right? Who else would it be? But I didn't want to believe it. And I *didn't*, not really. Not until they said that about him cutting her."

"People don't want to believe threats against them are real," he said. "I see it all the time. It's a natural response."

She squeezed her eyes shut. "It's so awful. Poor Jen."

"I'm sorry."

She looked up at him. No tears in her eyes, but he saw the pain there. He wanted to reach out and take her hand, but that was the last thing he could do. She was his client.

"Corby's trial was a bad time for me," she said. "There was so much pressure . . ." She trailed off. "It was big news here in Dallas. Four women raped and murdered over an eighteen-month period. The college campuses were practically on lockdown. Police were under a lot of pressure to arrest someone, and they did, which was good, except— between you and me—I think they may have rushed things. When it got handed over to the DA's office, it was disorganized, and it fell to Jen and me to pretty much piece everything together."

"What, you mean the evidence?"

"Yeah, I mean, they *had* him. No question. But some of the paper-work was hurried." She sighed. "It happens in high-profile cases sometimes, but it makes things harder in court." She squeezed her eyes shut again. "And God, it *was* hard. The worst case I ever worked on. It was all-consuming."

"I bet."

"It didn't help that there was this media spotlight on everything. We worked a lot of long days. Long nights. And every morning, I had to go into that courtroom and sit right across the aisle from him. And sometimes he would just *stare* at me when the jurors weren't there. I fucking hated it. I've never been so relieved to get to a verdict."

Erik watched her intently, his blood simmering at the thought of that shitbag murderer intimidating her that way. Erik had wanted to get his hands on the man for days, but now he truly felt the urge to throttle him.

The waitress was back with two beer bottles, each wrapped with a neatly folded napkin. She set down the beers and then a glass for each.

"Something to eat?" she asked.

"We'll start with the egg rolls," Brynn said. "Then I'd like the sesame chicken, the spare ribs, and the ginger broccoli."

The woman looked at Erik.

"Vegetable lo mein," he said.

"That's it?" Brynn asked.

"Yeah."

The server left, and Brynn poured her beer, tipping the glass to minimize the head.

Erik watched her, waiting for her to keep talking about the trial. Her hair was still damp and had made little wet spots on her shoulders. She looked so anxious sitting there, and Erik hated Corby all over again.

"Finally, the jury came back with a verdict," she said. "Guilty on all counts, just like we expected, but I've never in my life been so relieved. I never wanted to see him again. Or read about him or even think his name after that."

And yet she had. She'd kept tabs on him. She knew his nickname in prison. And she knew he'd had no visitors, besides those few reporters chasing an interview.

"All this stuff, it's dredging everything back up again."

"I know." He watched her, wishing there was something more that he could say.

"I'm glad they came, though," she said.

"You mean Gorman and Leary?"

"Yeah. Actually, I'm surprised they reached out to me. We're not exactly chummy with the cops around here, in case you haven't noticed."

"What's that about, anyway?"

"It goes back to this case Reggie had here in Dallas. Hector Bell." She sipped her beer. "You really want to hear this?"

"Yeah."

She took a deep breath. "Hector was thirty-one. He'd used up two of his three strikes and was out on parole when he got pulled over for a busted taillight. He was driving an old Buick and had an envelope in the front seat stuffed with five thousand dollars in cash. The cop who pulled him over asked about the money, and Hector said he was on his way to buy a car. He had the Buick's title in the envelope, ready to make the trade."

"Sounds legit."

"It was. So the officer ran him through the system, then returned to the window and demanded that he hand over the money. Hector refused. The cop asked him again, this time showing him the drop bag he promised to plant on him if he didn't comply. The bag had enough coke to guarantee Hector a one-way ticket back to prison if he didn't cooperate. Hector happened to have his cell phone recording the whole exchange, but the officer didn't know that until much later."

Erik shook his head.

"Reggie blew it out at trial, revealing a scam that involved three dirty cops, who sullied the reputation of the whole department. The three cops got fired, Hector got a walk, and Reggie got a ton of media coverage in Dallas. The case was a boon to his career, but when the dust settled, he decided to pick up stakes and move his practice to a place where he wasn't hated by everyone with a badge." She took another sip of beer. "So that's it. That's the case that made any lawyer from Blythe and Gunn a pariah around here."

The server was back with the egg rolls. Brynn divided the order and slid a plate in front of him.

"You're going to like these," she said, spooning mustard from a tiny jar.

Talking about Reggie seemed to improve her mood. Or maybe it was the food. She had the appetite of a linebacker, but somehow she managed to stay in shape.

"Looks like your case is off to a good start," Erik said.

"Where'd you hear that?" She chomped into her egg roll.

"I slipped into the courtroom and watched for a while."

"Slipped?" She dabbed the corner of her mouth with a napkin. "You guys don't *slip* anywhere. How come I didn't see you?"

"I'm unobtrusive."

She snorted and picked up her beer.

"You were preoccupied with your jury selection. Nice job, by the way. I think you made a good impression on those people."

"Yeah, well, Reggie's a good teacher."

"Is that how he got you? I know it wasn't all about money." Erik reached for the mustard and spooned some onto his plate.

"That's hot," Brynn warned.

He added another dollop.

"Reggie approached me after the Corby trial. I'd taken a leave of absence because I'd become so immersed in everything."

"What constitutes a 'leave' for you?" he asked.

"I was gone three weeks."

Erik bit into the egg roll. Holy *shit*. His eyes watered, and he reached for his beer.

Brynn smiled. "Told you."

Erik waited until he could talk again. "That's not a leave, that's a vacation."

"Well, for me, it was a leave. I went to Port O'Connor to visit my mom and her husband. Very restful. Reading, jogging, fishing every morning at five A.M. Napping in the afternoon. Of course, my mom and I got to bickering, but I knew that would happen. I love her to death, but we drive each other crazy."

"And your dad? Where is he?"

"No idea. He left when I was little and hasn't kept in touch."

She dipped the last bite of egg roll into some mustard and ate it without flinching. "Anyway, Reggie tracked me down the third week. He laid out his argument and persuaded me to move to Pine Rock and join his firm. So I did. I switched to private practice, bought a house, met a guy. Everything was great."

A young waiter showed up with a tray of steaming food. He unloaded the dishes, and Erik asked for a water.

"Wimp," Brynn said. She scooped food onto her plate and gave his lo mein a disapproving look. Erik already had buyer's remorse after seeing her barbecued spare ribs.

"You were saying?" he asked. "Everything was great?" Erik had definitely sensed a "but" coming.

"But then I started doing it all over again."

"What's that?"

"Putting in the hours, the evenings, the weekends. Skipping time off. Neglecting my friends, my boyfriend. So—big shocker—he met someone. I found all these sext messages on his phone."

Interesting. From the conversation in the car, Erik had thought the guy broke up with her.

"You found out he was cheating? That's why you dumped him?"

"I'd suspected he was cheating for months." Brynn stabbed a bite of broccoli. "I dumped him when I realized I didn't care."

Erik watched her.

"And I started thinking, you know, there's a pattern here. My problem isn't the job or the boss or the city." She leaned back against the booth. "It's me. I throw myself in, immerse myself in work, block out everyone and everything that isn't my job."

"Maybe that's why you're good at it."

"It is, I know. Work's great." She shook her head. "It's the rest of my life that's a wreck."

———

Brynn lay in bed, staring at the ceiling, listening to the faint hum of downtown traffic twelve stories below. She'd stayed in this apartment many times before. In this exact bed, in fact. And the noise had never bothered her. If anything, it had lulled her to sleep after a long workday.

Not tonight, though.

She kept thinking about that white truck. It was out there somewhere. James Corby was in it. Was he prowling the streets, watching her, waiting for his next window of opportunity? Or was he on the move, headed far, far away from the marshals and detectives and Texas Rangers who were scouring the state for him? Maybe he'd completed his revenge quest. Maybe he'd taken his last trophy and was on his way to enjoy his newfound freedom south of the border.

She thought of the digital pictures Erik had shown her, all the different images of what Corby might look like now. As if she needed a reminder. As if Corby's stone-cold eyes weren't permanently etched into her brain.

Brynn stared at the ceiling fan as it churned the air. She felt hot. Sticky. She kicked the covers off, swung her legs out of bed, and grabbed some cutoffs from the chair in the corner. Then she stepped into the hallway to check the thermostat.

And Erik.

The living room was dim, and she poked her head around the corner to see him sitting on the sofa, his arm stretched across the back. His suit jacket was off. He had his sleeves rolled up, and the light of the television cast him in a bluish hue.

"Still here?" she asked.

He just looked at her, and she felt a flush of embarrassment at the dumb question.

She padded into the kitchen and opened the fridge. Wine, Gatorade, water, beer. Nothing tempted her.

"Want anything?" she asked.

"I'm good."

She grabbed a water and joined him in the living room, sinking into the oversize armchair beside the sofa. Close but not too close. She wasn't wearing a bra under her T-shirt, and it was dark, but she didn't want to give him an eyeful.

"I can't sleep." She twisted the top off her water and took a swig. Then she glanced at the TV. He was watching CNN, but he had the volume switched off and the closed-captioning turned on. "You can turn that up, you know. That's not the problem."

"I like it on mute so I can listen."

Listen to what? Traffic? Voices? Footsteps in the hallway? She didn't know how his job worked, exactly. The cameras at Ross's were a part of it. Erik had gone through that with her earlier tonight—sharing information, just as he'd promised. Instead of two monitoring stations—

one at each apartment—they had set up a designated control room in the spare bedroom at Ross's. And they'd assigned an agent to monitor the cameras full-time, versus an agent in each apartment "keeping an eye on" the cameras. The new setup would eliminate the possibility of someone slipping into the building behind a tenant while both agents happened to be distracted, which was how Bulldog had gotten in.

Security gap filled. Or so they hoped.

"What *is* the problem?"

She looked at Erik. "Huh?"

"You said my volume isn't the problem. What is?"

She put down her water and grabbed a *Vanity Fair* off the coffee table. "Just, you know, general insomnia."

She flipped through the pages and found the article she'd tried to get through earlier, an interview with some twenty-three-year-old actress from the summer's big blockbuster. Brynn had absolutely zero interest in the woman, beyond the fact that she was gorgeous and Liam had protected her a year ago. Did Wolfe Sec still work for her? Had Erik ever met her? Maybe he'd been on her detail and they were friends now. Friends with benefits even, if he was ever in LA.

Brynn was losing her mind. Truly. She needed *sleep*. She glanced at the TV.

"Are you watching this?" she asked.

"I'm watching you."

She looked at him.

"What's wrong, Brynn?"

"Nothing."

He picked up the remote and switched off the television. Then he leaned his elbows on his knees and looked at her.

"Talk to me."

His words sent a rush of heat through her body. His words and his eyes. They were dark and serious, and the only light now came from the glow in the kitchen.

And he was completely focused on her. He knew something was bothering her, and he was determined to pin her down on it. Maybe that was why she'd come out here.

"I can't go to the funeral," she said.

"Jen's?"

She nodded. "It's at ten o'clock, and I have to be in court at eight thirty. Not that I even want to go. I hate those things, but I should be there." She sighed and rubbed her forehead. "Jen took a chance on me when I was straight out of school. I was drowning in loans and desperate for a job, even though my GPA wasn't great and my résumé was thin. We hit it off, and she gave me a shot, and I owe everything to her. And now . . . I can't even make it to her funeral."

"She'd understand."

"She would. That's the irony. She never let her personal life get in the way of her work." Brynn combed her hand through her hair. "I'm relieved, if you want to know the truth."

"That you have an excuse?"

"I don't really want to see all those people from my past and think about Jen and how she died." Brynn sounded whiny, even to her own ears.

Erik reached over. He took the magazine from her hands and set it on the table.

Her pulse picked up.

"Brynn."

"What?"

"I know you're worried."

Worried didn't begin to cover it. She felt paralyzed by her own thoughts. And she couldn't stop thinking them. Every time she tried to sleep, her brain got stuck on this continuous loop.

"But we *will* protect you, no matter what. That's ironclad."

She laughed. "Why? You don't even like me."

"You're wrong."

He held her gaze, and her pulse sped up again. Her skin felt tight. There was something in his voice, his look.

"I won't lie to you," he said. "Corby is a serious threat. He's armed, and he's experienced."

"And he managed to escape from prison. And get the drop on a cop."

"Retired cop," he said.

"Same thing."

"No, it's not. Mick McGowan wasn't ready for him. He never saw him coming. We're prepared. We're trained, and we have the advantage."

She stared at him, not wanting to voice her doubts.

"You still don't believe me?"

"I want to, but . . . it sounds a little arrogant."

"Not arrogant, confident. It's not arrogance if you have the skills to back it up." He rested his hand on her shoulder. It felt warm and heavy, and her pulse picked up at his touch. "You need to trust us, Brynn."

He held her gaze, and she wondered what it would be like to kiss him. She could tell he was attracted to her, and he had to know it was mutual. But she sensed his frustration, as though he didn't *want* to be attracted to her.

He dropped his hand from her shoulder and stood up.

She stood, too.

"You should get some sleep."

It was a dismissal, and she felt a twinge of hurt.

Then he surprised her by walking down the hallway to her room. She followed him, and he stopped at the thermostat beside her door.

"You hot?" he asked.

"Not anymore."

She watched as he crossed her darkened bedroom. He parted the slats on the miniblinds and peered out. Most of the window treatments had been closed since she'd arrived, and after learning Corby might have access to rifles and not just handguns, Erik had given her strict instructions to keep everything closed at all times.

He returned to the door, darting a glance at her rumpled bed.

"You're off at midnight?"

"Yeah." He touched her waist, surprising her again. "And on again at eight."

She gazed up at him, and suddenly the air between them felt so charged that she couldn't breathe. His fingers were on her waist, burning a hole through her thin T-shirt.

"Good night." He stepped away, but she caught his arm.

"Wait."

She kissed him, going up on tiptoes to reach his mouth. She slid her hands up to cup his face, holding him there as he tried to pull back.

Cold panic shot through her.

But then he kissed her back, and every part of her body fired to life. His lips moved against hers, and then his arms were around her, thick and strong and lifting her off her feet. He turned and backed her against the bedroom wall, pinning her there while his tongue delved into her mouth.

It was hot. Explosive. Every nerve inside her was electrified by his firm lips and his hard body and the heavy weight of him leaning against her.

He tasted so good, sharp and male and musky, and she realized she was starved for the flavor. She wanted more. *Him.* She wanted his mouth and his stubble under her fingertips. She wanted his big hands that were sliding under her T-shirt, searing a path over her skin.

God, he was good. She should have known he would be. He was so capable at everything, so why would kissing be any different? She pressed against him, and his hand gripped her hip.

A faint noise made her pull back. "Erik—"

He cut her off, taking her mouth in another fierce kiss that made her dizzy.

She heard it again—a soft *snick*. She pressed her hand to his chest. "Someone's—"

He jerked back before she finished the sentence. Keys jangled as someone unlocked the door and entered the apartment.

"Trent." Erik looked at her, and the desperation in his eyes mirrored what she was feeling. They stared at each other, breathless.

"He's early," she whispered.

Erik stepped back, raking his hand through his hair as Brynn tugged her T-shirt into place.

Erik's gaze hardened. "Sorry. This won't happen again."

Then he turned and walked out, leaving her alone in the dark with her lips numb and her heart racing.

10

BRYNN OVERSLEPT.

Of course. Because after flailing restlessly for hours, it was just her luck to fall into a deep, dreamless sleep that even her cell-phone alarm couldn't penetrate.

She awoke with a jolt at 7:45 and spent fifteen minutes throwing on clothes and racing around the apartment, jamming files into her attaché case. She checked her watch as she hurried into the bathroom and surveyed her cosmetics on the counter. She had time for makeup or coffee but not both.

"Shit!"

"Help you with anything?" Hayes called from the hallway.

"No, thanks! Wait, *yes*." She opened the bedroom door and poked her head out. "Can you make the coffee?"

His eyebrows shot up.

"Four scoops, eight cups of water." She closed the door before he could refuse. The man had made it through the FBI Academy. Surely he could figure out a coffeepot.

Brynn did minimal makeup and ran the straightening iron through her hair, trying not to singe it. She gave it a few spritzes of hairspray. She grabbed some earrings—understated gold studs today. Then she slipped her feet into slingbacks and checked the mirror.

"Ready!" she called, rushing into the hallway.

Ross stood at the door, looking dashing and impatient in his navy Hugo Boss suit.

"We're late, Brynn. What's the holdup?"

"Nothing, I'm ready."

She spied her travel mug on the bar beside Hayes.

"Bless you," she told him, grabbing it on the way out the door. Skyler was already waiting at the elevator with the doors open.

"Wait, my briefcase!" Brynn glanced back at her apartment.

"Brynn, seriously." Ross looked exasperated.

"You guys go. I'm right behind you."

She hurried back to her place with Hayes at her heels. She retrieved her briefcase and relocked the door.

"Is the car ready?" she asked.

"Yes, ma'am."

Meaning Erik was waiting. Brynn's pulse skittered at the thought of seeing him, but she didn't have time to dwell on it as they raced for the elevator.

On the ride down, she closed her eyes and took a deep breath to steady her nerves. She felt totally discombobulated starting the morning this way. The elevator slid open, and there was the Tahoe.

Erik stood by the driver's-side door dressed in a dark suit. He wore his mirrored aviators, and she couldn't read his expression as Hayes stepped ahead and opened the back door.

"Thank you."

She climbed inside, and Hayes took the shotgun seat. Erik was driving this morning, no doubt to prevent her from staging another impromptu press conference on the courthouse steps.

"You're late," Erik said to Hayes.

"It's my fault. I overslept." Brynn glanced at her watch as they got moving. "We'll be fine."

Erik pulled into traffic, which was unusually heavy today, of course. Hayes muttered a curse.

They stopped at a red light, and Brynn took out her compact. Despite her makeup efforts, she still had shadows under her eyes. She dug a lipstick from her bag and carefully painted her mouth.

She glanced up, and Erik was watching her in the rearview mirror. He looked freshly showered and shaved and infuriatingly well rested.

This won't happen again.

She couldn't believe he'd said that. Why the hell shouldn't it happen again? And why did he get to decide?

He looked away. Then he made a call on speakerphone. The man who answered sounded like Jeremy.

"Hey, it's me," Erik said. "We hit some traffic. Should be ten minutes behind schedule."

"Roger that. We're just pulling into the prisoner bay."

"You talk to Joe?"

"Yeah, a minute ago. All three mags are up and running."

"Okay, see you in ten."

Erik ended the call, and Brynn kept her gaze focused on her compact so she wouldn't have to look at him.

"What's a mag?" she asked.

"A magnetometer. They've got one at each entrance. And everyone's under orders *not* to wave anybody through today."

She glanced up at the edge in his voice.

"That includes you and Conlon," he said. "No one gets special treatment."

She pointedly looked at her watch.

"The line at the back checkpoint is short," he assured her.

Pop.

"Get down!" Erik yelled, reaching back and yanking Brynn's jacket. "Get her *down*!"

Her chin hit the console as both Erik and Hayes forced her head down. Tires squealed. The SUV rocketed backward onto a median.

"What the—"

"Keep your head down! Hayes, *get on her*!"

And then Hayes was in the back seat, pushing her down onto the floor as the SUV surged forward. Coffee scalded her knee, and tires shrieked as they took a corner. Hayes's weight smothered her, and she couldn't see anything with her face against the floor.

"Erik!"

"What *was* that?" Hayes asked.

"Gunshot," Erik said.

"I didn't hear it."

"Call 911."

Hayes shifted his weight, and Brynn leaned away from him, struggling for air.

"What the hell was that? What is *happening*?" she screamed.

But Erik was on the phone with Jeremy. "Gunshot fired at Commerce and South Streets," he said. "I repeat, Commerce and South. Clear the bay. We're coming in hot."

Brynn got to her knees and tried to sit up.

"Down!" Erik yelled, reaching back to push her head down.

The SUV veered left, then right. Horns blared. Erik jabbed the brakes, swerved again, and Brynn's stomach lurched. She glanced through the tinted window and saw that they were speeding the wrong way down a one-way street.

They took another corner, and she braced herself against the door.

"Almost there." Erik's voice was tense but calm. "Brynn?"

"*What?*"

"You okay?"

She didn't answer. She couldn't. She could hardly breathe. She swept her hair out of her face and looked over at Hayes kneeling on the floor beside her. He was juggling his pistol in one hand and his phone in the other as he talked to the 911 operator.

They whipped into a parking garage, and everything went dim. Another sharp corner, and the squeal of their brakes echoed off concrete. They skidded to a halt.

"Where are we?"

Erik jumped out without answering. Then Brynn's door jerked open, and four big arms reached in to pull her out. Erik and Jeremy. Skyler stood beside the entrance, along with a sheriff's deputy, and both of them had guns drawn. Brynn's feet barely touched the ground as Erik and Jeremy took her by the arms and hauled her up several steps and through a door. And then she was in a gray cinder-block hallway, surrounded by cops in uniform.

Skyler reached for her arm. "This way," she said, towing her into a room.

"What—"

"In here." Skyler pulled her into a corner.

Then Skyler walked out, and Erik was there.

"Are you all right?" He cupped his hand against the side of her face. His expression was alert and tense. And yet *calm*, which seemed totally out of place with all the yelling and chaos in the hallway.

"I'm . . . yes," she managed. "What *was* that?"

"You didn't hear it?"

"I heard something. I don't know."

"Stay here with Skyler."

He ducked out the door, and Skyler came back into the room, gun still in hand as she looked Brynn over.

"Stay here."

"Wait!" Brynn grabbed her arm. "Where is Ross?"

"Upstairs already."

Skyler stepped out, closing the door behind her.

Brynn looked around. It was a small room, maybe five by eight. There was nothing in it besides a metal bench that was bolted to the floor. They'd stuck her in a holding cell for prisoners, she realized.

She sank onto the bench and leaned forward to put her head between her knees. She felt dizzy. Slightly nauseated, too. She stared at the pointy toes of her shoes. And she noticed the carpet burn on her knees. She sat up. Her thigh was scalded red from the coffee, and she tugged down the hem of her skirt.

Calm down, calm down, calm down. Deep breath.

She closed her eyes and counted to ten, trying to settle her nerves. She checked her watch: 8:35. She needed to call Ross. But her phone was back in the Tahoe, with her attaché case and everything else.

The door opened. She jumped to her feet as Hayes strode in, followed by Skyler.

"Here," Hayes said, holding out her attaché case.

"Thank you." Brynn looked from him to Skyler. "What is going on?"

"The sheriff's deputies are searching for the shooter."

"*Shooter?*"

"Erik said there was a shot fired. You didn't hear it?"

"I don't know." She looked at Hayes. "It sounded like a car backfiring, maybe. Did you hear it?"

"I heard something. Not sure if it was a gunshot but something."

Brynn's phone beeped with an incoming text, and she pulled it from her bag. Ross: *Where r u???*

She glanced at her watch. "It's eight forty. I have to get upstairs."

"You want to go up?" Skyler looked surprised.

"Yes. I'm late for court!"

Skyler stared at her for a moment. Then she led Brynn out of the room and down the corridor crowded with cops. Above the din of voices, Brynn heard sirens outside.

Several prisoners in handcuffs stood against the wall. Brynn scanned the faces but didn't see Justin, and her pulse picked up again as she checked the time.

They went to the front of the security line and stepped through the metal detector. Skyler stayed behind to talk to the guard manning the X-ray machine as Brynn and Hayes caught an elevator to the second floor. The doors to Linden's courtroom were closed, and Brynn's stomach clenched as she race-walked down the hallway, clutching her attaché case.

Hayes jogged ahead and reached for the door, and Brynn entered the packed courtroom. Every seat was taken except for the jury box. Brynn's gaze zeroed in on the defense table, where Justin sat low in his chair.

Ross turned around. He looked distraught at the sight of her. Justin and his mother turned then, too, both looking distressed.

Brynn strode down the aisle, and the *clack* of her heels steadied her as she took in everything—the murmur of voices in the gallery, the polished wood of the witness box, the etching of Lady Justice with her scales, watching over it all.

"What the hell?" Ross whispered when Brynn reached the table.

"Ms. Holloran." Judge Linden glared at her over the tops of his reading glasses. "Please approach the bench. Counselor?" He looked at Conlon.

She and Conlon approached.

"You're late, Ms. Holloran. We have a full docket here, as I'm sure you are aware."

"I apologize, Your Honor." She stood ramrod-straight as she faced him. "There was . . . an incident outside the courthouse."

Linden's chin dropped, and he scrutinized her appearance. He glanced at Conlon. "Counselors, in my chambers."

They walked to the door leading to his office. The bailiff stepped aside to let them pass.

"Not you."

Everyone stopped, and Brynn turned around to see the bailiff blocking Hayes's path.

"He's my personal security guard," she said. "Can he—"

"He can wait outside my chambers," the judge said.

The bailiff moved aside. Hayes glanced at Brynn, then stepped into a narrow hallway outside the judge's office. Once inside his chambers, Linden turned to face Brynn and Conlon, glaring up at Brynn now because she was a head taller.

"Does this incident have to do with the sirens I heard on my way in here?" he asked.

"Yes, Your Honor. There was a possible gunshot a few blocks away. Police are investigating, along with our security team."

His bushy white eyebrows snapped together. "I heard about your security team. Am I to understand that this supposed gunshot is related to the murder of Jen Ballard?"

She cut a glance at Conlon. "Possibly."

Linden crossed his arms and stared up at her, his expression hard. Several seconds ticked by as Brynn's heart pounded and sweat pooled in the cups of her bra. She must look terrible. Disheveled. Out of sorts. She could feel Conlon beside her, sizing her up and sensing a weakness he couldn't wait to exploit.

"In light of these events," Linden said, "do you wish to take a brief recess?"

Her mouth dropped open. She'd been late, and now he was offering leniency? She tried to see through his steely gaze.

"Your Honor," Conlon said, "the prosecution is ready. We'd prefer to move forward on schedule."

"I'm asking Ms. Holloran." The judge turned to Brynn, and it occurred to her that maybe he'd known Jen personally and that's what this apparent sympathy was about. "Well?"

"We're ready, too, Your Honor." She looked at Conlon. "The defense would like to move forward also."

"Very well, then." Linden unfolded his arms and reached for the door. "Let's not waste any more time."

11

THE MINI-MART at the intersection of Commerce and South Streets was an impromptu staging area for Dallas law enforcement. Police units and sheriff's department SUVs crammed the tiny lot, and uniformed officers milled on the sidewalk, sipping coffee and wolfing down breakfast tacos.

Lindsey pulled her unmarked Taurus into a gap beside a fire hydrant. She had no trouble spotting Erik Morgan, who towered over everyone. With his dark suit, mirrored sunglasses, and SIG Sauer at his hip, he looked like he should have been standing beside a president, not arguing with a potbellied sheriff's deputy in front of a Grab-N-Go.

Erik spied Lindsey and immediately broke off his conversation to walk over.

"I got your message," she said. "What happened?"

Erik turned to face the intersection. Rush hour had ended, but the sweltering air still was thick with car exhaust.

"At eight sixteen, our vehicle was en route to the courthouse. We had just pulled up to the stoplight when I heard a gunshot."

"Brynn was with you?"

"That's correct."

"Where is she now?"

"In court. We've canvassed the neighborhood, interviewing potential witnesses, but so far no sign of a white Dodge pickup or anyone resembling James Corby in the area."

Lindsey sighed. "Well, shit."

"I need that list of weapons, ASAP."

"I don't have it."

Erik stared down at her, clearly displeased, and Lindsey saw her reflection in his shades.

"You said McGowan's son was going to get it to you yesterday."

"I haven't heard from him." She glanced around. "What about surveillance cameras? There have to be at least a couple of traffic cams around here."

"Four," he told her. "And three ATM cams within this one-block radius alone. The footage is under review, but as of now, no leads. We haven't been able to get anyone to corroborate the gunshot I heard. We've interviewed store clerks, but a lot of the businesses weren't open yet."

"What about the dry cleaner's there?" Lindsey nodded down the block. "That would have been open."

"The attendant says she heard something, but she believes it was a car backfiring or maybe a nail gun. She doesn't think it was a gunshot."

Lindsey didn't bother asking if Erik was sure. She'd been checking up on the man. He was a former Marine and had spent his entire career undergoing rigorous weapons training. If he said he'd heard a gunshot, then he'd heard a gunshot.

She studied Erik's face—the tight line of his mouth, the hard set of his jaw. *Intense* seemed to be his default, but right now he looked extra uptight.

"I've got the address for McGowan's son," she said. "I'll track him down myself and get that list for you."

"Soon as you have it, send it over."

Lindsey glanced around. "You know, with all the police traffic back and forth to the courthouse, there have to be a lot of dashboard cams. Maybe someone caught something?"

"We're looking into it."

"Good. Let me know what turns up."

———————

What turned up was nothing.

No bullet holes, no chinks in the concrete, no spent cartridges anywhere near the intersection.

Erik gritted his teeth with frustration as he walked back to Brynn's apartment, still combing the street for clues. After spending the entire day searching, he hadn't found one shred of evidence of a shooter.

Not one shred *except* for his certainty that he'd heard a gunshot. Erik had been looking at Brynn at the time, so he'd been distracted, which was part of his frustration. He'd been distracted then, and he was distracted now. He kept picturing that look of pure fear in her eyes when he'd pulled her from the Tahoe and hustled her into the courthouse.

Another frustration: Erik hadn't been able to place the direction of the shot, which was inexcusable, given his training. *This* was why he couldn't afford to lose focus, not even for a second. The smallest distraction could have deadly consequences.

Erik neared the Atrium and called Brynn. He could have called Hayes to check on things, but he wanted to hear her voice.

"Hey, I was just about to call you," she said, sounding better than he'd expected.

"What's up?"

"What's up with *you*? I haven't seen you all day."

"I've had my hands full."

"Anything on the gunshot?"

"No."

Silence. Erik scanned the surrounding buildings as he reached the Atrium's driveway.

"Brynn?"

"I thought you must have, you know, discovered something. You've been gone so long."

"I'm still working on it."

"You don't sound happy."

"I'm not. Why were you about to call me?"

"Logistics. I'm going out tonight."

"Out?"

"I've got a business dinner with Reggie."

Erik tensed. "Why weren't we informed?"

"This just came up. How soon can we have the Tahoe ready?"

Right. Like it was just a matter of pulling the car around.

Erik swiped his way into the building and went straight for the elevators.

"Erik?"

"It's not that simple."

"I know, but can you accommodate me? This is important."

He wanted to accommodate her, absolutely. He prided himself on customer service. But he'd counted on her wanting to stay in tonight, just like he'd counted on having more time to pin down this threat before tomorrow. And now she wanted to spend the evening out at some dinner?

"It's at Oak Creek Country Club," she said, predicting his next question.

The elevator slid open, and he strode down her hallway, passing several women with yoga mats tucked under their arms. One of them definitely gave him the once-over.

"When?" he asked.

"Seven o'clock."

Erik halted outside her apartment. "That's in forty minutes."

No answer.

He let himself inside with his key and saw Hayes standing in the kitchen on the phone.

Brynn emerged from her bedroom with a waft of perfume, and Erik stopped cold.

Short black dress. Tall black heels. Her hair cascaded over her shoulders in shiny, coppery waves. She smiled and strode up to him.

"Hey, you're here." She slipped her phone into a little black purse. "This mean we can go soon?"

He couldn't speak. Go soon? Was she serious?

She gazed up at him, all innocence. She'd done that smoky thing with her eyes again and something with her mouth, too.

"We're not going anywhere," he told her. "I need to know more about this event. Is it a private club?"

"Some golf club." She rolled her eyes. "The client invited us. Very exclusive, so security shouldn't be an issue. It's a gated club within a gated community."

"Who's the client?"

She tucked her purse under her arm. "Potential client. We're hoping to close him tonight."

"Who's 'we'?"

"Reggie and me."

"Not Ross?"

"No."

Erik studied her face as his mind raced with logistical issues. She looked perfectly composed. The stammering, wide-eyed woman from this morning was long gone.

"Who's the client?" he asked again.

"Daniel Sheffield."

Erik stared down at her. "*Danny* Sheffield. First baseman for the Rangers?"

She nodded.

And it all snapped into focus. The last-minute dinner, the dress, Ross not going. Erik tried to rein in his temper—not just about the plan but also about the fact that Brynn seemed on board with it.

"Forty minutes isn't happening."

"But—"

"Not happening, Brynn. I need to run his record, check out this club, get people in place—"

"Run his *record*?" She fisted a hand on her hip. "He's our client."

"I thought you haven't closed him yet?"

"Whatever. We *will* close him. If I can get there in time to help Reggie negotiate." She glanced at her watch. "We need to get moving.

I can give you his record on the way. In case you haven't heard, he was recently arrested for punching a tabloid photographer outside a night-club, and he's about to fire his lawyer and hire us, *if* Reggie and I can convince him over dinner."

"Tell him seven thirty."

"Seven thirty! He and his agent are already over there, having drinks in the clubhouse."

"It's the best I can do, Brynn. Take it or leave it."

12

BRYNN'S LATENESS had just the effect she'd anticipated. As the maître d' led her to the table, Brynn noted that Reggie looked pissed off while Danny Sheffield and his agent looked well on their way to being toasted.

"So glad you could join us," Reggie said, standing up.

Danny didn't bother, just smiled up at her and pulled out the chair beside him.

"You must be Brynn," he drawled. "Have a seat."

"Thank you." Brynn smiled and took the empty chair next to Reggie, who managed not to react to her snubbing the client. He made introductions, praising Brynn's record and calling her the firm's "heavy hitter."

The conversation started flowing, along with the wine. Brynn darted her gaze across the room a few times and noticed that Erik and Hayes had somehow melted into the shadows without attracting attention. It probably helped that many of the club's members looked like they'd been tossing back Scotches since they came off the golf course.

It was a typical Reggie-led client dinner with a celebrity athlete. Brynn laughed at Danny Sheffield's jokes, feigned interest in his stories, and pretended to be impressed as he dropped a bunch of names she'd never heard. She demolished her medium-rare filet and carefully nursed the glass of merlot the waiter kept topping off. When the plates were cleared and the second bottle of wine was emptied, Reggie rested his elbows on the table and got down to business.

"You know why we're here, Danny. Our firm would like to offer you representation."

The ballplayer leaned back in his leather chair, which was more of a throne. The decor in this room had obviously been selected with male egos in mind.

Danny smiled smugly. "I've already got representation."

It was all so canned, and Brynn wanted to roll her eyes. Instead, she leaned forward.

"For your business affairs, you've made the right choice," she said. "Fischer and Evans is definitely the right firm for you on that front. But for criminal defense work? They're not a good bet."

"Is that right?" he said, soaking up the sales pitch.

"That's right."

"I been with them for years." He shrugged. "I trust them. What can I say? Takes time to build that."

"Time?" Brynn shook her head. "That's something you don't have right now, Danny. You're facing two years, minimum, and your trial's in nine weeks. You need a *real* defense team, or you're looking at hard time."

His smug expression faded.

"She's right," Reggie said. "It's time to make a choice here, Danny."

Danny looked at his agent. Brynn could tell he was close to a decision. Beside her, Reggie shifted in his chair, and she knew he was winding up for the big pitch.

"Be smart here, Danny." Reggie leaned forward. "Go with Blythe and Gunn. It's like I tell all my clients, you don't want to take a knife to a gunfight."

Brynn managed not to groan. Or reach for her wine. She hated Reggie's slogan almost as much as she hated giving clients the hard sell. But this particular client was half-drunk, so subtlety would have been a waste of time.

Danny turned to Brynn with a look that was both lazy and calculating. She'd been on the receiving end of looks like that before.

He nodded at Reggie. "I'll think about it."

"Don't think too long. Trials take preparation."

Danny looked at his agent. "We ready?"

"Whenever you are."

Danny flagged a waiter. "Hey, tell them to bring the car around."

Everyone stood up. Brynn stayed back as the men filed out, not wanting to get swept up in good-byes. Danny's agent started passing out cigars, and Brynn took advantage of the diversion to slip off to the ladies' room.

Once inside, she stood before the mirror and sighed. She looked tired. And wilted. Which was precisely how she felt after getting no sleep and being in court all day and then enduring a three-hour Danathon. And what about Hayes and Erik? They had to be just as tired as she was, only they hadn't had the benefit of a steak dinner. Guilt needled her as she smoothed her hair and freshened her lipstick. Her phone pinged with a text, and she dug it from her purse.

It was Hayes: *We're out front.*

Brynn rushed out of the restroom and nearly smacked into a broad chest.

"Hey there."

She smiled up at Danny. "Hey."

"You were planning to leave without saying good-bye, weren't you? I see how it is."

"Of course not. It was lovely meeting you. Thank you for dinner."

"I meant what I told Reggie."

"What's that?"

"I'm thinking about hiring you." He leaned his hand against the wall above her. "You might be just the woman I need to get me off."

Brynn wanted to gag. Instead, she smiled. "Our firm's record speaks for itself. We hope to get your business."

He smiled and dipped his head down. Brynn ducked under his arm.

"Thanks again for dinner," she said, striding down the hall.

Erik stood beside the door, watching her. He shot a look over her shoulder, and if looks could incinerate, Danny would have been a pile of ashes.

Without a word, Erik pushed open the door. The Tahoe was waiting with Hayes behind the wheel. A red Ferrari rolled to a stop, and a valet hopped out.

Brynn ignored the obnoxious car and the even more obnoxious man who slid behind the wheel. She reached for her door, but Erik beat her to it.

"Thank you."

He didn't respond as she climbed inside.

They made their way home through the tree-lined streets of one of Dallas's wealthiest neighborhoods. No one spoke. Brynn was tense, Erik was silent, and Hayes just seemed oblivious to the mood as he navigated across town.

Brynn busied herself scrolling through her phone until they reached the Atrium.

"I'll park. You take her up," Erik told Hayes.

"You sure?"

"Yes."

Brynn rode the elevator up with Hayes.

"Please tell me you got some dinner," she said.

"Not yet."

"I'm *so* sorry. I'll order you a pizza."

"Really, I'm fine." They stepped off the elevator. "I'm off in an hour."

Still, she felt guilty as they walked down the hallway.

"Hey, you mind if I stop for a sec?" she asked. "I need to talk to Ross."

"Sure, go ahead."

She rapped on the door. It was almost eleven, but Ross was a night owl.

He answered in jeans and a sweatshirt, beer in hand. "Hey, nice dress." He looked her up and down. "How'd it go with Sheffield?"

"Fine." She walked past him. "Where's Skyler?"

"In the control room. That's what we're calling it now."

She turned to Ross. "Danny's still deciding."

"Damn, I thought we had him."

"I think we will."

"Well, cheers to clients with money." He lifted his beer. "You want a brew?"

"I just stopped by for an update. You hear anything from Bulldog?"

"Not tonight."

"Seriously?"

"Seriously. But don't sweat it. He'll come through."

"I'm sweating it, Ross. I mentioned Perez in my opening statement today."

"He'll be here in time to testify."

"How do you know?"

"Because I know Bulldog. Calm down. Let me show you what I've been working on while you and Reggie were wining and dining."

Brynn followed him to the coffee table, where he had legal pads spread out around his computer.

"I've been going through Conlon's open line by line and studying the wit list. I think I've figured out who he's going to call."

Conlon's witness list was ridiculously long, and if he called everyone on it, the prosecution's case would take months. That wasn't going to happen. Conlon was using the age-old tactic of burying the important names under a mountain of others. The trick for the defense was to figure out where to focus limited time and resources.

Ross handed her a legal pad with a list of names. Most were eyewitnesses who had been near or inside the pizza restaurant at the time of the shooting. One name jumped out.

"Dr. Peter Garvey." Brynn looked up.

"I think he's the heart of Conlon's strategy."

"Why? The eyewitnesses are much more of a threat to us. We talked about this."

"Yeah, but I've been analyzing Conlon's opening statement. He mentioned the ballistic evidence, which means Garvey. And we know he's got to put up some sort of forensic science, even if it's thin."

It was true. Today's jurors had watched so many *CSI* TV shows, they expected to see forensic evidence at trial, even in cases where police had other slam-dunk evidence, such as a taped confession. Forensic evidence was so crucial now that many juries had difficulty convicting without it.

"What makes you think he's going to go with Garvey versus some of the other experts? He's got a dozen listed."

"Garvey's a last-minute addition. I think they're banking on the fact that we won't have as much time to dig up dirt on him. Bulldog ran down everybody already, but we need to go deeper with this guy."

If there was any dirt, Bulldog could probably find it. Anything from a closet drug addiction to a blemish on the record of the crime lab where Garvey worked could damage his credibility on the stand.

Brynn handed back the legal pad. "Call Nicole, too. Get her on it."

"Why?"

"Bull's preoccupied. And why not use both? If Garvey really is the heart of their case, we need to go for the jugular."

She left Ross to his work and returned to her apartment with Hayes. Still no Erik. She retreated to her bedroom, and relief set in the instant she closed the door.

Brynn kicked off her heels. She stripped off her dress and tossed it onto the bed, then went into the bathroom and turned the shower to hot. She twisted her hair into a knot and stood under the spray, letting the water sluice over her tired muscles. By the time the bathroom filled with steam, she'd relaxed enough to face whatever else this day wanted to throw at her.

She put on a T-shirt and cutoffs. It was the same shirt as last night, only this time she wore a bra.

Memories flooded her. Erik's hands on her skin. His tongue tangling with hers. His stubble under her fingertips as she pulled him down to kiss her. Her cheeks warmed thinking about it.

And then she thought of his words. *This won't happen again.*

She'd thrown herself at her bodyguard. It was exactly what she'd warned Ross about. And even though Erik had been very, *very* into the kiss, he clearly regretted it now and probably thought she was an idiot.

She'd misread his signals last night, which wasn't like her. Evidently, he had some sort of moral code that prevented him from getting close to her, even though he seemed attracted to her.

No. He *was* attracted to her. Physically, at least. She'd felt proof of that last night.

Brynn walked out of her bedroom and found Erik at the dining table in front of his laptop. He'd taken off his suit jacket and rolled up his shirtsleeves, and she tried not to stare at his muscular forearms.

"You want to order takeout?" she asked.

He didn't look up. "I ate."

He did? When? Maybe he'd managed to have a burger while she and Reggie were eating steaks. Although that didn't seem like something he'd do, being so opposed to distractions while on duty.

She stopped beside the breakfast bar to watch him.

He glanced up. "What?"

"You have a problem you want to tell me about?"

"No."

She went into the kitchen and grabbed a bottle of water. "You *don't* have a problem with me? I'm just imagining this . . . hostility since dinner?"

He leaned back in the chair, meeting her gaze. "A problem with you? No. I have a problem with the guy you work for."

"Sheffield?" She waved him off. "He's a spoiled egomaniac. I can handle him."

"I know. I saw that." His gaze hardened. "I was talking about Reggie."

"Why do you have a problem with Reggie?"

He stared at her but didn't say anything.

"Really. Speak up."

"It's none of my business."

"So?"

"Okay, fine. I don't like the way he uses you."

"*Uses* me?"

"Uses your looks to land clients. Why do you put up with that?"

She bristled at the disapproval in his voice. "Our track record lands us clients. We have a very high success rate. Reggie built his reputation with clients like Danny Sheffield, which is why we get so many referrals."

He stood up and walked over to where she stood beside the breakfast bar. Without her heels on, she was much shorter than he was, and she felt distinctly disadvantaged. She crossed her arms over her chest.

He stepped past her and opened the fridge. "Then why does he dangle you out there like that?"

She laughed. "Oh my God, do you even hear yourself?"

"What?" He grabbed a bottle of water and leaned back against the counter as he twisted off the top.

"You don't think your boss uses *you*?" She stepped closer. "You don't think Liam Wolfe *uses* you guys with your combat fatigues and your muscles and your mean-looking guns?"

He tipped his head back and laughed.

"What the hell is so funny?"

"Our muscles? Like we strap them on when we come to work?"

"You know perfectly well what I mean," she said. "You guys show up looking like SEAL Team Six, and it intimidates people. That's your boss *using* your looks to get clients."

His expression grew pensive, as though he was considering her point.

"And anyway, Reggie didn't *dangle* me tonight. It's called introducing me to the client. Danny Sheffield has a well-deserved reputation for being a hothead. He shoots his mouth off, gets into bar fights, punches paparazzi. Reggie wants him to know that if he hires our firm to represent him, he'll get a woman in the courtroom to smooth some of his rough edges, and he definitely needs that to win over a jury."

"So you admit he's using you?"

"As an attorney, I sometimes *use* the fact that I'm a woman. If I don't, you can be damn sure someone will use it against me to make me look weak."

He just watched her.

"I freely admit it, Erik. I've been known to use sex appeal. I wear heels and skirts to work because it gets people's attention. I tower over men whenever possible. I assert myself because people *like* strength. They respond to it. They respect it. You, of all people, should understand that."

Erik looked at her, his expression unreadable, and she felt frustrated with herself for caring what he thought.

"You know what? I don't need to defend myself to you." She turned away, and he caught her arm. He gazed down at her, and she felt the heat of his touch all the way to her bare toes.

"You're right, you don't." He took a deep breath. "I'm sorry I offended you."

"Whatever." She shook his hand off. "I'm going to bed."

Erik stared after her as she disappeared into her bedroom.

She was dead-on accurate.

His looks did help him do his job, and he was being a hypocrite. He intimidated people, and it was completely intentional. If a potential threat took a look at a target's security team and backed down or decided to change targets, all the better.

Erik leaned his head back and sighed. He'd pissed her off. He should have kept his thoughts to himself, but instead, he'd spoken his mind. He wasn't thinking straight tonight.

The instant he'd seen Brynn backed up against the wall by that asshole, Erik saw red. He'd wanted to deck the guy when he tried to kiss her. And if she hadn't given him the slip, Erik *would* have decked him.

For the first time since he'd started this job, he felt rattled. Not because of some idiot ballplayer but because he felt his discipline sliding. He was getting distracted, which made him prone to mistakes. And he knew damn well this job left no room for error. What had happened this morning was proof of that.

Erik's phone vibrated in his pocket, and he pulled it out. Jeremy.

"Are you at Brynn's?" he asked, and Erik caught the tension in his voice.

"Until midnight. Why?"

"I just sent Keith over to cover for you. You need to come see this."

13

THE PARKING garage beside the Ames Theater had nearly emptied out for the night by the time Erik pulled in. He found Jeremy on level six, leaning back against his gray pickup.

Erik parked the Tahoe next to him and got out, surveying the area.

"Not a bad view," he said grimly.

"Look at this."

Jeremy led him to a corner beside a stairwell. The parking spaces were empty, and over the four-foot wall of concrete, Erik had a view of the downtown skyline.

The Atrium was a sparkly tower in the distance.

A ball of dread formed in Erik's gut. "That's got to be, what, two hundred meters?"

"Two fifty," Jeremy said.

As a former Marine sharpshooter, Jeremy would know.

This building was well beyond the area they had canvassed earlier. Jeremy handed him a pair of binoculars. Erik assessed the scene. From this elevation, he didn't have a view of the Atrium's entrance. It was blocked by the overhang that covered the apartment building's driveway. But he *could* see where the driveway met Commerce Street.

So could a shooter.

"Now look at this," Jeremy said.

They walked down the row of empty parking spaces. Before they reached the end, Erik knew what he was going to see. Sure enough, between two tall office buildings was a narrow view of the intersection in front of the mini-mart.

"That's an even longer shot," Erik pointed out. "That has to be three hundred meters."

"Yep."

"Corby has no military training. And he's not a hunter." Erik looked at his friend. "This setup doesn't feel like a fit. Everything he's done till now has been up close and personal. Like *very* up close. A shank in the gut."

"You checked your e-mail lately?" Jeremy pulled out his phone and opened a message. "This just came in," he said, handing the cell to Erik.

It was a forwarded message from Lindsey Leary. Erik scrolled down and saw the exchange between the detective and someone named Shawn McGowan, who had to be Mick McGowan's son. The man had provided investigators with a list of missing items from his father's gun cabinet.

"Glock twenty-three. Beretta nine-mil. An FN Five-Seven?" He glanced up at Jeremy. It was the type of gun used by many Secret Service agents. Erik preferred a SIG P229, but the Five-Seven was a serious piece of hardware.

"Keep going."

"A Remington twenty-two. A Winchester twelve-gauge. Shit, a Remington seven hundred."

A deer rifle. The military version was the M24, a favorite of snipers.

"He have a scope on it?"

"Lindsey asked that, too, and yeah. Shawn McGowan told her it's a Leupold."

"Fuck."

Jeremy didn't say anything, but Erik could tell he felt the same. A scope like that didn't make the shot easy for someone like Corby. But it made it possible.

Erik glanced around the parking lot, looking for cans or food wrappers or cigarette butts, any sign that someone had used this location as a sniper hide. They walked back to the other side, away from the overhead parking lights, and Erik pulled out a penlight to examine the concrete.

"Any evidence he was here?" He looked at Jeremy.

"Not besides the view. But it makes sense. People park here for the theater, so it's busy evenings and weekends but empty most mornings. And did you notice the camera setup on the way in here?"

"There isn't one," Erik said.

"Exactly."

Erik combed his flashlight beam over the area, illuminating dirt and grit but no trash to speak of. He'd repeat the procedure on the levels below, too.

"I don't like the rifle," Jeremy said. "And I sure as shit don't like the scope."

"I don't like how the fucking marshals have been after this guy for a week, and still they've got nothing." Erik looked at Jeremy. They'd worked together so much he could tell his friend knew exactly what he was thinking. The marshals couldn't be relied on to make this problem go away.

"It's time to ramp this up," Erik said.

"We need to talk to Liam."

"We need more agents, more cameras, and much less visibility."

Jeremy lifted an eyebrow. "She's not going to like that."

"You talk to Liam. I'll handle Brynn."

Lindsey eased down the darkened street, scanning the dilapidated houses separated by chain-link fences. Torn-up cars sat on lawns. Some homes looked deserted. Others were clearly inhabited, and shadowy figures lounged on sofas, watching the street from their porches. Lindsey was in an undercover ride tonight, but she still stood out like a parade float.

She passed a utility easement littered with abandoned fridges and construction debris. The next section of the neighborhood was even less inviting, with several of the homes boarded up and covered in gang graffiti. This neighborhood was a literal dump, caught between a rash of foreclosures and the promise of gentrification that hadn't yet materialized.

Lindsey checked her phone and squinted at the curb. No painted numbers, so she'd have to go by the dropped pin on her navigation app. She eased into the shadow under a tree and rolled to a stop. After checking her weapon, she got out.

The humid night air smelled faintly of sewage. A dog barked in the distance, and Lindsey glanced around cautiously before emerging from the shadows and crossing the street. She stepped onto the overgrown lawn of a desolate one-story with plywood over the windows.

James Corby's former home. The notorious serial killer had rented the place for nearly five years before his arrest. The house had fallen into disrepair, but even when Corby lived here, it was a far cry from the manicured campuses and landscaped apartment complexes where he'd trolled for girls.

Many criminals stayed within their comfort zone, but not Corby. He slipped in and out of wealthy neighborhoods, raping, torturing, and murdering with ruthless efficiency. Lindsey believed his job had provided a key advantage. As a cable installer, Corby had learned to move through vastly different neighborhoods without drawing attention. He'd overcome the natural human reluctance to trespass. And he'd learned to be elusive. All skills that served him well as a predator.

Lindsey stared at the dark front door, matching it to the crime-scene photos she'd seen in the case file. The yellow tape that had once crisscrossed the entrance was long gone. The property had changed hands several times in the intervening years.

Another glance around. An orange ember glowed on a porch across the street, letting Lindsey know she wasn't alone. She ignored it and crossed the yard to the side gate beside the shared fence. The gate stood a few inches ajar. Lindsey pulled. It didn't budge, and she gave it a hard jerk to unstick it from the weeds.

On her left, the fence was swallowed by a dense tangle of vines. She moved along the side yard, noting the weathered boards and chipping paint. It was dimmer here and danker, and the overgrown lawn was a minefield of trash. Crumpled beer cans lined the base of the house, and Lindsey stepped over a section of gutter as she entered the backyard.

The lot was deep and dark and sloped down. From the Google map she'd viewed, she knew the property backed up to the utility easement she'd passed earlier, which connected homes on this side of the street to a nearby trailer park that was a hot spot for meth busts.

Lindsey stood for a moment and let her eyes adjust. She didn't know what she was looking for, exactly. The marshals had been here already and found the place empty. Neighbors hadn't seen Corby, and most had never even heard of him. Or so they claimed. If they did know him, they'd been unwilling to talk about it to anyone with a badge.

A shudder moved through her as she scanned the gloomy yard. She wasn't sure why she'd come here, but after studying the crime-scene photos, she'd felt compelled to see it with her own eyes.

Another distant bark started a chorus throughout the neighborhood. Lindsey touched her front pocket, checking for her pepper spray. Picking her way through the weeds, she moved farther into the shadows until she reached the steep slope. She took out her mini-Maglite and beamed it around. She'd walked right past a fire pit, little more than a charred patch of ground surrounded by old tires and tree stumps. Bits of foil and bent spoons littered the area.

Lindsey stepped around a stump and aimed her flashlight at the place where the tangle of vines ended. It was where the fence ended, too. The lot dropped off sharply, and the stench of stagnant water was stronger here. A scrap of white caught Lindsey's eye. It was a cigarette butt, and the white contrasted sharply with the freshly turned soil of a shallow hole. Lindsey stepped closer and crouched down, taking out her phone. The hole was about the size of a shoebox. She snapped several pictures, then stood and tucked her phone away. A breeze moved through the trees, and she caught a whiff of cigarette smoke.

"This is private property."

She whirled, her hand instantly on her holster.

The gravelly voice belonged to a giant man holding a slender cigarette. He squinted at her as he brought it to his mouth. She aimed her light at him, checking his body for the telltale bulge of a weapon. His dingy muscle shirt showed off sausage-like arms covered in faded biker tattoos.

"Who the fuck are you?" he asked.

"Detective Leary." She shifted her jacket to show him her badge, as well as the butt of her pistol. "Who the fuck are you?"

"Call me a concerned citizen."

Lindsey checked his eyes to see if he was on something. "Where do you live?" she asked.

"Nearby."

"Have you seen any unusual people in the area over the past week?"

"You're looking for that guy. The fugitive."

"Have you seen him?"

He gave her a crooked smile, revealing a gap in his teeth. "What's it worth to you?"

"I don't know. What's it worth to you? Want me to run your name?"

The smile faded. "Nah, I haven't seen him. Police were already here asking."

"Any unusual cars in the neighborhood? Maybe a white pickup truck?"

"No."

Lindsey's phone vibrated, and she pulled it from her back pocket, still keeping an eye on the guy's hands. She recognized the phone number.

"Nice talking to you. Let's go." She nodded, indicating for Sausage Arms to go ahead of her. He flicked his cigarette away before turning and tromping back to the side yard, and Lindsey had a view of his hairy shoulders.

He squeezed through the gate. Lindsey followed. He gave her a last look before sauntering across the street toward the house with the darkened porch.

Lindsey tapped her phone. "Leary."

"This is Alec Mason, with the *Star*. I got your message at work."

"Mr. Mason, hi." She returned to her car, checking up and down the street before getting inside.

"You said something about a homicide investigation. Who are you, exactly?"

"I'm with the Sheridan Heights Police Department," she told the reporter as she took out a notepad. "I'm investigating the murder of Judge Jennifer Ballard."

"Then you're looking for James Corby," he said. "And I'll tell you what I told the marshal who contacted me. I haven't talked to the man in years."

Lindsey felt a pang of disappointment. So the marshals had already tapped this lead.

"That's not exactly why I called," she said. "I'm interested in your interview with Corby. I understand you went to see him about nine months after he was convicted?"

"I did. My paper wanted a feature."

"And what did you talk about?"

He didn't answer right away, and she wondered if he was going to stonewall her. The other reporter she'd reached out to hadn't even called her back. She figured this guy wouldn't have bothered if he weren't willing to talk.

"Mr. Mason?"

"We talked about his conviction, mostly. I mean, I started him with small talk to get him comfortable. But that didn't take too long. The guy wanted to rant, and I was happy to listen."

"What did he rant about?"

"His trial. The justice system. How everything was rigged. The police, the attorneys, the jury."

Lindsey jotted all that down. "He thought the *jury* was rigged?"

"He thought everyone was against him. The prosecutors were crooked. The detectives were liars. The people at his work—"

"The cable company?"

"Yeah, they were in on it, too, according to Corby. Every person, every step of the way, was part of some big conspiracy to put him away for murders he didn't commit. Like I said, the guy was on a rant. And I'm no psychologist or anything, but he seemed pretty paranoid."

"And did you find him . . . . credible?"

"I found him intelligent," the reporter said. "But that's not the same as credible. I mean, there was the blood on his boot. There was the necklace, the media clips in his house. I'm sure you're familiar with all the evidence against him. It was really overwhelming. The two lead lawyers—Ballard and Holloran—they put on a convincing case."

Lindsey tensed at the mention of Brynn. It was the first time she'd heard Brynn referred to as one of the lead lawyers. Jennifer Ballard was the true lead, but apparently some people had the impression they played an equal role. Maybe Corby thought so, too.

"Back to your conversations with Corby," she said. "Did he ever mention any friends?"

"He didn't have any."

"Coworkers he talked about by name? A distant relative?"

"No."

"Maybe an ex-girlfriend?"

"No." A pause. "Did you ever see him in person?"

"I haven't had the pleasure."

"Well, he's got this stone-cold killer thing going on. I could never figure out whether it was a persona or his real personality, but I'll tell you, it makes your skin crawl. He has this way of staring at you when you're talking to him. Or even when you're not talking to him. Trust me, he's not someone you ever want to meet."

"And you only met with him that one time?"

"That's right. I hope to never see him again. The day I heard he got out, I went and bought myself a handgun, and I've had it with me ever since."

"You believe Corby is a threat to your safety?"

"Hell, yeah. He's on a revenge quest. He's a threat to anyone he wants."

14

LINDSEY LEARY arrived Friday morning at 7:45 sharp, and Erik tapped the timer on his watch as he let her into Brynn's apartment.

"One sec," he said, leaving her by the door. The detective looked impatient. She'd tried to meet yesterday, but Brynn had canceled to work on her cross-examinations. Lindsey had insisted on seeing Brynn this morning before court.

Erik rapped his knuckles on her door.

"She's here. You ready?"

"Yes!" came the muffled reply.

Her voice sounded rushed, and Erik's suspicions were confirmed when Brynn stepped out of her bedroom in a pinstriped skirt, heels, and an oversize Astros jersey. She brushed past Erik and ducked into the guest room.

"Be right with you, Lindsey!"

Erik propped his shoulder against the door and watched as Brynn frantically combed through the closet. She grabbed a silky gray blouse on a hanger. "Damn it. What time is it?"

"Seven forty-eight."

Brynn billowed past him with the blouse. "Hey, Lindsey. Want some coffee?"

"I'm good." The detective looked Brynn up and down, probably wondering about her fashion statement. Lindsey wore practical flat shoes and another one of those dark pantsuits that concealed her sidearm.

"I have to steam while we talk," Brynn said. "I need to be in court in forty minutes."

Brynn grabbed a bottle of water from the fridge. She plugged in the handheld steamer on the counter and hung the shirt from a cabinet knob.

"This shouldn't take long." Lindsey pulled out a bar stool. "I had something to ask you and something to tell you."

"Ask away."

Lindsey shot a look at Erik. She might have preferred to talk to Brynn in private, but he wasn't going anywhere.

"I talked to one of those reporters you mentioned who interviewed Corby in prison."

"Oh, yeah?" Brynn ran the steamer over the shirt. "Mason or Dewitt?"

"Alec Mason."

"Any good leads?"

"Not on Corby's whereabouts, no." Lindsey darted a glance at Erik. "But he said something else I've been working on. It had to do with Corby's prosecution."

"What about it?"

"Well, he told me Corby was on a rant. Very paranoid and resentful about all the forces conspiring to make him look guilty for something he didn't do. He claimed he was framed for the crime."

"Damn, I wish I had a dollar for every defendant who's told me that *exact* same thing."

"Yeah, I know. But I started looking into it, and I noticed a lot of the key evidence presented in Corby's trial was circumstantial."

Brynn whirled around. "You can't be serious." She laughed. "You actually believe that Corby was framed?"

"No, not at all. But this reporter said Corby was adamant that the detectives were liars, et cetera, and it occurred to me that Corby went after McGowan first, as soon as he got out of prison."

Brynn's brows knitted together. "What are you saying, exactly?"

"I'm just speculating. The only real physical evidence against Corby was the victim's blood on his boot and the girl's necklace found in his house, right? Just hypothetically, what if that evidence was planted?"

Brynn stared at her.

"I never knew McGowan," Lindsey said. "I have no point of reference, which is why I wanted to ask you, since you worked with him. You were on the front lines together. What's your take?"

"My take? On whether a veteran police detective with a sterling reputation planted evidence to frame a suspect? Holy shit, Lindsey." Brynn shook her head. "I mean, I see why you're asking me now that I've switched sides, but . . . you really believe this?"

"No. That's the point." She crossed her arms, looking defensive now. "I'm exploring ideas. Corby did it, obviously. The evidence is overwhelming. But that doesn't rule out the possibility that some piece of evidence was planted. You know, as an insurance policy. Everyone was under the gun on this thing. You know how high-profile it was and the kind of pressure everyone was feeling."

"Uh, *yeah*. I felt the pressure, too."

"So do you think it might be possible McGowan or someone did something to ensure a conviction? It might help explain this deep-rooted hatred Corby has for everyone and why after escaping from prison he set off on a killing spree instead of going on his merry way."

Brynn stared at Lindsey, speechless. She looked at Erik.

"Look, I hope I'm totally off base here. Floating this theory—I can't think of a faster way to lose friends with Dallas PD. Or any PD. But I wanted to at least ask for your thoughts on this. You've been on both sides, so you're more open-minded than most."

"My thoughts . . ." Brynn shook her head. "My thoughts are that it's highly improbable. Not impossible but improbable. You're catching me off guard here, and I don't know what to say." She looked at Erik, as if she expected him to jump in. "Erik?"

He tapped his watch. "Six minutes."

Brynn rolled her eyes and turned back to Lindsey. "What was the other thing? You said you had something to tell me?"

Lindsey looked at Erik. "Yeah, this is for both of you. I wanted to pass along that I went to Corby's house, and I think he's been by there."

"When?" Erik asked sharply.

"I don't know. The marshals said they've had the place staked out, but I didn't see anyone when I was over there."

"They set up surveillance cams," Erik told her. "They thought it might be more subtle than having a car there, sitting on the house. What makes you think Corby was there?"

"It might not have been Corby, but someone was definitely there recently. I saw a shallow hole in the backyard. Fresh dirt. Looks like someone dug something up." She looked at Brynn. "Isn't it true they never recovered Corby's murder weapon? Or most of his souvenirs? I told the marshals I think he may have gone back for them."

Brynn's face paled as she leaned against the counter.

"What did the marshals say?" Erik asked.

Lindsey shrugged. "Not much. If he *was* there, it must have been before they got their cameras installed, so it had to have been right after his escape."

Erik would find out. And shit, another missed opportunity.

He looked at Brynn. "Two minutes," he said, and went to give the apartment a once-over. He did a sweep of Brynn's room and snagged her briefcase off the bed. They didn't have time to double back this morning if she forgot something.

When he returned to the kitchen, Lindsey was gone, and Brynn was standing by the sink, still in her baseball jersey.

Erik set her briefcase on the breakfast bar. "I unplugged your hair flattener."

"My straightening iron? It's on a timer." She grabbed the shirt off the hanger and hurried into the guest bathroom. "What do you think?" she called.

Erik didn't answer, not sure why his opinion should matter. He'd never met McGowan.

She leaned her head out. "Erik?"

"I don't know any of the players. What do *you* think?"

She came out, still fastening the top buttons. "I think the marshals are a bunch of morons! How could Corby get back there without them seeing?"

"Maybe it was his first stop after getting out."

"How does he keep evading everybody? You said these guys were professionals. Why is it so hard to find one fucking person?"

Clearly, Lindsey's visit had shaken her, and now she was going into court that way. Today was supposed to be a big day, too, and she'd been up half the night working.

She grabbed her briefcase. "Let's go."

———————

Brynn watched the jurors' body language with a sinking heart. They were hanging on the witness's every word.

"Take your time, Mrs. Marek." Conlon gave the witness his sympathetic dad smile. "We understand this is hard."

Lisa Marek dabbed her nose with a tissue. "Sorry."

Beside Brynn, Ross tapped his pencil on a legal pad. He was good at body language, too, and clearly he could see the damage being inflicted by the prosecution's main eyewitness.

"What happened after you heard the gunshot?" Conlon asked.

"He just . . . crumpled. Right there on the pavement."

"And then what happened?"

"The driver sped across the parking lot and drove away."

"And after you saw the driver leave the scene, what did you do next?"

"I got out my phone and called 911."

"Thank you, Mrs. Marek." Conlon looked at Brynn. "Your witness."

Brynn stepped up to the lectern and gave the woman a gentle smile. She was walking a fine line here. Lisa Marek was a mother in her forties, which gave her something in common with many of the jurors. Brynn couldn't appear combative, even though the woman's testimony was potentially a knockout blow to Justin. Through a photo array, Marek had identified Justin as the person behind the wheel of a blue

Chevy Malibu in the parking lot of Tony's Pizza House, and Justin had a blue Chevy Malibu registered to his name.

"Mrs. Marek, you testified that you never saw Justin Sebring before the night of March fifth, when the murder took place, is that correct?"

"That's correct."

"And you never saw his picture in the newspaper or on television?"

"That's right."

"Do you watch the news?"

"Not usually. Just the Weather Channel."

"So after the traumatic events of March fifth, you didn't turn on the news to see if the murder you'd witnessed was being covered?"

She glanced at the jury. "Oh, well, yes. I watched the next day. Becky and I were glued to the television."

"And what about the following day?"

"I watched it some."

"And the day after that? March eighth, the day Justin Sebring was arrested in connection with the crime?"

"I didn't see that. Like I said, I don't normally watch news."

"So even though all four local networks covered the story and ran a photo of Justin Sebring, you're sure you didn't see his picture on TV that night?"

"Yes."

"What about any other time after that? Any other media source?"

"I'm sure."

Brynn lifted an eyebrow at this bold statement. "Okay, so when police showed you the photo array and you identified Justin as the man driving the Malibu, that was based solely on what you witnessed at the pizza restaurant and nothing you'd seen in the media, is that correct?"

"That's correct."

Brynn stepped out from behind the lectern. "Mrs. Marek, let me direct your attention to the photograph of the parking lot in front of Tony's Pizza House." She turned to face the jumbo screen where Conlon had displayed a photo of the parking lot. Conlon's investigator had been on the stand earlier with a tedious explanation of how the shot was taken from the same booth where Lisa Marek had been sitting, at exactly the same time and under the same lighting and weather conditions as the night of the murder.

"You testified that this is the view you had of the crime scene while you were having dinner at Tony's Pizza House with your daughter, at ten twenty P.M. on March fifth, is that correct?"

"Yes."

"That's a little late for dinner. Do you and your daughter typically have dinner at ten twenty?"

"We were on our way home from a school play."

"And was this your first time to eat at Tony's Pizza House?"

"No, we go there a lot. It's in the neighborhood."

"I see. Would you say you're regulars there?"

She shrugged. "We go maybe twice a month."

"Do you know the staff?"

"We know some of the servers, and we know the owner, Tony. We've been going there for years."

"And do you always sit at this booth facing the parking lot?"

"Sometimes. We like to get a booth when they're not busy."

"Mrs. Marek, you testified that the booth where you were sitting gave you a clear and unobstructed view of the blue Chevy Malibu that Seth Moore was standing beside when he was shot, is that correct?"

"That's correct."

"The same view shown here in this photograph." Brynn picked up a laser pointer and aimed it at the screen. "And do you see a blue Chevy Malibu in this photo?"

"No."

"Because it's not an actual crime-scene photo, right? It only shows the view of the parking lot from your booth, correct?"

"Objection," Conlon said. "Asked and answered."

"Sustained." Judge Linden looked at Brynn.

"Mrs. Marek, do you see Justin Sebring in this picture?"

"No."

"Do you see anyone you recognize in this picture?"

She looked confused. "Well . . . no."

"Do you recognize the person here?" Brynn used the laser pointer. "This person standing in this shadowy corner of the parking lot here?"

"No."

"What about this man here?" Brynn moved the pointer. "Looks like he's getting into his car as the picture is taken. Do you recognize him?"

"No."

"You don't recognize Tony Martelli, the owner of the pizza restaurant you've been going to for years, whom you said you knew personally?"

"Objection." Conlon was on his feet. "Your Honor, the state objects to this visual stunt. The defense is manipulating this exhibit to confuse the witness."

"Your Honor, this is the state's own exhibit. How can they object to it?"

"Judge, the defense is referencing facts not in evidence. Ms. Holloran hasn't established who the person in the picture is. How can we know if it's Mr. Martelli?"

"Sustained." Linden gave Brynn a sharp look. "Rephrase the question, Ms. Holloran."

Conlon sat down.

"Mrs. Marek, can you positively identify the person"—Brynn aimed the pointer—"seen here getting into this car at the edge of the parking lot?"

The witness no longer looked tearful. She was a deer in the headlights. "I'm not sure. I mean, I can't see anything, really. It's all shadowy."

At the word "shadowy," Conlon winced. It was only slight, but Brynn caught it. She hoped the jury did, too.

"Thank you. No further questions, Your Honor."

"Mr. Conlon?" The judge arched an eyebrow.

Conlon started to get to his feet, then changed his mind. "Nothing further, Your Honor."

Linden smacked his gavel and announced the lunch break. The jury filed out, and Brynn took a deep breath as she gathered her files.

"That was beautiful," Ross said as he packed his briefcase. "You *nailed* it. Conlon was pissed."

"Don't get cocky, Ross."

"Why the hell not? You had his own witness saying it was too dark to see shit."

Spectators and reporters vacated the gallery, and Brynn stood back to wait.

"We need to brace for this afternoon," she said. "He's calling the forensics guys."

"How do you know?"

"Because he's out of eyewitnesses. He's bringing out the big guns next, so we have to be prepared."

Ross shook his head. "This is so you, Brynn. Celebrate for a nanosecond. Can't you just be happy we crushed their best eyewitness?"

"No."

Glancing at the exit, she spotted Erik. His gaze locked with hers over the crowd. The bottleneck cleared, and she and Ross finally reached the door.

"We need to meet with you two," Erik said.

"Who's 'we'?" Brynn asked.

"This way."

Keith appeared on the other side of Ross, and Brynn let the two bodyguards guide them down the hallway bustling with lunchtime traffic.

"Where's Jeremy?" Ross asked. "He didn't mention any meeting to me this morning. I have a lunch date."

"Cancel it," Erik said, stopping beside a gray door.

Erik led them into a narrow corridor, passing a series of conference rooms designated for attorney-client meetings. It was the place where many plea bargains happened, known by lawyers as Hail Mary Hall.

Erik opened one of the closed doors. He made eye contact with Brynn as he ushered everyone inside.

Liam Wolfe sat at the head of the table. He got to his feet as Brynn entered the room. Dressed in business casual with a sidearm under his jacket, he looked like a police detective visiting the courthouse to testify. Brynn glanced around at the other faces. Jeremy, Skyler, Trent. Almost the entire team was here.

"Ms. Holloran." Liam shook her hand. "Good to see you again."

"You, too," she said, maybe a little too sarcastically, as she took in the situation. Someone had taken the time to reserve this room. And order sandwiches. This meeting would clearly take the bulk of the lunch break.

The door opened, and Reggie stepped into the room. He nodded hello and set his briefcase on the table beside Liam. Then he shed his suit jacket, clearly expecting to be here a while.

"Why didn't you tell us about this?" Brynn asked him. "I was planning to have a working lunch."

"I didn't know, either, until an hour ago." Reggie looked at Liam. "I'm told this is important."

"What exactly—"

"Have a seat. We'll explain," Liam said, pulling out the chair beside him.

Brynn sat down, fuming. She didn't like being ambushed. Erik took the empty chair on her other side.

"Well, at least you're feeding us," Ross said, grabbing a seat near the sandwiches.

Skyler passed the sandwich tray around. Brynn declined the food and grabbed a water.

"Thought we'd catch you here at the courthouse," Liam said. "Easier to round everyone up."

The door opened again, and Lindsey Leary walked in, followed by a man Brynn didn't recognize. Liam stood, and Brynn's heart gave a lurch when she saw Liam and the stranger side by side. Their resemblance was uncanny.

"I'm Mark Wolfe," the man said, nodding at Brynn.

"I'm . . . Brynn Holloran. And this is—"

"Reggie Gunn." Reggie stood and shook the man's hand.

Ross introduced himself and did the same.

"Did you say Wolfe?" Brynn asked. "As in . . . ?"

He looked her directly in the eye, confirming what she'd known at a glance, that he had to be Liam's brother.

"My brother is a criminal profiler," Liam told her. "He offered to give us some help with our analysis."

"Analysis?" she asked.

"The letter you gave us."

Brynn shot a look at Erik.

"Mark works in the Cyber Crimes Unit at the Delphi Center crime lab," Liam said. "Before that, he was with the FBI's Behavioral Analysis Unit, known as BAU."

"We're still conducting some forensic tests on the samples," Mark said, "but I wanted to relay what I have so far."

"I'm sorry, *samples*?" Brynn looked at Mark. "As in, more than one?"

"We recovered two similar notes from Judge Ballard's desk," Lindsey said.

"Two?"

Lindsey nodded. "Both were anonymous but contained similar wording to the one you received." She opened the folder in front of her and passed over two sheets, both photocopies of a note on lined paper. Brynn's stomach knotted as she recognized the block handwriting: *I HAVE EYES ON YOU.* The second note said, *YOU CAN'T HIDE FROM ME.*

She glanced at Mark, who was watching her closely. His eyes were brown, but he had the same piercing stare as his brother.

Unsettled, she turned to Lindsey. "These were in Jen's desk?"

"At her office, yes."

"When did she get these?" Reggie demanded.

"We don't know," Lindsey said. "Her clerk wasn't aware of them.

Said she'd never seen them before. They were stashed in an unmarked manila folder in a drawer filled with office supplies."

Brynn passed the notes to Ross. "Did you ever get any—"

"No," he said tersely. "I answered this before. I haven't gotten anything."

He glared at Liam, as if the security specialist had somehow conjured up the notes.

"I understand yours was placed on your windshield," Lindsey said to Brynn. "Based on that, we're thinking something similar happened to Jennifer Ballard, maybe on the way to work, and she collected the note and stashed it in a folder when she got to her office."

"But she never told anyone about these notes," Brynn stated.

"Not that we've been able to find," Lindsey said.

"So we don't know when she got them. And they're anonymous. I assume you fingerprinted them?"

"No prints except the judge's," Lindsey said. "And no DNA."

"What about Mick McGowan? Did he get any of these notes?"

"Not that we've found."

Brynn looked at all the faces around the table, ending with Erik, who sat calmly beside her, watching her reaction.

She turned to Liam and smiled. "I'm sorry, but . . . what am I missing here?"

"Ma'am?"

"I must be missing something." She folded her hands in front of her on the table. "Almost the entire team is assembled here for this meeting. Everyone's tension level is through the roof. And you've brought a criminal profiler up here all the way from the Delphi Center"—she turned to Mark—"which is four hours away in San Marcos, if I'm not mistaken?"

He nodded.

"And on a Friday, no less. All so we can talk about three little slips of paper that aren't even signed?" She zeroed in on Liam. "What aren't you telling us?"

Liam watched her for a long moment. Then he looked at his brother. "Why don't you start with the notes?"

Mark nodded. "As Detective Leary mentioned, we have only the recipient's prints and no DNA on the samples recovered from Judge Ballard. We had the same results with your sample. However, we were able to trace the paper." He paused. "It comes from a four-by-six notebook with perforated sheets. This particular type of notepad is carried in the prison commissary at the Stiles Unit in Beaumont, and James Corby purchased four such notepads over the course of his incarceration."

Brynn stared at him. "That's it? That's the basis for this whole panic?"

Liam's brow furrowed. "No one is panicking."

"What we are doing," Mark said, "is viewing this as a potential communication between James Corby and his victim."

"Based on *paper*?" Brynn shook her head. "That doesn't prove anything. Thousands of inmates had access to that same type of notepad, not to mention all the other places those notepads are sold. It's not direct proof of anything."

Everyone was watching her, and she realized she sounded like a defense attorney. She looked to Reggie for support, but he was uncharacteristically silent.

Mark leaned forward. "Ms. Holloran—"

"Call me Brynn."

"This is not a trial, Brynn. We are not here to prove that Corby did something beyond a reasonable doubt. We are here to assess the threat to your safety"—he turned to Ross—"and yours. And after analyzing these communications, I can tell both of you with confidence that I believe these messages came from James Corby and were somehow smuggled out or mailed out and delivered to you and Judge Ballard on carefully selected dates. And I believe they are yet another example of Corby communicating with not just you but also the public."

"The public?" Ross asked.

"Yes. That's all part of this." He paused. "You may recall during the trial how the lead detective in the case, Michael McGowan, testified that they'd uncovered a stash of media clips Corby had collected. He'd been following his case closely and saving everything he could. He kept all of it in a box under his bed. Corby was obsessed with his own publicity."

Brynn's stomach tightened. She not only remembered the testimony, but she also remembered seeing the box itself in the evidence room when she'd been preparing for trial. The box had contained a thick stack of news clippings about Corby's gruesome killings.

"Corby grew up a loner," Mark continued. "He was starved for attention. From a psychological standpoint, he fed on all that media excitement while he committed the murders and even through his arrest and trial. Then he went away to prison, and all the interest disappeared, except for a few crumbs here and there."

"So . . . you're saying he's hungry for attention again?" Brynn asked. "That's what this is about?"

"A big part of it, yes."

"I thought it was about revenge," Reggie said impatiently. "Which is it?"

"Both. But revenge might be too simplistic," Mark said. "At the core of Corby's self-image is his belief that he's smarter than everyone. He outsmarted his victims, the police, his fellow inmates who played chess with him, then his prison guards. His ego was greatly inflated by the attention he received while committing these murders and evading the police for so long. But then the police apprehended him. The prosecution outmaneuvered him. Everyone bested him in a very public way, which he certainly found humiliating. He went away to prison defeated and deprived of the spotlight he'd been enjoying. But now he's reemerged."

"You're saying this whole thing—his escape, killing Jen and Mick—you're saying it's like a comeback," Brynn concluded.

"You could call it that. He's proving, once again, that he's smarter than everyone. He escaped from prison. He hunted down the lead detective and the prosecutor who put him away. He managed to kill them *and* evade police, and he's proud of what he's accomplished. He's feeding on the attention again."

Brynn felt a headache coming. She looked around the room at all the faces focused on her. Except for Ross, who was staring down at the table, his skin a sickly shade of white.

She huffed out a breath. "So . . . back to the notes. You really believe they're from him?"

"Yes." Mark was adamant. "I also believe they are communicating something dangerous."

"What? That even from behind bars, he can get someone to smuggle some notes out and stick them on people's cars?"

"That he can reach you whenever he wants," Liam said. "He wants you to know he's watching you, that you aren't safe anywhere."

She looked at the criminal profiler, who'd once worked for the FBI and now worked for one of the nation's top crime labs. "And you think this is his mission now?" she asked.

"He's proven it, Brynn. That's what concerns us," Mark said. "That's what makes these communications so threatening. The vast majority of people who make threats never attempt to carry them out. And those who do often fail. That's a fact. What's different here is Corby's track record. His experience. His success." Mark looked to Ross, then back to Brynn. "He's killed before, and we feel certain he'll attempt it again."

"I want the FBI involved," Reggie said. "These marshals are incompetent."

"The Bureau *is* involved," Liam said. "They have agents on the task force, which also includes people from the sheriff's office and several local police departments."

Lindsey leaned forward to look at Reggie. "We shared the letters with the task force as soon as we discovered them. We're doing everything possible to cooperate with the other agencies involved here, and we expect the same courtesy from them. Apprehending this suspect is everyone's top priority."

Brynn looked at the profiler again. The man was serious. Calm. Composed. And absolutely convinced of what he was saying about Corby's mission.

Reggie's phone vibrated on the table. He got up to take the call, giving Brynn a dark look as he stepped out of the room.

Mark spent another few minutes describing further tests that would be conducted on the notes to prove they'd been sent by Corby. Brynn tried to listen, but her mind kept going back to Jen and the horrible details of her death. And then there was Lindsey's theory from this morning, that some of Corby's rage toward the authorities might actually be justified.

"Brynn?"

Erik's low voice beside her jerked her back to attention. He was watching her intently, a look of concern on his face.

"That about covers it," Mark was saying. "I'll continue to work on my assessment, but the rest of the test results won't be back for another few days. I'll notify you as soon as we have something." His gaze rested on Brynn, and silence settled over the room.

"Well." Brynn glanced at her watch. "This has been . . . educational. But Ross and I have to get back."

Mark looked at his brother.

"With all due respect," Liam said. "It seems like you're not getting the gravity of the situation here."

"Actually, I am." She gave a thin smile. "I'm definitely getting it. Because in exactly"—she checked her watch again—"six minutes, I have to be in a courtroom to defend an innocent teenager who stands to spend his life in prison for something he didn't do. What happens this week will affect his entire future, as well as the lives of his family members. And every day of his trial, I've been distracted by threats from a homicidal maniac who has somehow eluded every cop in the state." She glanced at Lindsey, then Liam. "So yes, I'm fully aware of the *gravity* of the situation and the consequences if any one of us here fails to do our job."

She stood and looked at Mark. "Thank you for coming and for sharing your analysis with us." Then she looked at Erik, who was already on his feet. "Could we get back now? The last thing our client needs today is the judge finding his lawyers in contempt of court."

Erik had no trouble keeping up with her long strides as she navigated the crowded hallways back to the courtroom.

Brynn was shaken, and despite her glib comments and casual shrugs, Erik could see the truth. He'd learned to read her. He'd picked up on all her little tells—the tap of her fingers, the twitch of her mouth. She tried to appear confident, but Erik could see she was scared.

He wanted to pull her out of the traffic flow and tell her that yes, the danger to her was very real, but he'd protect her.

And what would that get him? Probably an angry shove and a thorough tongue-lashing.

She sliced through the crowd, glancing at him as they neared the courtroom. "What?"

He said nothing.

She looked back at Ross. "Come on."

Erik paused beside the door and caught her arm. "Shake it off, Brynn. You're ready. You've got this."

She gave him a puzzled look. "How would you know?"

"Because I do."

15

THE AFTERNOON was a marathon, and by the time Linden dismissed everyone, Brynn was tapped. Erik had disappeared somewhere, so Jeremy accompanied both her and Ross down to the prisoner bay, where the SUVs were waiting.

Erik was behind the wheel of the Tahoe. He got out and reached for Brynn's door as Ross and Jeremy slid into the Expedition.

"Just you?" she asked him.

"That's right."

"I'd rather ride up front, then."

She walked around to the other side and stashed her attaché case on the floor. Erik wasted no time getting them moving and navigating the congested route out of the parking garage. Brynn kicked off her heels and leaned her head back against the seat. Her feet were screaming, and her shoulders were in knots. She was craving a cold margarita or a hot bubble bath.

Or a massage from someone with strong hands. She glanced at Erik's on the steering wheel and sighed.

"Rough afternoon?"

"Horrible," she said. "The state rested its case."

"Already?"

"I should have seen it coming. I knew they were haystacking us—"

"Haystacking?"

"Putting so many names on the witness list. We didn't know who they were going to call, but we knew they couldn't possibly call everybody. The prosecutor made a clever move by calling only a handful of people so he could wrap up on a Friday, which means jurors have the entire weekend to ponder his case against Justin before the defense has a chance to put anyone on the stand."

"Sounds bad."

"It is. And today was Conlon's best day. This afternoon, he put up evidence of gunshot residue on Justin's hands and trace amounts of the victim's DNA on Justin's shirt."

"I thought it was a drive-by?"

"Not exactly." She closed her eyes and squeezed the bridge of her nose. "It was a drug deal gone wrong. The victim was standing right beside the car when he got shot, so it happened at very close range, hence the blood—according to Conlon. The bottom line? It's not looking good for Justin."

It was an understatement. In truth, it looked dismal. Because of Conlon's slick timing, the jury was going to spend the entire weekend mulling the evidence of Justin's guilt.

Feeling deflated, Brynn stared out the window at the sidewalk crowded with evening pedestrians. Downtown cleared out early on Friday afternoons, but people drove in, too, for the nightlife.

Erik cleared his throat. "So. I had an idea."

"What?"

"You up for a run?"

"A run?"

"Yeah, I was thinking you might want to blow off some steam, and we could go jogging. I know a nice outdoor track in a secure area."

Her eyebrows shot up with surprise. "Outdoor?"

"Yeah. With birds and trees and fresh air," he said, parroting her words from Sunday. "You up for it?"

"Um, yeah, but I don't have any clothes with me."

"I grabbed your workout gear from the chair in your bedroom."

He'd gone all the way back to the apartment? Now she really couldn't say no. Plus, she was sick to death of being cooped up. It was making her stir-crazy. She looked over her shoulder at the back seat, and sure enough, there was a shopping bag she recognized, alongside a duffel that probably belonged to him.

"Did you bring my sports bra?" she asked skeptically. If not, she wasn't running anywhere.

"Everything's in there. I threw in your earbuds, too."

"And where is this secure area?"

"A friend of mine's DEA, and they've got a training campus about twenty minutes from here. They have a track, a firing range, an O-course."

"What's an O-course?"

"Obstacle course. This place has everything. My friend offered to get us in on a visitor's pass."

"Did he, now? Well, wasn't that nice of him?"

"You interested?"

"That depends. You're not going to make me climb a rope or scale a wall or anything, are you?"

"The O-course is optional."

"I opt no. The track will be plenty for me."

He glanced at her. "So are you in?"

"I'm in."

The training campus was beautiful—wooded paths, lush green grass, glimmering fish ponds—and being outdoors was heavenly. Even the distant *snap-crackle-pop* coming from the pistol range added to Brynn's feeling of tranquility as she and Erik pounded along the track.

It was five miles, though—a little feature Erik forgot to mention, probably because the distance was hardly noticeable to someone in prime athletic condition.

Which he was. Wow. After changing into her workout gear and stepping out of the bathrooms near the trailhead, Brynn had been struck speechless by the sight of him stretching his legs against a tree. Wide shoulders, lean waist, muscular arms. She'd noticed it all before, but the details of his body were even more obvious as they stretched together and then started jogging side by side. In an olive-green T-shirt and cargo shorts, he looked like a Marine, which made him fit right in with all the law-enforcement types using the track.

Mile one was fabulous. Erik set a nice, doable pace, and Brynn had no trouble keeping up with him. But the heat was a factor, and by mile two, she was soaked. At mile three, her quads started to burn, and by the time she reached the four-mile marker, she was fighting a cramp in her side.

Just when she was about to wimp out and walk, a water fountain came into view.

"Water break!" she yelped, sprinting ahead.

He caught up to her, of course, and gave her a look of concern. "We can walk the rest, if you want."

"I'm fine!" She guzzled some water down, then dipped her forehead into the cool stream.

"You sure?"

She stepped back to give him a turn at the fountain. "Absolutely."

He took a brief sip, then straightened and looked her over. "No need to push."

"I'm not."

He lifted an eyebrow in a way that told her he knew she was full of bull.

"Let's go," she said.

He started up again but at a more relaxed pace.

"You usually do four, so I figured five would be no problem. I wasn't thinking about the heat."

"I have a confession." She darted a look at him. "I usually do two miles. The four is just this week. You guys shamed me into it."

He looked at her. "We shamed you?"

"Yes! You're all muscle-bound action heroes."

"I don't know about action heroes. But we try to stay in shape."

"Are you kidding? Your whole team could be out of a comic-book movie. I mean, Hayes could be Captain America."

She glanced at him, but she couldn't read the look on his face now. She was definitely affected by all those long glances and hard stares. He had the silent badass thing going, and it totally worked for her. He had to know that, since she'd practically jumped him the other night in her bedroom.

Thought you might want to blow off some steam.

How thoughtful was that? Not just that he'd listened to what she said but that he'd noticed something she needed and rearranged his whole day to get it for her. She felt touched.

"So," she said, wanting to keep the conversation going. "Will we get to see this friend of yours? I'd like to thank him for getting us in here."

"He's really more my brother's friend than mine. They went through training together."

"Your brother's a DEA agent?"

"Yeah."

"How come I didn't know this?"

He didn't respond, but the answer was obvious. Brynn knew almost nothing about his family because he was so guarded about his personal life. Meanwhile, everything about hers was on full display.

"Tell me about the rest of your family," she said. "I need something to get my mind off this heat."

He gave her a wary look. "What do you want to know?"

"What do they do?"

"My dad was a lieutenant colonel in the Marine Corps. He's retired now, does some consulting for the Pentagon. My brother Jake is in the Marines, too. Just promoted to captain. And then there's Brad, the youngest. He's DEA."

"Damn. What a bunch of underachievers."

He smiled slightly.

"Are you guys close?"

The smile faded. "Not really. They're all back east. I travel so much that I don't get back there very often."

Brynn thought that was a shame. She'd always wished for a big, traditional family, and so many people who had them let the relationships go. Brynn was close to her mom and sister, but she wouldn't recognize her father in a lineup. He'd walked out when she was three, and she hadn't seen him since.

"So your mom was a teacher," she said. "Sounds like you guys are all about public service."

He didn't comment.

"You ever miss it? Being part of something big like that?"

"What, you mean the Corps?"

"And the Secret Service."

He got quiet, and the only sound was the rhythm of their breathing and the distant pop of gunfire. Brynn waited. Was he finally going to tell her why he'd left that job?

"There are a lot of downsides," he said. "The politics, the bureaucracy, the bullshit. I like working for Liam. Wolfe Sec is lean and agile. Any operation can turn on a dime in response to a threat. It allows us to be creative."

Brynn had never thought about personal security as creative. Her work was creative, too, although most people didn't realize it.

"Is working with Liam your dream job?"

"There are some negatives. I'm on the road a lot. My hours are crazy. I'm hardly ever home."

"Now, there's an interesting point. Where do you live, anyway?"

"I've got an apartment near headquarters. It's basically a crash pad. There's nothing to it."

"Hmm."

He cut a glance at her. "What's that mean?"

"You don't see your family. You're rarely home. Do you ever get lonely?"

"That's not something I think about."

Which was different from a *no*. Maybe he dealt with it the same way she did—by doubling down on work.

He glanced at her. "You want your music? Might pass the time easier."

"What, you don't like to converse while you run?"

"Not usually."

"Figures."

"What?"

"You don't like to talk about yourself."

"Yeah, well. Not everyone's as extroverted as you."

"Actually, I'm a natural introvert. I used to be painfully shy."

He laughed.

"You don't believe me?"

"If you say so."

"Really," she said. "I was always the quietest kid in the class. Until I hit fourth grade."

"What happened in fourth grade?"

"Kids started teasing me about my red hair. I don't know what prompted it, but it kind of caught on." She blew out a breath. "There was this one kid, Shannon Snyder. He was merciless. He came up behind me in the lunch line once, pulled my hair, and called me fire crotch. I didn't even know what he meant. But the way he said it, I could tell it was something bad, and it made me really mad."

"What'd you do?"

"I turned around and stomped his foot as hard as I could."

"Excellent." Erik smiled.

"Yeah, *not* so excellent when I got sent to the principal's office."

"Let me guess. Detention?"

"I got off with a stern warning." She glanced at him. "I discovered the benefit of having a clean record. But that's how my shy phase came to an end."

Erik smiled again, and Brynn tried not to get distracted and miss a step. He was so handsome when he smiled, and he didn't do it much. But he seemed relaxed out here with the grass and trees and distant gunfire.

Brynn imagined what it would be like if they could be this way all the time.

They rounded a curve, and *finally* the five-mile marker came into view. Brynn sprinted ahead to reach it first, then halted and bent over, gasping for air.

"Five miles," she wheezed. "I haven't done that in ages."

Erik's big running shoes appeared in her field of vision. She stood up to face him, dismayed by his easygoing expression while she gasped for oxygen. His face was slick, but he wasn't even winded.

"You good?" he asked.

"Good? No. But you don't need to get the paddles, if that's what you're worried about." She staggered over to a water fountain and slurped some down.

When she stood up, he was watching her calmly, hands on hips. He eased closer, towering over her, and her stomach fluttered as he reached up and tucked a lock of hair behind her ear, the same hair that had brought her so much grief in fourth grade but was now a socially acceptable shade of auburn.

"I'm glad you're not shy anymore," he said. "And I'm sorry people tormented you in school."

"I'm over it."

"If I had to guess, this Shannon guy probably took some crap for having a girl's name, and he was looking for someone to pick on."

"Hmm. You might be right about that."

"I'm also guessing he had a secret thing for you."

Her heart sped up as he gazed down at her. His eyes were a warm brown, and she wondered what he was thinking. She wanted him to kiss her. She wanted to kiss him, but she'd already done that. The next move was his.

But he didn't kiss her. He turned away, and they started walking back to the parking lot in silence. When they reached the SUV, Erik dug a key fob from his pocket and unlocked the rear cargo door. He twisted the cap off a water bottle and handed it to her.

"Thanks." She sighed and shook her head.

"What?"

"You didn't even break a sweat."

"Yeah, I did." He stripped off his T-shirt and tossed it in the back, and Brynn was again struck dumb.

His muscular torso was a work of art. And yet he didn't even seem to notice her gawking as he rummaged through his duffel and took out a clean shirt.

"What, you don't want to hit the O-course?" she asked.

"Do you?" He paused in the act of putting on the T-shirt, peering at her through the neck hole.

"Kidding."

He pulled the shirt on. "You sure? I could help you. It might be fun."

"My idea of fun is a margarita and a beach towel, not a chin-up bar." She wiped the sweat from her brow and looked up at him. "And speaking of . . . you have any plans tonight? There's this Mexican place called Emilio's not far from the Atrium. *Amazing* enchiladas."

Was she really doing this? Was she really asking her bodyguard out on a date after she'd kissed him in her bedroom? Evidently, she was. And he wasn't answering, so maybe he thought it was weird.

It *was* weird. Erik's job was to be with her, so it was almost like having a paid escort. Ick.

"Or we could get takeout," she suggested.

"Might be easier."

They climbed into the car and got moving, and Brynn tried not to overanalyze his response as they pulled out of the lot.

Easier how? Because it would be less like a date? Was he trying to put her off? He'd seemed so relaxed a few minutes ago, and now he'd tensed up. The fact that he was driving her around like a chauffeur just emphasized the awkwardness of their relationship.

Not that they had a relationship, not in the traditional sense.

He was her bodyguard. She was his client. Anything else was just . . . temporary friendship. Or a figment of her active imagination.

But she hadn't imagined that kiss. No, that had been very real. And he'd been very into it, if only for a few stolen moments before Trent interrupted them.

Brynn took out her phone and pulled up the website for Emilio's. "How about I place a takeout order?" she asked, trying to keep her tone light.

"Sounds good."

———

Erik glanced at Brynn in the passenger seat. For the past twenty minutes, she'd been scrolling through phone messages and avoiding conversation.

He'd damn near kissed her back there. He'd been a heartbeat away from dragging her against him and kissing the hell out of her when the sound of pistol fire had reminded him where they were.

He clenched his teeth. What was he doing? He was on duty. He was supposed to be protecting her, not lusting after her.

Erik concentrated on rush-hour traffic and tried to get his thoughts under control. By the time they reached the apartment, he was back in the zone. No more distractions, not for the next five hours. When midnight rolled around, his thoughts could go wherever they wanted, but until then, his mind was a lust-free zone.

His problem was, it wasn't just physical attraction pulling his mind off the job. It was everything.

He liked watching her work. He liked talking to her—not just about Corby or her trial but about anything at all. She could recite her damn grocery list, and he'd be riveted by her mouth and the sexy tone of her voice.

He even liked arguing with her, which seemed to happen a lot. She wasn't afraid to question him or challenge him, and every time she did it, she got his blood going.

He pulled into the driveway and parked behind a black Mercedes, where a woman was unloading shopping bags.

"Thanks for the run," Brynn said.

"No problem."

"Thank your brother's friend, too. It was nice of him to set us up."

"Sure."

Erik got out, scanning the surrounding area before opening Brynn's door. He'd been on the lookout for a white Dodge pickup for days now, but he hadn't seen a single one.

Trent was in the lobby as they entered the building, and Erik caught his eye.

"I need you to take Brynn up while I park," Erik told him.

"No problem."

Erik left her with Trent, and his phone buzzed as he stepped back outside. He didn't recognize the number, but he'd given his contact info out to quite a few people over the past few days.

"Erik Morgan," he said.

"Yeah, I got a message here from my supervisor," a male voice said. "Someone wanted me to call about a white pickup in the parking garage at the Ames?"

The Ames Theater. This would be the janitor Erik had been trying to track down. According to the building superintendent, he would have been coming into work Tuesday morning not long before the shooting incident.

"Are you Mr. Mathis?" Erik asked.

"That's me. I work in the theater four days a week. I was here Tuesday, but I didn't see any white pickup truck."

"Are you sure?"

"Positive. This note here says you're an investigator. Is that Dallas PD?"

"I'm with a private firm," Erik said as he got behind the wheel. "You remember what time you got to work Tuesday?"

"I get in every day at oh-seven-hundred," he said. "Seven A.M."

His words caught Erik's attention. The man sounded like former military, which would make him more observant than the average civilian.

"What about other vehicles?" Erik asked.

"What about them?"

"Did you see any vehicle that didn't belong there? Or any suspicious people hanging around there in the parking garage?"

A pause.

Erik sat behind the wheel, waiting. "Mr. Mathis?"

"There was a black Honda. About ten years old. It was on level three, parked right by the stairwell when I pulled in."

"You happen to get the model on that?"

"A Civic, I think. Or could have been an Accord. The back bumper was dented—I noticed that."

"Anyone in the vehicle?"

"Yeah, a guy was sitting there. Looked like he was reading something. Or maybe on his phone. I figured he was waiting for someone."

Erik started the car. "Listen, Mr. Mathis, are you at work right now? I'd like to swing by and show you a few pictures. It will only take a minute."

"I really didn't see much."

People always said that. And then they were always surprised by how much they did see. An in-person interview would help Erik get details this guy didn't even know he'd picked up.

With a little more convincing, Mathis agreed to meet, and Erik made a call to notify Trent before pulling back onto Commerce Street. He drove west a block, then got into the left-turn lane to catch the cross street that would take him to the Ames Theater.

Erik scanned the intersection as he waited for the light. The streets were busy with people coming home from work or heading out for the evening. Several sidewalk cafés were filled with happy-hour customers.

A man in a baseball cap caught Erik's eye. Medium height, medium build. Nothing unusual, except . . . something was off about him. His shoulders were hunched up, and he had his chin ducked low as he stared out from under the brim of his cap.

A horn beeped behind him, and he glanced in his rearview. He took the turn, then watched in his mirrors as the guy walked into the yogurt shop two blocks down from the Atrium. Erik caught a glimpse of his goatee.

The hair on the back of Erik's neck stood up.

Was it Corby? He looked a lot like one of those police drawings. It was hard to tell for sure at a glance, though. But he made a habit of following his instincts, so he dialed Trent's number as he turned onto a side street and circled the block.

"Are you with Brynn?" Erik asked.

"Yeah. Why?"

"You're in the apartment?"

"Yes."

"Don't leave there."

"What's going on?"

"Just stay there until you hear from me." He hung up and called Skyler. "Where are you? Where's Ross?" he asked.

"He's right here. We're about to pick up dinner. Why?"

"I just saw this guy—"

Muffled screams came over the phone. Erik swerved to the curb and jammed on the brakes.

"*Skyler?*" He jumped out and ran toward the Atrium. "Skyler, report!"

More muffled screams. Then Skyler's voice, "Man down! *Man down!*"

16

ERIK CUT through the crowd, his gaze locked on a commotion on the sidewalk in front of Bamboo Palace. A knot of people had formed there, and Erik's heart lurched as he saw Skyler kneeling on the pavement.

Ross lay on his side in a pool of blood, blinking up at the people gathered around him.

"Call 911!" Skyler yelled, shoving her phone at a bystander.

"Skyler!"

She looked up at Erik. "He stabbed him! Then he took off!"

"Which way?"

"East. Baseball cap, black hoodie, jeans." She stripped off her T-shirt and pressed it against the gushing wound at Ross's side. "I've got this. You go!"

Erik raced down the street, darting around people. He caught sight of the man in the ball cap as he ducked around a corner.

Erik sprinted after him, SIG in hand. He sidestepped a jogger and pushed through a knot of people clogging the sidewalk near a bus stop, then ran around the corner just in time to see Corby disappearing around a building.

Erik raced to the location. It was an alley, and he bolted down it as Corby neared the end, where he grabbed a milk crate and flung it into Erik's path before ducking around another corner. Erik ran after him, hurdling the crate and pulling the buzzing phone from his pocket with his free hand.

"Where are you?" Jeremy demanded.

"Corby's fleeing west on Pearl Street! I repeat, west on Pearl." Erik didn't take his eyes off his target as he tore after him. Horns blared as Corby dashed through traffic, then slid across the hood of a red Corvette parked at a meter.

"Give me a description," Jeremy ordered. "We've got the marshals on the phone."

Erik halted to wait for a break in traffic, then sprinted across, sliding across the hood of the same Corvette.

"Brown goatee, blue baseball hat, black hooded sweatshirt and jeans."

"Armed?"

"Skyler reported a knife. He just turned down an alley heading north. I'm in pursuit." Erik darted down the alley and spied a tall chain-link fence at the end, blocking off a construction site. Corby was nowhere, but Erik saw a gap in the fencing.

"He just entered a construction site. Pearl and . . . Fifth, I think. You copy?"

"Copy that."

He shoved his phone into his pocket to free his hands as he reached the fence. He yanked back the mesh and pushed through, snagging his T-shirt. Jerking it free, he paused to scan the site, a maze of concrete slabs and heavy machinery, dominated by a towering steel skeleton in the middle. Workmen stood around swigging water and peeling off orange safety vests as they wrapped up for the day.

No Corby.

Cursing, Erik skimmed the giant steel beams and bundles of rebar. He jogged up to the nearest worker.

"Hey, have you seen—"

A jackhammer drowned out the words, and Erik's chest vibrated with the noise.

On the far side of the job site, Erik spied a man in a black hoodie. He wore a yellow hard hat, but Erik knew it was Corby and charged after him. As if sensing someone behind him, the man glanced over his shoulder, then broke into a sprint.

Erik sidestepped a concrete barricade and leaped across a trench. Corby reached a gap in the fencing, squeezed through, and took off down the street.

"Shit!"

Erik raced after him, reached the opening, and plunged into the street, crashing into a businessman.

He looked in both directions and spotted Corby barreling through a line of people standing beside a food truck. Corby ducked into a building, and Erik glanced at the sign. Mulligan's Pub. Erik's gut clenched with dread when he thought of the potential hostage situation. Adrenaline fired through him as he raced to the door and yanked it open.

The place was dim and noisy. His eyes adjusted, and he heard a loud yelp, followed by shattering glass. Pushing through the crowd, Erik followed the noise to the kitchen, where he found a waitress kneeling by a pile of broken bottles.

"Son of a *bitch*!" she spat, looking toward the back exit.

Erik rushed past the her and plowed through the door. He was in another alley. Corby could have gone in either direction, but he seemed to be traveling more or less west. So Erik took off that way, toward Pearl Street. They'd made a loop, which might or might not have been intentional.

Erik reached Pearl and checked both directions. No yellow hard hat. No black sweatshirt.

A squeal of tires had him spinning around. A black car peeled away from the curb and swerved into traffic. The car sped through a red light as horns blared and drivers slammed on their brakes.

Erik yanked out his phone and called Jeremy.

"He's in a black four-door heading west on Pearl! Just crossed Sixth." Erik raked his hand through his hair and cursed as the taillights disappeared. "Repeat, a black four-door. I think it's a Honda."

"Copy that. Are you in pursuit?"

"No, I lost him."

17

BRYNN TURNED off the shower and heard noises.

Voices. Footsteps. The front door opening and closing.

She wrapped herself in a towel as someone pounded on her bedroom door. She rushed to open it and found a panicked-looking Hayes.

"What's wrong?" She peered over his shoulder to see two huge men standing in her foyer. "Who the hell are they?"

They had guns and badges and looked like plainclothes cops.

"U.S. Marshals," Hayes said. "Corby's in the area. There's been an attack."

"*What?*"

Hayes looked tongue-tied, and she pushed past him.

"Where is Ross?"

The marshals were stone-faced. If they knew who she was talking about, they didn't show it. Fear seized her, and she whirled around.

"Hayes! Where's Ross? Where's Erik?"

"I don't know."

Brynn stalked past him back into the bedroom. She dropped her towel and threw on some clothes, then returned to the hallway. The sound of sirens outside sent a chill through her.

"Where'd they go?" she asked Hayes, who was alone in the foyer now, talking on his phone.

She hurried to the window, parted the blinds, and peered out. Two police cars raced down the street below, sirens wailing as they whipped around the corner.

Brynn's heart squeezed. Whatever was going on, she couldn't see it from this side of the building. She ran back into the bedroom, grabbing her phone off the dresser as she rushed to the window. With trembling hands, she dialed Erik.

Then she heard his voice booming in the hall.

"Where is she?"

She turned around, and he was in the doorway.

"What happened? You're bleeding!" she yelped.

"Get away from that window." He crossed the room in two strides and yanked her back from the glass.

"Your arm's bleeding!"

"I'm fine."

"What the hell happened?" Her voice was shrill as she stared up at his sweat-slicked face.

"Corby attacked Ross."

"*What?*"

"He stabbed him."

Brynn's stomach seemed to drop to the floor. "Stabbed him? Is he—" She didn't want to say the word. "Is he alive?"

"I believe so. The wound is to his lower back."

Brynn felt dizzy. "What . . . where . . ."

"He's in an ambulance on the way to the hospital. That's all I know."

"Where did this happen? And what happened to you?"

Erik's jaw tightened. "I got there right after Corby fled. I tried to chase him down but lost sight of him for a minute. He had a vehicle waiting."

"You tried to *chase him down*? Why didn't you shoot him?"

"There were people around."

"But . . . how did he get to Ross? Where was Skyler?"

"They were on their way to Bamboo Palace. Corby jumped Ross from behind, stabbed him in the back."

Brynn put her hands over her eyes, horrified by the image. "Oh my God."

"Brynn. Take a deep breath."

She dropped her hands and stared at him. "Are you insane? Ross was *stabbed*. How can you be so calm and emotionless? You're like a robot!"

"Brynn, I need you to take it easy while we sort this out. You should sit down."

Fury welled inside her. "Don't treat me like I'm some hysterical female. I want information! Tell me how this happened."

"Erik?"

They turned to see Hayes standing in the doorway. "Jeremy's with the marshals. He needs you to call him."

Erik started toward the door, but Brynn grabbed his arm. "Wait. *Wait.* I have to go to the hospital."

"It's better if you stay here."

"No way. Which hospital?"

Erik just stared at her. She looked at Hayes. "Which hospital, Hayes?"

"Uh . . ."

Brynn strode past both of them. The closest hospital was probably

Methodist. She reached for a set of keys on the bar, but Erik cut around her and grabbed them.

"God damn it, Erik!"

He pocketed the keys. "You can't go. The area's not secured."

"Ross is in the hospital, and I'm damn well going!"

He put his hand on her shoulder like a clamp. "You are not going anywhere right now."

"But—"

"How much more proof do you need that you're in danger?" His grip tightened. "I will go to the hospital. When the area is secure, *then* I will come here and get you. Are we clear?"

He was right, she knew, but tears of frustration welled in her eyes, making her even more furious.

"Fine. Go. But don't even think about leaving me here all night. I need to be there, Erik."

"I'll be back. I promise."

———

Half the marshals in the state seemed to be milling around the waiting room. They were joined by local cops, sheriff's deputies, and even a few Texas Rangers in cowboy hats. Corby would have to be suicidal to show up here, but that didn't ease Erik's worry as he watched Brynn from across the room.

She wouldn't sit down.

Two empty chairs right there, but she refused to sit, just kept pacing back and forth between the elevators and the vending machine. Every ten minutes, she walked over to pester the poor guy manning the nurses' station.

Erik kept his eyes on her, but she wouldn't look at him. Which meant she was still pissed off.

You're like a robot. He wasn't sure why her words got to him, but they did.

Jeremy and Lindsey walked over. Lindsey's partner, Max Gorman, was talking to several uniformed cops by the door.

"What's the update?" Jeremy asked Erik.

"Still waiting."

"They're working on his kidney?" Lindsey asked.

"From what I hear, yeah. Think there's damage to the spleen, too."

Jeremy shook his head. They both had seen enough combat to know this was serious.

"How's the search coming?" Erik asked.

"Just talked to the head of the task force," Jeremy said. "His name's Art Caldwell. He's with the local marshal's office."

"He any good?" Erik asked, although he'd already drawn his own conclusions based on the shitty job they'd done locating Corby over the past nine days.

"Former Navy." He shrugged. "He's okay."

"They've got two canine teams combing the area between the apartment and the courthouse," Lindsey said. "And a FLIR helo just went up."

A helo equipped with forward-looking infrared radar could detect someone hiding in a bush or a ditch from five thousand feet in the air, which might have been useful if they were in a rural area. In an area like this, Erik figured it was a waste of time.

"You know, his description is a pretty close match with one of the digital pictures we've been circulating," Erik told Lindsey.

"Which one?"

"Shaved head, goatee."

"That should help."

He blew out a breath, frustrated beyond words at how close he'd been to grabbing the guy. If only he'd gone after him in those first seconds, before he even called Skyler. If only he'd been faster, Corby would be behind bars right now. Ross would be unharmed. And Brynn would be tucked safely in bed at home.

He glanced across the waiting room to see her once again badgering the nurse for updates.

The elevator doors opened, and a flush-faced Reggie got off. He went for the nearest huddle of cops, but Brynn intercepted him. Liam stepped away from the marshals to approach him.

"I want someone's head on a platter!" Reggie jabbed his finger at Liam's chest. "I want to know how this happened! What the hell am I paying for?"

Liam towered over the angry lawyer, absorbing the jabs. When Reggie finished his attack, Liam calmly started talking.

"Heads up," Jeremy said, and Erik turned around to see a man approaching him. Tall. Thin. He had a Glock on his hip and a U.S. marshal's badge on a lanyard around his neck.

"Erik Morgan? I'm Art Caldwell."

They shook hands, and Erik glanced past him to see Skyler coming out of what looked to be a private office or a staff room. She'd changed into a Dallas County EMT shirt but still wore her blood-stained jeans.

"I know you filled out a report," Caldwell said, "but I wanted to talk to you in person, get your impressions."

Erik gave Jeremy a questioning look.

"I got her," Jeremy assured him, meaning Brynn.

Erik walked with Caldwell to the room Skyler had just come from, catching her eye in the hallway. She looked stressed. Having a protectee injured on your watch was hell.

It was a small conference room with a sofa along one wall, probably so interns could collapse between shifts. Erik took a chair and checked his watch. Ross had been in surgery for nearly three hours.

"I put everything in my report," Erik told the marshal.

He opened a file and pulled out a mug shot of Corby. As he slid it across the table, Erik realized it wasn't a photo but a computer-generated sketch. Erik hadn't seen this version, and it looked like it had been created based on the description he had given.

"Our artist came up with that after talking to you and Vera Gomez."

"Who's that?" Erik looked up.

"The waitress at Mulligan's Pub. She got a pretty good look at him when he smacked into her."

Erik studied the picture, noting the blue eyes and the neck tattoo of an eagle. He'd altered his appearance since his escape by shaving his head, growing the goatee, and getting a tattoo, but he wasn't wearing colored contacts.

"That could be a fake tat," Erik said. "Prison doesn't have a record of it."

"Could be." Caldwell nodded. "Or maybe it's recent. We didn't see it in the surveillance footage from the prison. Then again, stopping to get inked up when you've got every badge in the state after you is a pretty bold move."

"So is stabbing a man in broad daylight. And taking potshots at a woman's car."

Caldwell frowned. "You're sure it was a gunshot the other day?"

"Yes."

"You seem confident in that assessment."

"I am."

Caldwell held his stare. Erik had no doubt the guy had checked his background and knew he'd served two tours in Afghanistan before joining the Secret Service.

"He's got a Remington seven hundred," Erik said.

"From McGowan's gun cabinet."

Erik nodded. "That's consistent with the weapon I heard. We believe he took the shot from the parking garage beside the Ames Theater. This evening, I was on my way over there to interview a possible eyewitness."

"Eyewitness?"

"A janitor who might have seen him there Tuesday morning in a black Honda with a dented bumper, which is the same make I saw today. But then all this shit went down, so I had to cancel the interview. I rescheduled him for tomorrow."

"We'll talk to him."

"Good. So will I."

Caldwell gave him a long, assessing look. "Listen, I won't bullshit you. I don't like you guys mucking around my case."

"Mucking?"

"You guys want to take money to protect these people? Fine, take their money. Makes the locals' job easier, so have at it. But as for investigating Corby? Don't. He's ours."

"Does he know that?"

Caldwell's expression hardened. "We're bringing him in. And if any of you hired guns gets in the way, you're going to find yourself in jail and facing federal obstruction charges."

Erik checked his watch. "Anything else you want to ask me about your fugitive?"

"Don't fuck with us, Morgan. Trust me, you do not want to be in the way when we take this guy down."

"When, not if?"

"That's right."

Erik nodded and stood up. "Looking forward to seeing that."

It was after eleven when Brynn finally left the hospital. Hayes drove her back to her apartment, and they rode the elevator up in silence. Brynn watched the digital numbers blearily, and the events of the past few hours tumbled through her mind.

The door dinged open at the same moment her phone chimed with a text. It was Liz, wanting another update. She'd called her after Ross got out of surgery, but that was nearly an hour ago. Trailing behind Hayes, she scrolled through her other messages and saw that she'd missed one from her mom, one from Faith, and three from Emilio's Café. The dinner order she'd placed earlier had completely vanished from her head.

Hayes took out his key and let her into the apartment. Brynn glanced up and for some reason was surprised to see it looked exactly the same as when she'd rushed out of here hours ago.

"Did you get dinner?" she asked Hayes.

"No, ma'am."

She gritted her teeth at the "ma'am" but didn't comment. "Who else is on tonight?"

"Trent."

Disappointment welled inside her as she remembered Erik was off. He always seemed to give the late-night shifts to everyone else.

Brynn dropped her purse on the coffee table. "Help yourself to whatever," she told him. "I'm going to bed."

"Yes, ma'am. Good night."

Brynn swallowed a bitchy comment as she walked to her bedroom. *You get snippy when you're upset.*

Erik was right. And she was feeling snippy in the extreme as she closed herself in her room and kicked off her sandals. Not bothering to turn on a light, she sank onto her bed and stared at the glowing phone in her hand. She debated calling Faith back. Reggie's assistant was keeping the rest of the firm updated on Ross's condition. Brynn had told Faith that Ross had pulled through the surgery. But she hadn't told her about the grave look on the surgeon's face when he'd finally emerged from the OR and given his prognosis to Ross's sister, who'd driven up from Austin.

"The next twelve hours are critical," the doctor had informed her. "We'll know more in the morning."

Brynn put her phone on the nightstand. She didn't have the heart to talk to Faith right now. She'd already spent an hour on the phone with Liz from the hospital. The conversation had felt cathartic at the time. But now the same storm of emotions that had churned through her in the waiting room was back again. Brynn closed her eyes and rubbed her forehead.

Her phone pinged. Cursing, she grabbed it off the nightstand and read yet another message from her sister: *You okay? You want to talk?*

No, she wasn't okay, and no, she didn't want to talk. *Home now and going 2 bed,* she replied. *Call u tomorrow.*

She stared down at her phone, and a dull ache expanded in her chest. She hated when she got this way—lonely but antisocial. She needed to talk to someone, but she wanted everyone to leave her alone. She'd been this way since she could remember, and it didn't make any sense. And the worst part was that her sister understood and no doubt knew that she was sitting here staring at her phone on the verge of tears.

She crossed the darkened room and flipped on the bathroom light. After splashing water on her face, she glanced in the mirror and was annoyed to discover she looked every bit as stressed and sleep-deprived as she felt. She patted her face dry with a towel, then traded the jeans and sweatshirt she'd worn to the hospital for her silky black PJs.

The door to the apartment opened and closed, and voices sounded in the hallway. Brynn went still.

Erik?

She listened intently. It was definitely Erik out there talking to Hayes. Had he stopped by to check on her? Anxiety filled her at the thought of seeing him right now. Her nerves were raw, her emotions right on the surface.

The front door opened and closed again.

Brynn stood there a full two minutes debating what to do. Her stomach growled at her, reminding her she hadn't eaten, and the tray of sandwiches she'd passed up at the courthouse was a distant memory.

"Screw it," she muttered.

She crept into the hallway. The living room was dark except for the flicker of the television. Someone was here, but was it Erik or Hayes?

She ventured into the living room and found Erik in front of the TV, his arm stretched over the back of the sofa. Instead of the bloodstained clothes he'd had on at the hospital, he now wore a gray T-shirt and jeans.

"Hi," she said.

"Hi."

She walked into the kitchen.

"Thought you went to bed," he said.

She didn't answer. He was watching her, but she couldn't read the look on his face.

She opened the fridge. "I thought you were off now."

"I traded shifts with Trent."

"Why?" She turned to look at him.

"He needed a break."

"Is he okay?"

"Yeah."

She turned and surveyed the contents of the fridge. Her stomach started to flutter, and suddenly food was the last thing she wanted.

"You sure?" she asked.

Erik walked into the kitchen and leaned against the counter beside her. Up close, she saw that his hair was damp, so evidently he'd showered when he stopped by his hotel. "Yeah, I'm sure. Why?"

"I don't know." She took out a bottle of wine. "I saw him at the hospital, and he looked sort of shell-shocked."

He folded his arms over his chest and gazed down at her. "How are you?"

"Me? Fine."

But she got a hot, tight feeling in the back of her throat. She took a glass from the cabinet and poured some wine.

"Brynn."

"What?"

He stepped closer. "How are you, really?"

"Fine. I told you." She plunked the bottle on the counter. "Want a glass?"

"No."

Of course not. No alcohol. No caffeine. He was such a Boy Scout all the time—no temptations, no cravings, no distractions.

Including her.

He stared down at her, and the intensity in his eyes made her pulse pick up. He looked edgy. Not nearly as calm as he'd been any of the other nights when they'd stood in this same kitchen.

She dropped her gaze to his broad chest and folded arms. She noticed the angry red scratch peeking out from his sleeve. Tracing her fingertip over his skin near the cut, she felt his body tense.

Just a few short hours ago, he'd been chasing a vicious killer who'd already left a trail of bodies in his wake. Erik had gone after him, without regard for the danger to himself and all the things that could have gone horribly wrong.

She glanced up at him. "You never told me what happened."

"Scratched it on some fencing."

"May I?" Without waiting for an answer, she lifted his sleeve to examine the cut. It was long but shallow, and she slowly ran her finger down the taut skin of his shoulder where the cut started.

His hand settled on her hip, drawing her closer, and Brynn's heart started to thrum.

She looked up at him. "What?"

He kissed her.

It was soft at first but quickly grew deep and hungry, and she felt a wave of relief that that last searing kiss hadn't been a one-off, because she'd convinced herself that maybe it was, that maybe she'd built it up too much in her mind.

But she hadn't built up anything. He really kissed this way, like he couldn't get enough of her.

Brynn slid her hands behind his neck and pulled him closer. She loved the way he held her. The way he took control. He shifted her so she was backed against the counter, and excitement shuddered through her.

He gripped her around her waist and lifted her onto the granite, and she gave a startled gasp as she clutched his neck. Their gazes locked. They were at eye level now, and she saw that intent look on his face again.

He slid his hands under her silky top, and she twined her legs around him, pulling him close. He bent forward to go after her neck.

"You taste good." His breath was hot against her throat, and lust shot through her as his fingers traced over her nipple. He pushed the fabric up and bent down, and the warm pull of his mouth made her moan softly.

He stopped what he was doing to look at her. "If you want me to leave you alone, tell me now."

She tightened her legs around him. "Don't you *dare* leave me alone."

Heat simmered in his eyes. He kissed her mouth again, dipping his hands below the waist of her pants. He lifted her up and slid them off her legs, setting her down on the cool granite. She watched the desire in his eyes as she wrapped her legs around him and pulled him close to kiss him. His hands slid over her bare thighs, and she ran her fingers through his hair, as she'd wanted to do since she'd first met him. She felt giddy finally getting her chance. She loved the way he tasted, the way he kissed her, the way his capable hands moved over her skin. He kissed her neck, her collarbone, and she tipped her head back to enjoy it.

His guard was down. She wasn't sure what had changed, but he was acting on all those pent-up urges she'd seen in his eyes since their first meeting. She soaked it all in—the heat, the anticipation, the rasp of his stubble against her tender skin. Everything he was doing made her feel drunk and needy.

"Brynn?"

"Hmm?"

"Hold on to me."

She clutched the back of his neck as he lifted her off the counter and walked her out of the kitchen. She buried her face against his shoulder, squeaking as they passed through the foyer.

"What?" he asked gruffly.

"I hope Hayes doesn't walk in."

"He's watching the cameras."

He carried her into her room, kicked the door shut, and lowered her onto the bed, and her heart lurched at the sight of his tall, broad-shouldered silhouette against the faint glow from the bathroom. Her room was dim, but she had no trouble seeing the determined look on his face, and she felt a rush of excitement to have him here alone.

He watched her as he unbuckled his belt. He took off his holster and put it on the nightstand, then reached into his back pocket and added his wallet to the pile of leather and metal.

He rested a knee between her legs, and the mattress creaked under his weight as he leaned over her.

"I'm on the pill," she whispered.

Heat sparked in his eyes, and she felt another rush of anticipation. "Good to know."

He kissed her as he parted her legs and settled his weight on her, and every nerve in her body seemed to fire to life. Everything about him was intoxicating—his mouth and his hands and the musky scent of his skin—and she felt wonderfully dizzy as he kissed her and pressed himself against her core.

Sliding her fingers under his shirt, she felt the smooth muscles of his back. His hand glided up her thigh, and she arched against him.

He pulled back, resting his weight on his elbow as he gazed down at her, his look unreadable. Was he having doubts? *Now?*

She pulled him down to kiss her, wrapping her legs around him again. She combed her fingers through his short hair, and his tongue tangled with hers as he moved against her, making her entire body ache and throb until all she could feel was a blinding *need*. She reached her hand between them and unsnapped his jeans. She got his zipper down and pushed at his clothes, but he caught her hand.

"Just wait."

"No. Now."

He pulled back and looked at her, and the serious expression in his eyes made her heart skitter. He kissed her gently. Then he shifted her legs and pushed inside her with a hard thrust.

Her breath caught. She squirmed under him. He didn't move, and she pushed.

"Brynn," he said through gritted teeth.

"*Yes.*" She wrapped her legs tight and pulled him closer, sliding her hands up his back.

He began to move against her. He set a pace for them, slow and deliberate, intentionally designed to make her want more. Every move had her body pulsing with need, and it felt good. So good. She started kissing him again, and that made everything more intense.

She wanted more. Faster. And he somehow seemed to know exactly what she needed, because he was giving it to her with his mouth and his hands and his powerful body, and she leaned her head back and surrendered to everything he was doing.

She loved the way his muscles felt under her fingers, the way his hand gripped her hip, the way his jeans rasped against her bare thighs as he drove into her again and again. His look of concentration—his utter *focus* on her—filled her with awe. In all her life, no one had ever made her feel this way.

"Brynn." He closed his eyes. "*God*, Brynn."

"Don't stop."

She clutched him against her, and it was too good, too hard, too much. She scraped her nails down his back, and a cry tore from her throat as she shattered and came apart. Another soul-deep thrust, and he came, too.

He dropped his weight onto his elbows, and she let her arms fall against the bed as she gazed up at him.

She couldn't move. Or speak. Yet every inch of her body was singing.

He stared down at her, breathing hard. Then he carefully pulled out and got up from the bed.

He whipped off his T-shirt and tossed it to the chair, then knelt down to untie his boots. She sat up on her elbows to watch as he took a small black pistol from an ankle holster and thunked it on the nightstand, adding to the growing pile of equipment.

"What—"

"Backup," he said.

He stripped everything off, and her heart leaped at the sight of him naked. He rested his knee on the bed again, leaned over her, and, without a word, lifted the hem of her silky top and eased it over her head. He dropped it to the floor and stretched out beside her.

Her heart was still thrumming as she looked at him. She ran her fingers over his chest. She didn't have the words for how she felt right now, and she probably wouldn't have told him even if she did.

He slid his arm under her shoulders and pulled her close, and she felt a warm glow at the intimacy.

She lay there in the darkness, breathing in his scent and listening to the sound of traffic twelve stories below. She closed her eyes and sighed. She felt loose and floaty. More relaxed than she'd been in days. Weeks. Maybe ever.

"Brynn . . ."

The tone of his voice chased away some of the euphoria.

"We have to talk."

And there went the rest of it.

Groaning, she rolled against him. She nuzzled his chest and kissed him. "First, let's sleep."

18

LINDSEY WAS pulling into her apartment building when she got a call from a familiar number. John Dewitt, the reporter. She grabbed her phone off the front seat, surprised he was calling so late. Then again, he was on California time. She answered the call as she pulled into a parking space.

"Hey, John Dewitt here. I got an urgent message?"

"Thanks for getting back to me."

"Yeah, who are you again? Your message was vague."

Which wasn't an accident. Lindsey dug a notepad from her purse. "I'm with the Sheridan Heights Police Department. That's a suburb of Dallas. You may have heard we've got a pretty intense manhunt going on here."

"James Corby. I had a call from a marshal wondering if I'd heard from him or sent him money or anything. Is that why you're calling?"

"Not exactly. I'm working on some background info, trying to develop a better profile of the fugitive, and I came across your article in *Lone Star Monthly*. It was a good piece." Not really, but she figured it wouldn't hurt to flatter the guy.

"It was pretty basic," he said. "I was saving the more in-depth stuff for a book, but the project never got off the ground."

"Why's that?"

"Lot of reasons. Corby stopped talking to me after the second interview. Then he lost his appeal. He wasn't on death row or anything, so the story wasn't getting the attention I needed to generate traction. And then I got the job out here."

According to Lindsey's research, Dewitt had been with the *Hollywood Insider* for two years. It wasn't exactly known for hard news, but that wasn't to say they wouldn't want something about a notorious murderer, especially if the story had film potential.

"With regard to your interviews," Lindsey said, "can I ask what you talked about?"

"The usual. His trial. His innocence. He was unjustly accused, and the whole world was out to get him. Guy is pretty paranoid."

"Did he mention any particular people he was close to? Maybe a friend from childhood or a relative?"

"No."

"What about groupies? I know some of these guys have admirers who follow their trials." Some famous murderers even get married while in prison.

"He mentioned a pen pal once."

Lindsey's pulse quickened. "Really?"

"Yeah, some woman. He said he never met her in person. I think they connected through one of those prison pals programs. Think most of them are people doing mission work—you know, trying to convert condemned prisoners to Jesus."

Lindsey was scribbling frantically now. A female pen pal.

"Did you mention this to the marshal who called you?"

"It was a brief interview, so no. Fact, I hadn't thought about it until now. Why?"

"Did Corby tell you her name?"

Silence.

"Mr. Dewitt?"

"Can we go off the record?"

Lindsey stopped writing. "I'm not a reporter, Mr. Dewitt. I can't make promises like that."

"Well, I mailed a letter for him once."

"To this woman?"

"Yeah."

It was strictly against the rules, and Lindsey could only imagine why the reporter had done it. Maybe he was trying to curry favor with the subject of his future book. A smuggled letter could explain how Corby managed to get those threatening notes to Jen Ballard and Brynn Holloran.

"You remember her name?" she asked.

"Ann Johnson."

"Is that Ann with an e?"

"I don't remember."

Lindsey smelled a lie. "What about her address?"

"I don't recall. This was more than two years ago. It's not like I took a picture of the letter or anything."

She suspected that was precisely what he'd done. Or at least copied down the address for future reference. After all, the guy was working on a project he hoped to make money on. And this pen pal was potentially an inside source. Any reporter worth his salt would keep her info on file.

The woman herself might be hard to track down, though. Regardless of spelling, she had a very common name.

"Was she in Texas? Do you at least remember that?" Lindsey didn't try to mask her impatience.

"Sorry."

She bit her lip, frustrated.

"Listen, I'd appreciate it if you'd keep me out of this," he said. "Corby's a nutjob, and I really don't want to get involved in this thing."

"It's a nationwide manhunt, so that's not really up to me."

"But—"

"And it's safe to assume you'll be hearing from the task force looking for Corby." Especially since Lindsey planned to call them up and tell them everything. She'd be willing to bet the LA marshal's office would haul this guy in for questioning as payback for holding out on one of their guys.

Lindsey checked her watch, ready to wrap up the interview and get moving on this lead.

"Just out of curiosity, your book about Corby—whatever happened to that?" she asked.

"Like I said, it never got off the ground."

"But what about now, with all this renewed interest in Corby's case?"

"Yeah, someone might do something, but it's not going to be me," he said. "The man's a psycho. I'd be happy if I never saw him again."

Erik lay in the dark with Brynn's leg draped over him and her head resting against his side.

His mind was reeling. He'd broken every one of his personal rules. Not just broken—he'd hammered them into oblivion. He needed to get up and get out of here before he made it worse, but he couldn't bring himself to move.

Brynn shifted and sighed, her breath warm against his skin, and Erik felt a knot in his chest. She was so damn beautiful, sleeping next to him that way. He needed to go. He needed to get up and get dressed and get the fuck out of her bed, but he couldn't do it.

He should get her to do it for him. If he pissed her off enough, she'd kick him out of here, and his problem would be solved—if only temporarily.

He glanced down at her, all warm and soft and curled against him. He ran his hand over her perfectly round hip.

She shifted again, and this time, he could tell she was awake.

"Brynn."

She sat up slightly and blinked into the darkness, then turned to glance at the clock. It was 1:33.

She looked at him, and his heart gave a kick at the sight of her all sleep-mussed.

Sighing, she lay back down and tucked her head against his chest. He combed his hand through her hair, letting it slide through his fingers.

"We need to talk, Brynn."

Another sigh. "So talk."

"We can't do this again."

Her body tensed, and he waited for what she'd say.

"So . . . this is a one-time thing?"

He caught the hurt in her voice.

"Maybe when all this is over . . ." He trailed off, not sure what he wanted to say.

She sat up propped on her elbow and looked at him. "What? You'll go back to jet-setting with your celebrities, and I'll go back to Pine Rock to practice law? Is that how this works?"

"I don't know. I've never done this before."

Her brow furrowed. "You've *never* gotten involved with a woman you're protecting?"

"Never even been tempted."

Her mouth dropped open.

"Why are you surprised?"

"I don't know." She combed her hair away from her eyes again. "I figured it was one of the perks of the job."

"It's not."

He sat up and leaned back against the headboard. She gazed up at him, and the vulnerability on her face made him feel like shit. He knew better than to let things go here, but he'd done it anyway.

He wanted her again. Right now, even though he'd barely recovered from last time.

He'd thought that caving in once would get her out of his system, but it hadn't at all. And he cursed himself for being so stupid.

She ran her fingertips over his abdomen. "What if we find ways to be alone together when you're not on duty? That wouldn't be a problem, would it?"

"It's already a problem."

Guys had been fired for doing what Erik had just done or, at minimum, reassigned. The prospect of turning her security over to someone else was unthinkable. He couldn't let it happen.

"You're concerned there's going to be fallout at work?" she asked.

"There will be. Don't worry about that. I'll deal with it."

"You know what that sounds like? A bunch of macho crap." She shifted onto his lap and straddled him, then slid her hands over his shoulders. "If there's fallout, I'll talk to Liam. I'm the client—he'll listen to me." She paused. "Whatever it is, we'll *both* deal with it."

Erik didn't say anything to that—he was too mesmerized by her perfect breasts right there in front of him.

"This so-called problem," she said, brushing her hair over her shoulder. "Is it a problem of distraction?"

He'd been distracted since the minute he met her. Years of training and rigorous self-discipline had gone right out the window. She just had to look at him with those deep blue eyes, and his focus was shot to hell.

"Because I don't think it's a problem," she said. "I mean, look at this place. The apartment's secure. We've got cameras downstairs. You've got a whole arsenal here on the nightstand." She leaned closer. "I feel very protected."

"There are still things you don't see."

"I'm willing to risk it."

Erik wasn't. And yet here he was, unable to slide her off his lap so he could get up and leave.

She tipped her head to the side, watching him, and he sensed she was devising a new line of attack.

"I want to ask you something, and you're not allowed to lie," she said.

She was trying to distract him. And he was letting her.

"What is it?"

"Why did you trade shifts with Trent?"

"He asked me. I told you."

"Yes, but you weren't being truthful. Not completely."

How the hell did she know that?

"No, he did ask me." Erik sighed. "But I was going to make him give me his shift anyway."

"Why?"

"After everything that went down, I didn't want you out of my sight. I wanted to be here tonight."

Not just here in her apartment—in her bed. He'd known exactly what he wanted when he walked through her door.

She smiled. "I knew you were lying."

"I wasn't—"

"Thank you for your honesty." She kissed him, letting her tongue linger over his bottom lip, and he knew he wasn't going anywhere right now. Or for the foreseeable future.

"And FYI?" she whispered. "I wanted you here tonight, too."

19

BRYNN WOKE up alone in the big bed. The room was light, and the traffic noise drifted up from street level. She lay beneath the cool comforter, listening to voices in the kitchen, but none of them belonged to Erik.

She refused to feel hurt. Or disappointed. He'd made it clear last night where he stood on things, and nothing she'd done had changed his mind.

She slid out of bed and took her time in the shower. It was Saturday, so at least she didn't have to be in court. She dressed and put on some makeup, then took a deep breath to brace herself before going into the kitchen.

She found Jeremy seated at the bar with his computer. The sight of him there instead of Hayes or Trent put an uneasy feeling in the pit of her stomach.

"Good morning," she said.

"Morning."

She went straight for the coffeepot, glancing over her shoulder at him. Jeremy had a super-ripped build, a military-short haircut, and pale gray eyes that seemed to notice everything. Like Erik, he was a former Marine. Also like Erik, he wasn't a talker.

Brynn opened the canister, and just the smell of ground coffee perked up her senses. She got the coffee maker going and turned to face him. Her first challenge of the day was going to be chatting him up and getting info.

"So." She smiled. "Who else is here this morning?"

"Keith is in the control room, watching the surveillance cams."

"I assume you reviewed them from last night?"

He nodded. "No sign of Corby near the entrances."

Brynn shook her head. "Amazing."

"What's that?"

"How he's managed to elude the marshals for so long. Not to mention the local police."

"They'll find him."

"You sound like Erik."

The coffeepot gurgled, and she went to the pantry to hunt up some breakfast.

"Would you like a Pop-Tart?" she asked.

"No, ma'am."

She eyed him across the kitchen. Did they do it to needle her, or was it just ingrained? She tore open the foil packet and slipped a chocolate-iced pastry into the toaster.

The coffee finished brewing, and she filled a mug. She dumped several scoops of sugar into it and then stepped over to the bar across from Jeremy.

"So where is Erik?" she asked, taking a sip.

"Out."

She sighed and tried again. "Where did he go?"

"Had some things to take care of."

She lifted her eyebrows.

"He'll probably be back by this afternoon."

Brynn tried to keep her reaction to herself. This *afternoon?* She sipped her coffee and waited for Jeremy to elaborate, but he didn't.

The toaster popped. Brynn put her pastry on a plate and broke off a bite. Jeremy watched her silently, probably horrified by her caffeine-and-sugar–infused breakfast.

She glanced at the clock. "It's eight, so Ross's sister is likely at the hospital. I need to call her for an update."

"I just talked to Skyler. He made it through the night, no complications, and they've moved him to a private room."

"That's *great.*" Relief flooded her, and she pressed her hand to her chest. "He's stabilized, then?"

Jeremy nodded.

Tears welled in her eyes, and she turned around to top off her coffee while she struggled for composure.

"What else do you know?" she asked.

"The doctor didn't tell the family much."

"Yes, but I'm guessing you know more, right?"

Jeremy was the head of Ross's security detail. He felt responsible for him. And there was no way he'd been satisfied with the hospital's vague *we'll know more when we know more* crap.

"Come on. Tell me what you have."

He closed his computer. "I talked to my friend who's a combat medic, told him about Ross's injury."

"Okay . . . but isn't a combat medic more familiar with bullet wounds?"

"Bullets, blades, shrapnel, burns. He's pretty much seen it all."

"What did he say?"

"Generally, the kidney is the bigger issue. If they can repair the damage and keep him stabilized, he should have a good outlook. And from what I hear, they were able to do that last night."

"So that's more good news."

"Should be."

But Jeremy continued to look morose. Clearly, he felt responsible for his protectee being in the hospital, even though he wasn't the man who put him there.

"How's Skyler doing?" Brynn asked.

His brow furrowed. "This has been hard on her. But she's tough. She was there all night with the marshals."

"I heard Liam pulled her off the team."

"Pulled her off protective detail," Jeremy said. "She's handling purely tech stuff now."

"You think it was the right call?"

"Yes," he said without hesitation. "And she understands that. She screwed up, so she's off."

"And the marshals are guarding him at the hospital?"

"So they say. I think they're mostly there to interview him when he's ready to talk."

"I need to go see him," she said.

"He can't have visitors right now."

"Later this morning, then."

"We should be able to arrange something this afternoon."

Brynn's uneasy feeling was back again. She took her plate to the sink. "You mean when Erik gets back," she stated.

"That's right."

She turned to look at Jeremy. "And where is he again?"

"He had something to take care of."

"What exactly?"

No comment.

She leaned back against the counter and stared at Jeremy. He didn't look away. Neither did she. Brynn had a sneaking suspicion about where Erik had gone, and she hoped to hell she was wrong.

"Jeremy, why are you here this morning?"

"Erik asked me to cover for him."

"And why'd he ask *you*?"

"I don't know."

"He could have asked Trent or Keith or Hayes, but instead, he asked you. Why do you think that is?"

Jeremy smiled slightly and crossed his arms. "I feel like I'm in a deposition here."

She shrugged. "I'm just curious why Erik would ask you, specifically, when you're not on my detail."

"He trusts me."

"Trusts you . . . not to hit on me? Or to keep me contained today while he's off on some mystery errand?"

"Both."

Wow. Honesty. She hadn't really expected him to answer. And his answer told her a lot, starting with the fact that he knew something was going on between her and Erik.

Brynn no longer felt uneasy. Now she was worried.

"Jeremy, you understand, right, that just because my firm hired your firm to provide security, that doesn't mean I'm under house arrest here. You guys can't *force* me to do anything."

He nodded. "We can recommend. And we strongly recommend that you stay here today."

"That doesn't work for me. I have places to go and things to do today."

Jeremy shook his head, and she could tell he regretted promising Erik anything.

"I know I'm going to regret this." He sighed. "Where do you need to go?"

"That depends."

"On what?"

"I'll ask you again. Where is Erik?"

20

LIAM WOLFE'S compound looked different this time, and Brynn wasn't sure why. Same almost invisible gate. Same towering trees. Same crack of rifle fire as they drove past the shooting range. Maybe *she* was different. Maybe the tumultuous events of the past week had changed something in her.

Brynn buzzed her window down and inhaled the warm, fresh air that smelled of pine. She reached out and let the wind race through her fingers. It felt good to be out here, even if the reason she'd come did not.

Jeremy drove past the big log cabin that housed Wolfe Sec headquarters and parked at the end of a row of trucks and SUVs. Brynn got out, looking around. No sign of Erik or the silver pickup he'd supposedly borrowed from Trent today.

Jeremy walked around the Tahoe. "I'll find out where he is," he said, seeming to read her mind. "Wait inside, if you like."

She opted to stay outside. Her attention was drawn to a black wooden fence on the other side of a grassy knoll. She walked over, watching with interest as several men dressed in black fatigues played with a pair of German shepherds. The dogs wore matching black tactical vests and looked like they were trained to sniff out bombs.

Brynn leaned against the fence and watched the dogs leap around, grunting and snarling at their handlers. Judging from the playful banter back and forth, it was all a big game.

"Hi."

She turned around, shocked to see Erik behind her.

"God, don't sneak up on me."

His eyebrows lifted.

Brynn looked him over. He wore the same gray T-shirt and jeans he'd had on last night, and she wondered if he'd come straight here after slipping out of her bed.

She crossed her arms and gazed up at him. She'd planned to give him crap about his exit, but now the concerned look on his face put a lump in her throat. He looked worried. Burdened. Was she too late? Had he already talked to Liam?

"I see you've met Gus and Gracie," he said.

"Who?"

"Our dogs."

"Oh." She turned around. "Not exactly."

A line of men in green military fatigues—trainees, she guessed—stood inside the corral now, eyeing the German shepherds warily. One guy wore what looked like a catcher's uniform, complete with chest padding and a helmet. Keeping his gaze on the dogs, he walked into the center of the corral.

"What are they—"

"Watch."

A sharp command, and the bigger dog raced across the corral, launching himself at the defenseless man. Brynn gave a startled gasp as the dog clamped onto the man's arm, growling and fighting as he tried to pull away.

Another command, and the female dog raced into the fray. She leaped onto the man's back and latched onto his shoulder. He struggled to shake her off, all the while trying to free his arm from the bigger dog's jaws, but the animals held on. Brynn glanced at the spectators, amazed that no one rushed to intervene as the attack dragged on.

A loud whistle. Both dogs released their grip. They ran back to their handler and, after a brisk command, sat obediently at his side. The trainee bent over, resting his hands on his knees as he caught his breath.

Brynn rubbed her chest. Her heart was racing. And she was sweating, she realized, just from watching the drill.

"That's terrifying," she said.

"That's the point."

She looked at Erik. "Why?"

"Stress training. To counter your natural flight response when you're under attack. You learn to control your reaction so you can stand your ground and fend off a threat."

"You've done this? Stood there and let dogs attack you?"

He nodded. "Animals are better for this than people, because we instinctively know they can't be controlled, so the danger feels real, and your limbic system kicks in—which is what you want. Enough drills with Gus and Gracie here, and your heart rate actually lowers during an attack so you're able to think straight and maintain motor skills." Erik looked at her. "Yesterday you said I was like a robot. That calm you saw? That's a direct result of stress conditioning."

She gazed up at him, at a loss for what to say. He'd been through so much training, so many life experiences she knew nothing about. She wanted to hear more. She wanted him to open up to her so she could see his world and truly understand it. But he wanted to shut her out.

Frustration welled up inside her, and she turned away.

"You look mad," he said.

"Mad?" She choked out a laugh. "That doesn't even begin to . . ." She shook her head. "I'm severely pissed that you took off without telling me and left instructions for Jeremy to keep me on lockdown."

"Lot of good it did."

"I don't know where you got the idea you could put me under house arrest, but it's not happening. I've got obligations to people, Erik. Not just my client but Ross and Reggie and our legal team."

"Understood. We're working on a plan."

She put her hand up to shield her eyes from the sun. "Is that why you're here? Is that what was so urgent that you had to talk to Liam in person?" She paused, trying to read his expression. "Because after our conversation last night, I had this insane idea that you might have come out here to quit."

He just looked at her.

"Erik! God damn it, I knew it. That's *crazy*. You can't quit your job because of me!"

"It's not you. I had a lapse in judgment."

"But I didn't realize when we . . . Look, I had no idea this was such a big deal to you. It won't happen again. We won't let it. We won't even think about it."

He arched his eyebrows.

"Not until this is over," she added.

"Brynn—"

"What? You're being an idiot! I won't let you do this."

He glanced around, and she realized their heated conversation was attracting attention from some of the trainees.

"Let's go over here." He took her gently by the elbow and steered her across the grass toward the business office. When they reached the side of the building, he pulled her into the shade.

"I didn't quit. Although that would have been the honorable thing to do." He rubbed the back of his neck. "The truth is, Brynn, I'm the best man for this job. I know that. And I'm not willing to hand it over to anyone else."

She stared up at him. He looked so conflicted, and she could tell he'd been torturing himself over this.

"Then why are you here?" she asked.

He looked past her. "Last night at the hospital, talking to the marshals, I realized we underestimated this thing. We misjudged the threat." His eyes met hers, and she could tell he felt personally responsible for something—once again—that wasn't his fault. "I came to persuade Liam to bring in more people."

She watched him, saying nothing. She wasn't sure she wanted more people. And she definitely didn't want them if they didn't include Erik. She could work with him, talk to him, negotiate with him. They argued, yes, but he also listened when she voiced her opinions.

Which was one reason she'd been surprised he'd left so abruptly and dumped her on Jeremy.

"Liam asked me flat-out if I had a personal relationship with you," he said.

"How did he—"

"He picked up on something. I don't know. He reads people."

"What did you tell him?"

"The truth."

She huffed out a breath. "I would have advised you to take the Fifth on that. It's none of his business."

"Yeah, well, you're not my lawyer." His gaze held hers. What was she, exactly? No longer just a client. "Anyway, it is his business."

"I disagree. How'd he respond?"

"I'm pretty sure he wanted to yank me off the job and reassign me."

She heard a "but" coming.

"But in light of new developments, that's not happening."

"What new developments?"

Erik stared down at her, and a feeling of dread came over her. What was it? She'd talked to Ross's sister less than an hour ago, and he was recovering in his hospital room, guarded by marshals. Was it Corby?

The door opened, and heavy boots sounded on the steps. Brynn turned to see Liam. He was in black commando clothes—no more business attire—and he had that warrior look she remembered from the first day.

"Brynn." He nodded at her.

"Liam."

He looked past her at Erik. "You tell her yet?"

"I was just about to."

"Tell me what?"

Liam's gaze settled on her. "Mark is here. Probably better if you hear it from him."

21

MARK WOLFE was in the conference room, files and papers arrayed in front of him. In contrast to his brother, he wore a dress shirt and a blazer, which Brynn took for his casual look.

The expression on his face was anything but casual, though. The former FBI profiler appeared dark and brooding. Skipping pleasantries, Brynn took a seat.

"What's going on?" she asked.

Mark looked at Erik as he took the chair beside her. "I was just going over all this with Liam."

"All what?"

"Liam knows the head of the task force, and we were able to get copies of Corby's files."

"Which files?"

"Those pertaining to his criminal case," Mark said. "I've been reviewing everything to come up with a fugitive assessment. That's basically a criminal profile but with a special emphasis on predicting what a fugitive might do. Where he's going, where he's likely to hide, people he might reach out to. It's a tool for police."

"What did you come up with?" she asked.

Mark paused and tapped his pencil, as if not sure where to begin.

"Did the prosecution team or Corby's defense team ever bring in a profiler on this case?"

His question startled her. "The police reached out to the FBI for something after the third victim. But they didn't get back with anything before the fourth murder happened, and soon after that, Corby was arrested. Why?"

"What about during trial preparation?" he asked, ignoring her question.

"I can't speak for the defense, but we didn't. There was so much physical evidence linking Corby to the murders that we decided to make that the backbone of our case. Juries like physical evidence."

"As opposed to profiling mumbo jumbo?" He smiled slightly.

"Well, I've never referred to it as mumbo jumbo, but yeah. Jen's case was based on three main elements," she said, ticking them off on her fingers. "The cable company records showing that Corby had been in three of the four victims' houses while on the job, a droplet of blood from the first victim that was found on Corby's shoe, and the fourth victim's necklace recovered from Corby's house. It was one of his souvenirs."

The necklace had been an especially powerful piece of evidence. It was a gold chain with an L-shaped pendant, and Jen showed jurors numerous photos of young, vivacious Lauren Tull wearing it around her neck. The pictures provided a stark contrast to the crime-scene photos that showed Lauren on the floor of her living room with her neck slashed open.

"In that case, I may be the first profiler to go through all this," Mark said. "And I've found some alarming details."

"Like what?" she asked.

"You mentioned the cable company where Corby worked. Police zeroed in on him as a suspect when they learned three of the victims had recently had cable work done, and the same technician had been to their homes."

"That's right. Our theory was that he scoped them out ahead of time, selecting victims whose homes would be easier to break into."

Mark flipped a page in his notepad. "The first three victims had sliding glass patio doors that had been pried open with a crowbar. Victim one was found in her bedroom. The next two in the hallway. Based on the sleepwear they had on, it looks like the killer broke in after they'd gone to bed. In victim four's case, she was wearing regular clothes and was attacked in her living room. She didn't have a slider, but the window on her back door was broken."

"Okay." Where was he going with all this?

"The victims were raped and then killed by asphyxia," he continued. "The killer also slit their throats and mutilated them with the knife."

"Yes, but I'm sure you saw that the cutting happened postmortem," Brynn said. "Even though the media dubbed Corby the Throat Slitter, the ME determined that the actual cause of death was asphyxia."

"I was just getting to that," Mark said. "The asphyxia."

"What about it?"

He flipped open a file beside him. "According to the ME's report, microscopic fibers were lifted from Lauren Tull's mouth and nose."

"Okay."

"That suggests to me that she was smothered. The first three victims were strangled manually. Another notable detail? The tox screens. All four victims had varying amounts of alcohol in their bloodstreams, but Lauren Tull also had trace amounts of a chemical called seven-aminoflunitrazepam, whose parent drug is Rohypnol, which confirms that she ingested Rohypnol before death. Were you aware of that?"

No, she hadn't been. They'd been dealing with a huge volume of investigative materials, and the prosecution team had divided everything up. Brynn's focus had been on other aspects of the case.

"You're saying he drugged her?" Brynn asked.

"I'm pointing out subtle differences in the MO. The method of entry, manual strangulation versus smothering, the trace amounts of Rohypnol in the fourth victim's system."

Brynn leaned forward. "But why would he change his MO?"

"I don't think he did."

Silence settled over the room. Brynn glanced at Erik and Liam. They seemed to be waiting for her to catch up.

"I see what you're suggesting." Brynn shook her head. "But you're forgetting a few things. What about all the evidence at Corby's home? The necklace, the blood on the boot, the news clippings."

Mark looked at her for a long moment. Then down at his notes. "Another thing to consider is Corby's build. He's five-five and weighed one hundred thirty pounds at the time of his arrest." Mark flipped to another page in his notebook. "The first three victims were blond and could be described as petite, all weighing around one hundred ten pounds. Lauren Hull weighed more than Corby—one thirty-five— and had brown hair. She was a different physical type from the others."

"So . . . you're saying she wasn't one of his victims? But police found her necklace at Corby's house."

"Are you sure?"

Brynn just stared at him. The implications of everything he was saying were making her queasy. She thought of Lindsey's theory that the necklace could have been planted.

Mark leaned forward on his elbows, watching her closely. "What if someone else killed Lauren Tull?"

"What's your scenario?" She tried to keep her voice even, but she was freaking out.

"Okay, hypothetically, say she met up with someone or had someone over, and he drugged her drink. The amount of Rohypnol in her system was pretty low. So imagine she comes to during the rape and begins to struggle and make noise. Then her attacker grabs a pillow and puts it over her face, ends up smothering her. When he realizes she's dead, he panics."

"And then what?" Brynn asked. "Poses her like the other victims, with the knife wounds and everything?"

"The term we use is 'staged,'" he said. "'Posed' is when the killer arranges the victim's body in a certain way to send a particular message. 'Staged' is when he tries to manipulate the scene to mislead police. That could be what happened here. He could have been staging the crime to look like the recent murders that had been in the news."

"But what about the necklace? You're saying the killer took her necklace and somehow got it into Corby's house?"

"Or someone else did."

His words hung in the air. *Someone*, meaning someone on the investigation. As a defense attorney, Brynn had plenty of reasons to be cynical about law enforcement, but what Mark was suggesting stretched the limits, even for her.

"It was a high-profile case," Mark said. "I've seen it happen. The public is scared. The police are under intense pressure. Maybe someone pockets some evidence as backup to make sure that when they finally find the guy, he gets put away. And if it *did* happen—or something close to it did—that feeds into James Corby's story that he was set up by police."

"You're defending him?" She couldn't believe what she was hearing. "You think he's justified in his revenge quest?"

Mark shook his head. "I'm not saying that. The prosecution put up convincing evidence that he killed three women. But as for the fourth, he might indeed be falsely accused. And the 'trophy' he supposedly took from her—the gold necklace—that was the key piece of evidence that sent him away for life, and there's a possibility it could have been planted. I'm telling you, that's the source of his rage now."

"You know, you're not the first person to come up with this," Brynn said. "Have you talked to Detective Leary?"

Mark's brow furrowed. "No. Why?"

"She came to me yesterday morning with suspicions that the necklace might have been planted."

Mark looked surprised. "Then you're right, I should talk to her."

"You should share this information with the FBI, too. Aren't they spearheading the investigation while the marshals are leading the manhunt?"

He nodded. "I spoke to agents on the task force this morning."

"Great. But I have to ask why we're so focused on this *now*. Even if you're right with this theory, James Corby still raped and murdered three women, then killed a prison guard, a cop, and a judge. Our first priority should be to find him, not retry his case."

"This is important now because it goes to motive," Mark said. "What is his endgame here? The man escaped from prison, so logically, we might expect him to try to get away, maybe slip into Mexico. But we have to look at who we're dealing with. I told you yesterday, Corby perceives himself to be smarter than everyone else. His conviction and incarceration—they're a source of humiliation to him. The investigators and the prosecutors outsmarted him. They beat him, but maybe it was a rigged game. And they can't be allowed to get away with that."

"This is still only a theory," Brynn pointed out. "You need more evidence before you can prove it."

"You're right," Liam said. "But we need to consider it, because it could be dictating his actions."

Mark opened another manila folder. "What's in here on Corby's childhood is pretty limited. But based on the psych eval, it's clear he grew up without a father and had a domineering mother who abused him, both physically and emotionally. The system failed to intervene and stop the abuse. Corby feels he's been wronged his whole life, and his incarceration is just one more unfair punishment. Now it's his turn. Killing a cop with his own gun, cutting out the tongue of the lawyer he believes lied in court to put him away, stabbing a prosecutor in the back—it's all symbolic. And it tells us something crucial."

Brynn waited. She tried to keep her expression blank. But her chest felt tight, and her skin was breaking out in a cold sweat. She glanced at Erik, who was still watching her closely.

"In James Corby's mind, he's justified," Mark said. "He believes the system is rigged against him, and he may be right. He wants revenge, and accomplishing that goal may be more important to him than whether he lives or dies."

"That's why we're focused on this now," Liam said. "A guy like that? He's a formidable threat, because his mission is more important to him than his survival."

"He wants payback," Mark said. "And he wants it to hurt."

As they left Liam's compound, Brynn didn't say a word.

Erik had volunteered to take her back in the Tahoe, and Jeremy would return later that afternoon in Trent's truck.

"You okay?" Erik asked from behind the wheel.

"No."

Brynn glanced in the side mirror, where she saw yet another vehicle was following them, this one containing the two new agents Liam had staffed for the job.

I need my best people on this, he'd told Brynn at the end of the meeting. *Jeremy, Erik, Keith. I'm also adding three additional agents, including myself.*

Brynn was still absorbing it all. They were at *nine* agents, even more than Liam had recommended in the beginning.

Of course, much had changed since then. Mick McGowan was dead. Ross was seriously injured. And Corby had proven his talent for evading the police.

Brynn had been wrong about everything.

She turned to look out the window, feeling frustrated, scared, and confused—three of her least favorite emotions.

"Since we're in the area," she said, "you mind if we swing by my house? It's only fifteen minutes away, and I need to pick up some files."

"No problem."

Erik made a phone call relaying their plan to the other agents and rattling off Brynn's address—which, of course, he knew. He knew everything, and she knew precious little about him.

That was going to change.

They took the highway headed south, and Brynn watched in the side mirror as the black Suburban followed.

"Want to talk about it?"

She glanced at Erik. With his mirrored sunglasses, she couldn't read his expression. But the concern in his voice tugged at her.

"I'm just . . . thrown by this whole thing."

"Mark's theory?"

"All of it. If he's right, then Lauren Tull's killer is still out there raping women. And he's crossed the line to murder at least once." She shook her head. Who was to say he wouldn't do it again?

"What do you make of his theory?" Erik asked.

She appreciated that he called it a theory instead of treating it as fact.

"I don't know if I buy it," she said. "I mean, Mick McGowan had a hand in everything—the evidence collection, the interviews, the back-and-forth with the victims' families. The man had a stellar reputation. I can't believe he would plant evidence."

"Maybe he didn't. Maybe one of his detectives did."

"Or maybe it didn't happen." She looked at him. "Yes, smothering is different from strangling. But it's not like Corby's a preprogrammed machine. He's a human being, subject to impulses. Who knows what he might do in the heat of an attack? Or he could have been experimenting with different MOs, refining his craft."

"Craft?"

"I've read interviews, and that's how some of them think of it. Serial predators. They talk like it's a profession."

The queasy feeling was back in her stomach. She glanced at Erik beside her.

He was in bodyguard mode again. No acknowledgment of the fact that they'd spent the night tangled up naked together. She looked at his hand on the wheel and felt a pang of yearning.

Brynn turned away, annoyed by her reaction. It wasn't like her to pine after a man.

To distract herself, she checked her phone. Ross's sister had left a message during the meeting, and her voice sounded tired but hopeful.

"Ross is awake," Brynn told Erik as she listened to the message. "Marshals just interviewed him, and then he took a round of meds. He might be up for visitors in the morning. I need to go see him."

"I'll take you."

"Thanks."

They rode in silence the rest of the way to Pine Rock. As they passed the familiar streets and neared her house, Brynn's anxiety started to lift.

They turned into her neighborhood. The 1940s tract houses had been built well before Pine Rock was a suburb of Houston, back when it was its own separate town, with an economy based on logging and oil. As the sprawling city came closer, more people moved in, and many of the little houses on Brynn's block were being torn down and replaced by hulking new construction. Brynn understood the appeal, but she had other ideas.

They reached a white clapboard house with black shutters. It was dwarfed by the two-story monstrosity going up beside it. Erik pulled into the driveway, followed by the black Suburban with black-tinted windows. The vehicle looked like it belonged in a presidential motorcade.

"Not exactly a low profile," Brynn observed as they climbed out.

"Not supposed to be," Erik said.

She crossed the lawn and led him up the steps to her front door, which was flanked by clay pots of shriveled petunias. Brynn unlocked the door and pushed it open, sweeping aside a week's worth of mail that had been dropped through the mail slot onto her refurbished wood floor. Erik followed her inside, peeling off his sunglasses. The other agents seemed content to wait in their SUV.

The house was warm and still, and the smell of sawdust lingered from her most recent project. Brynn scooped up the pile of mail and dumped it on the side table.

"I usually get a neighbor girl to come by when I'm traveling," she said. "But I didn't want a child or anyone else here in case someone came looking for me."

"Good call."

She passed through her living room, comforted by the sight of her beautiful suede sectional piled with plush accent pillows. Her favorite chenille throw was draped over the back, and Brynn ran her fingertips over the cool softness on her way into the kitchen.

"I'll just be a minute here," she said over her shoulder. "I need to do a few things and pick up some case files."

"Take your time."

She got a pitcher from under the sink and filled it with water. She glanced at Erik. He was in her dining room now, surrounded by ladders and drop cloths, surveying the freshly primed walls.

"It's a work in progress," she told him. "I'm going room to room."

"You're doing it yourself?"

"Yeah. In my copious free time."

He stepped over to the built-in corner shelf that she'd sanded but not painted. Once upon a time, it had probably been used to display someone's wedding china. Brynn planned to use it for books.

"How long you been in here?" Erik looked at her.

"Two years." Which made it pretty embarrassing that she'd only managed to finish the living room and the master suite. The kitchen had hardly been touched. It was mint-green tile and linoleum flooring. Brynn didn't mind the green, but the tile was chipped, and the grout was discolored, and she hadn't decided whether to pull it out or restore it.

Erik walked through the kitchen to her back door. He flipped the bolt and stepped onto the screened-in porch. Brynn had a wicker sofa out there where she liked to sip coffee or wine and do legal work.

She scooted past him and watered a fern in the corner. He was standing at the screen, scanning her backyard, looking for God knew what.

She wondered what he thought of her place. It wasn't nearly finished, but could he see her vision for it?

Brynn had grown up in a series of one-bedroom apartments, where she shared a room with Liz while their mom unfolded the sofa bed every night. After that, it was dorm rooms and shared apartments as she worked her way through law school. Brynn considered this her first real home. She'd earned the money for it. And when she pulled into the driveway each night, she felt a wave of pride, along with an underlying panic that was hard to describe. Sometimes she felt completely at home here. Other times she felt like someone from the mortgage company was going to show up and tell her there had been a mistake, and they were taking her loan away. She'd had dreams where it happened, and she found herself in a courtroom, arguing not to be evicted from her house.

She returned to the kitchen. Erik followed and rebolted the back door.

"It's nice," he said.

She shrugged. "If you don't mind paint cans."

"It's a three-two?"

"It was," she said. "Now it's a two-two. I had the master remodeled before I moved in."

"Mind if I . . . ?" He nodded toward the hallway.

"Go ahead."

He walked down the hall to her bedroom, her most personal space. And she discovered she didn't mind at all.

She watered the plants in front, then left the pitcher in the sink and went into the spare bedroom, which she used as an office. In the closet, she crouched beside a row of file boxes and removed the lid of the middle one. She found the brown accordion file she'd been looking for. It contained handwritten notes from Corby's trial. The official documents were still at the DA's office. But her case notes and doodlings and half-finished thoughts—she'd kept those at home.

Brynn grabbed the file and went into the master suite, which was her pride and joy. The big windows let in plenty of natural light, and she'd gone with muted colors that would relax her when she was home. In the center of the room was a king-size bed covered with a cloudlike duvet and satin pillows. Stepping into the bathroom, Brynn cast a longing look at her Jacuzzi tub, where she liked to soak in an ocean of bubbles after a long day. The spacious bathroom was decadent, and the Realtor had warned her that giving up a bedroom for it would hurt her resale value one day. But Brynn didn't care. This was her place, and she wanted it exactly her way.

She went into her walk-in closet and grabbed a tote bag. She threw in an extra pair of running shorts, then opened her lingerie drawer and selected a few pretty items—just in case.

She found Erik standing beside the shower in her unrenovated guest bathroom. He was fiddling with the window latch.

"Your lock's rusted out," he told her.

"I'll add it to my list."

"It's a security issue. Don't put it off."

He slipped past her and headed into the living room, where her other windows got the same inspection. Seeing him move around her home put a little tingle in her stomach, even though he was clearly here in bodyguard mode.

Brynn opened the fridge and was happy to see a six-pack of waters—enough for her and Erik and the agents waiting in the driveway. She grabbed the drinks, checked the back door, and returned to the living room, where Erik was standing over her pile of mail.

"Brynn."

His voice was sharp. She walked over to see what had his attention. He'd gone through the stack and found a slip of paper amid the bills and junk mail. No envelope, no postmark, just a note in blocky handwriting: *I'M WATCHING YOU.*

She clutched her hand to her throat. "He was here."

———

Erik let himself into Brynn's apartment and found Skyler at the bar on her computer. Keith was in the living room on the phone, and he gave Erik a nod.

"Hey," Skyler said. "How'd things go at the courthouse?"

"We're all set up. They adjusted the cameras so they've got some angles on the street now." He glanced down the hallway, then back at Skyler. She wore jeans and a black Wolfe Sec shirt. Her clothes looked fresh, but her eyes were tired and bloodshot. Since Ross's attack, she'd been demoted to tech duty, but she was keeping a stiff upper lip about it and had thrown herself into the task of improving their surveillance capabilities.

"Anything going on here?" Erik asked.

"She swam laps upstairs, then took a shower."

He heard Brynn's voice in the bedroom.

"Who's she talking to?" he asked.

"Reggie."

"In her *bedroom*?"

"On the phone."

Erik stepped past her and opened the refrigerator. He surveyed the contents, wishing he could grab a Coke for a jolt of caffeine. But he'd already blown his toughest rule, so the least he could do was stick to the easy ones. He grabbed a water, and when he turned around, Skyler was watching him with a concerned look.

"What?"

She cast a glance at Keith and lowered her voice. "Are you keeping your eye on the ball, Erik?"

"Yes. Why?" He swigged his drink.

"I'm worried about you."

"Don't be. How'd it go at the hospital? How's Ross?"

"Good," she said, not sounding convinced. "At least, that's what the doctors say. Personally, I think he looks terrible." She shook her head.

Erik didn't bother trying to persuade her this wasn't her fault. She wouldn't believe him, just as he wouldn't believe her if anything happened to Brynn.

"You're here until midnight?" Skyler asked.

"Yeah. Brynn said she had some trial work to do and wanted to order dinner."

"Oh, yeah? You better talk to her about that, because I think she's getting ready to go out."

Erik glanced down the hall. Brynn was still on the phone, but the door was open, so he figured she'd at least be dressed.

He went into her bedroom—the room he'd been in just before dawn today. All the lights were on now, and the room smelled like Brynn right after a shower.

She stood in front of the bathroom mirror, fully dressed, hair in soft waves around her shoulders. She had a mascara brush in her hand and her cell phone perched on the counter.

"Can we prove who bought the plane ticket?" she was asking. She caught Erik's eye and didn't seem surprised to see him there. He walked over and leaned against the doorframe.

"Bulldog's working on it," Reggie said over the phone.

"Because I'd really love to nail the guy."

"I'll let you know."

Brynn looked Erik up and down, and something in her expression made his pulse pick up. Or maybe it was her clothes. She was in jeans and a tight black T-shirt. No heels, just bare feet.

"But Perez isn't the reason I'm calling, Brynn."

"What is?" She leaned closer to the mirror and did her thing with the mascara.

"I hear that Judge Linden knew Jen. Under the circumstances, you could probably persuade him to give you a two-day recess."

"Why?"

"*Why?* Because one of the defendant's lawyers is in the hospital, and the other one's under threat of assassination."

Brynn leaned back and surveyed her reflection. "I don't want a recess. I'm ready now."

"You're a nervous wreck."

"Bullshit. I'm ready, Reggie."

"If you're not nervous, you should be. I would be, if I were in your shoes."

"Well, you're not me."

Erik sipped his water, enjoying the debate.

"I'm not asking for a recess," Brynn told him. "My client's been rotting in jail for five months."

"He'll be rotting a lot longer if you drop the ball this week."

She reached for Erik's water and took a swig. "Who's dropping the ball? Our star witness is here and ready to testify, thanks to Bulldog. I've got a world-renowned forensics expert who just flew down from New York. Momentum is shifting, Reggie, and I'm ready to do this. I don't want delays. I want to defend my client and get him his life back."

"Momentum helps, but it won't get you all the way there."

She handed back the water bottle. "Reggie, come on. We both know this case reeks. It's rotten to the core. Even Conlon knows it. He realizes he could lose."

"You're under stress, Brynn. Which means you may not be seeing this clearly."

"No, I am. I've *seen* the jurors, and you haven't. They don't like Conlon. He's coming off as smarmy and overconfident. They think he's a snake-oil salesman, and they're waiting for me to prove them right. These jurors are looking for reasonable doubt, and I'm going to give it to them."

Reggie didn't respond. Brynn looked at the phone. Then she looked at Erik.

"Reggie?"

"I'm here. It's your call, but you know where I stand."

"Thank you."

"Call me tomorrow."

Brynn disconnected and huffed out a breath. "Lawyers! They're so damn argumentative."

"You look nice," Eric said. "Where are we going?"

"To pick up Emilio's. I feel bad about forgetting my order last night, and I want to make it up to them." She squeezed through the doorway, brushing her body against his.

"Why are you all dressed up to go get takeout?"

"This is not dressed up," she informed him, sliding her feet into heeled sandals. "But yes, we do have another stop to make."

"Where?"

"You'll see."

"This isn't a game, Brynn."

"Fine, but you're not talking me out of this. I'm done standing on the sidelines."

22

LINDSEY PACED the conference room, her body vibrating from an overload of sugar and caffeine and adrenaline. The sugar came from the candy bar she'd eaten for dinner. The caffeine came from three cups of coffee. And the adrenaline came from the unshakable certainty that she'd just handed the marshals a major break in the case.

Calm down, she told herself. *Keep working*. Break or no, she couldn't let up until Corby was actually in custody. She stopped pacing and stared at the timeline tacked to the wall. There were still too many blanks, and she needed to fill in the gaps.

A knock sounded at the door, and Dillon leaned his head in.

"You've got visitors. They say you're expecting them?"

"Yeah, send them in."

Dillon stepped back to let Brynn into the room. His gaze lingered on her ass while Brynn's bodyguard gave him an icy stare.

"Thanks for meeting us," Brynn said, taking a chair at the table. Erik took the one beside her, watching the door as Dillon closed it.

"You're working late," Brynn said.

Lindsey sank into a chair across from them. "I've been here all weekend."

"Alone?"

"For the most part."

It was an interesting phenomenon that Lindsey should have expected. With every day that ticked by, she spent more and more time on this case, and her colleagues spent less. Max had practically disappeared, and so had the other detective.

"You know, each day Corby eludes capture, we look more incompetent," Lindsey said. "I think everyone here wants to distance themselves, let the marshals go down in flames for this."

Brynn stood up and walked to the bulletin board, where crime-scene photos were arranged in clusters. She zeroed in on several photos of Corby's fourth victim, Lauren Tull.

"I remember these," she murmured.

"From the trial?"

"These two were on her Facebook page. We used them in a trial exhibit."

Lindsey could see why they'd selected the pictures. Besides showing the victim in life, with a dazzling smile on her face, they also showed her wearing the necklace that was later recovered from Corby's house.

"I've been pursuing your theory about the necklace being planted," Brynn said. "I went back through my trial notes and found some evidence that makes me think you're right."

Lindsey felt a wave of relief. For the first time since she'd come up with this idea, she had some support. "What have you got?"

Brynn returned to her chair. "We had some issues with the necklace from the beginning. Jen and I did. For one thing, there's no crime-scene photo of the necklace in situ at Corby's house."

"No?"

"This came out in deposition. Detective McGowan, who was the lead, said the necklace was discovered in the inside pocket of a canvas jacket found in Corby's closet. The jacket is brown, so it vaguely resembles a jacket worn by someone sighted near one of the crime scenes, which is why police took it into evidence when they conducted the search warrant. We have a crime-scene photo of the jacket hanging in Corby's closet. And McGowan said the necklace was discovered later, inside the pocket, when they were going through items in the evidence room."

"You think he lied?"

"I don't know. At the time, I thought maybe it was a simple mistake—he found the necklace in the pocket, so he vouched for the jacket. Or maybe someone found the necklace elsewhere at Corby's place, but somehow the crime-scene photographer missed getting a picture of it."

"If that happened," Lindsey said, "maybe McGowan was trying to keep that critical piece of evidence from being tossed out on a technicality, so he made up the jacket-pocket scenario, and Corby knew that was bullshit—hence his hatred for McGowan."

Brynn smiled thinly. "Chain of custody is hardly a 'technicality.' "

Spoken like a true defense attorney.

"Here's the thing," Brynn said. "I saw Mark Wolfe again yesterday. The profiler has been analyzing the case files, and he reached the same conclusion you did."

"He thinks the necklace was planted?"

"Not only that. He takes it a step further," Brynn said. "He believes Corby didn't kill Lauren Tull at all."

Lindsey's eyebrows shot up.

"Wolfe found discrepancies between Lauren's crime scene and the others, and he believes someone else killed her."

Brynn launched into a detailed summary of Mark's theory. When she got to the part about fabric fibers being found on Lauren Tull's mouth, Lindsey was puzzled. When she got to the part about the Rohypnol, Lindsey was intrigued. And by the time she reached the part about the necklace, Lindsey was speechless.

"So Mark believes the killer staged the scene to look like the other recent murders that had been all over the news," Brynn said. "And investigators bought it and played right into his hands when they planted that necklace at Corby's house to beef up their case against him."

Lindsey watched her, absorbing everything. A notorious serial killer framed for one—but not all—of his crimes. The idea was potentially explosive.

"What do you think?" Brynn asked. "This is the theory you came up with, just taken a step further."

"A big step." She looked from Brynn to Erik. As usual, the bodyguard was silent. By Lindsey's count, he'd said zero words since stepping in here. "To be honest, this sounds like something a defense attorney would cook up. No offense to you."

"None taken," Brynn said. "But I didn't cook this up. And the more I think back on certain aspects of the case, the more I believe this idea has merit."

"And why didn't Corby's attorney come up with it?"

"I couldn't tell you," Brynn said. "But the guy's a public defender, and he hasn't exactly set the world on fire, career-wise. Jen and I rolled over him at trial. Also, there was so much other evidence against Corby—the first victim's blood on his boot, the media clips at his house, the fact that Corby had done work at three of the victims' homes. The jury was looking at a mountain of evidence when they arrived at a guilty verdict."

"My other thought is if you're right, if Mark is right, then Dallas PD has a problem on its hands."

"They've got a rapist and murderer roaming free," Brynn said.

"Correct, and his trail is ice cold at this point. They've also got a corruption problem." Lindsey leaned forward. "Walk me through how you think this might have happened. How did Lauren Tull's necklace end up at Corby's house?" She nodded at the bulletin board where the photos were displayed. "By your own trial exhibits, it looks like Lauren wore that necklace a lot. Are you saying Mick McGowan or some investigator took it off the body? I don't know if you've ever been to a murder scene, but it's a zoo. People, vehicles, cameras everywhere. I can't picture McGowan just reaching down and tugging a necklace off the corpse. Too risky."

"I agree," Brynn said. "More likely, he—or someone—found it elsewhere in Lauren's home. Maybe on her dresser or something. This person might have pocketed it to use later, as an insurance policy when they zeroed in on a suspect. I think he kept it and either planted it at Corby's house or somehow got it into the evidence room."

Lindsey paused to think about it. "Evidence rooms—especially for a large department—are crowded and sometimes chaotic places. And people are people, so things can get lost or mishandled, either by mistake or intentionally. The reality is, it happens." She sighed. "I'd have to see the logs from the evidence room to pin it down better."

"Any chance you can get a look at those?"

"I could try. I have some contacts over there."

For a long moment, she and Brynn simply stared at each other. Lindsey had never expected to team up with a defense attorney on anything, and yet here they were.

"Why is Mark analyzing this now?" Lindsey asked. "I mean,

whether Corby killed Lauren Tull or not, he killed the other three. And he's killed three more people since escaping from prison. What we should be focused on right now is how to locate him."

"I'm with you," Brynn said. "Mark thinks motive could be important in determining his next move."

"Tell me what you're working on in terms of locating him," Erik said.

Lindsey looked at Erik, whose priorities clearly were aligned with hers. "I'm convinced Corby has someone helping him, offering him refuge. Otherwise, he wouldn't have been able to pull all this off."

"Agreed," Erik said.

"I got a new lead from that reporter, John Dewitt, who interviewed Corby in prison, hoping to write a book about him."

"That guy is *helping* him?" Brynn asked.

"No. He's in LA working for some magazine now. But I wanted to see what he could tell me about the prison interviews."

"And what did he tell you?" Brynn asked.

"Two interesting things. One, Corby vehemently proclaimed his innocence. Said he was set up, and the whole crooked system was out to screw him over. In light of this new theory, maybe that wasn't all just noise. The other thing he told me, Corby had a pen pal."

"Who?" Erik leaned forward on his elbows.

"Some woman named Ann Johnson—not sure of the spelling. The reporter said Corby once asked him to mail a letter to her."

"And he *did* it?" Brynn exclaimed. "That little shit."

"My guess is he was trying to rack up some favors with Corby to get an exclusive or something. But it may be how those letters ended up with you and the judge."

"I got another one this morning," Brynn said.

"Where?"

"Her house," Erik said darkly.

"Did you share this with the marshals?"

He nodded.

"Back to this pen pal," Brynn said. "Tell me her name again? And do we know her address?"

"It's Ann or Anne-with-an-e Johnson—not sure of the spelling. And Dewitt claims he doesn't remember where she lives."

"He's lying," Erik said.

"I'm inclined to agree, but what am I gonna do? It's not like I can sweat this guy down. He's in Los Angeles."

"I'll talk to someone."

Someone meaning the marshals in Los Angeles? Or did he have a bodyguard friend out there? Whatever he meant, Lindsey didn't want to know about it.

"However she spells her name, it's extremely common, which doesn't help us," Lindsey said. "There are hundreds in Texas alone. It's like looking for a needle in a haystack."

"Why Texas?" Brynn asked.

"It seems logical because she probably delivered those notes to you and Jennifer Ballard. But you're right, she could live somewhere else, such as Oklahoma or Louisiana."

"Run the name against owners of a black Honda," Erik said. "That should narrow it down."

"We're working on that," Lindsey said. "The task force is doing everything possible to find this woman, because we think she'll lead us to Corby."

Brynn looked at Erik, then Lindsey. "We should let you get back to work." They stood, and Lindsey did, too. Brynn started for the door, but Erik stopped her and turned around.

"One more thing," he said to Lindsey. "If this necklace thing wasn't McGowan, then you've got a cop out there who knows the man he framed for murder is out of prison. He's bound to be getting nervous, and he's not going to like it if he hears you're digging into this."

"I'm aware," Lindsey said.

Erik pulled a business card from his pocket and handed it over. "If you're worried about anything, call us. Day or night, we'll get somebody on it."

She laughed. "You're saying *I* need protection? I'm a cop, for Christ's sake."

Erik nodded. "I'm saying be careful."

23

ERIK SHOWED up at Brynn's on Sunday night and found Hayes stationed in the lobby as part of her expanded security detail.

"She up there?" Erik asked him.

"In the fitness center, yeah."

Erik took the elevator to the top floor. The lights were on in the gym, but all the treadmills were empty. Erik recognized the tall, dark shadow standing beside the pool with his back to the windows. Tactically, it was a crap position, but he had a perfect view of the water.

Erik slipped through the glass door and stood in the darkness. The pool lights were on, and Brynn's body was a long silhouette gliding through the turquoise glow.

Erik walked up and clamped a hand on Trent's shoulder, making him jump.

"Shit, man! I didn't hear you come out."

"I noticed."

Trent shook his head, cursing.

"How's the shift going?" Erik asked.

"It's almost over." He checked his watch. "Only an hour."

"I got this. You can take off."

Trent glanced at the pool, looking hesitant. "You sure?"

"Yeah."

Another look at his watch. "Skyler's down in the control room," Trent said. "Are you here in the morning? Liam told me to report to the hospital to help cover Ross."

"Hayes and I are driving Brynn to work," Erik said. "I think she wants to stop by the hospital after, so I'll probably see you there."

"Okay, later, then."

Erik watched him leave, then lowered himself onto the end of a lounge chair near the side of the pool. He tipped his head back to look at the half-moon peeking through the clouds, and for the first time in hours, he felt his shoulders relax. A warm breeze swept over him, and he heard the distant hum of traffic at street level.

His gaze settled on Brynn. She did a quick flip turn and shot through the water, breaking the surface with a smooth stroke. Erik watched her, transfixed.

Watching Brynn was becoming an obsession, and it worried him. He liked watching her in court, arguing from the lectern. He liked watching her on the treadmill. On her sofa. In her kitchen. He liked watching her in bed underneath him, her head tilted back and her skin fever-hot as she came apart.

Maybe he was torturing himself being here, but he couldn't *not*. The threat was escalating, and he wouldn't put her safety in anyone else's hands.

She caught his eye as she reached for the edge of the pool. She stopped to look at him, and the water swirled around her.

"Hi," she said, panting. She wore her plain black Speedo, which shouldn't have looked sexy, but it did.

"Pretty late for a swim."

"Long day. I needed to burn off some frustration." She pushed up on the concrete, hitching herself onto the side of the pool. She reached up to squeeze water from her ponytail. "Trent said you were off tonight."

He watched the water slide down her shoulders and into the valley at the base of her spine. "I was running some leads down. I'm back on shift in the morning."

She looked away, and he didn't know what she thought of that. Did she want him to spend the night here? Or was it easier if he didn't? For him, it was hell spending the night at his hotel. But it would be worse here, passing the night on her sofa while she was in a bed only footsteps away.

"Why was it a long day?" he asked.

She shifted to face him, propping her knee up and resting her arms on it. "Trial stuff. Trust me, you don't want to hear it."

She was wrong, but he let it go.

"How was Ross? You stopped by there earlier?"

She frowned. "He's tired. He looked okay, though. Better than I expected. I didn't tell him about Mark's theory."

"How come?"

"I don't know. He was all pale and hooked up to an IV. I just didn't want to lay anything new on him right then." She reached for a water bottle beside the chair, and he handed it over. "Anyway, where were you?"

"I interviewed that janitor at the Ames Theater. He stands by his first statement. It was a black Honda he saw in the parking garage. Dented back bumper, like the one Corby used Friday. But we haven't been able to track down any black Hondas registered to an Ann Johnson."

She swigged her water. "Who is 'we'?"

"The task force." Not that he was a part of it formally, but they were cooperating.

She held his gaze, and he let himself look at her, all flushed from her swim, her hair slicked back from her face. His eyes went to the bead of water sliding between her breasts.

"Texas only?" she asked.

"They're expanding the search. I'll keep you posted."

"Thanks. Can you hand me my sweatshirt?"

He glanced around, then snagged the gray sweatshirt off the chair next to his and reluctantly handed it over. She pulled it on and stood up.

"Ready?"

"Sure."

She put on flip-flops, and they rode the elevator down to her floor without talking. The new camera they'd installed beside the elevator doors was up and running, Erik noticed.

He used his key to open the apartment, and the unmistakable smell of bacon made his stomach growl.

"Wait here," he said, leaving Brynn beside the door while he did a quick walk-through. When he was finished, she went into her bedroom.

Erik dropped his keys on the counter and glanced at the TV, which was muted and tuned to a local news broadcast. Nothing about Corby. But it was the end of the hour, and the manhunt had been the top story all weekend.

Brynn returned to the living room, still wearing the sweatshirt, but she'd changed out of her swimsuit and put on the frayed cutoffs she loved to wear.

"Someone make breakfast for dinner?" he asked.

"We had BLTs."

She had to mean Trent, and Erik ignored the twinge of jealousy.

"Want one?" she asked. "I made extra bacon."

"I'm good."

"You ate dinner?"

"I had a protein bar."

She rolled her eyes and walked past him into the kitchen. "So your team is working with the marshals now, I take it?"

"We're cooperating." He went into the kitchen as she took items from the fridge: beer, mayo, a cellophane-covered plate. She grabbed the loaf of bread from the basket on the counter and took out several pieces.

"Is this willingly or . . . ?" She trailed off as she dropped the bread into the toaster.

"We don't mind cooperating. They've got the best databases, so it makes sense to share intel."

She nodded, quickly slicing a tomato. She put the plate of bacon into the microwave. When the bread was finished, she slathered mayonnaise on it and assembled the sandwich—three layers tall—and Erik's mouth watered just looking at it.

"Get me a couple of plates, would you?"

He turned to the cabinet behind him and took down two small plates. She cut the sandwich into neat triangles, then arranged the sections on a plate and handed him one.

"Thanks."

"Bon appétit."

The dining-room table was blanketed with paperwork. Brynn set her plate on the coffee table. Erik took a seat on the sofa and left room for her beside him, but she took the armchair.

She grabbed the remote and turned up the volume as she chomped into her sandwich.

"Why was your day frustrating?" he asked again.

"Oh, you know. Work stuff." She shrugged.

Erik eyed the dining table as he ate. She worked harder than any client he'd ever had, going at it evenings and weekends. And if her house was any indication, she worked in her downtime, too.

Brynn's home had surprised him. He wouldn't have expected her to be a do-it-yourselfer. But he was learning that despite having read her file, there were plenty of things he didn't know about her.

She filled her time with work. Erik did, too, so he understood. The less time on his hands, the better. When he had a lot of free hours, it was too easy to think about everything lacking in his life. Such as a life.

"You really want to hear about my day?" she asked.

"Yes."

She nibbled on her sandwich and licked mayonnaise off her thumb. "Okay, you know Perez, right?"

"Your MIA witness."

"Except he's no longer missing. Bulldog brought him back from Las Vegas, and now they're holed up together in a two-room suite at the Four Seasons, on the law firm's nickel."

"So what's the problem?"

"I spent the afternoon with this guy. You know, running him through his testimony. This was originally Ross's job, getting him prepped for trial."

"And?"

She blew out a sigh. "And I've got a bad vibe."

"What do you mean?"

"Some people are good in front of a jury; some aren't. This witness could go either way, but I'm not feeling confident about it." She leaned back in the armchair. "I have a feeling Conlon's going to get to him."

"And you need him for what?"

"To alibi my guy. He's the heart of our case. We've got some forensics stuff to present, too, but this guy was supposed to be the emotional anchor. Perez swears he and Justin were at his girlfriend's apartment watching a Spurs game at the time of the murder."

"Perez's girlfriend or Justin's?"

"Perez's. They have a kid together."

"Can you put her on the stand?"

"I would. But she wasn't there at the time, so she didn't see Justin coming and going. It's all up to Perez." She closed her eyes. "I made a promise to the jury in my opening statement that I'd show them Justin wasn't guilty of this crime." She looked at Erik. "It's like a commandment with defense attorneys: thou shalt not disappoint the jury. And now I'm worried my main witness is going to fall apart on the stand."

Erik wanted to ease her mind, but he didn't know what to say. He knew jack shit about practicing law.

"Let's not talk about it anymore." She sighed. "I won't be able to sleep tonight."

Erik finished his sandwich down to the last crumb. Brynn rested her feet on the edge of the table, and he tried not to think about her shiny pink toenails. Her fingernails were pink, too. And he had to truly be losing his mind if he was noticing nail polish now.

"Trent tells me you guys are off to Hawaii next."

He looked up. "He told you that?"

"You're working for some actress who's on location?"

Erik pushed his plate away. "She's filming a new series. Something on HBO." Erik had never heard of the woman, but she'd been getting death threats. Or so her manager claimed. Erik had reviewed the case with Liam, and they both agreed there was a chance the manager was making it up as a publicity stunt. They'd find out soon enough.

Erik looked at Brynn, not happy that Trent was telling her all about their next gig. Now Brynn was focused on him leaving, when he was still trying to gain her trust. He didn't want her to think she had anything less than his full attention.

"Well, aren't you excited?" she asked. "I've never been to Hawaii, but I hear it's gorgeous."

"So they say."

Her gaze narrowed. "You don't like the travel, do you?"

"I don't think of it as travel. Not like you mean. If the job's done right, it's consistent no matter where we are. Location is secondary."

She tipped her head to the side, studying him.

"What?" he asked.

"Are you ever going to tell me why you left the Secret Service?" She didn't say "quit" this time.

"I can't talk about the details."

"Oh, come on. I'm a lawyer. I'm good at keeping confidences."

He shook his head.

"Then don't give me details," she said. "Broad brushstrokes are fine. What happened?"

"Why do you want to know?"

"Because. You know everything about me."

"Not everything."

"You know a lot. And I don't even know why you left the job you loved."

"How do you know I loved it?" he asked, even though she was right, and he *had* loved it, at least in the beginning.

"Because." She shifted on the chair to face him, like she was settling in for a story. "You went through a rigorous application process, then seven months of training, and then you spent years working your way up to one of the most sought-after assignments out there. And then—*snap*—you left. Something must have happened."

She'd been doing her homework. He watched her watching him with those bottomless blue eyes. And for the hundredth time, he wished she wasn't his client.

Erik felt a deep, consuming fear that his weakness for her was going to get her hurt.

Maybe he should open up to her. Maybe she'd understand where he was coming from and that he wasn't just some jerk who'd slept with her and now wanted nothing to do with her.

"You know, you talk about trust all the time," she said. "But it's a two-way street."

Brynn waited for him to say something. She'd learned to read his reactions, even though they were subtle. And she could see he didn't want to talk about this.

Which made her all the more determined to coax it out of him.

"Okay, so . . . broad brushstrokes." He gave her a stern look.

She nodded.

"You referred to our training. That's what it all goes back to, same as in the Marines." He paused. "We have a saying: The more you sweat in peacetime, the less you bleed in war."

The thought of him bleeding in a war or anywhere made her sick. But she kept her face blank.

"So training is key. People's lives depend on it." He leaned forward, resting his forearms on his knees. "We go through all sorts of drills—firearms, close-quarters combat, tactical driving. And it's not just a one-pass deal, something we do as trainees. It's ongoing. That's critical. These skills—especially the shooting—they have to be practiced over and over, until it's pure muscle memory. You follow me?"

She nodded.

"The average attack is over in less than three seconds. So there is no time—none—to hesitate or second-guess yourself. Your reaction must be instantaneous. It must disrupt the threat and save the life of your protectee. Three seconds. So we can't be slow on the trigger or sluggish or inattentive. That's what I mean when I say I have to be in the moment, every moment. In this job, there's no margin for error."

She gave another nod, and he paused to look at his hands.

"I was six years in, and I'd moved up the ranks. At this particular time, I was posted to a teenage principal."

Brynn lifted her eyebrow. Given the time frame, a teenager could have been one of four people in the president's or the vice president's family.

"For the sake of the story, we'll give her a code name. Butterfly."

"You guys really use those?"

"We do. Makes things easier over the radio. And every family's names begin with the same letter. Anyway, Butterfly was up in Boston visiting some friends over Christmas break, and we were with her. She told us she had plans to go out to dinner, but we'd already pretty much figured that was a ploy, because what she really wanted to do was slip out the back and go to a bar."

Brynn smiled. "She tried to ditch you guys?"

"All the time."

"Did she manage to do it?"

"On occasion, she did. She was actually pretty good at it. Which sucked, by the way. It never happened on my watch, but the few times it did happen, it was a shit show. 'Scuse my language."

"That is hysterical."

"No, it's not." His expression hardened. "Because one time when she tried to do it, somebody grabbed her."

"What do you mean, 'grabbed her'?"

"Some guy grabbed her in the back of the restaurant and locked her in the women's room."

"*Locked* her in there? Like held her hostage?"

He nodded. "This guy had been stalking her. He'd followed her all the way up from D.C., which was bad enough in itself. Then he saw his opportunity to get her alone without an agent, and he grabbed her."

Brynn put her hand to her chest. "You must have been freaking out."

"We were when we finally figured out what was happening. Due to some major gaps on our part, it took about ten minutes. And in the meantime, she's in there with him, and he's reading her a love letter."

"So he's crazy."

"Schizophrenic, as it turns out. It took another five minutes for us to send a female agent in to get her out of there. She posed as a civilian, let herself into the bathroom with a key, and pretended to be surprised to find them in there. Then she had the guy on the floor and cuffed in about four seconds flat."

Brynn shook her head. "I never saw this on the news."

"Nobody did."

"Was the girl okay?"

"Physically? Yeah. But she was traumatized. Scared the hell out of her. Scared the hell out of all of us." He looked down at his hands. "This guy had mental issues, which was dangerous enough. But if he'd been a foreign operator? Or someone with military training?" He shook his head.

Brynn watched him, wondering about everything he wasn't telling her.

"So . . . this wasn't your shift, but somehow you took the fall for it?"

"Shift doesn't matter. I knew about the guy, and he'd been on my radar for a while. I'd interviewed him, even. The reason he got to her was sloppiness, pure and simple. We were short-staffed across the board and cutting corners. People were skipping out on training routinely while supervisors looked the other way. On this assignment, we had too few people staffed, and the ones we did have were not on the ball. Every single agent on duty that night had worked over ninety hours that week. One had worked a hundred. You can't run a detail with people who are sleep-deprived and strung out on caffeine. Bottom line, it's dangerous."

Brynn watched his eyes. "What did you do?"

"I outlined a list of procedures that were being flat-out ignored because of staffing and budget issues, put it all in a letter, and handed in my resignation."

"You chose to leave?"

"I left in protest. But yeah, it was my choice."

"What happened to your protest letter?"

"Nothing. I'm sure someone buried it."

Not nothing. No way. Brynn would be willing to bet that letter had been buried only *after* someone made sure Erik was permanently blacklisted from the service.

"You know, Erik—"

"Don't say it."

"Say what?"

"I know what you're going to say, and I'm not interested in getting litigious. I left, end of story. And I'm better off where I am now."

She watched him, wondering if he really felt that way or if he'd just convinced himself. He couldn't go back now. His career with the Marines was over. His career with the Secret Service was over. This job in the private sector had to work out for him. Liam Wolfe's firm was one of the best in the business, and if Erik blew this opportunity, there was nowhere to go but down.

Brynn felt selfish for putting his job at risk. Sure, it took two to tango and all that, but she'd been determined to wear down his resistance. And she had.

He was watching her now, studying her reaction.

"You don't have to worry," she said, "about me saying anything."

"I know."

Did he really? He'd been slow to trust her, but he did. The last thing she wanted to do was break that trust.

Erik held her gaze, and she felt a familiar charge in the air, only this time it came with a zing of panic.

She wanted him to kiss her. She was suddenly swamped with memories, and she wanted him to make love to her again as he had the other night, when he'd been so forceful and tender, both at the same time. Just looking at him, she felt a bone-deep *craving* for him. It wasn't just his body or his hands or his mouth but his eyes that did it, the way he looked at her with such complete focus it made her heart melt.

She couldn't do this to him again. She cared about him too much. It was ironic, really. She wanted him close to her in every way, which was exactly why she needed to keep her distance.

She stood abruptly. "I should get to bed."

His gaze narrowed. "What's wrong?"

"Nothing. I have an early start tomorrow, so . . . thanks for talking."

He nodded.

She turned and walked away, leaving him alone with the TV until one of his teammates came to relieve him at twelve—which thankfully meant she wouldn't be bumping into him in the middle of the night.

"Brynn."

She turned around.

"I've been following the trial, and you're right about what you told Reggie."

She arched her eyebrows.

"The jury isn't buying what Conlon's selling. They want to hear your case. So good luck with Perez tomorrow."

Good luck? Wasn't he taking her to the courthouse?

"Aren't you driving me?" she asked.

"Yeah. I just mean good luck, you know, in case I don't get a chance to tell you tomorrow."

"You mean tell me something personal in front of Hayes."

He nodded, and for no logical reason, that hurt her feelings.

"I realize it's late in the game," he said, "but I'm trying to keep this aboveboard."

The *game.* Ouch.

"Hey, no worries, I understand." She forced a smile. "Good night."

———————

Erik felt itchy. Edgy. The constant low-grade tension he'd been feeling for days had ramped up tonight, and he couldn't shake it.

He didn't want to. The feeling was useful because it was instinctive. Erik had long ago learned to use his instincts, especially when they were trying to warn him.

Erik had given up on sleep at his hotel and returned to Brynn's apartment. Now he paused in the dim stairwell and listened.

No footsteps above or below. No groan of an elevator. At 0300, most of the building was asleep, and the hum of the AC duct overhead was the only sound.

He took the flights quickly. Reaching the bottom, he aimed his penlight at the recently installed surveillance cam. Everything looked in order. Erik slipped through the door and crossed the Atrium's deserted lobby, where the silence was broken by the gurgling fountain. He took the back exit near the parking garage and stepped into the muggy night, scanning the alley behind Brynn's building.

The alley had been a thorn in his side for days. The narrow strip of pavement had countless entry points, and short of setting up roadblocks, it was impossible to control traffic in and out, which created a security weakness. To make up for it, Skyler's team had installed half a dozen extra cameras at various corners, but Erik still wasn't satisfied.

Sticking to the shadows, Erik passed the entrance to the Atrium's parking garage. He made his way down the alley soundlessly, searching for threats. He passed Dumpsters and stacks of pallets where the air smelled of rotting garbage. He moved along the building adjacent to the Atrium's garage and emerged onto Commerce Street.

A small black four-door caught his eye. Engine off, no lights. It was parked at an empty meter a block from the Atrium, and a lone male sat behind the wheel. He wasn't moving or looking at a cell phone, just sitting there with his gaze trained on the building.

Erik approached from behind, careful to avoid his mirrors. He ducked low behind the car and waited. A minute ticked by. Two. He clenched his hand into a fist and made his move.

Erik pounded on the glass, and the man jumped.

"What the fuck?" he said, pushing open the door.

"You need to watch your mirrors."

Keith glared up at him. "Shit, Morgan. I could have shot you."

"First you'd have to notice me. Which you didn't."

He shook his head. "What's up, man? Everybody's asleep, right?"

Erik nodded, scanning the street in both directions. "Anything since midnight?" By "anything," he meant a black Honda or a white pickup truck.

"Caldwell made a pass around two, but other than that, nothing."

"Caldwell himself?"

"Yeah."

Erik was impressed. He would have expected the marshal to be tucked into bed next to his wife about now. Erik tapped on the top of the door.

"Stay awake," he said, and walked away.

Erik circled the block and approached the Atrium from the north this time. Traffic was light, but he could hear the distance whir of cars on a nearby overpass. Erik reached the six-story parking garage behind Brynn's building. He had been keeping an eye on it. The garage wasn't associated with the Atrium, and his team had no control over who came and went, so it was another source of concern. He checked the new security cams and looked around before taking the stairs to level two. He emerged from the stairwell and halted. Something was off. He stood motionless until he identified the issue. The light fixture near the elevator was out.

Erik surveyed the parked cars as he moved toward the shadowy alcove. He passed a row of steel cages where renters stored bikes, camping equipment, and other crap they didn't have room for in their apartments. When he reached the dim alcove, he took out his flashlight and crouched below the light fixture, noting the shards of glass on the concrete.

Thud.

Erik stood and turned, drawing his weapon. The noise had come from a nearby row of cars. Erik moved toward it, hyperalert for any sound or movement. No lights, no people. He reached the row and swept his flashlight beam between the cars. Beside the one on the end, he spied something small and white. A flattened cigarette butt. Erik knelt and touched the blackened end. Still warm.

An engine roared on the level below him. Tires shrieked. Erik ran to the wall and peered over as a black car sped down the side street and hooked a right onto Commerce. It was a Honda.

"Fuck!"

Erik made a call as he raced downstairs.

"Caldwell."

"I've got a black Honda on Commerce. It just exited a garage near the Atrium, and it's moving west. Where's your nearest unit?"

"Morgan?"

"Yes! I need a unit."

"Roger that. We've got someone on Pearl." Commotion on the other end as Caldwell talked to someone on a radio. "You said westbound?"

"Affirmative. Call me back."

Erik reached the sidewalk and ran for Keith's car. He pounded on the trunk before jumping into the passenger seat.

"Drive!"

"What? Where—"

"Pull a U-turn here."

Keith complied, pointing them westbound, and hit the gas. Erik quickly saw the problem. They were coming up on an interstate, which was near a major interchange. The only taillights in sight were a gray pickup and a white SUV. Had he turned off somewhere?

"Is it him? You saw him?" Keith was alert now, gripping the wheel.

"I saw a black Honda Civic."

The traffic light ahead went yellow.

"You're clear," Erik said. "Punch it."

Keith sailed through the intersection, glancing at Erik. They were almost to the interstate, which meant three choices.

"Hang a right," Erik ordered as Caldwell called back. "You have him?"

"No. We've got two units in the area, but they don't see him."

Erik scanned the cars ahead as they entered the freeway. Traffic was light, but there was no black Honda in sight. Keith pressed the gas, but Erik could already tell he'd made the wrong call. A major interchange came into view, and the choices multiplied.

"That interchange is a spaghetti bowl," Caldwell said. "He could be anywhere by now. Did you see the driver?"

"No, but there was someone staked out in the garage, having a smoke, with a clear view of the Atrium's north exit, the one facing the parking garage."

"You think it was Corby." It was a statement, not a question.

"Yes."

"That would be pretty ballsy, him getting so close after what went down Friday."

Which was exactly how Erik knew it was Corby. Everything he'd done till now had been a big fuck-you to law enforcement.

He heard Caldwell's muffled voice as he gave orders over the radio. After an endless wait, he came back on. "Morgan, I think we lost him. I've got two units there, and they're both saying it's a no-go. Wherever he was, he's gone."

"Head back," Erik told Keith. "We'll run the surveillance footage, see what we get."

"Why would Corby be there now?" Caldwell asked. "At three in the goddamn morning?"

"Maybe he's waiting."

Setting up an ambush, in other words.

"Shit. Who's taking Brynn Holloran to court tomorrow?"

"I am. Eight sharp."

"Okay, keep your eyes peeled," Caldwell said. "We'll be around."

So would Erik.

And his gut told him Corby would, too.

24

ERIK'S MOOD the next morning was extra-grim, and Brynn picked up on the tension as they rode the elevator down together. He and Hayes hustled her into the Tahoe at warp speed and then took a strangely circuitous route to the courthouse. Neither said a word the entire way.

Brynn didn't mind. She used the drive to calm her nerves and get in the zone. It was going to be lonely at the defense table without Ross. He was her support, her ally, always there to whisper a question or jot a note to help her through a cross-examination when she got stuck. The prospect of moving forward without him was more daunting than she'd admitted to Reggie, and she had hardly slept last night, tossing and turning with nightmares about her very first witness stumbling on the stand.

The nightmares didn't come close to reality. Perez crashed and burned.

He muddled through her questions with incomplete answers and inconsistencies, completely forgetting all the straightforward responses they'd painstakingly rehearsed together the day before. His testimony about his activities on the night of Seth Moore's murder was shaky at best, and Brynn knew that when Conlon got ahold of him, it was going to be a bloodbath.

It was. By the time the prosecutor finished his cross-examination, it had come out that although Perez had spent much of his evening at his girlfriend's apartment, he hadn't been alone. Perez revealed—to Brynn's utter surprise—that a female "friend" had shown up while he and Justin were watching basketball, and Perez had been with her in the bedroom for the second half of the Spurs game.

Justin's alibi was shredded.

When Perez finally finished his testimony and slunk out of the courtroom, Conlon looked triumphant, Brynn was reeling, and the jurors were eyeing her with suspicion, no doubt wondering what had possessed her to put Perez on the stand to kick off her case.

The jury was disappointed in her, Brynn could tell. One witness in, and already she'd broken a commandment. Linden smacked his gavel for the lunch break, and Brynn watched the jurors file from the courtroom with a knot of dread in her stomach. The bailiff led Justin out, and Brynn suppressed the urge to scream.

Her client had held out on her. It had happened before, and she should be used to it by now. But she felt gut-punched.

She grabbed her attaché case. For the first time all day, she was grateful to be alone at the defense table so that none of her colleagues could witness the disaster. She left the courtroom trailed by Hayes and saw Conlon duck into the men's room.

Brynn followed him. She glanced over her shoulder and noticed Hayes's worried frown as she pushed open the door.

Conlon stood at a urinal. The man beside him took one look at Brynn, then quickly zipped up and scuttled away.

"Counselor."

The prosecutor looked over his shoulder and scowled. "Well, well. You must really be desperate if you're looking for deals in the john."

"I'm not here for a deal."

"Oh, yeah?" He zipped up and turned around. "You sure? I've got an alphabet soup of evidence—GSR, DNA, the list goes on."

She smiled. "I'm here with a little reminder that witness tampering is a felony. My investigator knows about that plane ticket *and* the suite at the Bellagio."

He tipped his head to the side. "Damn, you *are* delusional, aren't you?"

"And if I can prove you knew about it, you will be disbarred. Oh, and sent off to prison, too, with some of the people you helped put away."

He shook his head.

"Have a nice day," she said, and walked out.

Erik surveyed the street from his lofty perch, searching for any sign of Corby or one of his known vehicles. The military-grade binoculars brought everything into razor-sharp focus as he monitored traffic and pedestrians a thousand feet below. No one looked up—not once—but Erik wasn't surprised. People never seemed concerned about or even aware of the possibility of being observed from above.

Erik's phone buzzed, and he dug it from his pocket.

"Hey, what's your twenty?" Jeremy asked.

"I'm on the roof of the courthouse."

"We just got a lead."

Erik's pulse picked up, and he waited, still peering through the glass.

"There's an Ann K. Johnson living in Fort Worth. Husband, Gary. He's got a black Honda Civic registered to his name. And get this— he's dead."

"The husband?"

"Yeah, Gary Johnson. Died a year ago. So maybe his wife's using his car."

"Or lending it out."

"Exactly."

"Sounds promising," Erik said. "The marshals finally got something."

"This came from Leary. She called me five minutes ago."

"Figures. That detective's sharper than all those marshals put together." Erik lowered the binoculars and skimmed the street in front of the courthouse. The sun blazed down on him, roasting him through his starched dress shirt.

"They're going to swing by the address," Jeremy said, "see if anything raises a flag. I'm planning to go, if you want to come."

"I'll stay here with Brynn."

"You sure? Isn't she in court?"

She was, along with two dedicated agents and a sheriff's deputy, but Erik wasn't going anywhere. "I'm sure."

"Okay. How's it going there?"

"Quiet."

Too quiet.

Erik lifted the binoculars again, unsure why he felt that way, but he did. Something was wrong. The air was too hot, too still, too saturated with sunlight. The conditions felt ripe for . . . something. He didn't know.

Jeremy picked up on his tension.

"Stay alert," he told Erik.

"Roger that."

25

"THE DEFENSE calls Joseph Rivas."

Surprise flickered across Conlon's face, but he quickly covered it. Brynn had done some haystacking of her own, and she could see the prosecutor hadn't expected her to call one of Justin's friends, who had at no time mentioned seeing Justin on the night of the murder.

Joseph Rivas was sworn in. The lanky nineteen-year-old wore black jeans—no rips, per Brynn's advice—and a belt to keep them from falling down his hips.

"Mr. Rivas, could you please tell us where you were on the night of March fifth?"

He cleared his throat and nodded. "I was at Justin Sebring's house playing Call of Duty."

"And was Justin there with you?"

"No, ma'am."

It was the only time Brynn didn't mind being called ma'am, because it made her witness seem respectful.

"What time did you arrive at Justin's house?"

"Eight fifteen. I went over straight after work."

"I see. And who answered the door?"

"No one. I just walked in. Aunt Sylvia leaves it open."

"Aunt Sylvia. Do you mean Sylvia Sebring, Justin's mother? Is she your aunt?"

"No, everyone just calls her that. She lets us hang there, eat, play games. Whatever. We come and go."

"Okay, so you arrived at the house, and did you see Justin's mother, Sylvia?"

"Yeah, she was in the kitchen."

"And where was Justin?"

"She said he was out watching the ball game—"

"Objection, hearsay." Conlon stood up.

Linden looked at Brynn. "Sustained."

"Was Justin there when you arrived?" Brynn asked.

"No."

"Were you surprised not to see him there?"

"No. I'd seen him earlier at work. He told me he was going to Perez's girlfriend's place to watch basketball that night."

"Mr. Rivas, where do you work?"

"Over at Chicken Stop. The one on Bissell Street."

"And you'd seen Justin there earlier that day?"

He nodded.

Brynn smiled. "Could you please answer yes or no, for the court reporter?"

He glanced at the judge. "Sorry. Yes. He came in at lunch, and we talked while I rang up his food."

"I see. And could you tell us what you wear to work, Mr. Rivas?"

Conlon stood. "Objection, relevance."

"Your Honor, the relevance will become clear in a moment."

Linden nodded. "Overruled."

"Mr. Rivas? What do you wear to work?"

"A red T-shirt with the Chicken Stop logo on the front. It's a yellow chicken."

"Before you worked at Chicken Stop, did you work at any other fast-food restaurants?"

"Burger Shack."

"And did you have a uniform there, too?"

He nodded. "A blue T-shirt with—"

"Objection, relevance." Conlon sounded annoyed now.

"Your Honor, as I said, the relevance will become clear momentarily." She shot Conlon a look.

"Soon, Ms. Holloran. Overruled."

"Thank you. Did either of your employers give you the shirt you're required to wear at work?"

"No, ma'am. I mean, they gave it to me, but they docked the money out of my first paycheck."

"And how many uniform shirts do you have for your current job?"

"One."

"Only one?"

"Yeah, I have to wash it at night if it gets dirty."

"And have you ever lost your work shirt?"

"No. I keep up with it."

"If you ever did lose it, would your employer buy you a new one, or would the new shirt come out of your paycheck, too?"

Conlon stood and made a show of tossing down his pencil. "Your Honor, once again, the state objects. This line of questioning has no bearing whatsoever on—"

"Sustained. Move on, Ms. Holloran."

Brynn glanced at the jurors. They looked confused, but at least Conlon's objections had drawn attention to her questions.

"Mr. Rivas, you said Justin dropped by Chicken Stop earlier in the day and mentioned plans to watch a basketball game with his friend, so was it odd to go to Justin's house that night, knowing he wouldn't be there?"

"No. Like I said, we hang there."

"Who is 'we'?"

"People in the neighborhood. You know. Whoever's around. Aunt Sylv doesn't care."

She nodded. "And when you arrived at Justin's house, did you see Justin's car in the driveway?"

"No."

"Did you at any time leave Justin's house that night, say, to take a break from video games?"

"Yeah, around ten, I ran down to the store on the corner to get a Gatorade."

She glanced at Conlon and was pleased to see he looked bored with this testimony. "And when you returned, did you see Justin's car in the driveway or parked near the house?"

"No."

"Okay, then what happened?"

"Then I was in the living room playing Call of Duty, and Justin's cousin showed up. His name's Joel, but we call him Stretch."

"Joel Sebring. And you know this man? Justin's cousin?"

"Yeah, he lives next door."

"Had you seen him recently?"

"Not in a while. He got popped for dealing meth and went away—"

Conlon leaped to his feet. "Objection, Your Honor! The state requests a sidebar."

"Counselors." Linden gave Brynn a stern look as she and Conlon approached the bench.

"Your Honor," Conlon said in a low voice. "I object to this entire line of questioning. I don't know who this Joel person is, but—"

"Your Honor, we've established that Joel Sebring is the defendant's cousin who lives next door."

"Your Honor, the defense is clearly trying to muddy the waters here by bringing up an outside party with a criminal record, whose presence has *no* bearing on the criminal matter at hand."

"His presence has bearing on everything, Your Honor, I can assure you," Brynn said. "If you'll indulge me just a few minutes longer, I will demonstrate the relevance."

Linden glared down at her over his reading glasses. "A very few minutes, Ms. Holloran. Make it quick."

"Thank you, Judge."

She felt Conlon's stare boring into her as she walked back to the lectern. Brynn could tell he still didn't see where she was going, but wherever it was, he didn't want her to get there. And despite what he'd told the judge, Conlon knew exactly who Justin's cousin was. The man had done four years for dealing drugs and was currently out on parole.

Brynn returned her attention to the witness. "Mr. Rivas, you said you were playing a video game when Justin's cousin Joel showed up at Justin's house. Could you tell us what Joel was wearing when he entered?"

He nodded. "Jeans. A black hoodie. And his work shirt."

"And how do you know it was his work shirt? Did he tell you he'd been at work?"

"No, but his shirt had the name of the car-wash place on it. Right across the front."

"I see." She glanced at the jurors, who were watching the witness, clearly intrigued by this new mention of work shirts. "And what did Joel do when he arrived?"

"We talked some. And then he went in the kitchen to get a drink. He threw his shirt in the wash and sat down, and we hung out for a while."

"You say he threw his shirt in the wash? You saw him do that?"

"I saw him throw it on the washing machine. It's one of those stand-up ones, and it's in the kitchen."

He meant stacking washer-dryers, but Brynn let it go. The jury was riveted now.

"Did Joel say why he took his shirt off when he showed up at his aunt's house to hang out?"

"Yeah, he said he was hot."

"And what about the hoodie?"

"He put it back on after he took off his shirt."

"Thank you, Mr. Rivas. No further questions."

Brynn had momentum. It put a tingle inside her.

Conlon tried to shake the witness on cross-examination. But he didn't make much progress, and soon it was Brynn's turn again.

She called her next witness to the stand, Henry Wheeler, a nationally renowned GSR expert who'd overseen a crime lab in Syracuse before retiring to write textbooks. After running through Wheeler's credentials, Brynn went straight to the topic of gunshot residue, guiding him through a series of questions that explained how someone could pick up gunshot residue from touching a surface where GSR had previously been deposited, such as a car steering wheel.

"This cross-contamination you talked about, Dr. Wheeler—is the same thing possible with DNA?"

Conlon shot to his feet. "Objection."

Linden lifted his eyebrows.

"Your Honor, the witness's textbook is about ballistics and gunshot residue, not DNA. This is not his area of expertise."

"Your Honor, Dr. Wheeler has multiple areas of expertise," Brynn said. "He possesses doctorates in microbiology and chemistry, and he used to run a crime lab. He's more than qualified to answer questions about DNA."

Linden gave Conlon a sharp look. "Overruled."

"Dr. Wheeler, is it possible for DNA to be transferred between locations in the way you just described for gunshot residue?"

The doctor nodded. "Yes, it happens a lot. You've got secondary transfer. Tertiary transfer."

Brynn cast a glance at Conlon, who was looking panicked.

"Can you give us an example of secondary transfer?"

"Yes. For example, a husband and wife share a bathroom. The husband comes home sweaty from work, wipes his face on a towel, then hangs the towel on top of a towel used by his wife. Now the wife's towel might show trace amounts of her husband's DNA."

"I see. Are there any other locations in a household where this type of transfer can occur?"

"Any number of places, if you've got multiple people sharing the same space. The bathroom. The laundry hamper. The washing machine."

Brynn looked at the jury. Their eyes were glued to the doctor. "This transfer of DNA can happen in a washing machine?"

"That's correct."

"What about if the dirty clothes in the machine are put through a cycle? Can trace amounts of DNA still be recovered?"

"Yes, that's right," he said. "They've done studies on the subject. When it comes to DNA, our methods of analysis are extremely sensitive now. Even after a cycle with detergent, trace amounts of DNA from bodily fluids can be found on the clothes."

"Bodily fluids, including blood?" she asked.

"Yes."

Brynn glanced at the jurors to see if they understood. Several did—she could tell by the appalled looks on their faces. Joel Sebring had taken his cousin's car to a drug deal, where he'd shot a man at close range. Then he'd gone over to his aunt's house to kick back and play video games before letting his cousin take the fall for the murder.

"And if an item of clothing with blood on it was put into a wash cycle with other items of clothing," Brynn said, "could those other items of clothing be contaminated with trace amounts of DNA from the blood?"

"That's quite possible, yes."

She glanced at Conlon. The prosecutor looked stricken. This one witness had raised reasonable doubt about every scrap of forensic evidence the prosecution had put forward—from the gunshot residue on the steering wheel and Justin's hands to the traces of the victim's DNA found on Justin's clothing. Brynn could have kept hammering, but she sensed it was better to quit while she was ahead.

"Thank you, Dr. Wheeler. No further questions."

Before Conlon could get up for his cross-examination, Linden hit his gavel and announced the afternoon break. Brynn watched the jurors file out. This time, when she left the courtroom, she was walking on air.

She turned to Hayes. "Did you *see* that?"

"I did, yeah."

She glanced around the crowded hallway, but Erik wasn't there. He'd missed her humiliation this morning, but he'd missed her redemption, too. It didn't matter, though. The jury had seen it, and that was what counted. For the first time in days, Justin had a fighting chance.

A deafening squeal pierced her ears.

"Fire alarm," Hayes said.

Someone grasped Brynn's arm, and she turned around to see Keith.

"What—"

"Get her out of here," Keith ordered.

They each grabbed an arm and propelled her down the hall.

"What? Where are we going?"

"In the event of an emergency, our orders are to get you to a secure location," Hayes said, plowing through the crowd.

"What location?"

"The holding cells downstairs."

———

Erik rushed down the stairwell, straining to hear over the earsplitting noise. Evacuees from dozens of courtrooms and administrative offices clogged the stairs.

"Hayes, report!" he yelled into his radio.

"We've got Brynn. One of the bailiffs said it's"—static blared over the radio—"threat."

"Hayes, repeat."

"It's a bomb threat. Someone just called it in."

Erik didn't like a bomb threat, especially one that was called in over the phone. *Callers don't bomb, and bombers don't call.* It was a saying he'd picked up during his training. Most phone-in threats turned out to be fake, whereas real bombers typically struck without warning.

"I don't like it," he told Hayes.

"You think it's a hoax?"

"I think it's Corby. Get Brynn to a holding cell ASAP." Erik pushed past the crowd, sliding down a banister. Five levels to go. "Do *not* leave her side. You copy?"

"Copy that."

"I'll be right there."

The holding cells were full.

People jostled her from every direction as bailiffs and sheriff's deputies pulled prisoners through the hallway. It was mayhem, with way too many sweaty, overheated bodies squeezed into way too tight a space.

Keith pulled Brynn against the cinder-block wall and shielded her with his bulk.

"All the rooms are full," he told Hayes.

"We can't stay in here." Hayes looked up and down the hallway, clearly unnerved by the crowd.

Brynn was unnerved, too. This part of the courthouse typically was run with careful precision, but the fire alarm's constant wail and the sudden evacuation of hundreds of people had turned everything topsy-turvy. Brynn couldn't help thinking of all the ways someone with nefarious intent might take advantage of the confusion.

A towering prisoner in an orange jumpsuit eyed her across the crowded corridor. He had a shaved head and tattoos circling his thick neck. He grinned at Brynn and unfurled a long, pierced tongue.

Hayes stepped closer, blocking the view. "We can't stay here," he said again.

"The armored car." Keith nodded at the exit. A uniformed cop stood in the open doorway, and beyond it, Brynn saw the Tahoe parked beside a traffic cone.

Hayes nodded. "Let's go."

Each grabbed an elbow, and they pulled her through the throng of people, pushing aside bodies as they made their way to the exit. The alarm was even louder outside, echoing off the concrete walls of the parking garage, but Brynn felt relieved as she managed to get a breath of fresh air.

Keith glanced around, hyperalert as he took out the key fob and popped the locks. "I'll take the wheel; you take the back."

Hayes steered Brynn to the back passenger door. She caught her reflection in the tinted glass of the window.

Corby loomed behind her.

Brynn's heart seized. Corby's eyes met hers in the reflection as he reached up, and Brynn spotted the weapon in his hand.

Boom!

A bone-jarring force slammed her to the ground.

———

"Hayes, report! *Report!*"

Nothing.

Erik pushed through the crowd and reached the first floor. But there was only one exit, and it expelled him onto the sidewalk on the building's west side. He cut through the mob, working his phone as he ran for the north side of the building.

Hayes didn't answer. Neither did Keith.

Erik traded his phone for his pistol and ran faster, his heart hammering as he dodged clusters of people. Even with the ongoing alarm and the chaos, he *knew* he'd heard a gunshot, and fear gripped him as he raced for the prisoner bay. Sirens filled the air as sheriff's cruisers and fire trucks responded to the emergency. A long red ladder truck pulled into the road beside the parking garage, blocking his view.

A man caught Erik's attention. The sidewalks were packed with people walking or milling around, but this guy was *running* right toward him.

Corby.

His gaze locked on Erik. Recognition flickered, and the man suddenly darted into traffic. Horns blared, and Erik took off after him. Corby had something in his hand. A gun? A knife? The man cut between two cars and bolted down the sidewalk as Erik dialed 911.

Erik sprinted faster, closing the distance as he relayed his position and told the operator he was in pursuit of the state's most wanted fugitive.

Corby reached a clear patch of sidewalk near the park. Erik halted and raised his weapon. *Shit.* Too many people. Erik took off after him again. Corby hurdled over a bench and ran into the park. He raced across the grassy lawn, jumping over people stretched out on towels and picnic blankets. He ran past a fountain, then veered toward a playscape crawling with children.

Erik cursed and poured on the speed. His legs burned. His lungs felt tight. His heart was about to burst as he sprinted as fast as he could. Corby cut through a swing set and hurdled another park bench to come out on Commerce Street, where traffic was stopped at a red light.

Erik saw the move before it happened. Corby raced up to a man on a motorcycle, punched him in the chest, and dragged him off. Erik reached the sidewalk just as the light turned green and Corby hopped on the bike.

Erik ran in front of an idling delivery truck and raised his pistol, aiming carefully at the motorcycle's back tire.

Pop! Pop!

Corby's bike tipped sideways, skidding out from under him. He slid across the pavement and tumbled into a parked car.

Erik bolted after him, tackling him when he tried to get up. They crashed to the ground, smacking into the tire of a parked pickup.

A fist connected with Erik's jaw, and his head snapped back. Erik struck back with a brutal left hook and caught a glint of metal as Corby's arm swung down.

Knife.

Erik grabbed Corby's wrist, squeezing it as tight as he could while using his other hand to shove his pistol against the man's neck.

"Drop it!"

But Corby didn't drop it. He struggled to hold the knife, straining against Erik's grip until his face was red.

"Out of the way! *Out of the way!*"

Shouts surrounded them, and Erik recognized a voice.

"U.S. Marshals! You're under arrest!"

Erik squeezed harder, felt the crunch of bone. Corby snarled, and the knife clattered to the ground. Erik heaved Corby up and onto his back, pinning his empty hand on the concrete beside him.

"Morgan! Move off! We've got this!"

Erik glanced up to see Art Caldwell in a black flak jacket. He had his pistol in a two-handed grip, aimed at Corby's head. Another pair of marshals ran up beside him, weapons drawn.

"Move off, Morgan."

Erik wasn't moving anywhere. "Cuffs," he demanded.

Caldwell glowered at Erik.

"Cuffs!"

The marshal nodded at one of his men, who tossed Erik a pair of handcuffs. Erik lifted the knee pinning Corby's thigh and flipped him onto his stomach. He jerked Corby's arms behind him and wrestled the cuffs on. Then he stood up and stepped back, breathing hard, as the marshals swooped down and hauled Corby to his feet.

Where was Brynn? Sirens wailed, and Erik felt a sickening pang of fear as he reached for his phone.

Caldwell crouched beside the knife, then frowned up at Erik. "Shit, did he get you?"

"No. Why?"

The marshal moved, and Erik saw the crimson-tipped blade.

"Then who the hell's blood is that?"

26

ERIK PLOWED through the doors and searched the emergency room. He didn't see her. He checked the hallways, the doorways, the vending-machine alcove. He cut through the rows of chairs, scanning the faces of everyone sitting and standing.

He spied her near the intake desk, arguing with a woman in blue scrubs, and Erik's heart lurched as he saw the blood on her white blouse. He moved toward her like a guided missile.

"I want to talk to your supervisor," Brynn was saying.

The woman looked pissed. "He's on break."

"Then I want to talk to *his* supervisor. Right now." She fisted a hand on her hip. "I've been here twenty-two minutes, and I demand to speak to someone in charge."

The woman glared at Brynn, then turned and disappeared through the double doors.

Erik stepped up to her, feeling like someone had two hands clutched around his throat.

"Erik, thank God! Hayes is back there."

"Are you okay?" He could barely get the words out as he took in all the blood on her. Her snowy white blouse was stained with it. Ditto her skirt and shoes.

"Corby came at us in the parking garage," Brynn said. "Keith shot him, and Hayes pushed me to the ground, but then Corby took a swipe at me, only he hit Hayes, and—"

"Keith shot him?" Erik took her arm, trying to calm her. Or maybe himself.

"He *missed*, Erik. And then Corby took off, but Hayes is wounded. It looks bad."

The doors opened, and the woman in scrubs was back, followed by a man in a white lab coat. The stethoscope around his neck told Erik he was a doctor, but the zits on his face suggested otherwise.

"I'm Dr. Heuer." The young man looked from Brynn to Erik. "What seems to be the problem?"

Brynn stepped closer. "The *problem* is that you have a twenty-six-year-old patient back there who was the victim of a vicious stabbing. His face is sliced open, he's heading into surgery right now, and I'm being told there isn't a plastic surgeon on staff in this entire hospital! How can that be possible?"

He turned to the nurse, and she stood on tiptoes and whispered something in his ear.

"There are, in fact, several on staff," the man said, "but no one on call at the moment—"

"*That* is unacceptable."

"I'm sorry, but—"

"Do you mean to tell me, if your wife was in there under the knife, you couldn't find a plastic surgeon to come stitch up her face? We are in Dallas, Dr. Howser."

"It's Heuer."

"There is a country club ten minutes from here, and I bet I could find half a dozen plastic surgeons on the nineteenth hole! You get on the phone and get someone over here. *Now.*"

He frowned at Brynn. "I'm sorry, and you are . . . the patient's wife?"

"I'm his lawyer! And I guarantee we will be suing this hospital if my client receives substandard care while in your facility. Now, do you want to get on the phone before one of your first-year residents botches up this man's face?"

The doctor started to say something, then changed his mind. He turned to the nurse. "Page Dr. Glenn. Tell him it's urgent." Another glance at Brynn, and he went back through the doors. Brynn turned to the nurse, who walked off in a huff.

"I swear to God, I'm going to punch someone." Brynn turned to Erik. Tears welled in her eyes. "Erik, I hate it that he was hurt protecting me."

He pulled her into his arms. He wanted to know what happened. But first he needed to hold her and convince himself that she was really okay.

Erik kissed the top of her head and looked around. Keith stood in the hallway, talking on his phone—probably to Jeremy, who was on his way over with Skyler. The rest of the team was stationed in another wing of the hospital with Ross.

Brynn pushed away and looked up. "What happened to you? Where's Corby? Keith said something about an arrest?"

"Corby's in custody."

She stared up at him, those blue eyes swimming with angry tears. "You're sure?"

Erik could tell she didn't believe she was safe and probably wouldn't for a very long time.

"I'm sure."

Brynn refused to leave the hospital until Hayes was out of surgery and in recovery. The ER doc had tracked down a plastic surgeon, who put fifty-two stitches in Hayes's face between his forehead and his left ear. Brynn felt sick just thinking about it but also deeply grateful that Hayes had pulled through the surgery and hadn't lost an eye.

At the insistence of a tall, extremely pushy U.S. marshal, Brynn had then gone to a DPD substation with Erik for a debriefing with various investigators whose names she was too tired to remember.

It had been more of an interrogation than a debriefing. Brynn had sat alone on one side of a table for nearly three hours, recounting the same series of events. Fortunately, she was good at dealing with people who covered the same ground repeatedly, trying to ferret out inconsistencies. But being good at it didn't make it any less of a pain.

She stood in front of a vending machine now, hungry, thirsty, and too bleary-eyed to even read the labels on the buttons. She fed a few dollars into the machine and gave the top button a jab. Nothing happened.

"Excuse me, ma'am?"

She glanced up to see a marshal she recognized from several interviews ago. He was young and had a buzz cut, and he'd spent most of the interview staring at Brynn's bloodstained blouse.

"Deputy Caldwell is ready for you now."

"Who?"

"Deputy Caldwell. He's in charge of the task force. He's ready to hear your statement."

"I already gave a statement. Twice." She tried another button on the machine, to no avail. "I'm waiting for my friend to finish *his* statement, and then I'm going home."

"Ma'am, Deputy Caldwell—"

"—can read the report," Erik said, stepping up to them. He looked at Brynn. "You ready?"

"Yes."

"But sir—"

"It's after one," Erik said, taking Brynn's arm. "She's done."

They headed for the exit at the end of a long corridor. Brynn glanced around and noticed a woman in handcuffs being led from an interview room. She had frizzy brown hair and a marshal on each arm, and uniformed cops were moving aside to let her pass.

Erik pushed open the door, and they stepped into the humid night.

"Who was that?" Brynn asked.

"Ann Johnson."

"They found her?"

"She has a house in Fort Worth. They think Corby's been shacking up with her."

"She talking?"

"Not yet, but she will. She needs to explain Mick McGowan's truck in her garage."

Brynn looked back at the door, a glowing rectangle against the dark backdrop of the police station. They were well into the graveyard shift now, and even the employee parking lot had mostly cleared out.

Erik led her to the Tahoe and opened the passenger door before she could do it herself. He helped her in and buckled the seat belt around her like she was a child. She must really look bad.

She tipped her head back against the seat as Erik went around and hitched himself behind the wheel. The SUV felt hot, and she buzzed the window down as Erik exited the parking lot. Warm air swept through the Tahoe, whipping her hair around her face as Erik picked up speed.

Brynn closed her eyes, and Corby's face flashed into her mind—the instant before Keith's bullet had missed him and Hayes had tackled her to the ground, saving her life. She thought of Hayes in the hospital with his head wrapped in gauze.

"You tired?"

She looked at Erik. "No." She glanced out the window. "More like wired."

She couldn't even think of trying to sleep now. Each time her eyelids drifted shut, all she saw was Corby, with those cold, dead eyes. She shivered.

Erik glanced at her and buzzed up the window.

Brynn didn't want to go home. She pictured the dining table in her apartment with all her trial notes from the Corby case spread out across it.

"Let's get drunk."

Erik looked at her. "What, now?"

"Why not? Oh, I forgot. No drinking on duty."

"I'm not on duty."

She stared at him. Nerves flitted to life in her stomach, and she had to look away. Of course, he wasn't on duty. Not anymore. Not with James Corby safely in custody.

Tears burned her eyes, and she clenched her teeth with frustration. What the hell was wrong tonight? She was so damn emotional, it was embarrassing.

She felt Erik's gaze on her, but she couldn't look at him. He and his teammates had risked their lives today. Hayes was seriously injured, and Erik easily could have been, too.

Erik had gone way beyond the job Reggie had hired him to do. He'd not only protected her, but he'd eliminated the threat against her so she could feel safe again.

Well. As safe as it was possible to feel in a world where men like James Corby existed.

Erik had risked everything for her. He'd given her so much. But now the job was over, and he'd be leaving soon. And the mere thought of it put an ache in her chest.

"Brynn?"

She looked at him.

"I'd take you to a bar, but it's last call by now. You want to go home?"

"No," she said before she could think it through. "I mean, yeah, eventually. Not yet, though."

He just looked at her.

"Corby's mug shots are all over my dining table, and—"

"I get it."

"I know it's silly, but—"

"I get it, Brynn."

Silence settled over them, and she stared out the window. He was off duty now. Soon he'd be leaving. A few minutes ago, she'd been dead on her feet, but now she felt a surge of energy. Or maybe it was nerves.

They neared the turn for the Atrium. But Erik didn't put on his turn signal and sailed right past it.

She looked at him. "Where are we going?"

He hung a right on the next street.

"Do you trust me?"

"Yes."

"Good."

He pulled into the parking lot of the two-story business hotel. It was definitely nerves, not energy, making her jumpy now. Erik cut the engine, and Brynn slid out before he could say anything that would make an awkward moment even more so.

He came around and retrieved the attaché case from the back seat. She'd tossed it there hours ago on the way to the police station.

"Thanks," she said as he handed it to her. Her phone was inside, but she refrained from checking it. Today she'd done enough talking to last two lifetimes, and the only person she wanted to think about was standing beside her, digging a room key from his pocket. Silently, he led her through the lobby to a first-floor room, then opened the door and let her inside.

The room was dark but smelled clean. He switched on a lamp, and she surveyed the space in the dim glow. Two queen beds. Table. Chair. Dresser and television. She noted the army-green duffel bag on the floor in the corner.

Brynn set down her attaché case. "Is it just you?" She looked at him as he tossed his suit jacket over the chair.

"Just me."

He removed his holster and set it on the dresser, and for a moment they just stood there, watching each other, a few short feet and miles of distance between them.

She glanced at the beds again and felt another flurry of nerves.

"Don't go anywhere. I'll be back." He took the key card off the dresser and walked out.

Brynn glanced around the room again, and her gaze landed on the duffel. It wasn't even full, and she thought of the ridiculous number of suitcases in her apartment a few blocks away. He traveled light, which didn't surprise her. He was on the move constantly, going from place to place with his job.

She heard the traffic outside and the faint hum of pipes upstairs, and a wave of sadness hit her as she checked out the dull space. She stepped into the bathroom and switched on a light. Glancing in the mirror, she was stunned by the reflection looking back at her.

Her hair was windblown—but not in a good way. Her blouse was missing a button and stained with blood from when she'd held Hayes's head in her lap until the paramedics arrived. Around them had been chaos, but Hayes had lain there, blinking up at her and gurgling his own blood as it seeped into his throat.

Brynn switched on the faucet. She washed her face and her neck, then noticed the blood on her bra, too. She kicked off her shoes, took everything else off, and turned on the shower, casting a furtive glance through the door to see if Erik was back. She kicked the pile of clothes into the corner and stepped into the tub to stand under the hot spray.

It felt good, but she didn't linger. She rinsed off and then grabbed a too-small towel from the rack. The towel didn't even begin to cover her as she wrapped it around her body and stepped out of the bathroom.

She spotted some of Erik's clothes hanging in the closet. Dress shirts, mostly, and a pair of dark slacks—attire for his shifts at the courthouse. One of the white shirts was wrinkled and had clearly been worn recently. She grabbed it off the hanger and slipped into it.

Erik's scent enveloped her, and she soaked it up as she stepped into the bedroom to snoop again. She glanced around, buttoning the shirt as she surveyed the place he'd called home all this time he hadn't been with her. She felt deeply lonely for him, living this way.

Brynn had no business getting attached to this man. But too late. She was already attached. And the bitter fact that he was leaving soon didn't seem to matter to her heart.

She stepped to the dresser, flipping up the cuffs of Erik's sleeves. His sleek black pistol was there in the holster. Brynn ran her fingertip over the grip, imagining him holding it in his big, capable hand.

The more you sweat in peacetime, the less you bleed in war.

She startled as the door opened and Erik stepped inside.

She smiled. "Hi."

He stopped cold, looking her over.

He eased the door shut behind him and flipped the latch. He had a can of Coke in his hand and a bottle of bourbon tucked under his arm, and the heated look in his eyes sent a ripple of excitement through her.

Brynn summoned her confidence and sauntered over. "What's this?" she asked.

"Jeremy's stash." He stared down at her. "You're in my shirt."

"You mind?"

"No."

She took the Coke and the bourbon from him, then turned and set them on the table beside a pair of plastic-wrapped cups. She felt his gaze on her as she tore open the plastic.

He popped open the Coke.

"Straight for me," she told him.

He poured a generous shot in each glass, then handed her one. She tossed it back, squinting her eyes shut as the liquid scorched her throat.

"God," she said, choking.

He smiled and shook his head, then leaned back against the dresser as he drank his down in a smooth gulp.

"Pretty good at that for a teetotaler," she said hoarsely.

"I never said I was a teetotaler."

He set the cup aside and watched her, his heated gaze moving slowly from her bare feet to her freshly scrubbed face, lingering on everything in between. She recognized the look—she'd been dreaming about it, in fact, since their very first kiss—and anticipation rushed through her at the thought of what it meant.

Still watching her, Erik unbuttoned his shirt, revealing a snug-fitting white T-shirt. He tossed the dress shirt onto a chair and then paused to look her over again.

"What?" she asked.

"What?"

"Why are you staring?"

He shook his head. "Because." He stepped closer. "I'm afraid if I touch you the way I want to right now"—he reached out and traced the back of his finger over her nipple, sending a jolt of heat through her—"I'll freak you out."

"You won't freak me out."

He eased closer. "I'll scare you."

"You don't scare me." She looked up at him, and his hand curved around her breast. His other hand slid around her waist and brought her in tight against him.

"Brynn?"

"What?"

"You are so fucking sexy. You have no idea." He crushed his mouth down on hers before she could respond.

Her whole body caught fire. From his mouth and his hands and his hard body pressed against her. His kiss was hungry and insistent, and she slid her arms around his neck and kissed him back the same way. He tasted like she remembered—that sharp, male *Erik* taste, only mixed with bourbon now. It reminded her of everything she'd been yearning for for days.

What had they been doing, wasting all this time? All these nights, they could have been together, and he'd stoically held her at a distance and kept all this delicious need locked up when they could have been enjoying it. Just the thought infuriated her, and she curled her nails into his neck and kissed him harder.

She bit his lip, and he jerked back.

"Ouch."

"Sorry."

"No, you're not." He kissed her again, harder and deeper, and his hands slid around to grip her butt. She rolled her hips against him, making him groan, as she scraped her nails down the back of his arm.

She went up on her tiptoes and kissed his neck, right under his ear. "I'm mad at you."

"I can tell."

He took her mouth in another searing kiss, lifting her up as he did and wrapping her legs around him. She thought he'd take her to the bed, but he turned her back against the wall, pinning her there as he pulled at her shirt. A quick yank of the fabric. Buttons flew, and then she was bared to him. He dipped his head down and cupped her breast, pulling her nipple into his hot mouth.

"Erik." She tightened her legs around him. "Harder."

Heat shot through her as he did what she asked. She reached down for the hem of his T-shirt, and he paused what he was doing to pull it over his head and toss it away. But then he was back again, stroking his hands over her breasts and making her crazy.

She loved everything he was doing to her, with his mouth and his fingers and the weight of his body. She reached between them, fumbling with his belt until she finally got it open. He shifted her in his arms and unfastened his pants, and she reached down to free him from his clothes. When she had him in her hand, she gave a hard squeeze that made him groan.

He took her mouth, delving his tongue inside her as he clutched her hips. She wanted him now, just like this. He paused to look at her and seemed to know what she wanted, because he adjusted her weight, leaning her back against the wall as he lowered her onto him. Pleasure blazed through her, and she tipped her head.

"Yes. More."

He shifted her hips as she clasped her legs around him. And then he started moving, pushing into her over and over, pressing her against the wall.

"Am I hurting you?"

"No."

Only he was. But it was a good hurt. The more power he unleashed, the more she wanted. She wrapped her arms around him, clinging to him as it went on and on, until she felt the room start to spin.

Was this what he'd thought would scare her? It didn't. It felt so amazingly good, and right, and she couldn't believe they'd resisted this. She kissed his shoulder, tasting his salty skin. Then she sank her teeth into muscle, spurring him on.

The tension inside her coiled tighter. She clenched herself around him, pulling him as close as she could, until she shattered and broke apart, and he seemed to know the instant it happened, because he went rigid, holding her through the aftershocks.

She let her head fall back against the wall. He pulled away and looked at her, his gaze intense.

Shifting her weight to one arm, he held her against him as he got rid of his pants and walked her the few steps to the bed. He lowered them onto it and kissed her forehead.

"Still with me?"

She nodded dazedly, coming down to earth, and he settled his weight on her and started a new, completely different rhythm. She held on to his shoulders, trying to catch her breath. She couldn't, though, because he was moving against her, deep and slow, building the fire all over again.

She closed her eyes and slid her hands over his arms, then up his back, loving the ripple of muscles under her hands, the sheer power of his body.

"Brynn."

She opened her eyes. He brushed her hair from her forehead, and the heat in his gaze sent a surge of joy through her. She'd never felt so desired, ever. And she'd never desired someone like this, with every cell of her body and every corner of her soul.

"More," she whispered.

He obliged, moving harder and faster as she clutched him to her and let the desperate need build and build.

"Erik."

"Tell me."

"Now. *Now.*"

He drove into her, smashing her world apart all over again as they came together this time. Then he collapsed onto his elbows, pinning her under him.

She stroked her hands down his sides, savoring his weight on her. His skin was slick and hot, and she felt happy knowing she'd done that to him.

He pulled away and rolled onto his back. She lay there, catching her breath. Then she rolled over and reached for him, but he got out of bed.

"Scoot up."

"Huh?"

"On the bed."

She scooted back and pushed down the bedspread. He swept all the covers to the end and then slid in beside her, pulling her flush against his naked body. She rested her head on his arm and sighed.

It was blissful. Heavenly. He brought her thigh up to rest on his stomach, and she turned to look at him.

There were so many questions churning inside her. She nestled her head against his chest, and silence settled over them. Was this their last night together? Second-to-last?

He ran his palm over her thigh, and his tenderness undid her. Not long ago, she never would have suspected this side of him. Or that she could ever develop such a strong connection with someone in such a short time. It felt special. She could admit that to herself. But what did he feel? She wanted to ask, but the idea scared her. She'd never been afraid to ask tough questions, but this time she couldn't find the words.

Brynn closed her eyes, fighting back tears. He stroked his hand up her thigh slowly, then back down again. And suddenly, the day was back, all of it, in horrible, vivid detail, and she pictured the shocked look on Hayes's mutilated face as the paramedics lifted him onto the stretcher.

"Hey." Erik gave her shoulder a squeeze. She looked up at him and realized her cheeks were wet.

"Sorry. I'm all weepy suddenly." She started to sit up, but he pulled her back down, snugging her against his chest. "Sorry."

"Don't."

"I don't know why I'm like this."

His hand stilled on her thigh. "Relief?"

"You think?"

"It's a powerful emotion." He resumed the stroking.

Relief. That was definitely part of it. And the release of all that fear that had been gathering inside her since she'd first learned of Jen's murder.

But it was more than relief.

It was uncertainty. And a whole different kind of fear of what would happen now with Erik. After all this time—thirty-three years—she'd finally met a man strong enough for her. He was fierce and hard and loyal and full of integrity. And the way he made love to her so intensely took her breath away.

And he was leaving.

He kissed her forehead and pulled her closer.

27

ERIK'S EYES opened at 0600, and the gray light of morning was already in the room. Brynn was curled beside him, her breast pressed against his side. He pulled the sheet up around her shoulders and stared at the water mark on the ceiling.

He was leaving soon. Not tomorrow but soon. And he dreaded the coming conversation with her.

He wanted to opt out of the job. He wanted to ask Liam to get someone else for Hawaii and give him something local. Or even better, he wanted to take a week's leave and spend every minute of it with Brynn.

He closed his eyes, cursing silently. When had he ever opted out of work? He hadn't. He didn't. That wasn't who he was, and he couldn't pick a worse time to change, given that he was already on the ropes. Liam had granted him a second chance, but Erik was under no illusions about his reasoning: he'd had a bad situation on his hands, and he'd needed skilled people. But Erik knew that if he dropped the ball again, he was history.

It was a sobering thought.

Or it should have been. But Brynn slid her thigh over his, and every work-related thought was replaced by this burning *need* that had been dogging him since he'd met her.

Would she be here for him when he came back? Erik traveled all the time, and she didn't seem like someone who would wait around for a man. Erik was well aware that there were plenty of guys who would step in when he wasn't around. Her ex. Ross. Danny Fucking Sheffield. The thought of her with any of them made him dizzy with jealousy.

Brynn moved again, and her eyes fluttered open. She gave a lazy smile. But it faded as she searched his face.

"What's wrong?" she asked.

"Nothing."

Guilt stabbed at him. He needed to handle this. Soon. But he didn't know how. Relationships weren't exactly his area of expertise.

But he was a problem solver. That's what he did. And he could solve this one, if he could get Brynn to trust him. That presented a challenge, though, because she was one of the least trusting people he'd ever met. She shifted onto her elbow and gazed at him with those blue eyes that were already filled with skepticism. She knew something *was* wrong.

Erik's phone pinged with a text. He reached across her and grabbed it off the nightstand. He read the message from Liam, then scrolled through another one he'd missed.

"Hayes did okay last night," Erik said.

"Oh, thank God."

"I've got a wrap meeting at oh-eight-hundred."

She tugged the sheet up. "A wrap meeting?"

"The team comes together to debrief, wrap up, address any loose ends."

"I see."

Something in her tone put him on guard. "What is it?"

"Nothing."

Now *she* was the one lying.

She sat up and looked around. "I've got to be in court at eight thirty. You mind giving me a ride to the apartment?" She slid from bed and grabbed his rumpled shirt off the floor, keeping her back to him as she pulled it on.

"Of course. I'll take you to court, too."

Brynn hurried up the courthouse steps before she could say or do anything stupid, like pelt him with questions. *When are you leaving? When will I see you again? How the hell are we going to make this work?* Because sometime between waking up beside him and kissing him good-bye just now, she'd decided she wanted to. If he had reservations, she'd just have to convince him.

Brynn shoved the thoughts from her mind to focus on the day ahead as she went through security. Conlon was already in the courtroom. As she passed through the gallery, the door to the judge's offices opened, and Linden's clerk stepped out.

"Counselors." She nodded at both of them. "The judge would like to see you in chambers."

Brynn shot a look at Conlon. He didn't appear surprised or even curious as he followed the clerk past the bailiff and into Linden's private office. The judge sat behind his desk, reading a document, as the clerk ushered them inside.

"Have a seat," Linden said.

Brynn sat, darting another look at Conlon, and for the first time, she noticed the gray pallor of his skin. He looked like he might be sick.

"Mr. Conlon? You had an important matter to discuss?"

The prosecutor cleared his throat, not looking at Brynn. "Yes, Your Honor. Thank you." He paused. "It has come to my attention that Joel Sebring was arrested last night." He glanced down at his hands. "He's being held on murder charges. Two murders, in fact. One of them is Seth Moore's."

Brynn's jaw dropped open. "What—"

"Seth Moore, whose murder *Justin* Sebring is being tried for?" Linden looked at Brynn. "Ms. Holloran, were you aware of this development?"

"No . . . Your Honor. I just—what the hell, Jack? Why didn't you call me?"

"I just found out this morning. A confidential informant who was arrested on drug charges yesterday implicated Joel Sebring in two separate killings."

"Implicated?" the judge asked.

"He claims he was there at the time."

Brynn stared at him. "He *claims*?" People would claim just about anything, especially if they were in the hot seat and facing incarceration.

"And how credible is this informant?" Linden asked.

"Very." Conlon tugged at his tie. "Apparently, he has evidence of these events on his cell phone. Video evidence. From what I understand, he was in the car when Joel Sebring shot Seth Moore."

The judge leaned forward, looking at Conlon over the tops of his glasses. "*In* the car?"

"That's correct, Your Honor."

Brynn stared at the prosecutor in shock. He still hadn't looked at her since dropping his bombshell.

"Ms. Holloran?"

She looked at Linden. "Your Honor?"

"I would suggest you make a motion to dismiss."

The next hour was a whirlwind.

Back in the courtroom, Brynn made a motion to dismiss the charges against her client, which the judge granted without a word of argument from Conlon. Linden had a brief conversation with the jury, vaguely outlining the situation and thanking them for their service before sending them on their way.

Justin was shell-shocked. His mother was a basket case. Sylvia waited in the courtroom, crying and wringing her hands, while her son went through the required procedures and then was released. After an impromptu press conference in the courthouse lobby—from which Conlon was conspicuously absent—Brynn led Justin and his mom to the back of the building so that they could slip out without being mobbed by reporters. They would have plenty of chances to talk to the press in the coming days.

By the time they parted ways, it wasn't even eleven o'clock, and it had already been the second-most tumultuous day of Brynn's career. After disentangling herself from a few lingering journalists, she slipped into the first-floor ladies' room to get some space.

She washed her hands and examined her reflection. She looked as bowled over as she felt. This case had been one of the most challenging of her life. And before it even got to the jury, her client had been miraculously exonerated, sparing everyone on his side an agonizing wait and the even more agonizing possibility of a conviction.

And Conlon was spared being reported for witness tampering.

Even in the confusion of the morning, that little detail hadn't been lost on Brynn, and she intended to check into it. She'd call Bulldog and get him to see what he could sniff out. But first, she needed to call Reggie.

The door opened, and Brynn glanced over her shoulder.

"Molly, hi!"

"Hi yourself." Molly grinned at her. "I hear you just caught the break of the century."

Brynn stepped over and gave Molly a hug. They had been friends since law school but drifted apart when Brynn moved to Pine Rock.

"Good news travels fast," Brynn said.

"Yep. It's all over Twitter. And probably CNN by now. That is awesome, girl. Now I know why they call you Reggie's good-luck charm."

She smiled. Reggie knew Molly from the Dallas days and had tried to recruit her down to Pine Rock.

"Hey, when are you going to come down and work with us?" Brynn asked.

Molly made a face. "Not anytime soon."

"I promise, you'd like the money, and we could really use your talent for appellate work."

Molly just looked at her.

"Reggie's not really a hard-ass," Brynn added. "Not as much as they say, anyway."

"Reggie's not the problem."

"What do you mean?"

"I could never work with Ross."

"Why not?"

Molly looked at her for a long moment. "Never mind. You don't want to know."

Surprise and intense curiosity buzzed through Brynn. "What? You can tell me. We've been friends for a long time."

Molly seemed to be debating. Then she glanced under the stalls. "I never told you this, but . . . a few years back, I went out with him one night. I woke up with a monster hangover and some ugly bruises. And I'd only had *one* drink. Or so I thought." She gave Brynn a meaningful look. "I have no idea what happened, but I know it wasn't good. And given the place I was in then? It could have been anything. Mitch had just moved out, and I was going through a wild phase. So I'm not accusing anyone, but I'm saying I don't remember a goddamn thing. And I don't know *why* I don't remember."

Brynn stepped closer. "Molly—"

She held up her hand. "Look, I heard about his attack. I know he's in bad shape, and I don't want to kick someone when they're down, but really, he's an asshole. I could never work around him. If he quits the firm? Then give me a call."

The door whisked open, and a bailiff walked in. She nodded at Brynn and Molly before going into a stall.

"Congrats again on your trial." Molly reached for the door. "Let's do lunch when things slow down."

28

BRYNN WATCHED in a daze as buildings and storefronts raced by. Her mind was spinning.

I don't remember a goddamn thing. And I don't know why I don't remember.

Was she saying Ross drugged her and raped her? *Ross?*

It seemed impossible. Brynn had known Ross for years. She knew he was a player, but she couldn't imagine him being capable of something like that.

Molly thought he was, though. She was so sure of it that she'd turned down a lucrative job offer with one of the state's top defense attorneys.

Brynn's stomach clenched, and she closed her eyes. Ross. *Ross.* The idea of him drugging and raping someone . . . And the implications . . .

Brynn's taxi pulled into the driveway of the Atrium. Her hands were clammy, and she wiped them on her skirt before taking out several bills for the driver.

"Keep the change," she told him, sliding from the cab.

She took out her key card and swiped her way into the building as wild thoughts raced through her head. She had to be wrong. It was lack of sleep. And the roller-coaster morning she'd had. Her brain wasn't functioning right. She pressed her hand to her stomach, wishing it would calm down, as she rode up the elevator to her floor. She let herself into her apartment and went straight to the dining-room table.

Mug shots of Corby stared up at her. His booking photo, his prison photo, an array of computer-generated drawings showing him in various disguises. Brynn had memorized all of them, and she swept them aside now as she searched through the paperwork. For days, she'd been culling through trial notes and transcripts and case-related documents Lindsey had sent her. She found what she was looking for: the search warrant for the initial suspect police had zeroed in on after the third murder, the meter reader who had been at all three of the victims' houses. Investigators had executed a search warrant at the suspect's apartment but had come up empty.

She skimmed the document, including the list of items investigators had told the judge they were looking for. The list included a heart-shaped locket, an ankle bracelet, a lock of human hair—all the souvenirs Corby had taken from his first three victims. Brynn flipped to the attached affidavit and scanned the legalese: *Affiant requests that a Warrant be issued forthwith to permit the search* . . . Brynn read the name of the officer requesting the warrant.

She whipped out her phone and looked up the number for Dallas PD. Her stomach did a nervous dance as she waited for the operator to put her through.

"Martinez."

"Hello. Is this Detective Jorge Martinez?"

"That's me."

"I'm Brynn Holloran, formerly with the DA's office. You probably don't remember me, but—"

"I remember you."

Brynn closed her eyes with relief. At least his voice sounded friendly. "Good. Listen, I'm checking up on some details related to the James Corby trial, and I see here that you were the officer who requested the initial search warrant?"

"The initial one, yeah. Mick McGowan handled the search warrant for Corby's place."

"Yes, I understand. I'm talking about the first search warrant for the suspect who didn't pan out." She took a deep breath. "I remember you guys used to call us sometimes, to give you a hand with the affidavits? I was wondering if you remember asking for help with this one?"

"Yeah, you know, I'm not much on paperwork. Truth is, I hate it. All that legal speak isn't my thing."

"I understand. So did you get anyone's help writing the affidavit?"

"Yeah, one of your guys over there. Foley."

"Ross Foley?"

"Yeah, him. Hey, I saw on the news about him—"

"Thank you, Detective. I appreciate your help."

Brynn hung up. Her heart was racing. Her legs felt noodly. She sank into a chair and stared at her phone. With trembling fingers, she called Lindsey.

"Hi, it's Brynn." Her quiet voice sounded strangely disconnected from her screaming thoughts. "I need a favor."

―――――――――

"Sure. What do you need?" Lindsey asked.

"Did you ever get the evidence-room logs? From the day after Corby was arrested?"

Lindsey grabbed an empty cubicle in the squad room and set her files down. This wasn't her department, but she'd been at Dallas PD all morning, meeting with detectives and filling out paperwork related to the Corby case.

"You mean the first arrest? Yeah, one of my contacts sent them over."

"I need you to check something for me."

Lindsey flipped open a file and found the papers. "This log's pretty lengthy. What name are you looking for?"

Silence.

"Brynn? You there?"

"Ross Foley."

She paused. "Ross?"

"That's right."

Lindsey frowned as she skimmed the list. "Yeah, he's on here."

"What's the date?"

"June tenth. The day after Corby's arrest. He was in the evidence room at ten fifteen A.M., signed out at ten twenty-five." Lindsey paused. "What's this about? Are you thinking *Ross* might have planted evidence?"

More silence.

"Brynn?"

"Ross had an interest in Corby being convicted."

"Okay," Lindsey said. That wasn't surprising—everyone at the DA's office wanted a conviction. "But what you're suggesting doesn't make sense. How would Ross know that Corby collected souvenirs? And where would Ross get the necklace?"

———

Brynn clutched her phone in her hand. Her heart was sprinting now, and she felt light-headed.

"People from the prosecutor's office weren't at Lauren Tull's crime scene," Lindsey continued. "I checked into that already. Detectives were at the scene, several patrol cops, the ME's people."

The killer. Brynn couldn't bring herself to point out the obvious. "I need to talk to you," she said instead. "It's important."

"Where are you?" Lindsey asked. "I'm at DPD downtown."

"Can you come to my apartment? I don't have a car. It's not far from you."

"I know. I've been there, remember?"

Of course, she had. Brynn's brain was muddled.

"It's important," she repeated.

"I'm on my way."

Lindsey left the police station and spotted Erik pulling into the lot. She rushed to intercept him.

"What are you doing here?" she asked. "I thought you were with Brynn."

"I'm meeting with the task force. Brynn's in court all day."

"No, she's not. I just talked to her. She asked me all sorts of questions about Ross."

Erik's brow furrowed. "What do you mean?"

"Honestly, I don't know. She wanted me to come by there and talk to her. She's got some theory that Ross planted the Lauren Tull necklace. You know what that's about?"

Erik just stared at her.

"I mean, it doesn't even make sense," Lindsey said. "How would Ross know about Corby taking souvenirs? Only the detectives knew that, and they kept that info under wraps for when they got a suspect."

Something flickered in Erik's eyes. Fear? Lindsey had to be imagining it.

He stepped closer. "Where is Brynn?"

Brynn combed through the mess of papers, making stacks and piles, as if organizing everything would somehow fix what was wrong. Her phone chimed. She saw the name and realized she'd forgotten to call Reggie. *Shit.*

"Congratulations!" Reggie boomed. "Why didn't you call me?"

"It's been a crazy morning." She sifted through the paperwork. She took everything related to Ross and her theory and shoved it into a file folder for Lindsey.

"Where are you now?" Reggie asked.

"At the apartment. Why?"

"I'm coming over."

"You're in Dallas?"

"I just closed Sheffield. We have a new client! That's two victories this morning, plus Ross getting discharged. Time to celebrate!"

Brynn froze. "Wait, what?"

"I'm bringing champagne. This day deserves a toast."

"Reggie, Ross is *out*?"

"They sent him home this morning."

"Home, as in here?"

"Yeah, his sister dropped him off. He's packing up today and going back to Pine Rock."

A sharp knock sounded at the door, and Brynn whirled around. She hurried over to check the peephole. Ross stood there, leaning his hand on the doorframe. No doubt he'd heard her in here on the phone with someone.

"Brynn?" Reggie said.

"Talk to you later, okay, Reggie?" She hung up and glanced around. She stuffed the file in her hand under her arm before opening the door.

Ross smiled. "Hey, tiger. Congrats." He leaned in for a hug, and Brynn played along. "I heard your good news."

"Yeah, you, too." She pulled away and looked him over. His complexion was sallow, and he seemed to be supporting his weight against the doorframe.

She pictured him struggling with Lauren Tull on her living-room floor, smothering the life out of her.

"So you're up and around already?" Brynn tried to sound normal. "How do you feel?"

"Pretty good, considering. They've got me on pain meds." Ross eased closer. "Are *you* okay? You don't look happy."

"I'm fine. Great. Reggie's on his way over with champagne. I've got to run an errand first." She slipped past him into the hallway.

"What's wrong?"

"Nothing."

He reached for her arm, and she jerked back. The file slipped loose and cascaded to the floor.

She crouched down to slap the papers back inside, and Ross bent over.

"Holy *shit*!" He clutched his side, gasping.

"Don't move! I got it!" Brynn snatched up the affidavit, the search-warrant inventory. She jammed everything back into the folder and tucked it under her arm, hoping Ross hadn't gotten a good look at the papers.

He seemed to be preoccupied with his pain.

"Don't pull your stitches." She stepped away from him, anxious to get out of there. She'd meet Lindsey in the lobby and talk to her at the police station. Anywhere but here.

"Brynn, what the hell's wrong?"

"Nothing. Talk to you later."

She race-walked to the elevator without looking back and hit the button. She stared at the glowing numbers, holding her breath as she waited for the sound of Ross returning to his apartment. She jabbed the down button again, then the up button. She didn't care, she just wanted off this floor. At last, she heard the sound of his apartment door opening and clicking shut again.

Brynn blew out a breath. She glanced over her shoulder at the empty hallway. She took out her phone and debated calling Erik. She should.

Ross had a gun. He'd borrowed it from a friend for self-protection. The realization turned Brynn's blood cold. She'd never thought Ross capable of using a gun. She'd never thought him capable of a lot of things before this moment.

A door opened behind her, and she spun around to see Ross in the hallway. He wore a gray hoodie now, and his hand was in one of the pockets. Brynn's heart lurched.

Dear God, where is the elevator?

Ross stayed beside his door, though, not moving closer.

"So, Brynn, what's your plan?" he called.

"Huh?"

"Your plan? You don't have a car here, do you?"

"Oh. No, Erik's picking me up."

The elevator dinged. The doors slid open, and Brynn jumped inside, bumping into a woman in workout gear.

"Brynn, wait." Ross started down the hallway. "Hold the elevator."

She stabbed at the close button, and the doors whisked shut. The woman beside her snickered. But then the car lifted, and she realized they were going up. She glanced around. There was also a man in business attire, who was probably headed to his apartment, while the woman in workout clothes was going to the fitness room. Next stop, Brynn would jump off and take the stairs down.

She dialed Erik's number, and he picked up on the first ring.

"Erik, it's me."

"Where are you?"

"I'm at my place. I've got a problem. With Ross."

"He's out, Brynn. He got discharged this morning. Are you alone at your apartment?"

The door slid open, and Brynn stepped out. The businessman headed down the corridor, and the woman disappeared into the gym. Brynn moved for the stairwell nearby.

The stairwell door opened, and Ross stepped through. Her stomach flip-flopped. He was sweating and breathing hard from the exertion of the stairs, but his eyes were alert. His hand was in his pocket, and she saw the outline of a gun pointed in her direction.

"Hang up, Brynn," Ross ordered.

Her throat went dry.

"*Now.*"

29

"BRYNN? *BRYNN?*" Erik cursed and swiped at his phone. He swerved around a slow-moving car, prompting a blare of horns behind him.

"Where is Ross?" he demanded the instant Skyler answered the phone.

"Ross? He's at home. Why?"

"Home at his apartment? Or Pine Rock?"

"They haven't left yet," she said. "Keith's picking him up at three and driving him back."

"*Shit!*"

"What's wrong?"

"Get to the apartment now. Ross is there with Brynn, and I think he might hurt her." Erik pulled an illegal left turn and stepped on the gas.

"*Ross* might hurt her?"

"Call Jeremy, too. I'll call 911."

"What the hell's going on, Erik?"

"I'll explain later. Just get there!"

Ross stuffed her cell phone into his pocket. "How's your boy, Brynn?"

She glanced around, but it was just the two of them in the foyer. The woman from the elevator was alone in the fitness room now, jogging on a treadmill with a pair of earbuds stuffed in her ears.

"I mean, come on, Brynn. Fucking your bodyguard? What a cliché." He shook his head. "Some people might even say that's unethical."

Brynn eyed the gun again and took a step back, but Ross reached over and plucked the file from under her arm. "Too smart for your own good." He folded the file in half and tucked it in the back of his pants, tugging the sweatshirt over it. "You should have let it go."

"Let it go? An unsolved *rape* and *murder*, and I should have let it go so you could frame someone?"

"It's not like Corby's innocent." Ross gave her a sharp look. "He got what he deserved. Guy's a sociopath."

"And you're not?"

"Actually, no. I didn't plan any of this. It just happened. And then what was I supposed to do? I was three years out of law school. I can't have rape allegations floating around me. I could get disbarred."

Fury welled inside her as she looked at the man she'd spent so many hours of her life with.

"You're a coward. You're a piece of shit and a coward."

"Save the lecture. Let's go." He poked her ankle with his foot. "Come on. Out the door."

Brynn pushed through the door to the rooftop terrace and was hit by a hot gust of pollution-tinged air. She stepped into the blinding sunlight, and Ross followed her.

"Where—"

"*Walk.* And keep your mouth shut."

Brynn glanced at the sparkling blue pool. It was empty. There was nobody out here.

"Go," Ross ordered, corralling her behind the concrete structure that housed the building's industrial-size air conditioner. No one in the fitness room could see her from here, and she felt a spurt of panic. She had to stall for time.

She stopped and turned to look at him. The gun was out of his pocket now, a big black pistol pointed right at her chest.

"Everything's about you, isn't it?"

"Shut up, Brynn."

"You think you're so clever, but you're digging your own grave here. You know that, right?"

"Keep walking."

She glanced at the wall ahead of her, and an icy wave of fear crashed over her.

"Been a rough day, huh, Brynn? You're probably thinking of hurting yourself."

She turned around, and the feral look in his eye made her throat close. He wanted her to step off this roof and disappear.

The sun blazed down on them. Brynn's back was sweating, and her mouth tasted like glue.

She had to stall him.

"Right. Sure." She choked out a laugh. "I just got my client off. You think anyone's going to believe I'm suicidal?"

He stopped and stared at her. "I think you're right. Better to make it look like an accident."

Her chest tightened as she thought of Erik. Where was he? And even if he got over here, how would he find her up here? The traffic sounds fifteen stories below seemed impossibly far away.

Brynn swayed backward, suddenly dizzy. She felt the too-still still-ness of the air. The pool beside her was as flat as a mirror.

Ross stepped closer. "Sorry, Brynn."

"You're crazy."

"Nope. Just smarter than you."

She glanced at the concrete wall, and her pulse started pounding so hard she could feel it in her ears.

She turned to Ross. "I'm not going to jump off a building for you. You're going to have to shoot me."

"Oh, I will." He eased closer. "But just know that if you don't co-operate, you'll die anyway. And while the cops are figuring out what happened, I'll be on my way to your sister's house."

Her stomach plummeted, like she was sinking in an elevator, down, down, down.

"You don't want those pretty nieces of yours to grow up without a mommy, do you?"

A flash of movement caught Brynn's eye. She tried to keep her gaze on Ross.

"You wouldn't do that."

"You don't know me as well as you think, Brynn."

She caught the sight of Skyler's dark head ducking behind the building. How did she get here? She had to be with Erik. Maybe they'd found her by using the surveillance cameras.

"Hop up there." Ross jerked his pistol toward the wall. "Go on."

"Drop the weapon, Ross!"

He turned toward the sound of Skyler's voice, but she was hidden.

"I've got a gun on you! Drop it now!"

Ross darted an angry look at Brynn.

Behind him, a shadow shifted. Brynn's heart skittered as she saw

Erik easing around the side of the maintenance building. He had his pistol raised and ready.

Ross looked desperate. His gaze hopped between Brynn and the far side of the pool, where Skyler was hiding.

"Three seconds, Ross," she called. "Either drop it or you're dead!"

Ross turned to Brynn. The desperation was gone, replaced by a look of utter calm.

"Three . . ."

Ross didn't move.

"Two . . ."

Erik leaped out from behind the wall, and Ross's arm jerked up.

Pop! Pop! Pop!

The barrage of bullets came from all directions, and Ross fell to the ground.

Brynn dropped to her knees. Erik sprinted toward her.

"Are you hit?" He clutched her in his arms, searching her face. "*Are you hit?*"

"I'm okay." She threw her arms around him. "What happened?" Her words were muffled against his shoulder. "Is Skyler okay?" She pushed away from him to look.

Skyler knelt beside Ross, checking his neck for a pulse, and Brynn had a flashback of her kneeling beside him on the sidewalk right after he'd been stabbed by Corby.

Skyler looked at Erik.

"Is he—"

"He's dead."

30

LINDSEY WADED through the sea of cops and CSIs and emergency workers. Even a few marshals were here, getting the latest news on what had to be one of the most bizarre cases they'd seen. She spied Erik over the crowd. He caught her eye and motioned for her to follow him into a hallway off the Atrium's lobby.

"This place is insane," she said over the noise.

"You should see the rooftop."

"I'll pass."

Even if she could get up there, she had no desire to see another bloody death scene right now. She'd already watched the body bag being rolled out on a gurney by the ME's people.

"How's Brynn?" she asked.

Erik frowned and rubbed his jaw. "I think she's in shock."

"Is she at the police station or—"

"Yeah, she's being interviewed. I'm on my way over there to pick her up and take her home."

"Home? You mean here?"

"Pine Rock. She needs to get out of here. I have to grab a few things from her apartment, and then we're out."

" 'We,' huh? I knew there was something up with you two." Lindsey smiled at him, but he continued to look grim as he scanned the packed lobby, hypervigilant as always.

"Listen, Erik, tell Brynn thanks for me, would you? If it weren't for her, we wouldn't have cracked this case. Ross Foley wasn't even on anyone's radar until she put it together."

Erik's expression clouded. "I'll tell her." He glanced over Lindsey's shoulder, clearly eager to finish his errand and get back to Brynn.

"Anyway, thanks to both of you." Lindsey patted his arm. "It was good working with you."

"You, too." He started to walk away, then paused. "And if you're ever thinking about a career change, give us a call."

Erik turned and walked off, cutting through the crowd of cops as Lindsey stared after him.

A career change? Her?

Something to think about.

———

Erik took Brynn home to Pine Rock because he knew it was what she needed. But the instant he turned onto her street, he changed his mind. The reporters and news vans camped out in front of her house had him pulling a U-turn and hopping back onto the freeway. Thirty minutes later, they arrived at his apartment, where they spent the next twenty-four hours ignoring the outside world while they stocked up on food, sleep, and time together.

It was a much-needed break, but Erik was worried about Brynn. She was too quiet. After a lazy afternoon in bed together, he went out to buy some steaks and a bottle of wine, hoping that cooking dinner with him might snap her out of her daze. When he got home from the store, he found her out on his balcony, wrapped in one of his flannel shirts.

"You all right?" he asked, stepping outside.

"Yeah." She smiled slightly. "Just enjoying the view out here."

"Pretty impressive, huh?"

"It is."

He looked across the crowded parking lot at a row of pine trees. It wasn't bad, really, if you overlooked the cars. But he wasn't home enough to spend much time out here.

He handed her a glass of wine and took the chair beside her. She looked so pretty sitting there on his balcony in the fading daylight, and he wanted to freeze this image of her in his mind to take with him.

"Brynn?"

"Huh?"

"I'm worried about you."

"Don't."

He set his glass on the table. "I'm sorry about Ross—"

"*Don't* say his name." She took a deep breath. "I don't want to talk about him right now. Or ever."

Erik was no psychologist, but he knew she needed to talk to someone. Maybe not him but someone. She'd spent an hour this morning on the phone with her sister, but something still seemed off with her. Erik would talk to Liam. He had to know someone trained in dealing with PTSD.

Brynn cleared her throat. "I was thinking."

"About?"

She sipped her wine and set the glass on the table. "I need to go in tomorrow."

"Okay. I can take you to get your car."

"Thanks." She sighed. "I need to meet with Reggie. I'm going to ask for some time off."

Erik took her hand and squeezed it.

"I've got to, I don't know, get my head straight," she said. "Recharge my batteries."

He nodded, waiting for her to continue. He sensed there was more.

She turned to look at him. "What about you?"

Damn. They needed to talk about this, but he hadn't counted on right now.

"I'm leaving soon," he said.

"When?"

"Friday evening."

They only had two more days together. But they didn't even have that, because Erik needed to spend most of that time at headquarters.

"It's a twelve-week job," he said. "I'll have a few days' leave after six."

"Six weeks?"

He nodded, watching her reaction. "I'll be back as soon as I can, and I'd like to see you. I'll miss you like hell while I'm gone, Brynn."

She smiled. "Promises, promises."

"What?"

"Nothing."

"You don't think I'm serious."

She shrugged. "It's okay. I mean, Hawaii, right? I doubt you'll have time to miss anything."

"Brynn, look at me."

She did, and the raw vulnerability in her eyes worried him. She'd had that look there since he'd seen her on the rooftop with Ross.

She tugged her hand away.

"Don't do that." He leaned forward and took her hand again. "Don't blow me off. I'm serious about you."

She looked away and shook her head.

"What? Talk. Because you obviously have something on your mind."

"Okay, you're right. Here it is, full disclosure. I don't have a good track record with relationships, Erik. Actually, my track record's pathetic."

"You're talking about your ex?"

"And pretty much every guy I've known since college." She sighed and folded her arms over her middle. "I don't communicate well. I let my work consume me. I shut myself off from people, and then they end up lying and cheating on me."

Erik dipped his head down and looked at her. "I'm not like that."

"I know."

"So what's the problem?"

"*Relationships* are the problem. People hurt each other, whether they want to or not. That's life."

She sounded so convinced, and his heart ached for her. She'd been burned repeatedly by people she trusted, starting with her own father, who'd walked out on her family.

Erik shifted his chair so he was facing her and unfolded her arms. He took her hands in his and looked her in the eye. "What if I tell you I have no intention of hurting you?"

She gave him a baleful look. "That's sweet. But even if you don't intend to do it, it happens. Trust me on this, because I think I have more experience with relationships than you do."

He smiled.

"What?"

"Come here," he said, pulling her into his lap.

"I'm too heavy."

"You're perfect." He arranged her legs over the side of the chair and looked at her, sliding his hand over her smooth thigh. "Give me a chance to show you how good we could be together. While you're busy trying to prove me wrong, we might actually build something solid."

She looked at him with those deep blue eyes.

"I don't trust myself right now, Erik."

"You don't have to trust yourself. You just have to trust me."

"I want to, but . . ."

"What?"

"I'm afraid of what could happen."

Now they were getting to the real issue. She looked uncomfortable, but at least she was making eye contact.

"I've never felt like this before, Erik. So emotionally . . . churned up. When I'm with you, I just . . ." She let the words trail off.

"I know." He touched her cheek. "Me too."

Relief filled her eyes. But then she looked troubled again. "I've always been the one to keep my distance. To end a relationship when it got messy or complicated. But the thing is, I don't feel any distance with you."

"Good."

"How is that good? This is a terrible time to start a relationship, and you're leaving anyway, so what's the point?"

He kissed her. Softly at first, but then he kept at it until her hands slipped around his neck and her tongue tangled with his. He slid his palms over her hips, kissing her and taking in everything about her that he'd come to need.

Slowly, he pulled away. "That's the point."

Friday came way too soon.

Erik was up before the sun. Brynn lay in her bed in the dark, pretending to be asleep as he dressed for his morning run and slipped out of the house. When he was gone, she got up and shuffled to the kitchen to make coffee. Now that the media had dissipated, they'd spent the night at her place, and she had to admit it was a relief to be home.

She took her mug onto the screened porch and curled up on the wicker sofa, letting her thoughts flow along with her tears as the sky went from black to indigo to gray. She was still in shock from everything, and her emotions were all over the map.

She'd been so wrong. About so many things. Days ago, she'd actually prided herself on her talent for reading people. She could read a jury. A witness. But those closest to her? Not at all. How had she been such a horrible judge of character?

Ross had left a gaping wound in her chest, and she didn't know whether it was his death or his betrayal that hurt worse. She closed her eyes to block it out, along with the self-doubt that had been plaguing her for days now.

She took a deep breath and snuggled inside Erik's flannel shirt. It was deliciously soft and smelled like him, and she planned to keep it when he left. She dried her eyes with the cuff and thought about today. They had a few more hours, and she wanted to make the most of them. She needed to hold it together.

The front door opened and closed, and she heard his footsteps. The screen door squeaked, and he stepped onto the porch. She'd expected him to be flushed and sweaty, but he wasn't at all.

"Thought you went for a run?"

"I changed my mind."

He seemed tense, but he didn't say anything, just looked at her. "There's coffee," she said. "I've got decaf, too, if you want me to make some."

The fact that she'd purchased something so pointless just showed how gone she was over this man.

"I'm good, thanks." He sank onto the sofa beside her, and it creaked with his weight. He pulled her into his arms, and she felt a rush of warmth. No matter how crazy her head was, his arms around her made her feel better. He pulled her close, and she settled her cheek against his shoulder, loving how right they felt together. She'd never had such a natural fit with anyone.

"When do you leave for the airport?" she asked.

"I'm not going."

"What?" She pulled back.

"I called Liam and told him to count me out."

"When?"

"Just now. From your driveway."

"But . . . you said you're the lead agent."

"Someone else can take the lead this time."

She squirmed back to look at him, and she could tell he was dead serious. He'd really done it. "What did Liam say?"

He shrugged. "He wasn't too happy. But I've never taken a vacation before, so he agreed to give me some time."

"Are you sure that's a good idea? I know you're already on thin ice with him, and I *know* how much your job matters to you."

"You matter more."

She stared at him, her heart thrumming. He was willing to risk his job for her. She felt a flood of joy and panic, both at the same time.

"How long do you have?" she asked.

"I don't know. As long as you need." He took her hand and laced their fingers together. "You're going through something right now, Brynn, and I want to help." He paused, as if trying to read her reaction. "I figure we'll take two weeks and go from there."

Brynn's head was spinning. She'd been prepared to say good-bye today.

You matter more.

"Say something," he said. "You look shocked."

"I am. In a good way. I mean, two *weeks*. What are we going to do?"

He smiled and squeezed her hand. "I have an idea."

Acknowledgments

A BOOK IS a team effort, and I'm lucky to work with the best in the business. Thanks so much to everyone at Simon & Schuster, including Jean Anne Rose, Abby Zidle, Sara Quaranta, Lisa Litwack, Diana Velasquez, Jen Bergstrom, Jen Long, and Carolyn Reidy. I'm grateful to the S&S sales team for their work and dedication. A very special thanks to my talented editor, Lauren McKenna, for her wonderful insights and her enthusiasm for this book. Also, I want to thank my agent, Kevan Lyon, for years of guidance and friendship.

And most of all, thank you to my family, whose love, patience, and support keep me going. I love you guys.

Epilogue

THEY WENT to Playa del Carmen because neither of them had been there, and they'd heard it was paradise. As luck would have it, it rained. Not gentle showers, but angry bursts of water that pounded down from the sky, and they spent three days holed up in their hotel room.

Which turned out to be its own kind of paradise.

On the fourth day the rain let up some. Brynn could tell Erik was getting restless, so at her suggestion they grabbed a taxi to Tulum. They explored the Mayan ruins in the intermittent drizzle, clambering over the slick rocks. Then they hiked down the steep path to the beach, where they sat on the sand and looked at the surf.

Erik held her hand—to Brynn's surprise, he was a hand-holder—but he didn't talk, and she liked that, too. They sat side by side with their knees up, staring out at the endless supply of waves battering the shore. On the way back, they stopped in town to eat ice-cream cones and buy postcards for Liz and her mom. Brynn told them everything was wonderful and didn't mention the rain.

"My sister wants to meet you," Brynn informed Erik as she mailed the postcards.

"Oh, yeah?"

"She said you must be really hot for me to run off to Mexico at a moment's notice."

He smiled. "What'd you say?"

She shrugged. "I said you were okay."

He grinned and pulled her in for a kiss.

Their fifth and final day was sunny, and Brynn dragged Erik out of bed at 7:45 to stake out the best lounge chairs by the pool. She lay there all morning, enjoying the balmy breeze from underneath the shade of an umbrella. Turned out, Erik didn't like lounging. He got restless again, and set out to walk the resort and check out their security setup.

Brynn's phone chimed on the table beside her. She checked the number and debated a moment before answering.

"Hey, Reggie."

"Hello." He sounded surprised she'd picked up. "How's Mexico?"

"Restful," she said, knowing what he really wanted to ask was when she planned to be back. "How are things there?"

He filled her in on new developments, including the news that her law school friend Molly was coming down for an interview.

"She's a genius at appellate work," Brynn said. "We'd be lucky to get her."

"I agree."

"Thanks for letting me know."

Brynn promised to call Molly and then jumped off the phone before Reggie could pin her down on her return date.

Brynn set aside her magazine and lowered herself into the negative edge pool. The water swirled around her, cooling her skin, which was already pink from the sun.

Brynn felt happy for Molly. She'd given up an opportunity years ago because of Ross, and now it seemed oddly fitting that his death should create a new opportunity.

Ross. She got a familiar tightness in her chest at the thought of him. Inhaling deeply, she ducked her head under the water and swam to the other end of the pool in one breath. She rested her arms on the warm tile and gazed out at the turquoise Caribbean.

She still couldn't believe Ross was gone, or that such a strange and twisted series of events had led to his death. And Corby was back in prison now, facing new charges for the murders of a prison guard, Jen Ballard, and Michael McGowan. Corby's girlfriend, Ann Johnson, was facing charges of her own for aiding and abetting a fugitive.

A splash behind Brynn made her turn around. Erik swam over and wrapped his arms around her from behind.

"I got us daiquiris for breakfast," he said, kissing her shoulder.

"I thought they didn't open until eleven?"

"I may have flirted with the waitress."

"You? Flirting?" She turned around in his arms. For Erik, that probably meant he'd uttered two sentences of small talk.

Brynn slid her hands up around his neck. He smiled down at her, but she saw the worry in his eyes.

"You okay today?" he asked.

"Why?"

"You were tossing around all night."

"I'm okay."

He kissed her softly, and Brynn's heart squeezed. He couldn't fix what was wrong, but it helped to know that he wanted to.

"I printed out our boarding passes for tomorrow," he said.

"Thank you."

Back to reality. Back to work and people and everything they'd managed to avoid for more than a week. Brynn took a deep breath.

"You seem tense," he said.

"I'm just thinking."

"About?"

"What happens next. This has been great, but it's not reality."

His brow furrowed. "I know what *I* want to happen. The more important question is, what do *you* want?"

"Why is that more important?"

"Because." He brushed a lock of hair from her forehead. "What I do is hard on relationships. The hours, the stress, the travel—"

"The bullets, the stabbings."

"It's not usually like that." He paused and searched her face. "Yours was an unusual case."

She trailed a finger over his shoulder where his cut was healing. It was going to leave a scar.

"I've seen people make it work, but you really have to want it." His arms tightened around her. "Do you?"

She looked up at him. "I've never wanted anything more."

The instant she said it, she felt weightless. The words were out now. No more hiding.

"I love you," she whispered.

He smiled.

"What?"

He pulled he closer. "I think I've loved you since that first day when you told me I wasn't your bellboy."

She pulled back. "You can't be serious."

"That whole car ride, that was it for me. I knew I was toast."

"I had no idea."

"I know."

She looked into his eyes. They were loving and tender, and she knew he really *saw* her, in a way no one else had. Hope began to edge out the fear. She was ready to commit to something hard. Hard was okay because they had something special together, and it was worth the effort, even though there were no guarantees, only possibilities.

"I'm counting on you to break my losing streak," she told him. "Can you handle it?"

He tipped her chin up and kissed her. "I can handle it."